Dear Robo I hope you enjoy
Vinnie Graziano

die laughing

Vincent Graziano

BOLD
FACE
BOOKS | WWW.**BOLDFACE**BOOKS.COM

Boldface Books

An imprint of Winoca Books & Media

www.winoca.com

Library of Congress Cataloging-in-Publication Data

Graziano, Vincent, 1953–

    Die laughing / Vincent Graziano.

        p. cm.

ISBN 978-0-9789736-6-7 (hardcover)

ISBN 978-0-9789736-7-4 (paperback)

    1. Italian Americans--New York (State)—New York—Fiction. 2. Undertakers and undertaking—Fiction. 3. Comedians—Fiction. 4. Little Italy (New York, N.Y.)—Fiction. I. Title.

    PS3607.R3995D54 2009

    813´.6—dc22

                             2009036366

Cover illustration by Curtis Fennell

For Johnny and Jemma

who lived it

Chapter 1

Frankie Grace often napped in a casket. He preferred the solid mahogany model B76, with the high-polished finish, champagne crushed-velvet tufted interior, and oversized pillow, but he had also tried out the solid cherry, hand-rubbed-finish satin interior and the copper with the adjustable plush mattress. So he was accustomed to confined spaces.

Still, the room he was being directed into, hardly more than a converted broom closet, was ridiculous. *Maybe one day I'll work this into a routine,* he thought. But not today. He was too agitated, caught in the midst of organized chaos as busboys and waiters scurried around him in the narrow corridor.

"Are you *sure* this is my dressing room?" Frankie asked the first kitchen staffer he could stop, a short fellow in a tall chef's hat. "I'm the entertainment for the Man of the Year gala."

Unimpressed, the man in the chef's hat pointed with a menacingly sharp cleaver, motioning Frankie into the tiny room off the kitchen. *No mistake.* He entered, hung his garment bag on the hook on the wall, and struggled to turn around beside the Pepto-Bismol pink lavatory to get the door closed behind him. He unzipped the bag, straightened the jacket on the hanger, and smoothed out the wide velvet lapels.

Above the tiny sink hung a square mirror lighted by a single

1

strip of dust-covered globe-shaped bulbs. An array of posters and a 1971 Playmate of the Year calendar tacked to the wall were the room's only decor. A decade's worth of *Look* magazines and a handful of kitchen towels were stacked on a wire shelf beside a grease-covered extension phone. Vinyl tile, avocado green, covered the floor. Scraps of lumber and odd-shaped tiles, leftovers from what appeared to be the club's most recent patch jobs, were heaped in one corner, and in the other was a toilet, absent a seat cover. *Great. Just great.*

Frankie could hear cleaver man yelling at his kitchen staff in words he didn't quite comprehend. From inside his broom closet, it sounded like pots and pans—maybe even knives, for all Frankie could tell—were being hurled across the kitchen.

Frankie's pager began to beep, and he unclipped it from his belt. *Dammit, not now—curtain's in ten minutes.* He'd only had the gadget for a week but already he'd learned how easily he could be located anywhere. He grabbed the phone and moved as far as the cord would take him toward the small window behind the commode, away from the clamor.

Laying a strip of plywood across the bowl, Frankie stepped on top. He opened the window and propped his elbows on the sill, trying to distance himself even further from the racket in the hallway. With the cord at its limit, he punched the number into the handset and waited for the voice on the other end.

"Strunz!" *Shithead.* Primo Grace's terms of endearment were usually followed by something like "You're as useless as tits on a bull," or "You do everything ass-backwards," or "Laughing turns to crying." Frankie waited for the admonishment.

"Strunz?" said the voice again.

"Yes, Dad, it's me."

"Where are you?"

Frankie needed to buy some time before he answered that question. "Hold on, hold on," he said. "Somebody needs to use the phone. I'll call you right back."

He disconnected the call just as someone knocked urgently on the door.

"Cheech, bubby, where are you?" It was Sal's unmistakable Brooklyn accent amid the din.

"Where the hell do you think I am? I'm in here—and who the hell are Cheech and Bubby?" Frankie opened the door, but there wasn't much room to invite Sal in.

"It's showbiz talk," Sal explained loudly. He surveyed the cramped space. "They call this a dressing room? Shit, this isn't even a closet. I won't hear of it. I'm your manager. I'm going to complain. I'll be right back." He turned to go and barely avoided sideswiping a waiter carrying a steaming chafing dish.

Frankie grabbed him and pulled him inside. "Sal, we have a bigger problem than this room."

Sal had that familiar what-are-you-talking-about look on his face.

Nearly nose to nose with his pal-turned-manager, Frankie pushed Sal toward the back of the makeshift dressing room, toward the poster-covered wall. "Do you know who that is?" he asked.

"Miss September?"

"No, *that* one." Frankie pointed toward one of the colorful posters.

Sal shrugged.

"It's Kosciuszko," said Frankie.

"So what?" said Sal.

"Kosciuszko. The Polish war hero."

"You're shittin' me," said Sal. "I didn't know there were any."

"Yes, a Polish war hero from the Revolutionary War."

Sal looked bewildered.

"The Kosciuszko Bridge, did you ever hear of it?" Frankie continued.

"Yeah?"

"Well, it was named after him."

"Really? You mean that bridge was here during the Revolution?"

Try another way. Frankie jabbed his finger at another poster on the wall. "How about this one? Do you see that picture? Do you know who *that* is?"

Sal shot him the same look of incomprehension.

"It's Bobby Vinton. Bobby Vinton, *the Polish Frank Sinatra*," he said slowly, waiting for their predicament to sink in.

Sal shrugged again, his expression blank.

Frankie reached over and pulled a ledger from the shelf. Dust flew. He opened the book, which contained handwritten entries of dues paid by members over the years. "Look at these. Do you notice anything?" He didn't wait for a shrug. "Librowski. Jowalski. Nowaski. All *Polish* names. This is a Polish social club. You booked me in a Polish social club, Sal. We're in the middle of P-fucking-*Poland*."

Sal raised his arms to question the problem. "Whaddya talkin' about? We're in Greenpoint, Brooklyn."

"Half my act is about Polacks," wailed Frankie. "Don't you get it? They're gonna kill me here."

"What's the difference? The other half ranks on Jews, and the other half ranks on Italians."

"I'll never get to the other halves. Polacks aren't going to appreciate Polish humor. These people don't *have* a sense of humor. They're gonna murder me."

The pager sounded again.

"My father," Frankie said. "Give me some quiet. If he finds out I'm doing a comedy act, *I'll* be the next customer at the funeral home." Frankie squeezed his way back around Sal, momentarily wedging both of them between the sink and the wall and tangling both their feet in the phone cord. He resumed his position atop the plank on the commode.

"Yes, Dad, it's me. Sorry, the connection is terrible here." Frankie covered the mouthpiece with his hand.

There was a commotion outside the door as Sal tried to block a troupe of accordion players from entering.

"Hey, we were told this was our dressing room," the leader said. "We go on in half an hour. I have to change and warm up."

Sal sized up the other members of the band. "Who the hell dressed you fruit loops?" he shouted over the clamor at the motley assortment of folk costumes. Two of the men were clad in skin-tight yellow pants with lace up the leg, tucked into black platform boots.

One guy wore moccasins and an embroidered saffron cape over a loose-fitting cambric tunic. All sported brightly colored vests and hats with braided red bands. "Try the ladies' room down the hall."

The troupe leader looked around. "No, I'm sure they told us to come here."

Frankie stalled for time again. "Just a minute, Dad—there's someone, ah, asking for directions."

"Look," Sal said, his voice menacingly subdued. "There ain't no room in here. My friend's gotta go outside just to change his mind. If you don't give me a few minutes I'll wrap that accordion around your head." He pushed the man out and followed, slamming the door behind him.

Moments later a practice session of "Roll Out the Barrel" echoed in the narrow hallway. Frankie put a finger in one ear as he strained to catch his father's question.

"Where are you?" his father asked.

Think, think. "I'm at church practicing with the choir." *Did he buy it?*

There was a moment of silence. "Okay," said Primo. "But Isabella Cianci has died."

"Mrs. Cianci the pastry lady?"

"Yes. She's in her apartment on top of the bakery. You gotta get her back to the funeral home and get some fluid in her."

"Now?"

"No, we have to wait."

"For a doctor to pronounce her dead?" Frankie asked.

"No, the doctor stops into the bakery for breakfast every day, so he signed the death certificate this morning over his coffee and brioche. But they're waiting for JB to come and see her. The word was he was going to be released today, but then there was a mixup in the paperwork. The feds can be clumsy when they want to break your *culones*. Finding out her son-in-law was getting out is probably what gave the old lady a heart attack in the first place."

There was an enormous clatter from the kitchen as a stack of pans hit the floor. Frankie strained to lean farther out the window and shouted into the phone, "Where is JB now?"

"The FBI still has him downtown."

"Um . . . what time did she die?" Frankie caught another polka starting up.

"Around eight this morning. What church are you in, anyhow?"

Just ignore the question. Frankie looked at his watch. Ten o'clock—dead in a small apartment fourteen hours. Not good.

"Dad, why did they wait so long?"

"You know that bunch, they hate to let go," Primo said.

Frankie understood. If there were a way to have a taxidermist stuff her, the family would keep Isabella in the apartment permanently, propped up against the oven. It was cases like this that made him want to get out of the funeral business in the first place. He knew what the rest of the night held in store.

"And bring help," Primo said. "You got five flights of stairs. And be prepared for her daughter, Annunziata. She's a handful. Never met a cannoli she didn't like, you know what I mean? Probably hysterical too. Oh, and whatever you do, don't stare at her lip hair. She's very self-conscious."

"Yeah, Dad, I'm on it."

"And for chrissake, tell your choir director to get some better music."

Primo hung up, leaving Frankie to think about the more pressing matter at hand. He shifted position, and the plywood plank slipped, sending him crashing to the floor. Sal opened the door to find his friend pinned between the bowl and the cinderblock wall. He pulled at his arm.

"Why did I let you talk me into being my manager?" moaned Frankie.

"Just grab my arm," Sal said. "And try not to ruin the tux. I only rented it for the show you're doing here—we got to have it back on Monday."

"Well, you can bring it back a day early. I'm gonna be dead in a few minutes anyway. It will be stained with blood—*my* blood. And believe me, blood stains."

Sal looked perplexed. "I don't get it."

"I do twenty minutes of my routine on Polacks and you book

me at a Polish social club. Are you friggin' nuts? These guys have been drinking warm beer since noon. The next time they roll out the barrels, I'll be *in* one."

Sal raised his eyebrows.

"Listen," Frankie instructed as he pulled on the jacket and clipped the tie to the collar of his powder-blue ruffled shirt. "You make sure the car's ready. Just in case. If you see me scratch my head, bring it around back. We'll make a run for it."

"Okay, I got you." He brushed Frankie's jacket. "Just promise, don't ruin the suit."

Frankie peeked into the dining room. Nothing fancy—more linoleum squares, brown, white, and an occasional red . . . wood-paneled walls, folding tables. No doubt there would be a bingo game here tomorrow.

"Did you ever see so many plaid shirts?" he asked Sal.

"Not worn with striped jackets," Sal answered.

The music came to a stop as the president of the group approached the microphone. He, too, was formally dressed, Frankie noted—though in a powder-blue tuxedo jacket paired with mint-green satin-stripe trousers that seemed to belong to a different suit. Frankie couldn't tell whether it was a unique fashion sense or a mixup at the dry cleaners.

The mic squeaked, sending a shrill vibration across the wires. "People, people . . . please can I have your attention?" the host intoned. "Welcome to the annual Kosciuszko Dinner for the Benevolent Association of the Eastern Division Lodge 230, in honor of Bazyli Chezernazcakyzi. To begin our show, let's have a nice welcome for the entertainer we've all been waiting for." He paused for dramatic effect. "All the way from Manhattan, New York, comedian Frank—E.—*Grace!*"

The emcee gave the cue by clapping his hands enthusiastically. From the audience came scattered applause that stopped long before the long-anticipated entertainer reached the stage. Frankie strode toward the dais, a platform raised about six inches higher than the linoleum floor. His last few steps were lonely. *Mental note to self: always reach the microphone while they're still clapping.*

The faint lights in his eyes, Frankie stepped to the mic. "Hey, thanks—thanks for changing my name. It's Frankie, not Frank E. Like I can't afford a middle initial."

No laughter. Not so much as a snicker. Not a good start. *Okay, lesson learned: never insult home-grown announcer. Move on.*

"I'd like to congratulate tonight's man of the year, but I can't pronounce his name."

Silence. Dead silence—a sound he was intimately familiar with.

"Hey, is that a last name—or a Polish eye test?"

Even deader silence.

"So, did you hear about the blind Polish lip reader? He couldn't find a job." A rumbling began. *So much for ad-lib.*

Undaunted, Frankie continued. "Hey, you know why it takes four Polacks to change a light bulb? Three to turn the ladder, one to hold the bulb."

About that time Frank E. Grace thought he saw the announcer whispering to someone offstage. Sweat began to form on Frankie's brow. *Think, stupid, change the jokes.* But he didn't have any new material.

"So . . . do you know how to tell a Polish bride at a wedding? She's the one wearing the clean T-shirt."

By that time a crowd had gathered around the announcer, who was doing his best to hold back the vanguard. Around the dining room a faint murmur grew to outright chatter. Frankie could see that some of the men were removing their jackets.

Think, stupid, be calm and think. Change the nationality.

"So, two Italians come from Warsaw . . ." *Jeez, where is this going? Move on.*

"Hey, they identified a body found in a trunk under the Brooklyn Bridge," Frankie offered, talking on autopilot. "Turns out he was the 1957 Polish hide-and-seek champion."

Was it his imagination, Frankie wondered, or was the emcee really turning purple in the face?

"Hey asshole," a voice yelled from the dining hall. "We're Polish."

"Okay, I'll talk slower." Frankie just couldn't help himself—it *was* a good line.

The crowd did not agree. The barrage started harmlessly—a crumpled napkin, an empty paper cup. Frankie ducked the first few items tossed at him.

"So you heard about the Polish cross-dressing transvestite who didn't have a thing to wear?" Chunks of kielbasa started flying in his direction. "You get it, thing, a thing?" Frankie repeated, "He didn't have a *thing* . . ." He pointed to his own zipper, to no avail.

"You suck!"

Hey, everyone's a critic.

"It's only a joke," Frankie pleaded. "Can't we laugh at each other? You wouldn't do this to Rickles."

Three groups had formed, as far as Frankie could make out. One was stage left, being held back by the announcer; one was stage right, with no barrier between them and the podium; and the other was in the center of the dining room gearing up for a frontal assault. I'll be damned, thought Frankie. A Polish Pinscher movement.

"So, I guess you don't want to hear about the two Polacks in a rowboat?"

It was the biggest sausage he had ever seen up close, and it caught him square between the eyes. Frankie was picking himself up from the floor when he caught sight of a group of younger patrons making their way toward the makeshift stage. The accordion player, clearly reveling in the entertainer's predicament, struck up an appropriately lively polka.

Frankie scrambled to his feet and made a dash for the door marked EXIT. His patent leather shoes, on loan from the funeral home, slipped and slid across the slick linoleum. As he crashed through the exit door, a thought occurred to him: *I never even had the chance to scratch my head.*

He looked both ways down the alley. No Sal. Where the hell was Sal? Frankie was entirely alone. I'll be found dead in this Polack alley in Polack Brooklyn, Polack New York, he thought, cut up into Polish sausage. He heard the angry footsteps of the crowd approaching. *I'm a goner now.* And then he caught a different sound—the rev of an engine. A monstrous roar. A squeal of tires.

He turned just in time to see the headlights of Sal's showroom-new '72 gold GTO turning the corner into the alley. The car came to a screeching halt and the passenger door flung open.

"Get in, *compare!*"

Frankie wasted no time. Sal floored the gas, leaving a fog of exhaust in his wake. There was an unmistakable look of success on his face. "I saved your ass," he said. "You owe me!"

With the help of 455 horses and an agile Hurst shifter Sal made his way like lightning through the maze of the borough's streets. Frankie had to hand it to Sal, the restaurant business had been good to his bank account. Back when they were both teenagers, when Salvatore Lucci, Junior, wasn't helping Salvatore Lucci, Senior, in the kitchen, he worked the floor as a waiter. That's where the money came in. Cash, as Sal always pointed out. Soon they were on the BQE, heading for the Williamsburg Bridge. In minutes they would be safe, on Mulberry Street, the motherland, Little Italy on Manhattan's lower east side. Only then could Frankie relax.

"Is it swollen?" Frankie asked, pointing to the side of his face that hurt the most.

Sal looked over at the black-and-blue welt forming beneath Frankie's eye.

"Nah, there ain't nuttin' there. But I think you need new material. That stuff is a little stale and it's gonna get you killed."

"It's not just the material, it's me. I was so nervous. I froze. I suck. I just suck."

"You're being too hard on yourself," Sal said. He turned up the radio and started to sing along. *"When you're down and trou-bled, and you need a hel-ping hand, and no-thing, whoa, no-thing is goin' right—"*

"Christ, this is great," Frankie said. "Are you trying to tell me something?"

"No, that's James Taylor singing," Sal protested. "It's the

number one song in the country."

"*That* is our country," Frankie said, as he pointed over the bridge. He reached for the knob and turned off the radio. They crossed the East River in silence.

As the car bounced off the Williamsburg Bridge onto Delancey, Frankie said, "Sal, we need to talk. I need a real manager. You're my best friend, but you don't know squat about show business. You own a restaurant—you're a cook, for chrissake. I need a manager if I am ever going to succeed as a comedian."

"First of all, I'm a chef."

"A cook."

"A chef."

Frankie cut him short. "You learned to cook from your grandfather. Did you ever go to culinary school? That's where chefs go."

"What are you talking about, cunnilingus school? What's that got to do with cooking?"

"Jesus, this is hopeless."

"Whatever."

Frankie rubbed his good eye. "Don't you understand? Since I agreed to let you manage me you got me booked as master of ceremonies of a zeppole-eating contest on Staten Island; a gig at a nudist colony in Pennsylvania where I almost got pneumonia; and an engagement party for a transsexual couple at your restaurant. I emceed a topless kazoo competition And now this gig at the Polish Copa."

"Hey, the tips weren't bad at the nudist colony, and some of those broads in the Poconos were worth a second look."

Ignore him, Frankie, make your point. "And how about the Ritz on Thompson Street? You said I'd be the opening act for Frankie Valli. On that we sold six hundred dollars' worth of tickets. The nightclub was a full three stories underground. People came by accident. They thought it was a train station, and who am I opening for?"

They answered at the same time. "*Rudy* Vallée."

There was an awkward silence as Frankie recalled the spectacle of trying to warm up an audience for a man who had sung through a funnel in the 1930s.

"I thought he was dead," Sal said.

"He was that night," Frankie countered.

"You're not being fair," said Sal. "I got you that date at Friar Tuck's in the Catskills. Not a bad gig for an upstart comic. We got room and board, two nights—huh, huh?"

"Yes, and they paid me five hundred," Frankie said.

Sal seemed pleased that he remembered, until Frankie continued. "Then I get called down to the West Side to see Nicky Knuckles, and he wants to know if I'm famous or something. And if I'm not famous, why should he pay a bar tab that you signed? Then he drops the aforementioned check on the table, and it seems a certain friend of mine, who shall remain nameless, was drinking champagne all night, not to mention buying drinks for the whole bar and signing for it."

"I thought I took care of that check." Sal sounded genuinely surprised.

Frankie continued. "And as it turns out, the bar bill came to one thousand four hundred seventy-five dollars, and they wanted their money."

Sal shrugged. "Hey, I got carried away."

"Right, I had to call my uncle Eddie to go to bat for me."

"Special Ed?"

"The same."

"A loser if ever there was one. They say he don't even know how to read."

"Yeah, but he's got a good heart."

"A loser, a dumb loser."

"Well, that loser got it squashed. All he had to do was mention some names, if you know what I mean."

A moment of silence.

"By the way," continued Frankie, "have you ever seen my Uncle Eddie play chess? You'd think twice about calling him dumb."

"Where did he learn to play chess?"

"A guard at Spofford Juvenile taught him. I tell you, Eddie's a genius."

Sal was not impressed. "I saw a show where a retarded kid played the piano like Beethoven or somebody. It's an aberration. I think they called him a servant, or something like that."

Frankie smiled in spite of himself. "Savant, you jerk."

"That's what I said. Let's get back to the matter at hand. You conveniently forget the San Su San. I got you that gig. What is it, three months now? Opening act once a week!"

Yeah, Frankie thought, a hundred dollars a show minus gas to Westbury, minus drinks. Net loss, a hundred dollars a night. *Let it go.*

Sal went on. "Listen, Frankie, I know I've made a coupla mistakes, but we all want something more for ourselves. You don't want to be carving up bodies for the rest of your life in some damp smelly basement of a funeral home. Well, me, too. I want something more. Do you think I want to drop dead at the back table, like my father, my head falling into a pile of potato peels? Remember that night?" He laughed and continued. "Just because my great-great-great-great-great-great grandfather fed the Romans doesn't mean I got to cook forever."

Then Sal moved in for the kill. "And one more thing, my dearest and best friend in all the neighborhood—wait, I take that back, in all the earth. I know I am new at the manager business, but there is one thing I know—talent, and you got it. You're funny. I told you since we were in third grade, you're too funny to be working for your father the rest of your life. You can make it to the big time, Vegas. I believe in you. Where you gonna find a manager who really believes in you? You can be there with the greats. I've seen you. I've heard you. You have it in you. One day you can host the Tonight Show. Carson can't live forever. You, of all people, should know that."

Frankie pictured Johnny Carson in a solid bronze casket, with gold handles shaped like golf clubs and a blue velvet interior customized to look like the curtains on the NBC Tonight Show set. He imagined putting last-minute touches on Johnny's makeup, and Johnny opening his eyes, looking at his watch, and imploring,

"Hey, it's eleven-thirty. I need a guest host. Frankie, you gotta get out there. The show must go on."

Sal continued, "Can you imagine hosting your own talk show?"

"Yeah, right. Who's dreaming now?"

"I mean it," said Sal, and it really sounded like he did.

Frankie remembered who his biggest fan was. He looked over at Sal. "So what was the name?"

"Of what?"

"Your great-great-great-great-great-great-great-grandfather's restaurant in Rome?"

"The Appian Way," Sal said.

Frankie nodded. "Did they do many funeral luncheons?"

Sal smiled. "Listen, Frankie, about tonight—I'm sorry. I didn't think about your routine and how that might not work so well at a Polish joint. We got to work on that, get you some new material. It'll come to you. Just keep writing all this stuff down like you always do. You're bound to find your voice. I'm telling you, a lot of big shots eat at Lucci's all the time. I'll make a connection some day that will get us both out of this place. I'm close to a deal right now. It was a secret. I was gonna surprise you."

Frankie didn't want to seem interested, but he took the bait. "What is it?"

"Let me put the finishing touches on it. A gig, a career-making gig. Just be patient."

The GTO cruised down Delancey, making a left down the Bowery to Hester and across Mott Street, to Mulberry.

"We're home safe," Sal said.

The Lower East Side was a haven to the Italian immigrants who had begun arriving at Ellis Island at the turn of the twentieth century. Row upon row of tenement buildings stretched as far as the eye could see, housing the influx yearning to breathe free. The area was the birthplace of the American Mafia, starting with the Five Points Gang and Frank Uale, and continuing through Genovese, Gambino, and, these days, Fortissimo and Ballsziti. Family connections were thick, and you had to be careful who you did business with—and how.

At street level were small storefronts housing trattorias, pizzerias, and salumerias, with balls of provolone and sopressata hanging in wait to clog a consumer's arteries. There were bakeries, butcher shops, and pork stores, Italian music stores, and more bakeries and restaurants. Here, sandwiched between the Isabella Bakery Shop and Lucci's Restaurant, stood the Grace Funeral Home.

The brownstone establishment was identified by a shingle over the door, a testimony to the aged brassworker who had bartered a portion of his prepaid funeral expense in return for fabricating the sign some sixty years earlier. The ancient artisan had not planned so well on the lettering, however, and by the time had constructed the frame he'd had to abbreviate.

The car came to a stop in front of the arched brick entrance, above which the sign read GRACE FUN. HOME. Some fun, Frankie thought. "Maybe this is not such a bad place anyway," Frankie mused aloud, dejected, to Sal. "Maybe I *am* destined to be a funeral director like my father and his father before him. It's in the cards, beyond my control."

"Destined my ass," said Sal. "Now listen to me. I won't let you give up. Look," he said, pointing north, up Mulberry.

Mulberry Street stretched south from Chinatown north to Houston. At the very end, beyond the rooftops on Houston Street, on the horizon, the glistening spire of the Empire State Building jutted up above the tenements. Sal pointed to it with a sweeping gesture. "You see that building? It's a reminder. Don't you ever forget there is something more out there, something bigger than us, bigger than this neighborhood, and it's waiting for us to grab it."

Frankie realized he would never be able to replace his childhood friend with a professional manager. He would have to play the hand he was dealt. That's the way it should be, he thought. If this neighborhood taught you anything, it was loyalty. "I'm sorry for doubting you," he said. "Of course you're my manager."

"*Yesssss!*" Sal pumped his fist in victory then threw his arms around Frankie's head, rubbing his knuckles into his hair.

"You won't be sorry, *compare*. You know I would do anything for you."

Frankie's beeper went off. He said, "Pull around the corner to the phone booth. It's my father again and I don't want to answer for why I'm wearing this tux." Sal obliged. Frankie dug out a dime from his pocket and called Primo, who answered, "Strunz?"

"Yes, Dad."

"Where are you? Get to the apartment, let's go, let's move. Turns out the son-in-law isn't getting released till Monday morning. Get her out of there before the Board of Health condemns the building."

Frankie walked back to the car. "You said you would be willing to do anything?"

"Yes, *compare*."

"Good. I need help. Mrs. Cianci is dead and I need help to get her down the stairs."

Sal said, "Isabella the baker, the pastry queen, her daughter Annunziata with the lip hair? Boy, did we have fun with that in school."

"Yes, that's her," Frankie confirmed. "And don't forget her name is Annunziata Ballsziti." He stressed the last name for emphasis.

"Jeez," Sal said. "I hate buying bread from her—I'm afraid I'm going to find a piece of that lip hair in it. It keeps growing, you know. It gives me the chills. Hey, is it true the hair keeps growing even when you're dead?"

"Look at her the wrong way and you'll find out. Remember, since you didn't get it the first time, she is Annunziata *Ballsziti*." He knew Sal would eventually get his drift. Johnny Ballsziti was highly respected in Little Italy, for all the wrong reasons.

"I remember her daughter too. What was her name?" Sal asked.

"I didn't know there was one."

"She didn't go to school here. They sent her off to finishing school somewhere."

"Does that mean she's Finnish now, not Italian?"

It took a moment, but then Sal laughed. "Finnish, hah, hah, that's good, that's funny. Hey, write that down. You could use that."

Frankie filed the line in his brain's comedy file cabinet, as was his practice. He turned to Sal again. "So, will you help me?"

"Jeez, Frankie, I don't know. I remember Mrs. Ballsziti is a mean one on a regular day. She can't be any fun to be around with her mother dead and all. She never smiles. I thought fat people were jolly."

"Would you smile if Johnny Ballsziti was your husband?"

"Hell no," Sal said, "Johnny Ballsziti is a crazy capo. The real thing. I heard it was an arranged marriage. They did that in those days."

Frankie nodded, and then laughed.

"What's so funny?" Sal wanted to know.

"I never could say his name right. Every time I tried to say hello, the *balls* and the *ziti* always got caught in my throat, something about the *s* and *z* together. I came out sounding like Daffy Duck."

"Be careful, Frankie. He's got a screw loose. And it's bound to be even worse now that Roscoe Keats and the feds have had him in custody. Word is he once had a guy's nuts cut off for calling him Johnny Balls. He's known for that, cutting guy's balls off. It's like his calling card. Rumor has it he keeps 'em on display in his café."

"I heard that too," Frankie said with a grim laugh. Then, "So, you'll help me move Mrs. Cianci's body?"

"For you, my friend and number one client, anything."

"Hey, thanks," Frankie said, adding as an afterthought, "chef."

Chapter 2

The cries of anguish could be heard from the sidewalk, quite an impressive feat, considering that Isabella Cianci lived on the top floor of a five-story walk-up and the mourners had been hanging around for nearly fifteen hours.

Frankie handed Sal a folding canvas stretcher. "Carry this, and when we get upstairs, you wait in the hallway until I call you."

"Why do I have to carry it?"

Frankie explained, "It's obvious. You are the assistant. I am the funeral director."

The hallway was dark, the staircase narrow. Flecks of missing paint revealed a jagged crack in the plaster wall that followed the rise of the metal handrail. With each step the pair took, the stairs squeaked, and the banister swayed with their slightest touch.

"Frankie, wait, I have to rest." Sal was panting.

"We're only on the third floor. You'd better lose some of that gut."

"Hey, it's not easy. I have to sample what I cook."

The harrowing screams from above threatened to shatter the plate-glass windows as Frankie and Sal approached the top floor.

"Frankie, Jesus, she knew she was dying, couldn't she come down a few flights?"

"Get all your jokes over with now, Sal. Remember, this is Johnny Balls—*zi*—ti's mother-in-law." Frankie pronounced it deliberately, trying not to trip over the *s* and *z* sounds that always got caught between his tongue and his teeth. "And whatever you do, don't stare at the hair on Annunziata's lip."

The odiferous sign of a decaying corpse was evident in the hallway as they reached the top floor. "Why did I agree to this?" Sal lamented. "I think I'm going to faint. The stink is getting to me. It smells like *bacala*."

Frankie agreed, but did not say so out loud. The smell of the salt cod fish could clear out a room. But not, apparently, in this case.

"I think I'll wait in the hall until you need me," Sal suggested.

The railroad-room apartment was typical of the tenements on Mulberry Street— three rooms, small, lined up in a row like train cars. The door from the hallway led into a kitchen, with a small bathroom next to the sink. Off the kitchen there was a parlor, which led into the third room, a bedroom. The parlor always had the obligatory couch, love seat, or chair that opened into a bed at night.

Mrs. Cianci's apartment, the last on the corridor, was easily recognizable by the number of shoes lined up outside the door. On an occasion like this, when there was a death in the building, the apartment took on the look of a clown's car, with a seemingly endless string of people coming and going. There were thirty, forty, maybe fifty people crammed into the tiny space—aunts, cousins, second cousins, second cousins once removed—*paisanos* sobbing and crying, one louder than the other, depending on the family relationship, a morose hierarchy. Aunts screamed louder than nieces, who in turn wailed harder than cousins—and those were just the women. The men huddled sheepishly around the kitchen table smoking cigarettes or guinea-stinker cigars. They poured steaming espresso into small cups already half filled with anisette. Frankie understood the need to drink.

The funeral director's arrival, in formal attire, was announced with great fanfare. "*I bacca morte è qui!,*" he heard a voice say. The undertaker is here. The kiss of death.

As word spread, the news sent the cacophony to a new high,

until the crowd separated to allow the rotund Annunziata Cianci Ballsziti to charge straight through the linked rooms like a bull at a matador. She rushed straight for Frankie. He braced for the impact. With less than twelve inches between them, she came to a halt, arms flailing. She wagged her index finger in his face. "You're not taking her! You're not taking my mother." The bereaved daughter raised her eyes upward. *"Dio, Dio,* God, why her, why my mother, why not me? Why did Mama die?"

Frankie wanted to suggest that her advanced age—ninety-six—had something to do with it, but he thought better of it.

A kindly gentleman seated at the table tapped on his arm. "Espresso?"

Then, miraculously, in a schizophrenic or hormonal moment—Frankie wasn't sure which—the screaming stopped long enough for Annunziata to ask a question. "Where are you taking my mother now?"

"Back with me to the funeral home, Mrs. Balls–zi–ti." Wrong answer, Frankie quickly realized.

"No, you sonofabitch, you're not taking her! Luigi, Mario, stop him, he wants to take my mother. No, no, you can't have her—" Then, a sudden calm. "Would you like a sfogliotella?" She picked up a crusty pastry shell filled with mascarpone cheese and covered with white confectioners' sugar, and shoved it under Frankie's nose. "It'sa fresh."

She was close enough now for him to see it. *No, no, look away, don't stare—she'll tell her husband.* He recalled Saturday mornings in the barbershop, where neighborhood historians had debated the actual length of Annunziata Ballsziti's lip hair. Some argued it was but an eight of an inch, while others insisted it was at least a half inch to three quarters. Rocco, the barber, and thereby something of an authority, reminded all that the curl at the end could easily straighten out into another inch or more, making the upside potential two, three inches or better. It was a double swirl, as he explained—very rare. They always deferred to Rocco's professional opinion. From his vantage point now, Frankie had to agree with the barber's expert analysis. He also noted the distinctive two-tone color of the oft-discussed moustache, black at the root, gray at the tip, as the end curled into the letter Q.

"Go ahead, have one. They're fresh," Annunziata repeated as she pushed the pastry toward him. A flurry of powdered sugar danced in the air, settling on his blue tux. Sal was going to love this, Frankie thought.

"You want something else? There's plenty of food." Indeed there was, dish after dish of cannoli, manicotti, an endless array of delicacies. "Our neighbors are so good to us. They thought we might be hungry."

When was the last time you were hungry, Frankie thought.

"Have something," she pressed.

"No, Mrs. Liphairballs–zi–ti—" *I'm such an idiot—recover, recover.* "I have to get busy. Your mother has been here all day..."

"Where else would she be? She lives here."

He refrained from correcting the tense of the verb. "Yes, but I think it's best we begin the work we need to do." *Mistake, mood change, high C.*

Annunziata effectively blocked his progress. "*Dio, Dio mio,* he wants to take my mother. The sonofabitch wants to take my mother!"

Frankie looked around, hoping one of the sixty people in the apartment could calm the woman down. Help was nowhere to be found. He tried in desperation to catch Sal's eye as the bereaved matron launched another salvo, a soprano wail that could have rattled the rafters of La Scala itself. *What am I going to—*

From the doorway, suddenly, a mellifluous female voice, as though introducing a duet, sounded a lovely mezzo note. "Mama, *sta ziti!*"

The whole village went quiet. Mrs. Ballsziti stopped midsentence. Frankie turned to see what angel from heaven had come to his aid.

"Mama," the angel said again. Her tone was soothing, reassuring. She captivated every eye in an instant. Frankie stared.

This had to be the *Finnish* daughter, no more than a few feet from him, a stunning young brunette, hair glowing, emerald green eyes sparkling, skin smooth and pale as a baby's bottom. He wished he had another comparison. His mouth remained open as he studied her full, sensuous lips. He was sure they were calling him.

Then panic set in as he thought of his mother's warning, delivered in her customary operatic style—If you want to know what a woman will look like in twenty years, look at her mother. He stared again, zeroing in on her upper lip. *Please God, no, don't let there be . . . .* He stared as if in a trance. Nothing. *Thank you, Jesus.*

Then he let his eyes move to see the entire package. A figure that wouldn't quit, breasts peeking milky white over the neckline of a black scoop-neck sweater. Beneath a short sheath skirt, the outline of shapely legs that started at the hips and went all the way down to the floor. Just the type he liked. Frankie was in love.

He continued to stare, slack-jawed, as the angel walked toward him. He caught her scent, a whisper of sweet perfume that momentarily made him forget the odor emanating from the bedroom. He was struck by the juxtaposition: a ninety-six-year-old corpse decaying in a nearby room, a buffet in front of him sufficient to feed a third-world country, and gliding before his eyes, the most beautiful woman he had ever laid eyes on. The philosophers, thanatologists, and poets always suggested some cosmic connection between death, food, and sex—and here it was. He was living it. These were the best ten seconds of his life, no doubt.

The angel reached out her hand. "I'm Caterina. It's my grandmother who has died."

Frankie shook her hand robotically. Her touch sent goosebumps up his arm. His knees nearly buckled. "So nice to meet you," he said.

Nice to meet you? What are you—at a party? Her grandmother's dead, stupid. Say something comforting. "I'm so sorry about your grandmother. I was explaining to your mom that it's best we remove her to the funeral home where we can begin our preparation process."

Preparation process? You clinical moron, what's wrong with you? What are you going to say next, I have to break rigor? I have to shoot her with fluid? Desperate, Frankie continued, "Perhaps you can have some of the people **go** into another room, so I can move the body." He didn't think he and Sal could maneuver the corpse past the food and through the crowd in the tiny apartment.

Caterina looked around. "There aren't many choices." Then she turned to her mother. "Mama, we'll have everyone come downstairs to sit with us."

Annunziata had become docile as a lamb under her daughter's direction. "They better take off their shoes."

"Sure, that would be a good idea," Frankie said. "How do we get them to leave?"

"Well," Caterina suggested, "why don't we say a prayer together at Nonna's bedside, then everyone can pay their last respects and leave so you can do your work."

That should have been my idea, thought Frankie. *I'm the professional.* Being around Caterina was apparently not good for his mental processes. "That's wonderful, Caterina," Frankie said. As he said her name he fell even more deeply in love. *Caterina.* He had heard the song over loudspeakers from Rossi's music store all his life, and now he was in love with the song, with her, with life! Sorry, Dad, he thought hastily. "Grazie. A prayer is a good idea."

She spoke to the masses, shepherding them out of the way. "*Venite, tutti.* Let us pray for Annuniziata's soul." Her words flowed like music. Like Moses leading the Exodus, she headed up the ungainly procession. Everyone started moving into the dead woman's room. (*Where was the fire department when you needed them?*) He was impressed. What poise, what panache, what . . . aplomb? *Mental note: look up aplomb.*

Frankie inspected the bed. Somewhere there in the folds of the bedclothes lay Caterina's dead grandmother. He moved toward the headboard and only then saw the small, wizened face with the complexion—or lack thereof—that accompanies death. Rosy cheeks had surrendered to shades of gray. Unlike her daughter, Isabella was thin. Her frail body scarcely made an impression on the mattress.

"She hasn't been eating," Caterina said.

Annuzniata plopped onto the foot of the bed. The mattress bent and the wood frame cracked. Frankie peered more closely at the corpse. Christ, he thought, she has lip hair too! It *is* hereditary! Life's not fair. Then he looked again at the angel across from him. Maybe she has her father's genes, he thought. Yes, that would be comforting; trading a cosmetic affectation for a sociopathic personality. His heart was pounding. I could live with it, he decided. For her I could do anything.

"Who will you pray to?" she asked.

"Perhaps Nonna had a special saint she liked," Frankie replied.

Caterina motioned toward the back wall. The assemblage of bedside mourners parted, revealing a bureau lined with lighted prayer candles flickering softly in front of a dozen porcelain saints, each missing a different body part. The Infant of Prague, with a broken crown, faced the door. St. Anthony was holding up one finger instead of two. Frankie took the gesture personally. *Same to you, buddy.* St. Christopher was still welcomed here, but he seemed to have lost the Christ child. St. Ann, missing a nose. *Mental note for the comedy file cabinet: a place in heaven for statue repair.*

Caterina offered an idea. "You know we have saints and prayers for every need or desire . . . once, to sell our house in Italy we were instructed to bury a statue of St. Joseph upside down in the yard. Isn't there a saint for mourning?"

There's a routine here, Frankie thought. This was no time to be thinking of his avocation, but he couldn't stop the internal voice harping on about the statue thing. Then he remembered: *Jesus, Sal—he's been waiting out in the hallway all this time.* "How about the Our Father, that's always a big hit," he suggested.

"Yes," said the love of his life. "That will be fine." Her lips parted.

Great teeth, Frankie thought. She was exquisite.

Not until an hour and twenty minutes later was the last prayer, the last scream, the last "why not me" heard from the fifth-floor bedroom on the corner of Mulberry and Hester Streets. Finally the room cleared. Each mourner who left took a tray of food, found their shoes in the hallway, and solemnly followed Annunziata downstairs to her apartment. Caterina, last to leave, showed no ill effects from the late hour or the family drama. She was the most perfect creature Frankie had ever encountered.

She paused at the top of the stairs long enough to rest one graceful hand on the banister. Frankie couldn't help but notice the effortless balance, the curving asymmetry of her hips as she stood poised on two steps. Contrapposto, the art historians called it. Michelangelo himself could have sculpted her.

She caught Frankie's eye for a fleeting second. *"Mille grazie,"* he heard those lovely lips say to him, before her figure disappeared down the flights of stairs.

O how happy my heart would be, if I knew that you loved just me—say it's true, say ya do, Caterina! Frankie found himself forming the words to the song into a silent prayer for her body and soul—mostly her body. Caterina was right—Italian Catholics had a patron saint for every need. You lose something, pray to St. Anthony; for hopeless causes, pray to St. Jude. Frankie sure knew that one. His father often prayed to St. Jude. So, why not his prayer? What broken statue could grant that one? *Why, St. Valentine, of course!*

✝

Frankie opened the door to the hallway and found Sal sleeping in the stairwell leading to the roof. His jacket was rolled into a ball on the stretcher where he rested his head.

"Hey, Sal. Wake up."

Sal opened his eyes. "I'm waiting out here all night, right after the daughter arrived. What took so long?"

"It's a long story. Come on."

Sal picked up the stretcher and followed Frankie into the apartment. It was dark inside, and eerily quiet. The earlier caterwauling had given way to muffled bouts of sobbing, now coming from below.

"Is it too late to change my mind?"

"Yes." Frankie proceeded to the bedroom and took the stretcher from Sal. In the moonlight from the one small window, he saw that all the color had drained from Sal's face.

Sal stood frozen in place. "Frankie, I got to go. I'm not cut out for this."

"Sal, you can't leave now. Just do what I say." Frankie unfolded the stretcher alongside the bed. He removed the handmade calico quilts from the bed, folding them and placing them on a chair. Under the covers, Isabella was fully dressed, as though she expected to sit straight up in the bed, get to her feet, and don her apron for a day's work in the bakery. But her lifeless face and hands had turned a deep plum color. Decomposition had already begun.

"This is too weird," Sal said. "I can't help you. I can't."

"Shush," said Frankie.

Frankie untucked the bedcovers from the mattress and folded them over Isabella's corpse. Then he tied the corners of the sheets, creating a gurney that could be lifted onto the stretcher.

He motioned to Sal. "Stand there," he said, pointing to the headboard.

"Why am I carrying the head end?" Sal looked down at the old woman's face. His eyes drifted to a spot above her top lip. "Jeez, the same hair her daughter has. Hey, you never answered me. Does hair keep growing after you die?"

"Be serious, or you're going to find out personally. Come down here, and you can take the feet."

The two switched positions.

"Just do what I do," Frankie instructed. He picked up the edges of the makeshift gurney. Sal reluctantly followed suit. Together they slid the body onto the stretcher.

"Christ," Sal said. "I need a drink."

"You've been known to drink for a lot less," Frankie said. He reached for the straps and brought them over the body. As he fastened the buckle at the top of the stretcher, Isabella's arm raised upward.

Sal started to hyperventilate and was about to collapse when Frankie steadied him. "Sal, come on, snap out of it. I need your help."

"Did she just give me the Italian salute?"

"It was the strap, stupid. Her arm moved when I tightened the straps."

What a colorful pair. She's deep purple, and he's Casper-the-Friendly-Ghost white.

Frankie covered the stretcher with a canvas. "Let's go," he said. "Pick up your end."

As Sal lifted the stretcher, there was an audible groan. Frankie said, "Sal, she weighs ninety pounds. What the hell are you groaning about?"

"That—that wasn't me." Sal gulped and broke out in a sweat.

"It's nothing," Frankie said. "A death rattle. It happens all the time, air exiting the lungs."

"Yeah, well, that's not the only place air is exiting. How the hell can anyone do this for a living?"

Frankie had asked himself that same question many times, mostly in the prep room when the hose attached to the trocar—the instrument used to aspirate the thoracic and abdominal cavities—slipped, covering him in bile and blood. At moments like that, only thoughts of a different future and the promise of a few well-deserved cocktails at Lucci's helped him through the task at hand.

Sal made the turn into the narrow hallway and shuffled his way down the steps backwards, one foot at a time, with the stretcher pinching into his waist. As he reached the fourth step, he yelled "Ouch!" and stopped.

Frankie looked annoyed. "Keep going, come on. What's wrong now?"

"I don't know. I have a sharp pain in my stomach." Sal looked down. "Frankie, her foot just came through the stretcher! Her toenail is digging into me. I think I'm bleeding."

Frankie stared down the steps and saw Isabella's foot buried in Sal's waist.

"Put the stretcher down on the landing." They lowered the stretcher, and Frankie leaned over. "You didn't strap her legs in, moron."

"What do I know? I'm a chef, remember?"

"Cook," muttered Frankie, buckling the straps and securing

the sheet around her legs.

"Jeez, you couldn't pay me to do this," Sal said.

"I don't intend to," Frankie answered. "Now lift."

Sal lifted his end of the stretcher and walked backwards, bumping into the wall and banister on the way out.

"You owe me big time," Sal said. "I better be your manager for life after this."

"Let's take her out through the back yard," Frankie directed. They carried the stretcher out of the building, maneuvered through the narrow alley where the hearse was parked.

Frankie unlocked the door to the funeral home, disappeared into the shadows for a moment, then came out rolling a gurney.

"This is as far as I go," said Sal firmly. Sal watched as Frankie maneuvered the stretcher onto the larger gurney and wheeled it down the darkened ramp into the bowels of the basement embalming room.

"This shouldn't take long—an hour or so." Frankie removed the tux jacket, unclipped his tie, and rolled up the sleeves of his dress shirt. "Where will you be?"

"At Bellevue, having my head examined."

Frankie nodded sagely. "A little late."

"What?"

"I said, *later*."

Sal squeezed past the hearse that blocked the alley, then turned back. "Frankie, how do you do it? I mean, I felt sick just helping you carry her. What you do now, how can you do it?"

"You don't want to know. You won't understand."

"Yes, I will."

Frankie stopped at the basement door. "Basically, to do what I need to do, I go into a functional coma. I do what I do by being someone else, by being somewhere else. I'm Abbot's Costello, I'm Jerry Lewis, I'm Rickles or Carson, someone, somewhere on a stage, far from where I am."

"Yeah," said Sal. "I can see that."

✝

It was late, past closing time. The busboy at Lucci's turned the last chair upside down on the table and rushed down the steps past Sal with a friendly "Hasta manana."

"Yeah, right, Pasta Faggiola, or whatever." Sal was in a daze, reliving the last few hours. He was feeling queasy and decided he was hungry. Sal was always hungry, though he ate even when he wasn't.

In the restaurant kitchen, he scrubbed his hands with Ajax. Not satisfied, he took a sponge and rubbed his hands under steaming hot water until they were nearly raw. Then, just for good measure, he scrubbed them again. He smelled his hands. No hint of bacala.

Satisfied, he poured olive oil into a frying pan and lit the gas stove. He took potatoes from the refrigerator, ran them under the faucet, peeled and sliced them, and dropped them into the sizzling skillet on the back burner. As the potatoes fried, he cracked three eggs and let the yolk drop into another smaller pan on the front. Mix and mingle, shake the pan, toss the new omelet into the air and catch it, mused Sal as he watched the eggs turn golden. The omelet was ready.

He reached for a loaf of crusty, seeded Italian bread from the Isabella Bakery. As he checked it for hair, he thought back to the unpleasant task he'd helped Frankie perform. The smell still haunted him; his stomach turned. He smelled his hands again. Ah, the fresh, clean scent of Ajax, he thought. No hair and no bacala. He placed the omelet into a healthy wedge of the bread, removed the potatoes from the open flame, and set himself a place at the nearest table. This was all anyone needed in life to be happy, he was sure. That, and a glass of Chianti.

He thought about his promise to Frankie about closing in on a big deal, a career-making gig. He hadn't been lying. He did have something up his sleeve.

Ever since the attempted assassination of Joe Colombo at an Italian-American rally uptown, neighborhoods like Little Italy had become quite the tourist attraction. A mob boss's creation of the Italian American Civil Rights League turned the media spotlight on the once sleepy neighborhood—unwanted attention, in the eyes of people like Johnny Ballsziti. When thousands of well-meaning Italian Americans took to protesting outside FBI Headquarters, the feds retaliated. High-stakes cards games and late-night craps sessions were raided; bookies and low-level shylocks were picked up. It was bad for business—*his* business.

The media attention also brought hordes of visitors to the streets of Little Italy who would never before have set foot south of Delancey. Busloads of curiosity seekers arrived every morning. They walked through the streets as if touring a movie set. At night, the neighborhood became a magnet for the rich and famous. Hollywood types and Wall Streeters alike sought vicarious thrills in the presence of the heirs of *omertà*. They patronized sidewalk cafés and trattorias, hoping to rub elbows with real-life mobsters. A slew of young wannabes, wearing spaghetti-strapped T-shirts and twirling gold keychains, added to the allure. Mulberry Street had become the place to be.

That's how Sal had met Tony Romo, owner of the legendary San Su San Night Club on Long Island. Romo had become a frequent diner in Sal's Mulberry Street establishment, Lucci's. Sal arranged for Frankie to audition at the San Su San and boom—Tony had hired Frankie to do the weekly show, as the opening act for his bevy of up-and-coming singers.

Sal was sure he would eventually make an even bigger connection. He always made sure to look over the patrons and check the reservation list. If a name jumped out at him, or if anyone looked like they might be in show business, they got a personal visit from the chef.

There was that night when he happened to overhear a group of diners discussing a movie they were producing. Sal sent a bottle of his best Chianti to the table, introduced himself, provided a fresh Italian cheesecake for dessert on the house, and plied his new friends with after-dinner drinks. They returned a second and third time, and each time he ingratiated himself even more. "I like the look of the restaurant," said one of the movie people. "Real authentic."

Of course it was authentic, from the empty wine bottles

hanging behind the bar, to the display case filled with stuffed mushrooms and fresh eggplants, to the hundreds of photographs that adorned the wall, framed glossies signed by baseball legends, political bigwigs, and the FBI's current Most Wanted list. The tables were adorned with red-and-white-checked cloths, and a vase of fresh flowers provided a centerpiece for each. A red horn—to ward off *mal'occhio*, the evil eye—hung from the broken arm of the Infant of Prague statue, which faced the door, as was the custom. Just for insurance, a rosary hung from the Infant's other arm. The Hollywood guy asked about using the dining room for a scene in a movie about Lenny Bruce, the comic, so Sal told them about Frankie. They'd said there might, just might, be a cameo role in one of the nightclub scenes.

Sal couldn't feel any better about the opportunity. He was just waiting for the call. He told them where they could catch Frankie's act, and they promised they would and get back to him. If Frankie got this role, the rest would be easy. Sal was sure of it.

The phone call he'd been hoping for had come a week later.

"Sal?"

"Yes."

"It's me, Sol Weis, calling from L.A. We're thinking of going out to the San Su San to catch your friend's act when we're in town."

"Hey, Sol, that's great." In his excitement, Sal drew blood from his cuticle.

"Well, we'll see. We may have a small part for him, as a favor to you, of course."

"Sol, thank you. You won't regret it."

"Hey Sally, baby, maybe you can do me a favor."

"Name it." *I smell a freebie*, Sal thought.

"We have some people flying in from the West Coast next week. I'd like to take them downtown, about eight people, can you pencil us in?"

"It's done, Mr. Weis." *Solly*, he wanted to say, but thought better of it. He did some quick calculations; eight people, thirty a head, plus wine. A small price to pay, Sal convinced himself.

A huge sense of satisfaction washed over Sal, due not only to the last morsel of omelet and his escape from the night's misadventures. He'd rescue Frankie Grace from the funeral racket yet. He smirked as he thought of Frankie telling him he didn't know the first thing about being a manager. Ha!

Chapter 3

Eddie Fontana was called "Special Ed," but never to his face. He had a hair-trigger temper that would have made his father proud. Eddie's mother died in childbirth, leaving his father to raise him. Mario Fontana was a man of the streets and had little time to raise a son. Little Eddie would tag along as his father held meetings in different stores in Little Italy. Eddie would sit at a sidewalk café dunking anisette cookies into a glass of milk, waiting for his father to appear. He noticed early on how the other men kissed his father on both cheeks after these meetings. His father was the quintessential mobster, impeccably dressed and manicured, with slick salt-and-pepper hair. Mario had also had the dubious distinction, in 1963, of being the last man to be executed by the electric chair in New York State. Timing is everything. Eddie was only sixteen years old then. There was no inheritance, Johnny Ballsziti had told him. In fact, to short-circuit any inquiry as to monies put aside, Ballsziti let it be known on the street that Mario actually *owed* a few dollars.

The nuns at Transfiguration School on Mott Street labeled Eddie slow as well as unrepentant. At their suggestion, he was shipped off to Hoboken to live with an elderly aunt. The nuns did not miss him, nor did his aunt, when he fled her confines at the first opportunity. As the sea beckons a sailor, Little Italy beckoned Eddie back. With the help of his father's former partner, Ballsziti,

33

Eddie moved back to Mulberry Street, into the apartment across the hall from Giovanna and Primo Grace. The apartment was JB's safe house, and to make room for the new tenant, JB had hundreds of cartons of illegal cigarettes moved into its back room. The apartment reeked of tobacco, and so did Eddie and everything he wore. Young Eddie splashed on copious amounts of cologne to cover it up. He drowned himself in Canoe. His efforts weren't completely successful. Even with the cologne, there was always an underlying note of tobacco, leaving him smelling somewhere between sweet and smoked. Still, there was never a question what to get Eddie for Christmas or birthdays. A bottle of Canoe, and he couldn't thank you enough.

JB didn't charge him rent on the income-producing apartment, and he often reminded his protégé of that fact. But it was Giovanna who made sure Eddie ate. She also did his laundry, ironed his clothes, and cleaned his apartment. She and Primo tried to get him to enroll in trade school, but Eddie preferred the school of hard knocks. The Graces were the only family he had, the only stability he knew, and he was a fixture in their home. And although they were only a few years apart in age, Frankie Grace grew up calling the other young man at the kitchen table Uncle.

Eddie spent his formative years in the mafia apprentice program, under the adept tutelage of Johnny Ballsziti. The life had a certain appeal. If he passed the course, one day he, too, would be a made man. Eddie's education included on-the-job training in peddling fireworks for Fourth of July celebrations, selling cigarettes imported from South Carolina without the required federal tax stamps, running numbers, collecting loan-shark payments, picking up JB's dry cleaning, having the oil changed in JB's car, and driving a certain tinsel-haired blonde to the Plaza Hotel then back home to Brooklyn two days later. It also required a number of hands-on advanced placement courses: delivering an occasional dead fish to someone's doorstep, or breaking an occasional leg. All with the promise that one day, he too would be able to afford Brioni suits and custom shoes, just like his late father had. That was JB's unspoken promise.

Eddie lived in hope: If I do what I'm told, when Johnny Ballsziti becomes *capo regime*—a vote by secret ballot—I will be right there with him. JB was the dominant force in his life. Any self-respecting don needed a gofer, and Eddie understood it was an entry-level position with the possibility of promotion. Being close to JB made him feel connected to his own father. He'd heard the rumors on the street that his father got the chair for a murder JB committed. But JB always gave credit where it was due, praising Eddie's father in front of all the men in the café.

"He was a stand-up guy, your father. He kept his mouth shut. He was old school."

Nothing could have made Eddie prouder.

Over the noise of Monday morning traffic, Frankie heard a distinctive whistle. Still bleary-eyed from the previous day's labors, he shaded his eyes and searched for the source. Across Mulberry Street, in the deep shadows, stood Eddie, a nervous chain-smoker, waving at him. Eddie wore his trademark short-sleeved, square-bottomed, bowling-shirt-styled dress shirt. He preferred to wear the loose-fitting garment that did not need to be tucked in. It hid a lot of sins. This one was orange, but he had them in all colors, mostly bright pastels, with his initials embroidered in cursive on the chest. Vinnie from B & G Clothing on Arthur Avenue kept a steady supply on hand for him. Eddie pointed to Frankie and then tapped his fingers like a quacking duck, pointed to Frankie again, then to himself. It was mobspeak. Frankie interpreted: I need to talk to you now.

He hustled across the street. Frankie could smell Eddie's cologne, still with the slightest hint of tobacco, from ten feet away. Eddie smiled as he approached.

"What's up, Uncle?"

Eddie always spoke in code. He lived in fear of being recorded and often moved his lips without making a sound. This technique he had learned from his mentor, JB. Frankie figured if the feds were waiting to learn anything from Eddie they were in a sorry state. Listening to one of his conversations left even those who knew him best confused. But Eddie liked to think the feds were watching him. It gave him an elevated sense of importance. It was all part of the underworld allure. Years of practice qualified Frankie to decipher the speech code and charades.

Eddie put his arm around Frankie's shoulder. "I spoke with my friend. He wants to meet you tomorrow. She's to be buried in a family cemetery in Queens." After that last word he nodded "no," then he pointed to his hand, then to his ear. He looked around at rooftops and passing cars. Then his lips moved, slowly enough to be read: Be careful, be careful, I don't like it, he mouthed.

"Don't like what?"

Eddie grimaced and put his hand over Frankie's mouth.

"Sorry," Frankie said.

Eddie grabbed Frankie by the arm and led him over to Mott Street. His head was down so no gremlin agent could read his lips. He whispered, his voice barely audible. "You know why our friend was away?"

Frankie shrugged.

Eddie pointed to his eyes: open, shut, open shut, open, shut.

Frankie didn't get it.

"The Brinks job, remember the *Brinks* job a few months ago." Eddie said aloud, out of frustration.

Ah, blinks, sounds like Brinks, thought Frankie. He recalled the largest armored-car robbery in history, from the Federal Reserve Bank on Liberty Street, where five million in newly minted currency was stolen in broad daylight. It was a professional heist, well planned and executed, and no one got hurt.

"What about it? What's the Brinks heist got—"

Eddie cringed again, looking north, south, east and west. Frankie got the message. "They think JB had something to do with it, but he didn't," said Eddie. That was loud enough for anyone to hear. Play that in court, you flatfoot.

Eddie was agitated now. He pulled Frankie into the hallway of a nearby tenement. "Frankie, you should know better," he whispered. "If you understand me, just nod. It's counterproductive if you repeat what I say out loud."

That made sense, Frankie thought.

"Listen, there's something going on. JB didn't do the heist. Here's how it went down. Three professionals from Canada pulled it off, but they were smart. They knew they could never get back to Toronto with five million in hot money. Every flatfoot from Washington to friggin' Niagara Falls was looking for them. They reached out to JB. He paid them twenty percent clean money. How much is that?"

"A million," Frankie answered.

"Right, I knew that." Eddie continued, "And they went back to Canada. They were smart, not greedy, you know what I mean?"

Frankie nodded, "I guess."

"Anyway, the feds know JB is involved, but they can't prove it. And now JB's got the problem of cleaning the laundry, if you know what I mean." Eddie looked out the hallway to the neighboring fire escapes. They slipped out of the hallway after checking the street and continued walking.

"They've been trying to put him away for thirty years," Eddie said in a hushed tone, "but he's too smart for them. They got everyone else, one at a time, all the capos got sent up or went missing—but not Johnny. He's too smart for them. They got him locked up as a so-called material witness for months now, no charges, nottin'. I thought this was America. Anyway, his lawyer finally got a judge to order his release, and now this thing with his mother-in-law. So, he wants me to tell you to meet him at the café tomorrow morning to discuss the funeral. Did I tell you the cemetery is in Queens?" He shook his head 'no' then pointed to his hand, then his ear.

"Yes, so? St. John's is a lovely place. The old lady will be very happy there."

Frustrated, Eddie pulled Frankie into another hallway. "Hey *capo dosta,* you ain't hearin' what I'm sayin'. Not Queens, Italy."

"Italy? That's a bit far from Queens," Frankie said.

"I'd guess it is," Eddie said. "Now do you understand why I'm worried?"

Frankie thought about it. "You worry too much. There is

nothing so unusual about burying someone in Italy."

"Shush!" Eddie looked over his shoulder, put his head down, and covered his lips.

"What's the big deal?" asked Frankie.

"First of all, Isabella comes from Nola, that's in Naples." Frankie wasn't making anything of this conversation.

"JB wants her buried in—" He pointed to his upturned hand, then his ear, repeating the motions several times.

"Hand, ear, no, palm, ear, palm . . . Palermo?" Frankie shouted like he had just answered the sixty-four-thousand-dollar question.

"Jesus Christ, Frankie! You're killing me here."

Eddie's whispers were barely audible with his hand over his mouth. "I don't know. I got a funny feeling about how he plans to clean the laundry, a real funny feeling. I don't want you or your family to get into no trouble." Eddie made more lip movements, pointed to his eye, then, flapped his arms like a bird, then pointed to Frankie's nose.

Frankie was proud of deciphering this one. The nose thing had helped. "The feds will be watching like a hawk," he guessed out loud.

"Frankie, Frankie, when you gonna learn. You're gonna get us both pinched."

Okay, I'll play. "Uncle, you got to calm down. You've smoked three cigarettes in ten minutes."

"What of it? I don't pay for them."

"Uncle, can I ask you something?"

"Anything, kid." He looked out the hallway, up the street, down the street, up the buildings' fire escapes, rooftops. "Anything, but don't ask out loud."

He couldn't mean that. Frankie asked, "Why do you put up with this, Zio? He uses you. You're a nervous wreck. You don't take care of yourself. He has you running all hours of the day and night. You know, my mother doesn't go to sleep until she hears you coming home."

"Hey, I'm paying my dues."

The dues must be high, Frankie thought. Eddie was always a

nickel short of having a dime.

"One day, the books will be opened and JB promised to make me a made man, a man of respect."

"And where is this book I keep hearing about? Is it in someone's basement in Brooklyn or something? A library? It is an actual book, like a registry of card-carrying Mafia members or something?" Half these guys don't even know how to write, Frankie thought.

"Frankie, don't!"

"I mean, you're with this guy since you are a kid. What do you have to show for it? Do you have anything put away?"

"He takes care of me, if I need something. He got me a deferral from the army. If it wasn't for him I'd be fighting those Korean mooks in Nam."

Wrong enemy, wrong war. Frankie ignored it. "How did he do that?"

"I don't know. He told me he had a connection with a guy on the recruitment board."

"Eddie, you have a punctured eardrum. You weren't eligible."

"Eligible?"

Move on. "Still, Eddie, do you have a pension plan, hospitalization, sick leave?"

"Hey, don't be funny. This is serious. Just come with me to the café tomorrow, ten o'clock. Don't be late. He don't like that."

"Okay, Zio. I'll be there."

"Now listen, I'll walk out of the hallway first. You count to fifty, then you walk out and go the other way. Got it?"

"I think so."

"How's your mother?" He lit another cigarette.

"She's good, Uncle."

"I love that woman and your father too; what they did for me I will never forget. I would never hurt them."

"I know that," Frankie answered.

"And you, you still doing the comedy stuff?"

"Yes, still working at it."

"Rough field, Frankie; and be careful. If your father finds out, he ain't gonna be too happy. He ain't got no good sense of humor, that guy. Then again, there ain't much of no good opportunity to laugh, doing what he does."

On this Frankie agreed, double negatives and all. Eddie threw his arm around Frankie's neck and planted a kiss on his cheek. He took one more glance out the hallway from the bottom of the stairs and left.

"Remember, count to fifty, then walk that way."

Maybe, Frankie thought, as he watched Eddie walk down Mott Street, looking over his shoulder, he's not as dumb as everyone thinks. After counting to ten, Frankie left the hallway and walked up Mott Street. Just to keep Eddie happy.

Chapter 4

Giovanna had given birth to Frankie, the Graces' only child, in 1950. The restless baby could not wait for his debut and got turned around in her womb looking for a way out. Frankie's breech birth was the reason Primo Grace constantly reminded his son that he did everything ass-backwards. It proved a difficult delivery, requiring the skills of no fewer than four midwives: Pasquelena from 2-A, Zizilena from 3-B, Angelina from 4-B, and Lena from 4-C, widows all.

When Giovanna's time had come, Primo ran first for the doctor and then the car to drive her to hospital, while the Lenas escorted her down the stairs to the sidewalk. But when Primo backed out of the alley—in the hearse—the superstitious quartet, appalled at the mode of transportation, refused to let his wife get in. Giovanna was caught in a tug-of-war—the Lena four on one side, and Dr. Copolla and Primo on the other. All four Lenas feigned heart attacks on the sidewalk. Copolla insisted there wasn't much time.

At last Giovanna got in the front seat of the hearse with Primo, while Dr. Copolla stopped a taxi and the women piled in with him. They never made it to the hospital. On Broom Street, in front of Our Lady of the Rosary Church, Primo pulled over and started screaming. The taxi screeched to a halt and its occupants rushed toward the hearse, entering from five sides. A few minutes later, they eased Giovanna from the front seat and laid her in the back

41

of the hearse. There were Lenas on the passenger side door, Lenas on the driver side door, Lenas at the back door. They were moving around, back and forth, in and out, in a complete frenzy.

The delivery was complicated not only by the fact that the baby had turned in the womb but because each thrust forward caused Giovanna to slide backwards on the hearse's rollers, the mechanism that normally facilitated sliding a casket in and out.

Soon, however, Primo heard cheers and shouts. "Maschile, maschile!" It was a boy.

The first-time father had been more than a bit surprised by the mop of red hair on his newborn son, but the Lena four assured him blue eyes and red hair were not unusual in Italy. "Although, more in the north of Italy," they added apologetically.

Their assistance with Frankie's special curbside delivery henceforth entitled them to open access to the Grace table any time of the day or night, a fact that annoyed Primo on more than one occasion. They were de facto grandmothers. Any attempt to dislodge them was met with fierce resistance. Once, hoping to speed their exit so he would be able to utilize his small bathroom without surrendering his self-respect and dignity, Primo tried the Ex-Lax strategy.

"Put these in their coffee," he proposed, confident of his wife's support. He reveled in silent anticipation, anxious to see firsthand the effect the unexpected chemical alteration would have on the morose faces around the table. The quartet always looked a bit constipated anyway. His mind raced with glee at the thought of seeing them squirm when the internal eruption began. He joined them at the table. The grim-faced neighbors looked bewildered. He understood their skepticism, for he had never before sought to join the coven. He sat, staring them down, not tipping his hand, waiting until one by one they would make a lame excuse to return to their own apartments. Soon he would be king in his castle, able to take his place of honor, having successfully fought off the invaders from upstairs.

Stare at them he did, and they at him. He was certain that their ancient abdominal cavities, lined as they were with years of garlic, wine, pasta, plum tomatoes, and anisette, would be easy prey to the apothecary's over-the-counter remedy. Giovanna stared too, not at her friends, but at her husband. She was appalled, upset at the thought that she would be an accomplice to such a ruthless act. The moment Primo felt his stomach grind, the second he heard the first faint groan from his lower intestine, he realized that the tables had been turned. "Et tu, Giovanna!"

Primo bounded across the table in an effort to get out the door, his destination the bathroom in the funeral parlor below. Nearly knocking over Lena 4-C on the way out, he crawled between the chairs and dashed into the hallway and down the steps, a man with a mission. In the solitude of the tiny bathroom in the basement of the funeral home, he had time to relive the events of the past half-hour and contemplate what had gone wrong. Perhaps, he thought, his plan had worked after all. He was alone, a king on his throne.

As for his wife, she played it right down to the end, never letting on that she made the switch—the first rule of any successful sting operation. She would excuse herself later, claiming it was an innocent mistake, but some part of him knew the truth.

In the first-floor apartment above the funeral home, overlooking Mulberry Street, Frankie sat at the Formica-topped kitchen table listening to the weekly ritual of his mother arguing with the exterminator. She refused to pay for his service. Looking very much like an insect himself, he made his way around the kitchen, metal vat in hand. Her complaints fell on unsympathetic ears as the beleaguered bug man tried to explain politely that there was no way to completely rid the apartment of roaches. She took no solace in knowing there were roaches in Egypt; that was the Pharaoh's problem. She was not swayed by his attempts to explain that roaches had survived thousands of years or that they preferred clean houses. She did not take this as a compliment. Instead, she insisted on battling the bug with borders of poisonous powders sprinkled strategically around the perimeter of the apartment. Lethal liquids were sprayed in the most remote recesses where powders did not reach. Frankie noticed the bugs getting bigger over the years, building up immunity. He kept his opinion to himself.

He marveled at his mother. Living above the dead had not diminished her spirit or optimism. Her chiseled features were regal, her face blessed with character. Prematurely gray, she was tall, graceful, and full of energy. She spent her life pursuing an obsessive-compulsive cleaning disorder. From morning to night the three rooms of the little apartment were mopped, vacuumed, and dusted. The windows were cleaned, the closets were organized, the laundry was done, and the bathroom was scrubbed. When she was finished, she would begin again. In between, there were dinners for family members mourning their dead. It was part of the deal; mourners ate with the Grace family. Often that meant having a dozen people crammed around a table for four. This was Giovanna's chosen career, a labor of love, complemented by her songbird's voice that echoed through the hallways as she went about her chores. An opera enthusiast, she put her own libretti conversation to music. Her simplest sentences were often sung in the recitative, non-melodic style. For Frankie, hearing her sing "Good morning," "Good night," "Dinner is ready," or "Be careful with that girl" was a welcome, joyful antidote to the general state of depression and wailing that awaited him daily.

With a wink, Frankie acknowledged the exterminator, who ran his finger in little circles on his temple, indicating Mrs. Grace was not all there. After dismissing the exterminator, she resumed her ironing. A towel padded the table, and the cord from the iron ran underneath to where it plugged into the wall. The gliding motion of the iron lulled Frankie into a sense of well-being. No one pressed shirts like his mom, and there was never a shortage of supply.

"These are you father's," she said, pointing to six long-sleeved white shirts already on hangers. "These two are yours, and those are Eddie's." She pointed to a basket of short-sleeved, pastel-colored garments. After shirts, she moved on to underwear.

"God forbid you get hit by a car, your underwear can't be wrinkled," she sang.

"Ma, if I get hit by a car, wrinkles won't be the only thing in my underwear." She did not respond.

"Later, I want you to bring some manicotti to Eddie. Put them in his refrigerator. The door is open."

Frankie nodded. He stared across the kitchen through the window. A narrow, flat roof separated the buildings. The fire escapes from the floors above landed just outside. On the wall of the adjacent building there was a large mural of the Bay of Naples.

"Who painted the mural, mom?"

"Your grandfather Francesco. He lived in this apartment before us, died here too."

Great, now tell me he died in my bed. Why not, I don't have enough trouble sleeping. "Where did he die?"

"Don't ask," she trilled lightly.

He stared, transfixed by the mural. His grandfather had displayed real talent with a brush. He painted the bluest of waters, upon which dozens of fishing boats with colorful sails appeared to be swaying. Whitecaps danced below the hulls. There were two figures in the mural, one an elderly man in a fisherman's hat sitting on the dock staring out to sea, the other a young woman. Their images were somewhat blurred.

"When you were young," she explained, "you would sit out on the roof on a beach chair, and your grandfather would run a hose up from the basement, so you could cool off on hot summer days. Do you remember?"

Chairs were still gathering soot on the roof. A garden hose still ran up from the basement and was held in place by a wire hanger. He did recall running under the nozzle's spray, but he replied, "No."

"What's wrong, Frankie?" She stopped her ironing for a moment and sang, "You're quiet today. That's not like you."

He nodded agreement. "It's everything. I know Dad has plans for me, but I have my own plans and they're not working out either. Maybe I'm just fooling myself but there's a voice in my head that's always whispering punch lines to me. I really want to do comedy." Not to mention that the thought of spending his life running the funeral home downstairs sent chills up his spine.

Giovanna said, "He only wants what's best for you." She

believed his desire to be in show business was frivolous, a phase he was going through. After all, Frankie was still young. For her part, she was willing to give him some space. It was better that he get it out of his system, so he would have no regrets in the future. She had told her husband as much. She placed a shirt on a wire hanger and walked into the bedroom of the small apartment, maneuvering gingerly around the four-poster bed that took up the entire room. One of the bedposts was loose, but Frankie didn't know how to tell her.

She opened the closet door and hung the shirt at the end of a row of suits. Primo had five suits—black, blacker, black pinstripe, blacker pinstripe, and black-on-black shadow stripe. On the door, a tie rack held twelve ties. Most were black and silver, striped from left to right, but a few were silver and black, striped right to left.

It sometimes occurred to Frankie that his father could dress in the dark, and everything would still match.

"Some of these suits may fit you soon," said Giovanna melodiously. He didn't want to think so, for that would portend a future in black.

In the kitchen there was tapping on the steam pipe coming from the funeral home below. Tap, tap, then three more quick taps. It was their Morose code, as Frankie called it.

Giovanna said, unnecessarily, "Your father is coming up." When he was ready to eat, Primo would signal on the pipe that ran from the funeral home's basement to the top floor. Giovanna cleared the laundry from the table. Water was already boiling in the pot. It was Monday, which meant fusilli macaroni. She poured the pasta into water. In three minutes, the time it took for Primo to walk upstairs, the noodles were ready, al dente, just the way Primo liked them. She placed the dish of pasta, covered with red sauce, on the table just as Primo walked in. In a well-choreographed process, practiced nightly, he handed her his jacket, and Giovanna placed it on a hanger. He moved to the table, and she moved his chair in. He loosened his tie, and she tucked a cloth napkin around his neck. All the while, he never took his eyes off his son.

"You did a good job on Isabella," said Primo. "She came out

nice. Maybe too much of a smile." He twirled the pasta around his fork as Giovanna poured a glass of wine. He asked his son, "Why do you always make people smile, like they're happy or at a party or something? You make them smile too much."

Frankie wondered if anyone could ever smile too much. Well, maybe the dead, with his help.

"Johnny Balls wants to discuss the funeral tomorrow morning," Frankie reported, to change the subject.

Primo took a sip of wine. "Please don't call him that. It's Mr. John Ballsziti. Do you think you can handle that without getting yourself killed? Don't be funny, especially with him."

Frankie nodded. "I'll make sure it's by the book."

"Is there anything else you want to tell me?" his father asked.

Frankie did not respond. Had he missed something at Isabella's apartment? What had he screwed up now?

"Let me jog your memory," Primo said. "Was a certain guy I know, who is supposed to be a professional funeral director, seen at a nightclub making funny, like some kind of circus clown?"

Technically, it wasn't a nightclub—a difference without a distinction.

His father continued, "Was this certain person in the company of another person who is nothing but trouble?"

His father's ability to get information always amazed him. Frankie stood by the door, his face hot.

"Now listen, Frankie, we are funeral directors. Your grandfather Francesco was a funeral director and his father before him. I am a funeral director, you are a funeral director. This is a serious business. There is no place for funny business. We don't laugh. Your grandfather didn't laugh, his father didn't laugh."

Frankie looked at his mother.

"Three generations, not one smile," she confirmed, in song.

That's a long time to go without laughing. "Sorry, Dad. It won't happen again." *Not quite like that, anyhow.*

Primo rose and walked round the table and put his arm around Frankie's shoulder. "Look, I know it's this Sal kid putting these crazy thoughts in your head. You know he's a little off. Try to understand son. We're morticians—it's not what we do, it's who we are."

"I'll do better, Dad," he said halfheartedly.

"Okay, you have a big day tomorrow. You come back and give me a full report from Mr. Ballsziti. I'm going to the Knights for a meeting."

Giovanna took the napkin off his neck; he tightened his tie. She handed him a hairbrush and opened the bathroom door; he held out his hand, she shook a few drops of Vitalis into his palm; he matted it through and combed his hair in the mirror. She helped him put on his jacket; he adjusted his cuffs. She ran a lint brush across his shoulders as he headed out the door. Like a well-oiled machine.

He gave Frankie a soft pat on the cheek. "No laughing, promise?" he said. "Laughing turns to crying."

After Primo left for his meeting Frankie helped his mother clear the kitchen table. Above the clatter of dishes in the sink came a shout from street level, which they heard through the open window.

"Giovanna, Pasquelena, Lena, Angilena, Zizilena!"

A moment later, a burlap shopping bag, attached to a rope, flew out from the fourth-floor window, falling to the sidewalk below.

"Mr. Vitagliano is here," Giovanna said.

On the sidewalk, the neighborhood butcher put five packages into the bag. He tugged on the rope, and in a moment, it was hoisted back up. It stopped at the first-floor window and Giovanna extracted a bundle with her name on it. She opened the package, revealing portions of chopped meat, beef, and pork, wrapped in deli paper. She took money from her apron pocket, placed it into the bag outside the window, and tugged on the rope, and the bag continued to the floors above.

"Thank you, Mr. Vitagliano," she yelled out the window. It sounded like music.

"Prego," the butcher said.

"He's such a gentleman," she remarked.

After making stops on the floors above, the bag descended once again. He heard Lena 4-C yelling. "You call that a leg of lamb? I've seen better legs on tables. It's coming back down. I don't want it."

"I'm sorry," Mr. Vitagliano said. "Tomorrow, I'll bring a better one tomorrow."

"He's very patient, too," Giovanna added.

Suddenly she froze dead in her tracks, her eyes fixed in space. With a precision that would make a sharpshooter proud, in one fell swoop, she lurched back, flipped the slipper off her foot, caught it in midair, swung it across her body, and slammed it on the bureau.

"I got you, you bastard! Three days you been playing with me, but now I got you!" She lifted her slipper to reveal her flattened prey. She had the smug look of a winner.

"Ma, how do you know it was the same one?"

"Oh, you can tell. Roaches are like people. They're all different. You can tell, if you live with them a while."

In his room, Frankie opened the Castro convertible and sat in bed. He took his notepad and jotted down "Italian roaches." He laid back and stared out the window at his grandfather's graffiti mural, his thoughts turning again to the two people on the dock. The man wore a button-down flannel shirt and held a pipe in his hand. Standing beside him was the tiny frame of a young woman whose long hair flowed backwards in a breeze. Frankie studied her. There was, he thought, sadness in her eyes.

Were they just strangers on a pier, or people his grandfather needed to remember? He knew that his grandmother had waited in Italy until her husband was secure in America. Then he sent for her. But she was not happy in the new land. She died a few years after giving birth to Primo. Pneumonia or homesickness, Frankie could never determine which from the late-night conversations he overheard from his bed. Francesco returned her to Italy for burial. He wondered if his grandfather ever found the promise he sought in America. For him and his wife, life ended the way it began, in separation.

The quaint façade of Naples stood behind the gentle bend of the harbor wall. It was the closest Frankie had ever been to Italy. He wondered if his grandfather had come to this room to sit and gaze out of this very window. Perhaps in more melancholy moments he had done just that. Perhaps it made him sad to recall the home and family he'd left behind in pursuit of his dream. Or perhaps it served some other purpose, reminding him never to forget where he came from.

One thing Frankie knew for sure. His grandfather had a greater sense of adventure than his father. To leave all you knew, the safe harbor, for a dream! From his room, he could hear a tenor's voice through the speakers mounted outside Rossi's music store. The speakers lent each voice a scratchy quality. He tried to place the singer. Caruso, he guessed. He didn't need to understand the lyrics; the music went right to his soul. Listening more closely, he could hear someone singing along from the street below—Biaggio, a local crooner, who, had it not been for a conflagration overseas that interrupted his training, might now be singing at La Scala. Instead, he had found himself fighting the Germans at a place called Bastogne. Ah, well, the best-laid plans. Now, Biaggo was content to entertain his friends at Larry's Bar and dream of what might have been, in a neighborhood replete with might-have-been stories.

Frankie was happy that there was no visitation in the parlor below—a rare night. From his foldaway bed in this small room, Frankie thought, maybe it's not so bad to fall asleep staring at the Bay of Naples, while Italian music seeps up through the window. Maybe it's supposed to be this way.

Chapter 5

Frankie donned a freshly pressed suit and tied a double Windsor knot in his navy blue tie. He wiped a smudge of mud from the tip of his right shoe. This is what I get for following in my father's footsteps, he thought. Mud on his shoes came with the territory. It was important he make a good impression. Eddie was already having coffee at the kitchen table when he stepped out of the bedroom.

"We're gonna be late," Eddie said. They each kissed Giovanna and walked up Hester Street to the headquarters of Mr. Johnny Ballsziti.

There were butterflies in Frankie's stomach. Meeting with JB was special. He'd never been invited to the inner sanctum before. He followed Eddie into the café and waited for his eyes to adjust to the dim light. The dozen or so old-timers playing cards at the back tables lifted their heads for a moment, as did the two pool shooters on the other side. They recognized Eddie first, and then Frankie. All was safe. They went back to their games.

"Did you see that?" Frankie was surprised.

"See what?"

"All those guys, they all scratched their balls when we came in. What did they do that for?"

"That's for luck," Eddie said. "You're the undertaker. When they see you, they scratch their balls because they think you're

51

sizing them up. It's an old custom a Pope started."

Frankie laughed at the thought of a Pope scratching his balls. *Maybe that's why they wear those long vestments.* Frankie remembered walking down Mulberry Street with his father. Everyone would greet them respectfully, but if he turned his head quickly enough, he would inevitably spot a man with his hand on his crotch. Eddie's explanation made sense to him. It was protection.

Johnny Ballsziti was seated in his usual chair at his usual table in the Marconi Social Club, the café affectionately known by neighborhood residents as the Ammazza Tutti Society. *Kill Everybody.* JB started his day at eight a.m. with breakfast at the bakery. His henchmen would wait outside until he finished, then drive him around the corner to the café. JB didn't like to walk.

There was little that went on in his neighborhood that JB didn't know about or sanction. It was his job to know. His eyes and ears were all over. At first glance, the café itself was indistinguishable from dozens of similar establishments in the area. Windows always blacked out, a *Members Only* admonition painted on the door, each café named after some obscure charter member, each one with the same décor—dark woods, frosted mirrors, dim lights, and a layer of dust. But this one was different in one important respect: this was Johnny Ballsziti's place, his haven, and today he was back in it as though nothing had ever changed.

Someone was always watching him, too. The feds had been trying for ages to catch JB in the act. One photo, one conversation, one wrong move was all it would take to put him away for good. But Johnny Ballsziti was too smart. All those mirrors gave him eyes in the back of his head. As an added precaution, thanks to a cousin who worked for the phone company, he had the premises scanned for recording devices on a weekly basis.

Ever vigilant, JB took no chances, especially at this time of year with so many unfamiliar faces in and out of the neighborhood. September was a busy time of year on Mulberry Street. The Mafia calendar year began in mid-September with the ten-day commemoration of the beheading of San Gennaro, the patron saint of Naples. Running the feast took great organizational skills. As thousands of lights were being strung from building to building, vendors came into the café by the dozens to procure their allotted spaces. The process was well established—each solicitor handed an envelope to one of JB's nephews at the door. If the contents checked out then the other nephew would escort them to JB's table for a statement of purpose and conditions. All very official, except there were no written contracts; none were needed. When all was agreed, JB would simply state, "Okay, you have the space in front of the music store." Or, "Your booth will be on the corner across from the delicatessen." This year, thanks to his unscheduled sabbatical courtesy of the FBI, there was a lot of ground to make up.

It took a few moments more for Frankie's eyes to adjust completely to the dark interior of the Marconi Social Club. He took in the scattering of card tables toward the rear, where even at this early hour a few games were in progress. In one corner, a nine-ball table was centered under a frosted glass light fixture suspended from the ceiling by a length of aluminum chain. The bar was dull walnut with a brass footrest running along its base. A red stainless steel espresso machine, for which he could tell no expense had been spared, occupied a good portion of the counter. Top-shelf liquor bottles lined the mirrored backdrop, standing guard behind whiskey glasses, stacked one upon the other. A color television set with fuzzy reception, the tips of its rabbit ears wrapped in tinfoil, was mounted in the corner on the front wall. The bartender was, no doubt, an aged veteran of the Italian army. If Frankie had to guess, he would bet that he limped. Soon enough, he confirmed that his assumption was on the money. Frankie could not help but notice the giant glass jar at the end of the bar. It was filled with olives floating in a clear, viscous liquid. He looked closer. On second thought, he *hoped* they were olives. He swallowed hard.

At the farthest corner table, nearly in the dark, sat the proprietor, Johnny Ballsziti. His was the only armchair in the room, leather, with a padded seat and back. JB was no a slave to fashion. He wore a bulky, threadbare sweater, wrinkled pants, mismatched socks, and old shoes unevenly laced. A slovenly, unshaven guy, as Frankie recalled. Frankie began to sweat.

Two life-sized portraits occupied the wall behind JB—one of wrestler Antonio Rocco and the other of welterweight boxer Andy Thomas. Thomas might have made it all the way to the top, but in 1923 he took a blow to the head by Johnny Clinton in a qualifying match that ended his career and his life. He was a local boy, and nearly fifty years later, he was still remembered here.

Without asking, the bartender packed black coffee into a portafilter and attached it to the espresso machine. The lights flickered when he activated the machine. Local lore had it that the New York City blackout of 1969 was caused when all the espresso machines in little Italy were activated at the same time. Steaming hot water wheezed through the filter, spitting out a stream of coffee captured by small demitasse cups. He placed the cups of espresso on the bar in front of them.

"Oh, no thanks," Frankie said, "I don't like the taste of—"

Eddie leaned in. "Just drink it," he said, with a ventriloquist's contorted lips. "Don't insult him."

The bartender proceeded to add two, three, four spoons of sugar to each small cup, waiting for a sign to stop.

"Eddie, I won't be able to sleep for a week." Frankie whispered.

"Just drink it," Eddie said again. "Like this." He swallowed the contents, one sip, two, gone.

Frankie followed his uncle's example but choked as the strong, hot liquid went down his windpipe instead of his esophagus. JB waved them over. Frankie gagged as he walked toward JB's table. As he approached, JB became more clearly visible. His clothes were ragged, his eyes were overwhelmed by scraggly brows, and stray hairs protruded from every orifice. *What is it with this family and facial hair?* "Are you sure this is the most powerful man in New York?" Frankie whispered to Eddie. "He looks like a stumblebum."

"That's just what he wants you and everyone else to think. You see, that's how smart he is. But don't kid yourself. If he pulls on his earlobe, those two guys will dismember you and bury the pieces under the West Side Highway. He never has to say a word, just pull his earlobe." Eddie nodded toward the two sumo wrestler types who stood expressionless by the door, like the lions guarding the Forbidden City. "Those guys are JB's nephews, Bull."

"What's the other guy's name?"

"Bull." He answered.

"Jesus, where's their neck?"

"They don't need one."

One of the brothers Bull was clipping his fingernails, while the other had his left hand deep into his open zipper, pulling on his right shirttail. He repeated the process on the other side, attempting to achieve perfect symmetry. Undeterred by an audience, he had no compunction about performing this shirt-tucking ritual inside the café or on the sidewalk in full view of passersby or diners. Day or night, inside or out, feeling his shirt bunched up prompted this corrective measure. In this instance a full circular tuck was also called for, so he lowered his pants halfway down his thigh to get unimpeded rear access. Frankie felt compelled to laugh but his inner voice, usually comedic, advised otherwise.

JB was staring at the television, where President Nixon was addressing the nation's concerns over inflation and the Vietnam War from the White House briefing room. There was a bowl of assorted olives on the table—black, burgundy, green, liguria, kalamata. JB loved olives. There were toothpicks but he chose to use his fingers instead. That guaranteed that no one else would help themselves to his treats.

Eddie led Frankie to the table and leaned over to kiss JB on the cheek. *I'll wait till he shaves, thank you very much,* Frankie thought to himself, but Eddie pulled him closer. *Hey, when in Rome . . . or little Italy.* He did the same.

JB stared at him for a moment, then motioned for Eddie to come closer. He whispered in his ear. They both stared at Frankie.

Then Eddie responded, "I'm sure, probably the north."

This seemed to satisfy JB, who invited them to sit. He held up his hand, not ready to talk until Nixon finished, then gave his commentary. "Do you believe this prick? And they call *us* crooks. Lorenzo, shut that off."

Lorenzo raised a broomstick to the television and hit the off button.

"Anyway," JB said, "my wife said you did nice at the house, you prayed and everything and you were dressed real formal." The table was littered with olive pits. JB gathered them into a pile, making little patterns as he spoke. A gunk of gaeta was lodged in his teeth. "Would you like some espresso?"

Please say no, Eddie.

"Is everything going all right, boss?" Eddie asked.

Good going, Eddie, change the subject, move on, no more espresso, please!

JB waved his head dramatically left and right. "How can things be all right? This feast is making me crazy. It gets worse and worse. This guy don't want to sell sausages because he's too close to that guy who sells braciola. That guy don't want to sell jelly apples because he's too close to the guy with the cotton candy. The priest wants a piece of the action from the gambling in the church courtyard. Talk about Mafia, there's the *real* mob. I'm gettin' the shakedown, straight from Rome. I tell ya, they invented extortion."

"I know, JB, it's not easy."

San Gennaro—who was martyred for his faith in 305 A.D.—could never have known that each September, the ten-day celebration of his beheading and the subsequent boiling of his blood would constitute a major source of income for the mob on Mulberry Street in the twentieth century. Each year the street would be decorated with lights strung across the street from Bayard to Houston. Concessionaires would line the sidewalks on both sides of the street as hundreds of thousands came to sample the foods of Little Italy and enjoy the parades of marching bands, civic groups, and church and municipal dignitaries.

The festivities would kick off with a grand procession, when a bust of the saint was carried through the streets and devout visitors pinned money to its vestment. Proceeds from the take on the vestment, as well as from the gambling in the churchyard, the selling of sidewalk space to vendors, and commissions on beer, soda, bread, and meat had filled the coffers of the Mafia crime families since the festival's inception in 1926. The cash flow was tremendous. No wonder San Gennaro was revered—though a statue of St. Ditmas, patron saint of thieves, might have been a better choice for honoree.

"Now, Bella," JB continued. "Get a load of this; she wants me to get insurance for the angel after what happened last year. I said, what, are you friggin' crazy? I ain't insuring no friggin' angel." He looked right at Frankie. "Can you believe that—insurance for an angel?"

During the annual parade, the Ladies Auxiliary of the San Gennaro Society would select a young girl, dress her as an angel, secure her to a special wired girdle, and send her winging her way across the street on a cable connected to the fire escapes. All the neighborhood mothers vied for the honor of having a daughter thrown out of the window as the feast angel. It was one of the highlights of the festival.

"Well, after last year . . ." Eddie began hesitantly.

JB continued. "Is it my fault they picked a girl who looks like Two Ton Tony Galento? I mean, did you see the size of that kid?"

It was the most exciting thing that had ever happened at the festival, and just thinking about it made Frankie laugh. The ladies' committee had made the mistake of choosing Annette Grandulose. A zeppole lover, the girl could be found on any given day during the feast waiting for the mixture of flour and dough to come out of a vat of hot oil, to be coated with confectioner's sugar. She'd eat a dozen in contest-winning time.

On the appointed day, the busty members of the Ladies Auxiliary held Annette Grandulose in place while others struggled to get the girdle around her. She was an unusually reluctant candidate who needed some coaxing, prodding, and outright pulling in order to get her to the window. Even then, she needed a little push. The poor girl's eyes bulged out of their sockets as she stared out the second-floor window. Her arms stiffened against the window frame and she braced her legs against the sill, fighting off all attempts to get her airborne. When they finally sent her launching out the window, the wire snapped. Looking more like Tarzan than any angel, she crashed into the dignitaries leading the parade. The domino theory kicked in, as the force of the healthy twelve-year-old, accelerated by a drop of twenty feet, caused row upon row of people to fall backwards. She slammed into Assemblyman Basso, who, lucky for her, was there to break her fall. She, in turn, broke his nose, collarbone, and third lumbar vertebra. Nonetheless the assemblyman was considered a hero, and the neighborhood was eternally grateful. They returned him to office and stood behind him even during his trial for embezzlement and tax evasion. The old-timers didn't forget their friends.

"Frankie, Frankie Grace." He heard his name.

"I'm sorry?" he said.

"Have a cup of espresso," said JB.

"No, no, thank you Mr.—" *be careful, moron, say it slowly—* "Balls...ziti."

"I got just the thing, then," said JB. He pointed to Eddie. "Get us two grappa."

Eddie walked to the bar and returned with two drinks in pony glasses. JB picked up one, Frankie the other. His eyes began to water as the fumes, reminding him of turpentine, invaded his nose.

"Go ahead," JB coaxed, "It's good for you; puts hair on your chest."

Just what I need, thank you very much . . . quiet, drink, stupid!

In one swallow, the clear liquid burned a path down his throat, and Frankie realized the smell wasn't the only thing it had in common with turpentine. Sweat seeped from his every pore.

"Frankie," JB said. "About my dear dead mother-in-law. You know, I'd like to have her buried in her beloved Palermo. It was her wish. Tell me, what's involved in such a transaction?"

"Well," Frankie started. The potent distillation constricted his vocal cords. His voice cracked like he was going through puberty all over again. He coughed, cleared his throat, and continued, two octaves higher. "We have to get the death certificate, and then obtain permission from the Italian consulate on Park Avenue. They have certain requirements, of course."

"And what would those be?"

"Well, they telex the town where the burial will take place and wait for the clearance."

"Clearance?"

"Formalities," Frankie explained. "Make sure there is a cemetery plot and all that."

"Fine, no problem."

"And we'll need a letter from the medical examiner stating that Isabella did not die from a disease, and we'll need certified copies of the death certificate." Frankie's eyes watered as Eddie poured another round of grappa into his discarded glass. Johnny pushed the glass toward Frankie, who grudgingly took another swallow.

"What happens then?"

"Well," Frankie started, his voice rising to the next register, "for one thing, the casket has to be sealed in a three-inch-thick plank box with a zinc liner."

"Zinc?"

"Oh, yes, sir, and the zinc has to be hermetically sealed as well."

Ballsziti looked to Eddie, of all people, for some help with "hermetically."

Frankie understood. "Soldered," he explained. "Welded, by fire. Airtight."

"Ah," Ballsziti said. "That's good. What happens then?"

"Well, we take the airtight box to the Italian consulate and they place the wax seals on the edges, and then give us the permits to go to JFK."

"JFK?"

"Kennedy Airport. There they check the paperwork and permits, weigh us in, and that's it, she's off to sunny Italy." He regretted those last words; it wasn't like she was going on vacation. "Where she will rest in eternal peace," Frankie added in a more solemn tone.

"Weigh you in?"

"Oh, I didn't mean weigh us in, as in me," Frankie explained. It wasn't getting clearer. "You see, they charge by the pound, so they weigh the casket. But your mother-in-law was so thin. She can't weigh more than ninety pounds."

"That dear old lady." All were quiet as JB made the sign of the cross. Eddie did the same. Bull and Bull followed, as did the card and pool players. It was contagious.

"Fine, that's good," continued JB. "Now, I want you to make sure she has a good casket, bronze, the best. That's a heavy one, right, and waterproof? That's important. If the plane goes down, I don't want her to drown." He did not wait for a response. "She was worth it, that dear old lady."

Frankie looked at Eddie. "Well, bronze is expensive, and the outer box with the zinc is also expensive."

Olive pits flew in all directions as Ballsziti slammed his fist down. "Money means nothing to me when it comes to that woman— understand?"

Frankie nodded.

"I mean, who can think of money at a time like this?"

You'd be surprised, Frankie thought.

"And we are going to do this on Thursday. Are we all set?"

"Let's see, a week from Thursday should work."

"No, I mean *this* Thursday. Is there a problem?"

Frankie's eyes bulged. "But . . . well . . ." He struggled to think clearly. "It takes a long time to get the proper permits."

JB shrugged. "You don't understand. I said *Thursday*. Do what you gotta do, pay off who you gotta pay off, but get it done. Capisce?"

Frankie nodded. He was breaking out in a sweat. What if he couldn't pull it off? He wasn't sure who would kill him first, his father or Ballsziti. But then another angle occurred to him. "What about the opening day of the feast? It may not be too easy to have a funeral with all the commotion."

Ballsziti waved his hand. "She loved the feast. It's the last wish I can grant the old lady. What better sendoff can we give her than San Gennaro's feast?" He turned to Eddie. "What spots do we have in front of the funeral home?"

Eddie thought for a moment, then answered, "The sausage stand and Clara the rice ball lady."

"Another pain in the ass," JB noted. "They should be no problem. Get them—" he thought better of it, "—*ask* them, to close for an hour on Thursday. That's all I need, is to have them praying for rain." He pointed to the two empty glasses. Eddie ran to the bar and came back with two more glasses and a fresh bottle of grappa. JB motioned Frankie to move his chair closer.

"But," he said, "I have ulterior reasons as well." He leaned in closer and closer still until the combination of espresso, grappa, and olives on JB's breath was unmistakable. Frankie's head was starting to spin, and he wasn't sure he could still feel his toes in his dress shoes. "You may have heard that certain people have made a career out of trying to claim I am the head of some fictitious underworld gang."

Frankie coughed. *Yes, the Ballsziti Crime Family, so nice of them to name it after you.*

"I think I did read something along those lines," he said.

"Well, you know these people are going to be out in force with their cameras, making a mockery of an innocent woman's funeral. It will be a little harder for them to park with the feast going on."

"I guess," Frankie said. "But there is still the matter of the shurch. I mean the *church*. They will be all over that as well."

"Yes, I thought about that too. Here's what I suggest. You put in the obituary that Isabella is being buried in St. John's Cemetery. I have a crypt there. No one but us has to know where she's really going. Ain't that right?"

Be a jerk, say no. "Yes, I guess."

"Well, just make sure. Now, I will need four limousines."

"No problem, sir."

"Good. And as far as hearses go—"

"Well of course, that goes without saying. We certainly need a hearsh."

Judging from the look on his face, JB did not like being interrupted. "Now, as far as the hearse goes, here is what I want."

He leaned over and whispered into Frankie's ear. As JB's request got stranger Frankie's eyebrows rose higher and higher. Frankie looked to Eddie, who was nervously playing pocket pool.

"Do you understand what I want?" JB asked. Frankie nodded.

After one final round of grappa, Eddie leaned in and kissed JB. Frankie, attempting to do the same, tripped over his own feet, and fell into the table. He knocked over glasses and sent the piles of pits into JB's lap. Not a good first impression, he thought. Red-faced, he kissed JB and stumbled out behind Eddie. Turning at the last moment, he walked back toward the table.

"Mr. Balls . . . ziti, I just want to make sure. You did say the cemetery is in Palermo?" JB only nodded. "I always thought she was Neapolitan, not Sicilian."

JB shrugged. "No, she converted years ago."

Eddie was troubled by the conversation at the café. "Let's go eat something. I gotta think, and I can't think with all this noise."

On Mulberry Street, a carpenter's orchestra of hammers and electric saws filled the air as vendors constructed their wood-framed booths along the street. Frankie felt as though the hammers were all pounding inside his own head. Frankie and Eddie made their way through the maze of construction projects. Each vendor had paid JB thousands of dollars for space along the street. They would have ten days to recoup the rent, and all parties hoped there would be a profit at the end—as long as it didn't rain. Rain was the only thing that could dampen their enthusiasm and render their efforts useless. JB offered no refunds, no angel or rain insurance.

Frankie said, "Fine, we'll go to Sal's place."

"You're still tight with that guy? He seems a little off to me."

"Come on, he'll treat us right."

In front of Lucci's, Sal was arguing with a concessionaire. "What the frig are you building here, Yankee Stadium?"

The man continued his work. "You got a problem," he said, "take it up with JB."

Sal bit his tongue and went inside. Frankie walked in behind him with Eddie in tow.

"Christ, this feast is bad for my business. I gotta have this jamoke blocking my entrance for the next week."

"Hey, watch what you say about the feast," Eddie said. "You're gonna get yourself in trouble."

Sal shrugged it off. "I hope you guys are hungry." He looked in Frankie's direction. "Although you look a little green already."

He donned a white apron as they made themselves comfortable. From behind the bar he poured a cognac and handed it to Frankie.

"Eddie, what's your pleasure?"

"Club soda, no ice." He rubbed his head. "And a glass of red wine."

A waiter brought menus to the table. No sooner did he hand them out than Sal took them from their hands. "Leave it to me," he said as he walked into the kitchen. "I have good news for my friend here—and we're gonna celebrate with something special."

"What's wrong, Eddie?" asked Frankie, still woozy from the grappa.

"I wish I knew, but I got this uneasy feeling. JB is up to something."

"Maybe it's just your imagination."

"No, I got no imagination."

Sal returned from the kitchen carrying a platter. "You see this? This is bufala mozzarella." He pushed the plate closer to the two diners, slicing a fork through the milky white balls. "You see, like butter. You can't get this stuff anywhere but Paestum, Italy. It's the mozzarella capital of the world. Now, you go to La Luna's across the street, or other restaurants who claim they serve bufala mozzarella, but they don't. To be bufala it must be made from the milk of a water buffalo."

"So," Frankie quipped, "The other restaurants are literally bullshitting us?"

"Ha, ha," Sal said, as he spooned the delicacy onto their plates. "This is flown in once a week to Kennedy, and only goes to three of the top restaurants in New York. Thankfully, I got a cousin who works cargo at the airport and is able to commandeer a couple of cases."

Frankie poked his finger delicately into to the creamy cheese. It shimmered in the light with a slick glaze that beckoned him to partake. He was impressed. "Soft," he said. He placed a slice into a wedge of bread and ate. His eyes lit up. "Jeez, this is delicious, melts in your mouth. This is ecstasy."

"Told you so."

"So, you said something about good news?" asked Frankie.

"You got it, *compare*. You—"—he made a drum roll on the table with his hands—"are being scouted by Sol Weis and company from Hollywood, U.S.A.!"

"Say what?"

"You know I told you I was working on something big—well, you gotta practice up in a hurry, because soon you're gonna be performing for some real-life movie VIPs."

"Wow . . . I don't know, Sal. I've got no new material," Frankie said, the previous weekend's close call still fresh on his mind. "Besides, I've got probably the biggest funeral of my life two days from now, and if my father finds out I'm working on a comedy routine, it'll be a double ceremony."

"Hey, come on. You're committed for your regular gig at the San Su San tonight anyway. Think of it as a dress rehearsal. What can it hurt?"

Sal smiled. A waiter handed Sal another dish. "You see these?" He pushed the dish under Eddie's nose. "These are roasted peppers. I know because I roasted them myself. Now, you go across the street and he has roasted peppers on the menu, but really they're not; they're pimientos. They get them from a can." He served the orange and red peppers onto their plates and went back into the kitchen.

Eddie was resigned. "So now I know the difference between pimientos and roasted peppers. The day isn't a total loss."

"Lighten up, Eddie." Frankie's voice was muffled as he chewed the peppers and stuffed more mozzarella and seeded Italian bread into his mouth. He continued, "Jeez, you worry too much. It's a funeral. I do it all the time. I can understand why he doesn't want to turn it into a circus with all the feds watching. I'm just glad I didn't skimp on the formaldehyde. Anyway, what can go wrong? And if there was something going on, wouldn't you know about it? You're closer to JB than anyone." Frankie reached for more mozzarella. "This is really delicious, like butter. Try some," he said.

"Imported from Italy," Sal added.

Eddie lit a cigarette. He glanced around suspiciously at the other customers in the dining room. "You don't understand. JB didn't last this long by letting people know what he's thinking or planning. He keeps everything inside. Everyone is on a need-to-know basis. His right hand don't know when his left hand is playing with himself."

Frankie tried to follow the metaphor, contorted as it was. "By the way," he said, "What did he ask you, when you answered, 'north'?"

"Oh, he wanted to know if you were really Italian. After all, red hair, blue eyes, a guy's gotta figure you're an Irishman."

"Irish!"

Eddie laughed, "Yeah, God forbid, right."

"Those are rumors, ugly rumors," Frankie retorted. He knew there was the suggestion of a wee bit of the Emerald Isle in his bloodline that accounted for his fair looks. They drank a bit more of their wine. "I'd better run this by my father. You know he's by the book. I don't think we'd be breaking any law, but he'll get the state law code out and investigate."

"It don't matter," Eddie said. "Whose law would you rather break? The feds' or Johnny Ballsziti's?"

Frankie stopped chewing.

"Besides, the less your father knows the better."

When it came to his comedy dates, Frankie couldn't agree more. But when it came to funerals—well, that was a different matter.

Chapter 6

On the seventy-fourth floor of the World Trade Center offices of the Organized Crime Task Force, Roscoe Keats stood gazing out the window at the panorama of lower Manhattan. A prematurely bald, stocky man, he chewed on a cigar until it disappeared into his throat. No other law enforcement office in all New York had a view like this, he thought. He ought to be able to see every crook in the city.

Keats could have retired, full pension, five years ago, but that would have been admitting defeat. His persistence was about to pay off, he was sure of it.

"Honey, I'm sorry. I'll be working late," he said into the phone. "Tell him I will make it up to him. I'll take him to a ballgame." After a click, he hung up. She was angry.

There was a knock on the door. His deputy walked in, asking, "You heard the news? He's out—yesterday. Finally got a judge to spring him."

It only confirmed what Keats already knew. His head fell to his chest as he turned and took a seat behind his desk.

"I know, I heard his mouthpiece lawyer on the courthouse steps. 'Mr. Ballsziti is an elderly man, in failing health and constantly harassed by law enforcement. He is a kindly old gentleman who lives modestly off his wife's salary and knows nothing about the allegations against him.' What bullshit. I tell you, his lawyer is dirty too, slick and dirty. I know it, I feel it here." Keats pointed to his gut.

"You did your best," his deputy said.

There was no answer. Keats was in a trance, staring at the sizable cork bulletin board resting on an easel at the corner of his desk. Plastered to it were photographs of the who's who of the New York Mafia. The photos were arranged in a neat pyramid pattern, fifteen or so along the bottom, leading to twelve on the row above, topped by eight, then six, three, until finally just one reigned over all the others. Each picture was labeled with a name and status: Convicted, Missing, Dead. All but one, the one that got away. Mr. John Ballsziti, safe at the top of the pyramid.

A few years back Roscoe Keats had been tapped by no less a personage than Senator Robert Kennedy himself to head up a special unit concentrating on organized crime. For years Keats had devoted his career to breaking the mob's grip on the city of New York. Judging by the captions beneath each picture, he had been successful—but he felt differently.

"Roscoe, you okay?" The deputy walked to the board. He knew what his boss was thinking. "Hey, Roscoe, you did alright. You did a fine job. You put them all away, the button men." He started at the bottom row and traced the pattern upward. "The captains, the capos, they are all away, because of you."

Keats nodded. "Thanks," he said, "All but one, Mr. Teflon, Mr. Ballsziti."

The deputy took a seat in a chair across from Keats. "Don't blame yourself. This one is a little different, maybe a little smarter, keeps his own counsel. Never heard him on tape."

That was just what Keats did not want to hear—that some street-bred mob guy was, in the end, smarter than he was. That would make his degrees from Boston University, his time at Georgetown Law, and his training at Quantico worthless, wouldn't it? Keats scowled at the display featuring the hierarchy of the New York mob. And to think I helped him get to the top, Keats mumbled to himself.

He was right. Armed with RICO, the Racketeer Influenced and

Corrupt Organizations Act of 1970, the feds were at last able to make cases against the mob that had previously been impossible. It didn't hurt that the quality of the mob recruits had changed. Tell a low-level flunky these days that he was facing forty years in Marion Penitentiary, and what he didn't know, he would make up. From the bottom up, soldier after soldier gave up their superiors. One by one, under the direction of Special Agent Roscoe Keats, the dons of the American Mafia were shuttled off to prison, where they would remain until they died. As he considered the photos now, he was struck with the irony. "In a perverse way," he told his deputy, "I helped Ballsziti achieve his success."

Each time Keats put a capo away, Johnny Ballsziti was there to pick up the pieces of the leaderless family. He moved in, time after time, absorbing the remnants of the crew. As each chess piece toppled he grew more powerful. What Keats didn't accomplish with his newfound legal powers, Ballsziti took care of with a tug of his earlobe. Those were the photos labeled missing or dead. With the help of Roscoe Keats, Johnny Ballsziti was able to consolidate power like no one since Lucky Luciano. And, Keats hated to admit, he was just as smart. That thought stuck in his craw.

The deputy asked, "What are you going to do now?"

Keats stepped back to the window. The city bustled below him. "The money is out there. I know he was involved. I know he has it, somewhere. It has to show up."

The deputy lit a cigarette. "Maybe we're wrong about this. This heist took brains. This job was way over their pay grade. Maybe he doesn't know anything. Don't you think money like that would have surfaced by now? Some dumb flunky would have bought a car or something. Maybe we are wrong, and Ballsziti doesn't know anything. And now this thing with his mother-in-law dying and all, maybe we should let up."

Keats laughed. "You are so young, my friend." He pointed to Ballsziti's picture. "Nothing comes into or out of the city, from the airport to the docks, without this man knowing and approving. No truck delivers a garment, no cement is poured, no taxi gets a medallion, no liquor gets to the shelves without this man getting his tribute. Jesus, he gets a kickback on the flour used for calzones. He is top hat in his own game of Mobopoly. Are you trying to tell me he has no idea where five million in new bills is located? Think again, my dear friend."

"Well, what's the plan?"

Keats was stymied. "I don't know. I think I'll go to Mulberry Street, get a sausage sandwich."

An unmarked police car on Mulberry Street was as conspicuously out of place as brown shoes with a black tuxedo. The presence of the puke-green Dodge Dart with the blackwall tires sent red flags flying through the streets. Like monkeys screeching out a warning of danger through the jungle treetops, every shop owner was instantly deputized to track the movements of the intruder. They joined a silent army of housewives sitting by their windows or hanging clothes on the line. Anything unusual prompted a phone call to get the word out.

Beneath the sign of the Grace Fun. Home, massive flower arrangements were already being delivered hourly for the Cianci family. Wise guys from Philadephia, New Jersey, New Orleans, Chicago, Vegas and Los Angeles wasted no time in being represented by a floral display. Not to do so would be a sign of disrespect. But Frankie knew there would be no room for all of them in the tiny storefront. In homage to the dearly departed, many of the ornate floral pieces were shaped like a variety of Italian pastries. The giant gladiola cannoli was open to interpretation.

The obligatory floral wreath with a clock face set to the time of death, 8:08, was delivered. That number would be played on the ponies for a full week after the funeral. As the faithful gathered yearly at Houdini's grave awaiting proof of an afterlife, the people of Little Italy had their own ideas about what constituted proof. If there was a heaven, a God, the resurrection of the body, the deceased would prove it by letting friends hit the winning number. For this reason, no clue was overlooked. The time of death was an obvious choice for a two-dollar bet, the license plate number of the ambulance that took someone away, the address of the building where the deceased lived, an apartment number, a birthday. A death in the neighborhood was a financial boon to the local bookies. Between the flower deliveries and the construction projects on the sidewalk, Frankie was sick with contemplating the difficulties that lay ahead. Or maybe the lingering effects of the grappa had something to do with it.

A middle-aged man chomping on a thick cigar made his way through the streets and approached Frankie and Eddie outside the funeral home. "Excuse me," the man said as he looked up at the sign. "Is this where the wake will be, for Isabella . . . ? Her last name escapes me."

Frankie was quick to answer. "Cianci. Isabella Cianci. Yes, Thursday at Most Precious Blood."

That seemed to satisfy the inquirer. "And the burial?" he asked.

Frankie was again quick to answer, too quick this time.

"Ital—" He felt Eddie's elbow dig into his ribs. "It'll be at St. John's."

"Excuse me?"

"St. John's Cemetery, in Queens."

"Well, thank you," the man said, as he continued his stroll up the street.

Eddie pushed Frankie through the half-open door to the funeral home. "Sure, 'Why are you worried, Eddie?' Why am I worried? This thing hasn't even started yet and already you almost throw a wrench in it. Don't you know who that was? Don't you read the papers? That was Roscoe Keats—he has federal agent written all over his Irish face, and you can't stop blabbing. Can you try to keep your mouth shut for forty-eight hours?"

At dinnertime Frankie weaved through the crowd of workmen constructing booths and draping banners along Mulberry Street. He slipped into Lucci's, garment bag draped over one shoulder, ready to put the funeral business behind him for the evening. He hung the bag on a coat hook behind the door and took a seat at the family table near the kitchen, where Eddie had already made himself comfortable.

Sal emerged from the kitchen with a platter of freshly sliced Roma tomatoes and bufala mozzarella in one hand and a loaf of bread from the Isabella Bakery in the other. With the festival approaching, out-of-towners had already begun arriving. Little Italy was abuzz with anticipation, and the restaurant had been jumping all evening. Sal was in his element, and all the more fired up because, unbeknownst to Frankie, Sol Weis and party had just finished their dinner and were even now en route to Long Island to catch his opening act.

Sal slid the appetizers onto the table and moved to the bar to pour Frankie a cognac. He had debated whether to reveal the details to Frankie, but decided it would only make him nervous. "*Compare*, you ready for tonight? Shouldn't you be on your way to the San Su San?"

"As soon as my father goes to sleep. Then my mother will give me the keys to the hearse."

Eddie stopped picking at the tomatoes and mozzarella and put his fork down. "You drive the hearse to do your comedy stuff?"

"Hey, it's my only set of wheels. When I leave, I have to let the parking brake off and coast out of the alley so Primo won't hear me crank the engine."

"Jeez," Eddie said.

That reminded Sal. "Park it in the back this time." Frankie and Sal roared with laughter and Frankie choked on his drink. "Tell Eddie. Tell him what happened the first time you went there."

"Well, my first night working at the San Su San could well have been my last," Frankie related as he struggled to recover. "I mean, I drive out there, a real nightclub for the first time and I'm getting paid—not like working at The Improv or any of the SoHo dives. This is a paying gig. So, I'm in the lobby and I introduce myself to the maître d' and I'm just waiting. Then I hear some guy yell, 'What's that parked in front of the door?' Now, that rings a bell. Again, he screams, 'Who's the joker who parked a hearse out front?'

"The maître d' points to me and this guy, who's built like a tank, walks over to me and asks, 'You the comedian who parked that friggin' hearse out there?'

"'I'm sorry, I wasn't thinking,' I say. Meantime I see the veins bulging in his neck.

"'This is a nightclub,' he says, 'People come here to laugh and have a good time and you park a meat wagon outside. What are you trying to be, funny? Think you're a goddamn comedian or something? Who the hell are you, anyway?'"

Eddie and Sal laughed hysterically.

"Then, of course, the matîre d' says, 'This is Frankie Grace, Mr. Romo. He's the opening act tonight. The comic you hired.'

"So this guy looks at me like he wants to eat me alive," Frankie continued. "'Move the friggin' meat wagon,' he says, 'or you'll be riding in the back.'"

"You're a crazy bastard." Eddie stared at Frankie in amazement.

"For sure, I never thought I'd be working there again. I say, 'I'm so sorry, Mr. Romo. It will never happen again.' 'I think you're right,' he says, obviously meaning that was the end of the gig."

Eddie and Sal laughed until tears rolled down their cheeks.

"So what happened?" Eddie asked.

"I got a call a few days later," Sal explained. "Mr. Romo apparently got some compliments after the show and tells me to send Frankie back. Hey, Frankie, he says, isn't it great to work in front of a *live* audience?"

Frankie reached for a cocktail napkin and scribbled *live audience.*

The phone rang. "Yes, Mrs. Grace," Sal said. "I'll tell him." He hung up. "Your father's asleep. Go get the keys."

"And park in the back," Eddie howled as Frankie walked out the door.

✝

The show went off without a hitch this time. Reassured for the moment amid familiar surroundings, Frankie felt confident he'd be ready whenever Hollywood came calling. Bring it on, Sol Weis.

As he had done other nights after closing, Frankie stopped by the bar to say goodnight to Tony Romo and the few stragglers. Romo sat at on a corner stool with his head in his hands.

"See you next week!" Frankie called out, still jazzed from his performance.

He was surprised when Romo motioned him over. In the proprietor's hand was an envelope along with a bar check. Romo's glasses hung low on the bridge of his nose as he reviewed the tab. "Mr. Grace, do you realize this is a *dinner* show?"

"Um, I think so," Frankie replied.

"And during a dinner show, do you think people want to hear about cockroaches? But there you go, during a dinner show, talking about Italian roaches, Jewish roaches. What's wrong with you? You dense or something?"

"Jeez, I'm so sorry, Mr. Romo. It will never happen again."

"And furthermore. Do you know how much cognac you drink?"

Sensing a misunderstanding, Frankie said, "Oh, but I settle up at the register before I leave, Mr. Romo."

Romo shook his head. "No, you don't understand. It's Courvoisier, you're supposed to sip it, not guzzle it like Boone's Farm."

"It's my mother's fault. She put cognac on my gums when I was teething."

"Whatever," Romo said. He handed Frankie the envelope. "This is your pay for tonight and next week, too. Plus, I'm ripping up the bar tab."

"Next week? You don't have to pay me in advance, Mr. Romo."

"I'm not paying you in advance. There *is* no next week. Show's over, monkey's dead."

Frankie stood paralyzed. "What's wrong?" he asked. "Wasn't I funny? You don't have to pay me at all. I'll do it for free—"

"I'm not saying you was funny and I'm not saying you wasn't funny. I don't have to give you no reason. You're not a silent partner," Romo said. "I got enough of those. Just can't use you anymore."

Frankie was shattered. Where had he gone wrong? He went over his lines, looking for some clue to why he'd been canned. He relived all the jokes, the punch lines, the laughs. Could it have been that damned roach routine? He stood in disbelief, then turned to steady himself against the bar. He was just no good, that really *was* it. He lacked any sense of timing, couldn't tell funny from a hole in the ground. Yes, that was it. He just stank. Laughing turns to crying, he could hear his father reminding him.

The bartender obviously sensed another cognac would be in order, and he placed a fresh drink in front of Frankie, who watched Romo across the bar, waiting for him to smile and say he was just kidding. Romo remained silent as he took a stack of checks off the bar and sauntered off into his back office.

Frankie drained the snifter. "Keep 'em coming," he told the bartender, determined to have someone feel sorry for him. After three more he invited everyone to join his going-away party. The bartender obliged. Of the dozen or so people gathered in intimate conversation around the circular bar, none felt his pain. Before long, neither did he.

When Romo returned to the bar, he couldn't help but notice that Frankie was in a sorry state.

"Mr. Romohomojo," Frankie called, "What did I do wrong? They laughed. I was funny. Wasn't I funny?" he asked the crowd at the bar, his speech slurred.

"Frankie, go home. You can't even talk, you're tongue-tied."

"I'm not fung fied, damminit," he fired back.

Romo spoke to the bartender. "Eighty-six him." Dreaded words to an aspiring alcoholic. They were cutting him off.

"Thass okay. I'll go where I'm wanted. I can hold my alcholiqua. Give me my sheck," he slurred. The bartender was about to hand him the bill, but Romo shook his finger back and forth.

"No check," the bartender said. "Courtesy of Mr. Romo."

"Thass good, cause I ain't paying." Frankie stumbled toward the door.

Romo motioned for the bartender to follow him out.

"Get him some coffee," he ordered. "See if you can find him a taxi." The bartender followed him out to the parking lot, but Frankie brushed him off as he fumbled for the keys in his coat.

"I'm alone. Leave me okay." Frankie was sure he meant something like that.

"I never met a drunk who wasn't," said the bartender. "Come back in. Mr. Romo wants you to come in and have coffee. Listen, I'll let you sleep it off in the back room."

"Mr. Romojohomo don't want me. You heard him."

Frankie staggered out to the hearse and after a few tries got the key into the ignition. As he pulled across the curb and out of the parking lot, he nearly ran down the longsuffering bartender, who stood on the sidewalk motioning for him to put the headlights on.

Somewhere on the Northern State Parkway Frankie dozed off. The hearse swerved off the road. The cobblestone curb gave him a sudden jolt, and his eyes opened just in time to see the stone wall of the overpass looming in front of him. Instinctively he turned the wheel to the left, sending the other side of the vehicle smashing into the unyielding granite. There was a crunch of crumpling sheet metal, a squeal of tires sliding, and a heavy thud somewhere in the vicinity of his forehead. The collision took all of five seconds, and it had an effect more sobering than any cup of coffee.

Frankie took stock of himself. His head had come to rest against the steering wheel, and a trace of blood flowed down his brow. He began to cry. He chided himself for his stupidity. Was he really willing to die on that lonely road just to spite Romo? His self-indulgence came to an abrupt halt, too, as he recalled the sound of crushing metal. He fumbled for the door handle and fell out on the pavement. Picking himself up and stumbling around to the wrecked side of the vehicle, even under the dim streetlight he could make out the damage. The right rear quarter panel was demolished . . . the rear panel of the hearse that his father had forbid him to use for personal transportation . . . the hearse that they needed on Thursday for a funeral . . . the funeral of Johnny Balls's—*there, I said it*—mother-in-law. He considered the mangled mess. He was in deep shit indeed. Thursday, he thought, that should be no problem. Right.

Thursday. Frankie had no time to feel sorry for himself. He got back behind the wheel and slowly worked to disengage the smashed hearse from the ditch and the wall. Shifting between drive and reverse, he rocked it to and fro until it bolted onto the road surface. With a final lunge he heard the distinct sound of metal being ripped from its housing. Not encouraging. He managed to drive away, leaving nothing behind but a smear of black paint on the gray stone and one side of the hearse beaten up like crumpled tinfoil.

Once on the highway again, to his credit, Frankie remembered to thank God. *This could have been worse.* Far, far worse. God had to be watching over him. God had helped him. But now he needed Eddie.

✝

Frankie parked the hearse two blocks away on Baxter Street, as inconspicuously as he could manage, and walked up to the café. At two in the morning there were three tables of card players in the back and an intense game of chess going on across the corner of the bar. Eddie Fontana had taken on an opponent imported from the Marshall Chess Club on West Tenth Street. They sent their best, twice a week, in a vain attempt to defeat Little Italy's champ. When it came to the royal game, Special Ed was no slouch.

Eddie stood waiting, hands clasped behind his back, as his opponent frowned and moved his pawn forward. He turned momentarily when Frankie walked in. "What happened to you? Looks like you saw a ghost. Some stiff get up and walk out on you?"

The men in the café laughed as they scratched their collective balls. Eddie swiftly captured his opponent's knight. His opponent took a deep breath, scratched his head and bit his nails, and leaned into the game board to study the maneuver more closely.

Frankie approached the game table, pale, disheveled, still trembling. As Eddie looked closer, he saw the ruined suit, the blood coming from above his eyebrow. Blood equaled serious.

"Hey nephew, you okay?"

"I need a favor," Frankie said.

Ah, the magic word, favor, the coin of the realm. Favors were how wise guys got through the day—they traded favors, a mob barter system. One good turn deserved another. You do this for me now, and I'll owe you one. Eddie started to walk toward him, then turned back to the chessboard, where his opponent had just countered his move. He studied the board and responded by moving his queen to an unprotected opening. "Check and mate," Eddie announced. A chorus of "Shit, mother, shit" arose from the Tenth Street onlookers. Eddie left the losers to bask in defeat.

Outside, as they walked toward Baxter Street, Frankie rubbed his aching head and related the whole sorry tale. They turned the corner on the dark street, and Eddie surveyed the damage. "I'm no body-and-fenda man, but it looks like your father's gonna kill you." How astute, Frankie thought.

Nonetheless, Frankie was glad that Eddie understood the problem. "This kind of thing takes time to repair—and I need it by Thursday for Isabella's funeral." Eddie hadn't thought about the funeral—that certainly put the situation in a whole new light. For a moment, Frankie considered telling his father, dare he say, the truth.

"The truth!" Eddie shouted. "Whatta you, nuts? Get in and drive!"

Frankie, his faculties fully restored by now, did as he was told. He had nothing to lose. After a series of lefts and rights, Eddie directed him to a commercial district on lower Canal Street. They made a left onto Christie. The streets were deserted.

"Go slow," Eddie said, as he scanned the numbers on the factory buildings. "Here, *here*—pull in here."

Frankie eased the hearse up onto the sidewalk in front of a trio of huge overhead garage doors. Eddie got out and walked over to an adjacent entry door and pressed the buzzer. A minute later the door opened a crack. Light flooded out onto the black street, and Frankie could make out the figure of a man talking to Eddie. Not long after, the bay doors rumbled open, winched by a giant overhead chain and pulley system, shattering the silence. Eddie motioned for Frankie to drive the hearse into the open warehouse. Enormous fans hung from the ceiling, circulating fresh air throughout the garage. All the windowpanes were blacked out. Frankie had a moment of panic as a police cruiser turned onto the street, stopped, and pointed its floodlight into the garage.

"Everything all right, Pete?" an officer yelled.

"Fine," Pete yelled back. "No problem."

"Okay," the cop said, "And thanks for picking up our dinner check at Cha Cha's."

"My pleasure," Pete said.

"Are we still good for the Yankees tickets?"

"Stop in on Friday."

"Thanks, Pete." The officer waved good-bye.

Pete gave a signal, and the giant doors rattled closed. There were a dozen men busy working in the garage. Some had blowtorches, others had saws; some were working with the hoist to remove engines from cars, others were uninstalling radios, and still others were removing bumpers and grillwork. None, Frankie observed, were putting parts back.

"This is my nephew," Eddie said. "We got a little problem."

The lanky man with the grease-smeared face placed his hands inside his coveralls and adjusted his balls. Then he wiped his nose, rubbed the grease on his coveralls, and extended his hand to Frankie. The man's name was Pete the Mic, short for mechanic. Frankie shook his hand reluctantly, considering where it had just been. But he needed help, and this was no time to be finicky. The Mic examined the damaged hearse and ran his hand over the back panel.

"We don't do repairs here, Eddie, you know that. We're strictly production."

"I know, but this is a favor. Didn't I do you a favor recently? Didn't I take your spinster sister out for dinner?"

"Yeah, and she paid for dinner, and you banged her."

"Well, I was a little short that night."

"That's what she said." The Mic continued to inspect the damage, relenting at last. "Okay, bring it in Saturday and I'll try to get to it."

"No," Eddie said, "You don't understand. We need the thing

back by Thursday morning, at the latest."

"You gotta be kiddin'," Pete protested. "I'm already behind on orders. I gotta have these cars stripped and crated and brought to the pier by Friday night. I gotta answer to people."

"That's why they call it a favor. Come on," Eddie cajoled, "do this one thing for me, for the kid. He'll give you a discount when the shylocks finally catch up with ya. He'll make you look pretty. The kid does wonders with bullet holes."

"They won't kill me. I'm worth more alive."

"Whaddayasay?"

"It means I gotta have two men, working round the clock, and pay 'em overtime."

Eddie took that for a yes. "Thanks," he said, pushing Frankie toward the door. "I owe you one."

"Yeah, call Marie," the man yelled to Eddie.

"The things I do for you, Frankie," said Eddie when they were alone. "I may have to take that dame out again."

They walked over to Dave's Corner Diner on Canal Street. Dave's was a twenty-four-hour eatery, an institution. The sun began to peek through the long east-west corridor and the trickle of trucks and taxicabs turned into a rush-hour flood. Frankie told him the story of how he was fired from the club. Eddie said he could not recall ever having been fired.

"You have to have a job first," Frankie explained. He needed a cheeseburger and vanilla egg cream to replace the electrolytes depleted by the cognac. He didn't know the exact scientific reason, but he needed grease.

"I'll take care of this, Frankie," Eddie offered. He waited, then reached into his pocket.

Frankie stopped him. "It's on me, Eddie. It's the least I can do." Frankie laid a twenty on the counter. Seeing it, Eddie had six hot dogs with mustard, sauerkraut, and onions and a chocolate egg cream.

Frankie couldn't shake the feeling of dejection after his swan song at the San Su San. He had awakened with a pounding headache that still lodged between his temples. He was disoriented. Was it a dream, or had he been fired? And—*oh, Christ, the hearse. Did I bang up the hearse?* Then he remembered—the Northern State Parkway and Pete the Mic and the whole sorry scene. It was real. He was in deep.

He had to rouse himself to face the never-ending rounds of flower deliveries, and the paperwork he knew his father would need help with. Only late in the afternoon did he take a break and slip away next door to Lucci's. He didn't relish telling Sal what had happened.

Sal had a full crew working the dinner shift, and he was nowhere to be found. With dignitaries arriving in advance of the feast, business was unusually brisk for a weeknight. Not a single booth or table was open. Frankie slipped into the kitchen to find Sal shouting directions at the cooks, who were listening to the Yankees game on the radio over the din of rattling pans and the chop of flashing knives.

"How may times I gotta tell ya, don't let the pasta stand in the water . . . drain it and get it on the plate! And not too much garlic in the carbonara!" Sal stopped short when he saw Frankie leaning dejectledly against the pantry. "Whoa, what's up? Who died?"

"I'm fucked. I've been fired. Romo let me go. I must have sucked. I'm sure I sucked. I thought I was doing great there."

Sal was puzzled, given the encouraging report he'd already had from Weis. "Jeez, c'mon, it can't be that bad. I thought there was *really* something wrong. "You'll get another shot."

"That's not all. I banged up the hearse. If I don't get it fixed by tomorrow morning my father is going to kill me. He may have to wait in line because Ballsziti is also going to kill me. Maybe that's a good idea anyway. I'm better off dead. There is no comedy in my future. There *is* no future. This is a nightmare." He banged his head repeatedly on the door jamb.

Sal was accustomed to Frankie's mood swings. "Listen, pour yourself a strong one, and we'll talk in a minute. I have something to tell you. But I've got to seat this party of—"

The radio broadcast suddenly caught his attention. "—more on that early morning fire that destroyed a legendary Long Island nightclub. I'm Brian Ross. More information in just a moment after a commercial break."

Sal turned to the guy who was busy chopping onions. "Hey, what'd you hear about this?" Frankie stepped over to the radio as Sal turned the volume up.

"Um, they said it burned to the ground about four in the morning, just after closing."

The commercial ended and Ross came back on air. "I spoke earlier with Anthony Romo, proprietor of what was once the most famous club on Long Island, the San Su San in Westbury. He was notified of the fire at his home around daybreak. When asked his plans, he had no immediate answer. It's just fortunate no one was injured. The police are still investigating the origin of the fire, which seems to have been started by kitchen grease. We'll bring you more as details develop."

Frankie paused and frowned. "Kitchen grease?"

"And now, here's Mark Wilson with sports. . . ."

Sal shut off the radio. "Don't you get it, you dummy?" He whacked Frankie's head with a wooden macaroni spoon. "I'll bet it was a torch job. The shys must have had him by the culones. Maybe he had a problem with the ponies or somethin'. Either way, Romo knew what was going down. He saved you the ride out there next week. Or worse."

"Jesus," Frankie said, as the gravity of the situation registered. What if he'd taken the bartender up on the offer to sleep it off? They might just now be uncovering the charred remains of one Frankie Grace of Mulberry Street, Manhattan, traced only by the license plate of a black hearse parked in the lot. He wondered how quickly a human body would incinerate when it was that soaked in alcohol. He felt bad for Mr. Romo—wondering what demons he fought. But he felt better for his sense of self-worth.

Rejection to redemption, he thought, as the hammer blows inside his head finally settled down to a dull roar.

Chapter 7

Even during the best of times it was not easy to hold a wake on Mulberry Street. Between trucks dropping off produce to the local markets, suppliers delivering raw material to the sweatshops, and the typical tourist traffic, trying to conduct a meaningful funeral service was challenging. The feast multiplied the problems tenfold, as vendors raced to get all their wares in before the street was cordoned off for the official start of San Gennaro.

Every inch of sidewalk was lined with food concessions: sausage and peppers, beer and soda, cannolis, clams, Charlotte Russe, Italian ices, every imaginable sort of delicacy. On Thursday morning, vendors were already starting to hawk their wares to draw customers in. "Fresh stromboli! Getcha manicotti here!"

Clara Pella, who sold homemade arancini, was positioned directly in front of the funeral home—where she had adamantly insisted on opening for business. If Johnny Ballsziti wanted her to close, she expected a discount on the rent. She had the lungs of an opera star. "Rice balls," she shouted at intervals, "come and get your rice balls!" Revelers on one side of the funeral home door, mourners on the other: the irony did not escape Frankie.

Frankie helped place the last pastry-shaped flower arrangement in the small chapel. The perfume of so many flowers assaulted his olfactory sense. How they would find room for all the mourners, he couldn't imagine. He stole a final glance at Isabella, may she rest in peace. He was proud of his handiwork. She'd taken the fluid nicely. Frankie had debated whether or not to remove that single hair protruding from her upper lip, and tempted though he was, decided against it. No one would recognize her without it, he concluded.

He adjusted the mood lighting to somber and wiped any traces of dust from the large capodimonte holy statues that occupied every corner of the room. The life-sized porcelains often came in handy when he was practicing his routine.

Primo stood at the door awaiting the Ballsziti family. "They're coming," he warned Frankie. "You look terrible," he said. "Are you okay? Snap out of it. This is a big call. We got to get this right."

Today, JB had no choice but to walk. With no room on the sidewalk, he strode down the middle of Mulberry Street, leading his entourage, as if it were a bizarre rehearsal for the saint's procession that would take place on the same route that day. Somewhere behind him, Caterina walked with her mother, who was dressed in black from her shoes to her veil—a color that was usually slenderizing, thought Frankie, but not in Annunziata's case. JB was approached by cronies offering condolences.

The shrieks and wails, overpowering even the noise of the street vendors, started up moments before the family entered the funeral home. They intensified as Frankie made last-minute adjustments to the cheesecake-shaped flower arrangement at the foot of the casket. Exhaust fans from the restaurant on one side and the bakery on the other sent the intoxicating aroma of mostaccioli and cannelloni into the funeral parlor, overpowering even the sweet-smelling gardenias.

He heard the screams grow closer and turned to see his father trying to restrain Annunziata. Good luck, he thought. The bereaved daughter broke away and ran toward the casket as though she were attacking a buffet table. *If she slips, I'm a veal cutlet.* He sidestepped the rush like a matador, leaving the job of pulling her off the casket to JB's nephews. Bull and Bull escorted Annunziata to a love seat, which she fully occupied by herself.

Then Frankie saw her, his Caterina. The smell of food from the restaurant filled the room. Here it is again, he thought—food, death, and sex. She was wearing a clingy black dress that stopped mid-thigh and accentuated her every curve. The gauzy mantilla obscuring her hair and face made her even more alluring. She was even more beautiful than he remembered. As she approached the casket, he extended his arm to greet her. He studied her face; still no sign of five o'clock shadow. He was in a trance. She was a natural beauty. Nice coloring.

Her mother shouted, "Mama, Mama! *Compagna mia!*"

Caterina, elegant as Jackie O, approached and knelt in prayer. God, she must be adopted, Frankie thought. He hoped. Frankie and Primo waited for some comment about how the deceased looked. It was always nice to hear "Good job," "Peaceful," or the supreme compliment, "Looks like she's sleeping."

It was Caterina who finally spoke. "I've never seen Nonna smile . . . " She added, "so much."

Primo shot Frankie an I-told-you-so look.

As mourners entered the chapel and locals arrived to offer respects, vendors on the street went on about their business, oblivious, continuing to promote their wares. Each time the door opened to admit a guest, it was in perfect sync with Clara's broadcast, "Get your rice balls!"

Frankie surveyed the crowd as the chapel began to fill. Eddie stood by his side as he opened the door for mourners. "I thought there'd be more wise guys," he said to Eddie.

"Nah, JB is too smart. He knows he's being watched, so he told them all to stay away. He even takes the cards off the flowers after he reads who sent 'em. If the feds raid the place they won't know his associates."

"Raid the place?"

"It could happen," Eddie said.

"That's all I need," Frankie said.

"You don't look so good," Eddie observed.

"I'm a nervous wreck. Have you heard from Pete?"

"Pete who?"

"Pete, Pete, the guy with the hearse," he whispered.

"Oh, the Mic. No, not yet. I called but he wasn't there. I'm sure you got nottin' to worry about." Clearly Eddie had bigger things on his mind.

"I'm a dead man. A dead man."

Frankie slumped miserably into a chair and listened to the Italian version of a Gregorian chant. *They might as well go ahead and bury him too.*

The women of Mulberry Street elevated crying to an art form. Frankie was all too familiar with the technique—these were the morbid lullabies he fell asleep to each night. It was a unique sound that began in the lower intestines, gathered strength in the stomach, and picked up thrust in the lungs before blasting out the esophagus through the oral cavity. The force of the wails shook the torchière lamps and rattled the porcelain statues. To prevent any lull in the sobbing, the women collaborated to create a crying tag team, with one row of mourners crying out while the others inhaled. Inhaling was important because it determined the quality and duration of the exiting moan. Inhaling properly took years of practice so that the breath was drawn in sharply, which in turn caused the vocal cords to wheeze as they constricted the windpipe. A lot of agony and effort, considering many of the women, funeral groupies, did not even know Isabella.

Father Colapetra, a middle-aged parish priest with a horseshoe-shaped hairline, entered the funeral home dressed in his simple brown cassock.

JB motioned to Frankie. "Tell this guy to keep it short. No need for a lot of bullshit."

Frankie relayed JB's request to the good father and slipped twenty dollars into the priest's hand. Colapetra looked at it, then took another thirty from his own pocket and handed it back to Frankie. "Do me a favor. Give this to Eddie. Tell him I want the Giants with the points this Sunday."

"Do you think the Giants have a chance Sunday?"

"I'm praying."

Then he surveyed at the flowers in the room, his eyes coming to rest on the floral wreath with the clock. "And put five dollars on 808."

"Bless you, Father."

"By the way," Father Colapetra said, "she's smiling too much, I can see it from here. But it was nice that you left the hair on her lip."

"Just keep the sermon short, Father."

He did, leaving the family and friends of the deceased with a memorable final thought. "It is at times like these," the Father said, "that we understand what is important in life—"

The door opened as a latecomer arrived, and everyone heard the chant, "Balls, balls, rice balls!"

Early that morning Roscoe Keats had made his way up the five flights of stairs to the roof access across the street from the Grace Funeral Home. He brought a dozen doughnuts and three steaming coffees for the stakeout team already in place. He took the binoculars and peered through them, focusing on the funeral home entrance. Noting and recording who attended funerals and weddings—and who didn't—provided law enforcement a useful insight into the current mob hierarchy, so it was no surprise they'd taken a keen interest in the rites for Isabella Cianci.

The younger agents thought they'd made it to the rooftop unobserved, but Keats knew better. In this neighborhood, unmarked vans and men on roofs who weren't flying pigeons did not go unnoticed, certainly not by the legion of loyal housewives going about their daily chores.

"She saw us," said Keats, pointing with his chin to a woman pulling in clothes from a line strung across an airshaft. "That lady who just put down the laundry basket."

"Well, these friggin' pigeons circling all around us are like a warning system! It's like they're trained!" the agent complained.

"I wouldn't be surprised," said Keats dryly. He took another look through the binoculars. "What have you seen so far?"

"Well, JB is there, Special Ed just walked in—he's in the black bowling shirt with the plaid jacket—some low-level guys, too. It's not the gathering at Appalachia yet, but it's early."

"I don't see his bulldog nephews though," Keats noted.

"Right, Bull and Bull. That is interesting."

"They'll show," Keats said. "They don't want to miss the luncheon afterwards. We just need a little luck, just a little luck."

Keats felt, more than heard, the thump as a pigeon left a calling card on his head. He looked up—only to be hit with another, square on his forehead. The rooftop agents tried unsuccessfully to conceal their laughter. "Quiet!" he hissed at them. "Damned Italian pigeons."

They finished their coffee and doughnuts in silence. Meanwhile, one of his younger protégés radioed his counterpart on the ground. "No one important yet?"

"Sit tight, they'll be here. I'm sure of it. Keep the cameras going."

"Hold it." The agent flattened himself against the ledge and trained his binoculars down the street. "I see something; a limousine is making the turn down Hester, and, one, two, three . . . *six*—six flower cars."

"Bingo!" The ground agent adjusted his headset.

"This is it. This is it."

The cars stopped in front of the funeral home. "Are you rolling?"

"Affirmative. We have clear view, cameras are rolling."

Primo stood on the street, tapping his foot on the sidewalk. "Frankie," he said, "I'd like to begin the funeral. Is there something missing?"

Look stupid.

Primo clarified things for him. "Well, the limousine is here and the flower cars are here, but I don't see the hearse. Aren't we supposed to have our hearse here?"

Frankie looked at Eddie, who was standing nearby. It was the moment of truth.

"Dad, I've got to tell you something."

Primo was geared up for bad news. From his son, he had come to expect it.

"About the hearse, Dad—"

Then he heard a whistle, like Roy Rogers calling for Trigger. He saw Eddie giving him the high sign and pointing to the corner. Frankie had never been so happy to see anything in his life. He looked up to heaven, thanking God and Jesus and Mary and all the angels all over again, along with his Uncle Eddie. There was not a trace of damage to the glistening black chariot as the Mic drove it past them, dodging the street vendors and stopping beside the funeral home.

"You had it Simonized," Primo said. "Good thinking. Let's go in and start the funeral."

Primo entered the funeral home as Eddie and Frankie converged on the hearse. It looked brand new in the sun. Even Eddie was impressed.

"How'd you bang out that panel so fast?"

"I didn't," Pete said from the driver's seat. "National Funeral Home Livery had a hearse the same year and make. We borrowed it last night and switched the panels. Let them worry about it."

"You're a genius," Eddie said.

"Call my sister," was Pete's only reply before slipping away into the crowd of festival goers. The chauffeur opened the curbside door of the hearse and waited as cameras clicked away.

Inside the Grace Funeral Home, the mourners were preparing to depart for the church. Father Colapetra offered a final blessing, well-wishers paid their last respects, and Annunziata again grew inconsolable, ready to throw herself onto her mother's casket. It had become a routine by now. The Bulls were getting a workout holding her back.

"Nunzie!" JB exclaimed. "Basta. Enough!"

Now I know where his daughter gets it, Frankie thought. He had seen Caterina command that same sort of cooperation from the headstrong Annunziata. Like a faucet being shut off, the hysterics stopped, and Annunziata said a quiet prayer.

Outside, Primo pulled the hearse around and positioned it in front of the limousine. He signaled to Frankie to clear the sidewalk and escort the family to the car.

"I'll make sure the casket is closed properly," JB told his wife. "You go ahead." He turned to confer with Eddie. Frankie figured it must have been important; their lips were moving, but they made no sound. Eddie looked pale as he crossed the room.

"Frankie," Eddie explained, "JB wants to put a few special sentimental items in his mother-in-law's casket."

Like his wife, Frankie mused. Eddie seemed a bit unsettled at the prospect; maybe it was his customary squeamishness with corpses. "No problem, just give them to me and I will place them." Frankie organized the pallbearers to load the floral arrangements into the flower cars. Eddie gave a nod, and JB motioned to the stairway leading to the basement lounge.

Caterina took Annunziata by the arm as Primo arrived, on her other side, to lead her to the limousine. On the sidewalk, he maneuvered her between the sausage concession and Clara's rice balls, around the zeppole vats, and past the calzone stand.

"Rice Balls!' Clara yelled as the doleful group passed by. Annunziata accepted two, free of charge.

As the redoubtable Annunziata made her way to the limo, her flowing dress suddenly caught on a nail protruding from one of the stalls. The fabric tore thigh-high, revealing an imposing scaffold of black silk undergarments. The agents on the rooftop snickered as they saw Primo Grace give Mrs. Ballsziti's ass an indelicate but necessary push to help her into the limousine. It wasn't the surveillance they'd come after, but it was a hell of a lot more entertaining.

A full city block away, around the corner from the funeral home and out of view of the cops' cameras, a trio of station wagons made their way down Mott Street and came to a halt outside Vitagliano's Butcher Shop. There, JB's nephews Bull and Bull were waiting on the sidewalk. They scanned the street up and down until they felt everything was clear, then signaled to the occupants of the cars. The doors opened, and three men in dark sunglasses, each carrying a brown leather satchel in either hand, emerged. They carried the bags into the shop. It took three trips until, satchel after satchel, all were transferred inside. When everything was secure, Mr. Vitagliano, in his bloodstained white apron, escorted the men past the walk-in freezer, toward the back door, and down a narrow flight of steps.

At the bottom of the stairs, Tony Branca, the neighborhood handyman, took over. With a flashlight in one hand and a broomstick in the other, he motioned to the couriers. "Follow me. Watch out for the rats. They wear saddles down here."

Bull took out a snubnosed pistol. "They won't bother me," he said.

"Professional courtesy?" asked Tony.

"Huh?" Bull didn't get it.

Like an urban safari guide, Tony led the eight men through a maze of musty catacombs and moldy underground passages that connected one building to another. They passed through a hidden jungle of leaky hallways, abandoned coal chutes, and steamy boiler rooms before finally emerging into the basement lounge of the Grace Funeral Home. Johnny Ballsziti was waiting to lead them upstairs.

Frankie handed off the last of the elaborate floral sprays and turned to see half a dozen men in suits standing at the head of the casket, bearing heavy canvas satchels imprinted "U. S. Treasury."

"Your mouth," Eddie whispered to Frankie. "Close your mouth."

After studying the space available in the casket JB did some quick geometric calculations and turned to Frankie. "It's best we lay these mementos on the bottom."

Frankie was frozen in place. Bull One turned the lock on the front door, while Bull Two monitored the sidewalk activity through the slit between the curtains.

"Let's go, let's go," JB ordered. "Get her out for a minute."

In a daze, Frankie approached the casket. He slid his arms under the corpse and gingerly removed it. He held the body like he was carrying a bride across the threshold. The dead Isabella's head rested on his shoulder, her lip hair tickling his ear. He didn't know whether to laugh or cry. He recalled the Gospel According to Primo—laughing does turn to crying. He felt faint as he watched the men stuff the satchels beneath the casket mattress. It took considerable effort to force all the bags into place.

When the strangers had replaced the bedding and fluffed the pillow, they nodded to Frankie, who still held Isabella in his aching arms. It could be worse, he thought. It could have been Annunziata. With the assistance of Bull and Bull, Frankie placed Isabella back in the casket. With its newly raised bed, however, the lid would not close. It kept hitting her nose.

"Turn her head sideways," JB said. He didn't get to the top by being stupid.

Frankie placed his hands on Isabella's waxen face and tried turning her head to the side.

"It won't move," he said, "She's firmed up."

"She was never helpful," JB said.

"Maybe we don't have to put her back in, boss," Bull One offered.

"What do you mean?" JB asked.

"There's a furnace in the basement," Bull Two said.

"Hey, that's my friggin' mother-in-law." He thought for a moment, considering it, then said, "Take the pillow out from under her head."

Frankie obeyed, knowing that JB needed closure, of sorts. With the pillow gone, the casket shut. *I guess that's not the first time an Italian was known to keep money under the mattress.* JB sent his mob couriers, in the company of the Bull Brothers, back down the way they had come. "Meet me at church," he ordered. He knelt down and said a quick prayer—whether for the safety of his mother-in-law's immortal soul, or for the delivery of his hidden cargo, Frankie could only guess.

The Bulls unlocked the front door again. JB rose and exited to rejoin his wife, pausing for a moment in the doorway beneath the sign of the Grace Fun. Home to light a cigar. Not once did he glance upward at the men on the rooftops.

✝

Frankie was apoplectic. "Eddie, do you know what I just did?" he hissed. "Do you know what you got me into? I just committed a crime. I could go to jail for life. I—"

Eddie shook him by the shoulders. "Get a hold of yourself. I had a bad feeling all the while. I'm sorry he involved you in this, but you're involved now."

"Eddie, what are we going to do?"

Eddie did not release his grip on Frankie's shoulders. "You're going to do the only thing you can do. Don't say *nothing*. For once in your life, do just what you are told, and when you get to the church, say a prayer that he gets away with this."

"I'd better tell my father."

"No, what are you, stupid? I told you, the less he knows the better. If he gets called to testify, they can't get him on perdury."

Jesus! Testify, perjury: these were not good words. Frankie felt sick.

The sound of camera shutters was audible even inside the doorway of the funeral home. The feds were falling all over themselves trying to catch a glimpse of someone important, but in this they had been sorely disappointed. No one who was anyone had showed up. JB had made sure this funeral was by invitation only.

As he walked out the door Eddie announced, "We're ready to go, JB." He looked up and was about to wave to the film crew on the roof, but a sideways glance from Ballsziti stopped him.

"Eddie, don't do that," JB commanded. "Don't rub their noses in it."

Eddie desisted.

JB covered his mouth with his hand. "The kid knows enough not to mention this, right."

"I'm sure," Eddie said.

"I hope you're sure. Not to no one, and that includes my daughter."

"Of course, JB."

Frankie organized the pallbearers on each side of the casket. On his cue, they lifted. The six hefty men groaned aloud as they struggled to balance the weight. "This is friggin' heavy," said one who looked like he could've been Annunziata's twin.

"What the fuck is in here?" another questioned.

"It's bronze, idiots," Frankie replied.

They squeezed through the door only to find there was no room to maneuver between the concessions. They rested the casket on the countertop of the sausage stand, where it became lodged. Primo, a model of professionalism, was devastated. He leaned over to help slide the casket along the plywood surface. It was wedged solid, the front metal edge biting further into the wood with each attempt. It wouldn't budge.

Clara, sure that having a casket stuck in one's booth was a bad omen, poured olive oil on the counter, then got behind and pushed. With one shove the casket slid into the arms of the pallbearers, who had gathered in front like a line of scrimmage to receive it. The pallbearers regrouped, hoisted the casket on their shoulders as best they could, and marched erratically toward the hearse. The weight of the casket swayed them right, then left, then right, then backwards. Primo shook his head. It was not textbook.

At last they secured the casket and its unexpected burden in the hearse, and the funeral assembly was under way. It was only a few short blocks to the Church of the Most Precious Blood. Annunziata was sobbing uncontrollably as she tried to throw herself from the window of the limousine. "Mama would have been so proud," she cried. A woman from the building across the street waved and blew a kiss. Festival goers pointed toward the passing vehicles, speculating as to what notable person had died.

At the church the process was reversed. The pallbearers, their black suits now dusted with white confectionary sugar, struggled up the brick steps. Thoroughly exhausted, they could hardly lift the casket above their knees. *That's all I need now,* Frankie thought, is to have the casket fall down the church steps and roll down Baxter Street. He made a mental note and filed it in the comedy cabinet: *runaway casket.*

After much difficulty, the casket was borne safely up into the sanctuary, and all waited in the aisle for Father Colapetra. Organ music echoed through the vaulted spires that ran the length of the nave. Above the altar, a figure of the body of Jesus Christ hung from a cross, with the skyline of Mount Calvary painted on the domed ceiling behind Him.

Ballsziti had paid extra to have a short mass. He was anxious for part two of the plan to commence. Nerves were evident as the organ music grew steadily louder and the mourners shifted about. They were not a patient crowd. Frankie slipped behind the altar into the sacristy in search of the absent priest. There he found Colapetra leaning over a table studying the *Daily News* racing section, a small pencil in his hand.

"Father!"

Colapetra looked up. "Oh, is it time yet?"

"A little past time," Frankie responded.

"Relax," he said, "She's not going anywhere. It's not like you have to catch a flight. Do you want some wine?" He pointed to a chalice.

"A bit early, even for me, Father."

Father Colapetra slid the pencil behind his ear and slipped his chasuble over his head. "Interesting," he remarked, staring at the paper. "Fifth race at Belmont, the horse's name is Napoleon, and Half a Loaf is running in the sixth. Do you think that is a sign, from heaven, like?"

"Father, don't take this wrong, but are you crazy?"

"Well, I know they are long shots but sometimes He works in mysterious ways. This might be a sign from God."

"A sign—are you serious?"

"Yes, Frankie, see, we're burying the baker, the pastry lady, and there's a horse named Napoleon, like the pastry; might be trying to tell us something."

"Father, do you think there is anything unusual about a priest with a gambling habit?"

Father Colapetra thought about it. "His will be done."

"Could His will be done a little faster?"

As he continued to vest, the priest explained, "You don't understand. I don't gamble for myself—I gamble for the church. Do you know how much it costs to heat this joint? Our take on Sundays is off. You know, the smaller the people fold the bills they put in the basket, the smaller the denomination. Luckily, last month I hit the trifecta! I had the sacristy painted and bought a new prie-dieu for the grotto. God is making the best use of my talent. I always had a knack for handicapping, mostly football and the ponies, and He sends me messages to verify my selections. For example, this horse named Napoleon, a clear sign."

Frankie gritted his teeth. "Is there a horse named Requiem for a Priest? Because unless you get this over with, they are going to be celebrating one for you!"

"I'm ready," he said as he added a last-minute check mark. "Is there anything special about her, anything they want me to say?"

"Isabella, you know. She was an institution."

"I'll work it in."

No one standing in the aisle seemed to notice when the organist segued subtly from "Amazing Grace" to the call to the post. It was a cue for Father Colapetra, who made his way from the sacristy.

"Dearly beloved," he intoned as he walked up the aisle to the casket, pencil still tucked behind his ear.

As he sat in back of the church, Frankie was impressed with the nexus Father Colapetra made between Isabella baking bread and Christ breaking bread. He spoke of the importance of bread in the liturgy, the bread of life, and the special place God must have in heaven for bakers. *A little hokey, but not bad for the last minute.* Quite a talent for improvisation, the priest had. It even took Frankie's mind off his predicament for the moment. That— and his unobstructed view of the family pew, where he rested his eyes on the back of Caterina's lovely head. Annunziata's sobs faded into background noise as Frankie enjoyed his brief respite.

After final commendation, Father Colapetra blessed the body, then knocked once on the casket with his knuckles. He winked at Frankie, who understood the final appeal to Isabella for luck at Belmont.

✝

With his mother-in-law safely returned to the hearse, JB accompanied his family into the waiting limousine. "Caterina," he said, "I see you giving goo-goo eyes to this Frankie kid. He's not right for you. He's trouble, *babana*, gambling. A bad seed. Once a week I have to stop some hood from breaking his legs. Stay away from him. You know, that formaldehyde stuff affected his brain or something. He's not right up here." He tapped his temple.

Caterina did not answer.

Still vested, Father Colapetra walked down the church steps. Frankie escorted him to the limousine that would transport Caterina and her parents.

"I'd rather sit in the hearse," the priest said.

"Not today, you wouldn't," said Frankie, suspecting this would be a funeral procession like no other. Eddie ushered Father Colapetra into his seat and, just before closing the door, quietly reached down to pull the alb on the priest's vestment, leaving it exposed outside the door saddle.

The cortege, led by the half dozen overflowing flower cars, made its way slowly along Baxter Street and onto Canal, a wider thoroughfare that led to the Manhattan Bridge. Frankie was at the wheel of the hearse, keeping one eye on the road and one in the rearview mirror. As he approached the bridge, three other hearses encircled him, followed by limousines weaving in and out of the lanes. With the skill of seasoned getaway drivers, each limo peeled out from behind its hearse and followed one of the others. The drivers of the flower cars scattered as well, each choosing a different lane and different procession to lead. In their midst an unmarked police car was doing its best to tail the casket.

"Jesus, we have a problem," Roscoe Keats shouted into the radio. "There are four hearses now and four limousines."

A voice came over the radio. "Which one do we follow?"

"That one—no, no, *that* one. We need backup, backup right away!"

Keats slammed his hand against the dashboard.

"That bastard! That sonofabitch!"

It was a funerary stock car race, right there in lower Manhattan. The black hearses swerved in and out of lanes, as limousines and overladen flower cars fell in behind them.

"Not that one," Keats shouted, as he pointed to one hearse. "It's all banged up," he explained. "That wasn't the one."

Four different funeral processions were headed toward the bridge. Keats shouted into the radio, "Just keep your eyes on Ballsziti's car—that one, the one with the white cloth hanging out, passenger side front. Just follow that car."

Frankie struggled to keep his cool and his bearings amid the circus. A blaring horn got his attention as he looked back to see an eighteen-wheeler barreling toward him in the right lane. He veered on two wheels, swerving unexpectedly onto Mulberry and breaking through a police barricade. The limousine following him fell in behind another passing hearse, while the Bull brothers' car did a one-eighty to catch up with Frankie's hearse. Frankie stomped on the brakes and came to a halt in the middle of the street, where the feast of San Gennaro was now in full swing.

As his limousine followed an empty hearse over the bridge, JB looked out the rear window in time to witness Frankie's unintentional stunt. He had every confidence his nephews would keep the plan on track. He also saw Keats and all the other unmarked police cars following him. For this he was grateful. They had taken the bait. He reached up and patted Colapetra on the shoulder. "You did a good job, Fata."

Chapter 8

The brothers Bull abandoned their vehicle right in the middle of Canal Street, wreaking havoc and stalling traffic further. They galloped down Mulberry on foot, barreling around startled pedestrians in an attempt to catch up to the runaway hearse. Frankie, determining there was no way to back out of the crowd, accelerated to a crawl. The hearse was already deep into the street, surrounded by a crowd of curious pedestrians, when the doors opened on either side. Bull jumped into the passenger side, while the other Bull forced his way into the driver's seat, sandwiching Frankie in the middle.

The hearse moved forward inch by inch amid the lunchtime throngs awaiting the saint's procession. People standing in the middle of the street and those eating at sausage stands flattened their bodies against the concession stands to make room for the intruding vehicle. Confused vendors scurried to remove cases of soda and bushels of peppers stacked in front of their booths.

The street band was making its way down Hester Street, preparing to lead the procession. The hearse cleared the intersection of Mulberry and Hester, midway through their ranks. Frankie, the Bull Brothers, the late Isabella Cianci, and five million dollars became inextricably wedged in the middle of the Neapolitans' High Holy Day parade. Half the band members, in their baggy, gold-trimmed black suits, peeked over their shoulders at the hearse suddenly tailing them. Figuring this was a new float sponsored by the local funeral home, the remnant of the band fell in behind and switched to a lively, New Orleans–inspired "When the Saints Go Marching In." Each rhythmic step tugged at the waistbands of their uniforms.

The road ahead was blocked by the platform that had been erected to accommodate the altar and the figure of San Gennaro. The wooden stage measured a full thirty feet long and fifteen feet wide, and the altar was decorated with strings of lights. A dozen chairs for the holy delegation from Naples had been placed atop the platform. The statue, a five foot, gold-plated bust of San Gennaro, was dressed in embroidered silk vestments, with a bright red-and-white silk cape studded with dazzling rhinestones. A bishop's miter crowned its head. The statue's fingers were raised in the sign of benediction, and its eyes were slightly raised to heaven, with much the same "Why me?" look that Frankie had seen so often on his father's face.

Driver-side Bull tried sounding the horn and flicking the lights so the hearse could move through the crowd, but his actions only added to the party atmosphere. The hearse slowed again to a standstill, engulfed by a crowd of tourists. Passenger-side Bull leaned out the window to buy zeppoles and a calzone. Driver-side Bull grabbed for a sausage-and-pepper sandwich. With one hand on the wheel, he bit into the greasy concoction. "Christ, I got *earl* on my tie," he growled.

In an effort to remove the portentous vehicle from the parade route, feast officials motioned frantically to driver-side Bull, some directing him one way, some directing him another, some urging him forward and around, others urging him to back up. A few of the hand signals constituted something other than directional assistance.

"Your sister's ass," was Bull's only response.

✝

Ahead, anxious as thoroughbreds at the starting gate, thirty men from Bari, Italy, waited for just the right moment to take their places behind the street band. Their expertise at carrying San Gennaro was legendary: a certain gait and cadence made it appear that the saint was walking above the crowd. Like dedicated postmen, they would allow nothing, not even a wayward hearse, to deter them. They waited as the band approached the altar playing "A Festa e' San Gennaro" and the "Marcia Reale."

Then, in a well choreographed routine, the crowd grew quiet as the president of the San Gennaro Society made his way to the altar. He welcomed the visiting bishop and handed him a proclamation from Naples, where a vial of the saint's blood was kept as a holy relic. On the coming Sunday, the feast day of San Gennaro, the Catholic faithful would wait in hope of a miracle, when the martyr's blood would liquefy as a sign of God's continued protection.

The bishop addressed the expectant crowd. "E un miraculoso!" Or, Let the games begin.

People cheered as the band kicked up, and on cue, the bearers from Bari lifted the platform with San Gennaro and his robed followers upon their shoulders. Slowly, like a barge leaving the harbor, they maneuvered the makeshift ark into the middle of the street, following the band. On this day, each had one hand on the support post and the other on his crotch, in deference to the hearse in their midst.

"Find an opening," passenger-side Bull yelled, as oil dribbled down his chin.

"There ain't none," driver-side Bull answered, as ricotta dripped down his.

They moved along with the parade. The members of the holy society, good Catholics, shot Neapolitan invectives at the hearse and its occupants. Its presence had no doubt cast a dark cloud on the feast. The second half of the band continued to play from behind the hearse as it inched up the street.

"Rice balls, get your rice balls!" At the sound of Clara's voice, Frankie slouched down into the seat.

The parade made its way toward the review stand, where an august group of officials awaited. The clerics on the platform waved to the dignitaries perched high on the stand. The honor guard followed, carrying the American and Italian flags. The dignitaries saluted. As the statue of San Gennaro passed by, the dignitaries blew kisses toward their beloved patron saint.

Then, to the chagrin of all, the hearse passed right in front of them. Trying not to be obvious, the dignitaries looked at each other. There was no protocol for such an occurrence. A salute was not called for, nor a kiss. They all came to the same conclusion: make a sign of the cross. It only made sense. Frankie looked in the rearview mirror just in time to see them all go from the sign of the cross to the scratching of the balls. It never failed.

The crush of revelers made it impossible to move, and the tension was building. As the hearse approached Grand Street, passenger-side Bull saw an opening. He threw his considerable arm across Frankie's chest. "Take this left," he said to his brother.

Driver-side Bull made a sharp turn onto Grand Street, and soon they were free. A look in the rearview mirror revealed an orchestra of Italian salutes.

"We suppose to go to Brooklyn now?" asked driver-side Bull.

Frankie took a deep breath. "Yes, Union Street," he said.

It was an unusually quiet ride, even for a hearse. Normally, Frankie would practice his comedy routine on the way to the cemetery, but the two men next to him did not have a sense of humor. There was no answer to his questions as he tried to break the ice.

"So, are you guys brothers?"

Silence. *Yeah, like a different mother could spit out these two.*

Passenger-side Bull clapped his hand over Frankie's mouth and held it there for a minute. Frankie took the hint: they were not into conversation, so he turned on the radio. Driver-side Bull turned it off. Passenger-side Bull dozed off, his massive head coming to rest on Frankie's shoulder. The smell of garlic was nauseating.

At the South Brooklyn Casket Company, they watched a fork-lift lower the casket into a zinc-lined wooden box. The machine tilted under the casket's weight.

"Jesus, you got a healthy one in there," the man said.

Frankie gave him a warning sign, motioning his head toward the two hulking types watching the process. The operator got the message. Being near retirement, he kept his mouth shut and went about the job of sealing the zinc.

When the box was returned to the hearse the rear bumper scraped the shop floor, but the car leveled off when Frankie, Bull, and Bull got in the front seat. At that point, the whole chassis bottomed out. The overloaded vehicle pulled out of the warehouse, sparks flying from the bumper, as they cruised along Fourth Avenue and over the Brooklyn Bridge to the FDR.

When they arrived at the Italian Consulate on Park Avenue, a man with a handlebar mustache was waiting. Frankie showed the documentation; everything was in order. Handlebar Mustache disappeared into the back of the hearse, where he melted a red candle over the metal straps that secured the outer box. Into the hot red wax he placed the seal of the Italian Consulate. If this seal were broken or damaged, Alitalia would refuse to ship the remains. It was routine for Handlebar Mustache, and he paid little attention to Frankie or his guests. The consul put his signature to the documents, and Frankie began to breathe easier. In an hour this whole ordeal would be over.

Next stop, the Alitalia cargo terminal at John F. Kennedy Airport. When the clerk weighed the box, the cost of shipping came to $3,900, more than three times the customary rate, and he began to act suspicious.

"Ma perché, perché?" he asked. *"Troppo pesante."* Why so heavy?

Frankie understood why the man questioned the heavy delivery. If the clerk kept it up, it could blow the whole plan out of the water.

"Ah, capisco," Frankie said, lighting on the solution. "Mama, their mama, *grosso come loro.*" He pointed to the two expressionless men. He puffed his cheeks with air and poked out his stomach as far as he could, miming. *"Their* mama," he said again.

The man looked at the outer box, then at the brothers Bull. He laughed a little. No so hard to understand after all. *"Ah, io capisco, allora. Troppo pesante come loro!"*

Whatever that meant, it was good enough for Frankie. The clerk affixed the final stamps to the shipping documents and the casket, at last, was loaded on the flight to Palermo.

"Make it look good," Frankie said to the Bull boys. "I told him she was your mother, so wave good-bye to her."

They did. *Hmmm, they do understand English.* It was another quiet ride back to Mulberry Street, where Bull and Bull gave the hearse back over to Frankie, who wisecracked, "Guys, it's been great. I promise, when I get my talk show, you guys are my first guests."

They glared at Frankie, not amused.

There was a message from Father Colapetra, back from Queens with the family. He was upset. Hare Lip won the fifth race at Belmont, and he missed it.

After returning the hearse, a frazzled Frankie made his way to Lucci's, where Eddie and Sal were waiting. "That was quite a show," Sal said. "You had to see their faces when your hearse passed the review stand. Those guys were scratching like they had fleas. You singlehandely made 'em forget all about the fallen angel. It was great!"

Frankie was quiet as he sat down next to Eddie. Sal brought drinks. "What's the matter with you guys? You don't look so good."

Eddie just said, "I'm sorry, Frankie. I'm so, so sorry. I had a feeling, but I didn't know for sure. I couldn't say anything, and even if I did, it wouldn't have changed anything. You woulda had to do what you were told."

Frankie let his head fall to the table. Eddie continued. "It's done now. It's over. We didn't get caught."

"Caught?" Sal said, eager to hear more.

Frankie didn't raise his head. "I just helped Johnny Ballsziti ship five million in cash out of the country."

Eddie smacked him in the head. "That's how you will get caught. You don't go around telling people."

"I'm not people," Sal protested.

"You just forget it," he said, addressing Frankie. "It never happened. Don't be making conversation about this."

Sal sat down, impressed with the news and eager to hear more. Enlightened, he said, "So, he *was* involved with the Brinks job."

"Hey, what did I just say? Ain't I making myself clear? I don't want him talkin' about it."

Sal continued, ignoring the prohibition. "I didn't think JB was that smart."

Eddie took exception. "Yeah, well, he's plenty smart, smarter than those federal agents who followed a bunch of empty hearses all over the nine boroughs. For all I know, they're still driving around out there. JB is the man, and he's getting ready for the day when they do catch up with him. He's got a million thousand different names and identifications in Italy, with money stashed all over the place. If it ever comes to it, they will never find him for a million thousand years."

Sal threw his hands up. "Hey, sorry if I insulted your idol."

"Guys, guys, come on," said Frankie. "We have enough problems here."

There was quiet for a moment. Then Eddie said, "Frankie, it's over. Done. Just forget it."

"We're not home free yet, Eddie. A lot can still go wrong on the other side."

"In Italy?" Eddied scoffed at that. "Don't make me laugh. That's JB's backyard."

That night Frankie couldn't sleep; he drifted through one nightmare after another. He was in the basement embalming room. The whole room was blinding white—bleached-white octagon tiles on the floor and walls, cold white porcelain table, institutional white slop sink. Every step echoed. A large, clear glass tank stood behind him. Against the wall, white cabinets housed rolls of cotton, bottles of chemicals, and clean, pressed white sheets. Primo soaped down the table. He waited for Frankie to help slide a body off the stretcher onto the embalming table. Beneath the plastic morgue sheets, cold and damp, a human form sprawled, motionless.

"I'll take care of this one. You just watch," Primo instructed. Frankie didn't mind being an observer. He never liked to see a dead man's face for the first time, always stark, scary, always discolored, with deep purple skin. His father covered the face with a tissue. "No one ever dies with their mouth or eyes closed," his father lamented. "Only in the movies." Frankie preferred the movies.

The foul odor of the decomposing corpse mixed with the chemicals, causing him to gag. He heard the snap of rubber gloves. The tools of the undertaker's trade, shiny metal instruments that reflected the overhead light, were laid out on a tray beside the table. His father picked up the scalpel, held the man's arm back, and cut near the armpit. Not to worry, his father assured him, the dead are unfazed by this. Only the living feel pain.

Primo reached for the embalming fluid in the glass-front cabinet and poured it into the tank, adding water from the faucet. The opaque red liquid quickly dissolved. A rubber tube extended from the tank to a small feed inserted into the exposed artery. Primo turned the machine on, and the motor pumped its contents into the body.

The air was caustic, irritating. Frankie couldn't breathe. There was drainage, too, redder than anything he had ever seen. It ran down a beveled edge at the side of the table, finding its way through a tube leading into a drain in the floor. As the motor hummed, the purple hue faded from the body, and Primo moved on to the next task. He reached for a can of Gillette Foamy shaving cream, squeezed some onto his palm, and lathered it in. He ran a razor across the man's face. It scraped like sandpaper. With a large, soapy sponge, he massaged the limbs. Each stroke sent more red flowing into the drain. He continued to work until the tank was empty. He flipped the switch. All was quiet.

Primo dabbed Vaseline onto a small piece of cotton and placed it under an eyelid. "Eyes usually sink when someone dies," that's what he said. "This puffs them a bit, makes them look more natural." Vaseline was also a good moisturizer. He closed the eyes and the mouth, taking extra time with the lips. Lips must be perfectly closed, he instructed, not pulled or clenched; they should look natural and relaxed. People notice lips the most. He stepped back.

"Do you think he is smiling too much? Can't have too much of a smile." Primo didn't wait for an answer. "No, just enough," he said, "just enough. He looks better already."

Better is relative, Frankie thought.

"Finished," Primo announced at last. He stepped back from the table to admire his handiwork.

"Hey, this stiff looks familiar." He motioned Frankie closer. Frankie didn't want to move, but his father pulled him in toward the body. "Look, don't you recognize him?"

Frankie stared at the corpse on the table. It was his own. His face, his body, dead on the table. He screamed. He turned to his father, who had suddenly morphed into Johnny Ballsziti. JB was laughing at him, laughing and laughing and pulling him ever closer to the table. Frankie screamed again and again until he woke up, shaking, in a cold sweat.

There was banging on the wall from the adjacent bedroom. "Frankie, go to sleep, goddammit," his father yelled. "You're dreaming again."

He did, but moments later he was awakened by the sound of a bedpost banging against the wall. The image that appeared in his head was almost worse than the dream.

Chapter 9

For Frankie, it wasn't *if* the other shoe would drop, but when. He bought a copy of *La Repubblica*, fully expecting to find a front-page story complete with images of Interpol and local *polizia* surrounding Isabella's casket. Stack upon stack of American money, all the evidence they needed, would be strategically spread across the table for the photo op. Frankie would not need a translator—the picture would tell the story. Getting the money out of the country was one thing, but plenty could go wrong in Italy, and it could all easily be traced back to him. He envisioned different scenarios in which he was accused of the robbery, and in each one he had no choice but to take the fall. He was certain JB would clearly explain to him his options, or lack thereof.

He thought about the beautiful Caterina. What would she think if she found out he'd shipped millions of dollars out of the country in her grandmother's . . . Jesus, he needed to see her again. Was there some protocol for how much time should pass before he asked her on a date? And he foresaw at least one major problem—her parents would not take well to their daughter dating the undertaker, the ultimate portent of misery.

The people of Little Italy were a religious lot, deeply rooted in superstition. They believed that someone could give you the evil eye and cause you harm or bad luck. Being *overlooked* was the root cause of any unforeseen malady. Leading this sect was Annunziata

Ballsziti. Not only was Annunziata a believer in *mal'occhio,* the evil eye, she was a devotee. She had earned her credentials to remove or place the evil eye during a solemn ceremony performed by an accredited mal'occhian. According to the old wives' tale, the secret accreditation ceremony could only take place on Christmas Eve, in a ritual preformed by an elder practitioner.

Annunziata had been a working practitioner of the art for more than forty years. People came to her for everything from a headache to a bad day at the track, and she would confirm they were being overlooked. Yawning was the determining factor. The more she yawned, the stronger the ill wishes, and the harder it would be to remove them. To counteract the curse, she would murmur a quiet prayer while holding some item of the afflicted's belongings.

On any given day, the late Isabella and her daughter Annunziata wanted no part of the Grace family. They began each morning by pouring salt on the sidewalk, most of it on the funeral home section, to ward off evil spirits. They went to great pains to protect themselves and their business from the mal'occhio. Salting the sidewalk or hanging a red horn over the register were quick fixes. Only a quirk of fate had situated the bakery shop directly adjacent to the funeral home, a fact the family bemoaned every day. But not even her strongest hexes were sufficient to staunch Frankie's yearnings.

✝

At the bakery, there was no extended mourning period. Too many restaurants depended on her for their bread and pastries, so Annunziata went about her business—seven days a week—as her mother would have wanted.

On Friday morning Bull and Bull waited in front of the bakery for JB to appear and have his customary breakfast. Ballsziti barely nodded to them as he left the apartment building and entered the bakery.

No one acknowledged JB's presence except the cat, who hissed as he came in. "Calma, calma," Annunziata urged, sotto voce.

JB sat at his usual table, head turned toward the door, averting his wife's stare. "Caffè," he growled.

The espresso machine squeezed out the last drop of demitasse, and she brought it to the table, still glaring at him.

"What, what?" He knew that look.

"You told Caterina the undertaker boy is no good. Why? *Stunata,* yes, but not more."

"Why, you want him involved with our daughter?"

"God forbid," she said. "But I don't like what you're thinking. I don't want that on my conscience."

"What do you know about what I hear on the street? Don't question when I say something, because I know things that you don't. Now, get me my biscotti."

She moved behind the counter and reached into the display case for his favorite anisette treats. She passed them before the cat, who obligingly ran his sandpaper tongue across their equally rough surface. She smiled. The cat did, too.

She brought the twice-baked anise-flavored cookies to the table. "Don't choke," she said. That was about as loving as she got.

He ignored her as he savored his morning repast.

✝

Later that morning, Frankie peered through the bakery's display window and saw Annunziata, who he hoped despite their mutual dislike would be his future mother-in-law, wedged behind the counter. She was sampling the anisette cake. Caterina was nowhere in sight. Frankie wondered how the bakery could be profitable, considering all Annunziata ate.

Armed with a bouquet of flowers tucked behind his back, he plucked up the courage to enter. The countertop was filled with trays of freshly baked breads, dozens of cookies, and a dazzling array of pastries. The rich aroma of chocolate-covered cream-filled cherry-on-top delights mixed with the pungent smell of cappuccino and espresso and the sweet scent of the flowers he carried, leaving Frankie in a dreamlike haze.

She was polite enough as the door chimes rang, innocent enough as she limped behind the showcase, layering a dozen almond-coated cookies in a cardboard box for her customer. She barely acknowledged Frankie as he stood by the door, the omen from hell. The cat lounging next to the register glared at him, adding to his nerves. *What would a witch be without her familiar?* He shifted his weight from foot to foot.

While the customers browsed she finally came over to greet him. "What?" she said. "Are you looking to get paid already?"

Frankie tried to reply, but nothing sensible would come out. It wasn't worth it, all this angst. He started to bolt. The internal debate raged—ten seconds were ten hours—until his yang took over his yin and he got hold of himself.

"These are for Caterina," he blurted out. He brought the bouquet of gladioli from behind his back and placed it on the counter. At the sight of the flowers Annunziata stumbled backwards against the espresso machine. Frankie realized he might've made a slight logistical miscalculation. With the abundance of arrangements, how could she have recognized this one little bunch?

The color drained from Annunziata's face, and her eyes bugged out of their sockets. She was confused, disoriented, on the verge of hyperventilating. Had it not been for the witnesses present, she would have suggested an appropriate place where he could stick his gift. But ever the consummate businesswoman, she forced a smile for the benefit of the few customers milling about. The smile exposed her evenly spaced, tightly clenched teeth.

"*Grazie!*" The word came sardonically from deep in her throat.

Jeez, thought Frankie. Not like the original customers could get any further use out of them. He bowed politely and backed up into the door, then through it, leaving the bell chiming in his wake.

With a nod and a raised eyebrow, Annunziata lifted the bouquet from the counter, using but two fingers as if it carried the plague, and disposed of it in the trash. She exorcised the ill-gotten glads with a series of machinations and incantations, jabbing with her pointer and pinky finger extended outward. Flowers left over from a funeral—they would no doubt translate into trouble, a bad day at the register at the very least.

Undeterred, Frankie returned to the funeral home. He knew

he would have to call Caterina. It took him another hour to find the courage and pick up the phone.

"C-C-Caterina," he stammered. "It's Frankie Grace. Did you like my flowers?"

"Flowers?"

So much for that tactic. "Never mind. I thought—I thought you would like to get away from all this madness in the neighborhood. With your grandmother's funeral and all. I mean with the feast crowds and everything. I thought you might like to get away."

"What did you have in mind, Paris?" she answered coolly.

He took a deep breath. "We could to to Chinatown."

"Chinatown?"

"Yes. We can giggle over moo goo, talk over thai foo, laugh over lum yem, flirt over flaming duck."

She laughed. "Please, spare me the alliteration," she begged.

"But you'll join me for dinner this evening?"

To his amazement and joy, Caterina agreed. She sounded a bit hesitant at his suggestion of rendezvous point, but the only word Frankie took away from the conversation was Yes.

Caterina understood as she turned the corner to find Frankie leaning against the hearse, nattily dressed in a sport jacket, gray slacks, and loafers. Baxter Street was quiet at night, and the presence of the funeral wagon would not draw attention there. It was, in fact, the only car parked in the commercial factory district. Under the street lamp, as the last rays of sunset faded, Caterina saw Frankie's face melt into a welcoming smile as she approached. She was skeptical, but Frankie assured her that no harm would come from riding in the *front* of a hearse. He gently guided her into the front seat, her long hair flowing, her dark eyes piercing the twilight and Frankie's heart at the same time.

They made their way to Chinatown, where he parked the hearse on another out-of-the-way side street. They walked the three city blocks to Chinatown's main thoroughfare, talking and laughing as they went. Chinatown was the place to take a date—plenty of food and prices so low you could afford to eat again in an hour, which was good because in an hour you would no doubt be hungry again.

It was the most incredible night of Frankie's life. On the happiness meter, nothing else had even come close. After dinner they strolled through Columbus Park, stopping to relax on a wrought iron park bench. Frankie stretched his arm across Caterina's shoulder. She leaned against his chest, listening to the steady beat of his heart as they sat feeding stale fortune cookies to the grateful pigeons. They laughed as they unfolded the paper slips salvaged from the crumbled cookies; his read THERE ARE BIGGER THINGS AHEAD, hers, LEAVE NOW. *I can't even get a break from Confucius,* Frankie thought.

"Would you like to go for a ride?" he asked. The night air was turning chill.

She shrugged.

He took that for a yes and escorted her back to the hearse. *Where do you find a woman like this? Brave, daring, beautiful.*

They drove across the bridge and far south along Brooklyn's Belt Parkway until they found a space at the water's edge. The night was serene. A cloudless sky held countless stars, and the full-faced man in the moon was smiling brightly over the Hudson. Frankie inhaled deeply, taking in the salty sea air, the marshy smell of low tide, and the musty remnants of dead flowers in the back of the hearse. Not the most romantic combination. Still, he slid across the velour seats and embraced Caterina. He ran his fingers lightly across her cheek, and she laid her head on his chest. They gazed out toward the open sea, watching tugboats guide freighters in and out of the harbor until she at last broke the silence.

"So, why are you always in trouble?" A real icebreaker.

"It just happens naturally, I guess. It's not like I plan on it."

There was a pause as she digested his answer.

"What is it you want out of life, Caterina? What is your dream?"

She thought for a moment. "I'd like to continue my studies. I've been accepted at the American University of Bologna Business School. I like business management of some kind or other."

That ought to come in handy running her Dad's empire.

She must have read his mind. "My father's ways are not my ways," she said. "But he is my father and wise enough to get me away from all this."

"I guess." Frankie could understand how seeing her father's name plastered on the front pages of the *New York Post* or the *Daily News* could interfere with her development as a productive member of society. She was different from other girls he'd dated, who measured success by a two-family house in Brooklyn, where they would rent out the upstairs and live in the damp finished basement, complete with a large television, genuine vinyl recliner, plastic-covered living room chairs and couch, and a dehumidifier. "Do you see yourself selling pastries like your mother and grand-mother?"

"No, retail doesn't really excite me. I have some other ideas though. My grandmother had some wonderful recipes. There must be a way to make better use of them."

Business plans did not excite him. He leaned over and kissed her. She let him. Then she asked, "And what about you? What's important to you?"

He kissed her again, if only to keep her quiet. He didn't want to answer. "It's getting late," he said. He was flushed, his heart was pounding; hers too. They both agreed it was the MSG in the Chinese food.

"But you still haven't answered," she remarked as she returned his kiss.

"I'm not sure yet. I'm confused, really confused. Maybe I'd like to jump on one of those freighters and travel around the world, one adventure to another. Never knowing what tomorrow will bring." He whispered in her ear. "You are beautiful." She was. On the hearse radio Tony Bennett was singing, "*When Johanna loved me, every town was Paris, every day was Sunday, every month was May.*" What a moment! Frankie thought. No matter if it's bad for business, it's good to be alive.

"But you have a good background, a good family business waiting for you," she said. *They got to her, those capitalist bastards.*

"I know that's the way it seems, but I'm not sure it's for me."

"Not sure? Well, what then?" Each word sent her warm breath into his ear, right to his heart. It tickled, too. Unlike her grandmother's lip hair tickle, this was a welcome sensation that gave him goosebumps. He loved the feeling.

"I just don't know if I'm cut out for funeral work," he hedged.

"It must be pretty depressing. It takes a certain kind of person, a special person. Someone has to do it, and I guess it can be gratifying to be a caregiver."

"I know, I know, but maybe it's not for me."

She pressed him. "Well then, what *does* Frankie see himself doing in ten years?"

The night sky was like a velvet cloth sprinkled with diamonds. Her perfume was intoxicating. The hearse windows had started to fog up. "Well, I think about being a comedian. I think I'd be good at that."

It was getting colder. Her eyes opened a bit wider.

"Show business?" she asked. *Not a good tone.*

"Yes, I think I could be a comic."

"Really?" she said. "Can you actually make a living at that?"

"I don't know, never thought about actually making a living." It was true. He hadn't.

"Seems kind of iffy to me; not very practical."

Change the subject, stupid. You're losing her. Too late.

"You are odd, Frankie Grace, really weird. You have so much going for you, a profession where you can make a difference in people's lives, so much waiting for you, and you do the weirdest, weirdest things."

The moon was full, but to howl now would only confirm her suspicions.

He kissed her lips and neck passionately and worked his way down to her breast, his hands leading the way. Flushed with excitement, he came up for air and looked her in the eye.

"What are you thinking about at this very moment?" she asked.

"Bufala mozzarella, imported from Italy." *Did I say that out loud?*

"Excuse me?"

Oh shit, I did. "Nothing," he said. He laid his head on her lap, stretched out across the hearse's bench seat with his feet out the window, and looked at the stars. She stroked his hair, curling it in her fingers.

"What were you thinking?" she asked again.

He didn't answer, but as he sat in the hearse, tasting her, smelling the night air, his truthful answer would have been food, sex and death, though not in that order.

Their good-night kiss, on the quiet street around the corner from the bakery, was interrupted by a loud knock on the car window. Frankie turned to see a man holding a badge and identification. Three letters jumped out at him: F–B–I. He rolled down the window.

"Are you Frankie Grace?"

He had to think, but he wasn't fast enough to lie. "Yes," he replied.

"Would you please come with me? We have some questions for you."

Frankie's hands began to shake. He looked over at Caterina, worried.

"I'll tell my father."

"No, don't."

"Okay, I'll tell *your* father."

This no was emphatic.

"Who then?"

"Tell Sal in the restaurant. And give him these," he said, handing her the keys. "He'll know what to do."

Chapter 10

Frankie fidgeted in the back seat as the car made its way toward the local FBI field office. He wasn't handcuffed; that was a good sign. The stoic agent alongside him did not look like he would welcome small talk; the driver either, for that matter. His two escorts were intimidating—intentionally so, he guessed. They struck Frankie as the Bull Brothers' WASP counterparts.

The black sedan entered an underground parking lot under the south tower of the World Trade Center. There was still no conversation as the two agents led Frankie to the elevator. Once inside, one of them pressed the backlit button for the seventy-fourth floor. The only sounds to be heard during the ascent were the hum and click of the elevator mechanism. When the doors opened at their destination, Frankie was escorted into an interrogation room.

"Sit tight," one of the agents instructed.

"Yes, sir." Frankie replied.

Time dragged on as Frankie sat alone in the nondescript chamber. The room was bare, containing only a small table with a writing pad and four uncomfortable chairs. The only interruptions in the unadorned gray walls were a large picture window on the wall behind the table and a smaller one in the exterior wall from which Frankie could see all of lower Manhattan, alive with lights, and in the distance midtown, the spires of the Chrysler and Empire State buildings. Frankie looked at his watch; it was midnight. *Be calm,* he told himself. Be careful what you say, take the fifth, drink a fifth, whatever, don't volunteer anything.

As he waited for someone to arrive, he decided to do what he always did when he was nervous: think funny. He looked directly into the interior window and did his best Cagney impersonation, complete with an exaggerated attempt at the actor's hallmark body movements. He talked to imaginary coppers, more boldly than he would have if they'd been in the room. "You dirty copper, you killed my brother, you dirty rat, you dirty copper."

For stylistic feedback, he stared at his reflection in the large window. Then it hit him like a brick: that was no window; it was a two-way mirror. He was giving a show, and the audience hadn't even paid for tickets. He turned red with embarrassment. *Maybe it could work to my advantage,* he thought; it might make the insanity defense an option. He looked deep into the two-way glass but saw only shadows.

Roscoe Keats entered the adjacent room in time to see his agents laughing hysterically. "Roscoe," one of them asked, "do you really think this guy knows something? He looks like a wack-a-doo, if you ask me."

Keats nodded. "Oh, don't worry, he knows something. He knows plenty. Let him stew for a while. Enjoy the show. I hear he does a great Ed Sullivan."

Two hours later Roscoe Keats finally made an entrance. He seated himself at the table and dropped a file folder in front of Frankie. "Mr. Grace," he started.

✝

When Sal saw Caterina Ballsziti enter the restaurant, he disengaged himself from his lip-lock behind the showcase with a cocktail waitress from the Café Napoli. The waitress buttoned her blouse and hurried past her, out the door.

Unfazed, Caterina walked up to Sal. "I'm Caterina Ballsziti. Frankie is in trouble, and he told me to tell you." She relayed the events of the past hour.

"Jesus Christ," he said, "does anybody know?"

"He told me to let you know. He said you would know what to do."

Sal nodded. "Right, right, uh, are you hungry? Can I get you something to eat?"

"Is that your plan? To eat?"

"No, no. I know what to do. I'll call Special—" his voice faded as he thought better of it. "I'll call Eddie." He stared at her, very closely, searching for a trace of her ancestry along the line of her upper lip.

"Is anything wrong?" she asked.

"Sorry, no," he said. "I'll call Eddie."

She opened her purse and found the keychain. "The hearse is parked around the corner," she told him. "Frankie said you'd take care of it."

Sal took the keys and raced out the door, stopping only long enough to find Eddie and explain the situation.

The hearse was parked on Hester, right where she'd said. He drove it around the block to the alley, backing in as he'd seen Frankie do many times. The maneuver was a tight one, and he pulled out and backed in again to give himself room to open the door.

Primo Grace, ever sensitive to the sound of the motor, rose from his sleep and went to the window. He was livid at the sight of Sal wedged between the open door of the hearse and the wall. He knew that Lucci boy was up to no good!

Primo pulled on his socks and stumbled down the stairs, just in time to see Sal hightailing it out of the alley. "You sonofabitch!" he yelled. "What were you doing in that car? And where's my son? You tell that good-for-nothing strunz to get his ass back home."

As he stood on the deserted sidewalk clad only in T-shirt, boxer shorts, and black socks, the street sweeper truck caught him by surprise. As it brushed past him, gathering the evening's debris into its maw and spraying jets of water to wash down the dirt, Primo found himself thoroughly drenched. He swore every step of the way back up to his castle.

✝

Roscoe Keats made himself comfortable across from the weary Frankie Grace.

"Mr. Grace, you handled the final arrangements for the funeral of Mrs. Isabella Cianci earlier this week?"

Frankie was silent.

"It's not a trick question, Mr. Grace."

He nodded. "Yes, I thought at the time they were final."

"Who made the funeral arrangements?"

Silence.

"Was it her son-in-law, Mr. John Ballsziti?"

He did some quick figuring; that answer shouldn't get him in trouble. "Yes, it was."

"Where was she buried?"

Frankie looked uneasily at this watch. More than twenty-four hours since the JFK flight to Italy, enough time for the plane to land, and the casket to be taken to the family vault in the cemetery outside Palermo. It was too late for them to do anything now.

"She was buried in Italy, a small cemetery outside Palermo."

Keats pulled a newspaper obituary from the folder. "Can you explain why this obituary states the place of burial was to be at St. John's Cemetery in Queens? Did you do that?"

Think, stupid. "Uh, I did, and that was the original plan, but the family changed their minds at the last minute. It was too late to print a correction."

"At the last minute," Keats repeated.

Frankie nodded, "Yes, the last minute."

"Was there anything unusual about the funeral?"

"Unusual? No, not that I can recall. Let's see . . . the casket got stuck on the counter of a sausage-and-zeppole stand, and Clara the rice ball lady had to put some oil on the counter to help the casket slide across; the pallbearers were covered with confectioner's sugar; there was a big rip in Mrs. Ballsziti's dress; and, oh, yeah, the Festival of San Gennaro was going full swing. No, nothing unusual. Just your everyday, run-of-the-mill Italian funeral."

Keats scowled.

Don't be smart with them.

"Now, Frankie, I'm going to ask you a question, and I want you to think very carefully before you answer. Did Mr. Ballsziti put anything in Isabella Cianci's casket?"

Frankie turned beet red. "In the casket?" he repeated, stalling for time.

"Yes," Keats said, "in the casket."

I am screwed, screwed, screwed. "Um, there was a rolling pin and spatula, and a statue, as I can remember."

"A rolling pin," Keats repeated. "Anything else that you can remember?"

Play dumb.

"Let me be clear," Keats said. "Was any money placed in her casket?"

"Money?"

"Yes, money."

He took a moment. "Oh, money, of course. Mr. Ballsziti put some loose change in her hand. It's a common custom."

"Really?"

"Oh, yes, an Italian thing . . . in case there's a toll at the pearly gates." He laughed at his own cleverness. *Mental note for the comedy cabinet: putting things in the casket.*

"Loose change?"

"Yes, sir."

"So after church you went to the airport?"

"Well, no, I had to have the casket sealed at the casket company, and then I had to get the final clearance from the Italian consulate. It was all done by the book, sir." He was proud of that.

"I'm sure." Keats picked up the folder. "Were you alone?"

"Yes," he answered.

"Can you explain this?" From the folder, he removed a picture showing Frankie crushed between Bull and Bull in the front seat of the hearse. Both of them were eating.

"Honorary pallbearers," he offered.

"Cute," said Keats.

My first lie, or at least the first one I got caught in. "I really don't know why they came along. They were very close to Isabella and wanted to see her off?"

"Frankie Grace," said Keats, "I don't like you. I'm going to keep my eye on you."

There was a knock on the door as it opened. "This interview is over," the man said coolly.

It was past three in the morning, but the man at the door looked like he'd just stepped out of *Gentleman's Quarterly*: clean-shaven, tanned, hair slicked back, and impeccably dressed in a silk suit complete with a hand-painted tie and starched white shirt with a collar that ended practically at his belly button. The visitor looked Keats in the eye but did not extend his hand. "I'm Roy Silverschein," he said. "My client has nothing to say."

"Gee, how impressive," Keats said to Frankie. "No less a personage than the esteemed Roy Silverschein gets out of bed for you. The mob mouthpiece. You don't fool around, do you? You hire the best."

"We'd love to stay, have a chit-chat with you," Silverschein said. "Perhaps another time."

"Oh, there will *be* another time," Keats answered. "Anyway, I'm finished with him for now."

Silverschein waved Frankie ahead of him as he turned and to go. Keats reached into his wallet and took out a card. He held it out for Frankie. "If you remember anything, give me a call. It's not too late."

Frankie took the card.

Bull, Bull, and Eddie were standing alongside the Chevy Impala as Frankie and Silverschein left the World Trade Tower. Eddie tapped his foot nervously. Bull One ran a rag over the car's bumper. Bull Two tucked his shirt into his pants. Frankie was flattered: not only had Ballsziti sent his lawyer, he'd sent his own car.

Eddie rushed up and hugged him. "Are you okay? Did they beat you or anything?"

"I'm fine, Eddie, fine."

Eddie spotted Roscoe Keats standing on the promenade, chomping on a cigar. "Up yours," he yelled, his middle finger extended for emphasis. He looked Frankie over, top to bottom. "You're okay?" he said, "You're sure?"

Frankie nodded again.

"Come on," Eddie said. He opened the back door. "Let's get out of here."

On the way to Mulberry Street, Eddie peppered Frankie with questions: what did they want to know, what did they ask, what did you say.

"Nothing, really, Eddie, I said nothing."

The Bulls exchanged doubtful glances, but Eddie was satisfied with the debriefing. "It's gonna be alright," he said. "It's too late for them to do anything, or more importantly to prove anything. The casket arrived safely. The transfer has been made. The old lady made the deposit and is resting in peace."

Frankie was relieved. There would be no headline in *La Repubblica*, thank God. *Chi ha detto, non puoi portarlo con te?* he had heard his mother say. Who said you can't take it with you?

When the Impala pulled up in front of the darkened restaurant and Frankie stepped out, Sal unlocked the door and ran to hug his friend. "You okay? Did they torture you or anything?"

"I'm fine," Frankie said. "Relax." He was embarrassed.

"Come in," Sal said. "Eat something. You'll feel better."

"That's a good idea," Eddie agreed.

As Eddie questioned Frankie again, Sal brought out a dish of baked clams, the overwhelming smell of garlic preceding him. "Taste these," he said. "You see, the restaurant across the street just takes the clam out of the shell, dices it, then puts it back. Not here," he explained. "We add our breadcrumbs and a secret combination of spices that my grandmother learned from her mother who cooked for King Vittorio Emmanuel. The king loved baked clams."

"Do you have any idea what he's talking about?" Eddie asked, with a sideways glance at Frankie.

"Not a clue," Frankie answered, as Sal put the dish on the table.

"Could you use any more garlic?" Eddie asked.

"Hey, it's good for you. Puts lead in your pencil."

Frankie could have done without the reference to lead anywhere on his body.

Although he didn't think he could ever eat again, Frankie sucked a few clams off the shell. They slid down his throat. Hungrier than he thought, he dipped fresh bread in the juices from the serving dish.

"That's the best part," Sal said. He was happy his friend had not lost his appetite.

"Is there anything else you can remember?" Eddie asked. "Anything else you said? Tell me now."

He thought for a moment. "Oh, yeah," he said. He pulled Keats's card from his pocket. "He gave me this. Said if I thought of anything to call him."

Horrified, Eddie snatched the card from Frankie's hand. "Give me that. What, are you crazy?" He read it and put it in his pocket. "You don't want to be caught with that card. Jeez, what does he think, you're a rat?"

"Not me, Eddie. I didn't say a thing."

"Frankie, this is important. Think! Did you say anything? Anything?"

Frankie thought while he sipped at a glass of Chianti. "No, Eddie. That was it. I didn't say anything, but they know."

"It's okay. What they know can't hurt us now."

"I hope not."

"You done good, kid. I have to meet with our friend tomorrw. He was worried about you. He feels bad you went through this. That's why he sent us with his own car to get you. He was very happy today, too. The funeral in Italy went off without a hitch, and when I told him about you being picked up, well, jeez, he just felt terrible. He sent his lawyer down there on the double. You see, the old man worries about you."

Behind Eddie's back, Sal stuck his finger down his throat, pretending to gag. Eddie turned as he saw Frankie smile. Sal quickly poured more wine. "By the way, call your girlfriend tomorrow. She was worried about you too. Christ, she has some set of—"

"Hey," Eddie said, "watch what you say about her. That's Johnny's daughter."

"I didn't say nothing. She's beautiful, that's all I said." He glanced Frankie's way. "But, have you noticed anything about her?"

"Like what?" Frankie asked.

"I can't put my finger on it. She's beautiful, I'll give you that. But, I thought I saw something on her upper lip. Ah, probably a freckle. That's it. It was a freckle."

Chapter 11

"Strunz!"

Frankie adjusted the pillow over his head and tried to imagine why his father was calling his name in the prison corridor. He shook the bars of his cell and heard the sound of keys rattling outside. Then the jailer called for him again.

"*Strunz!*"

Startled awake, Frankie jumped out from under the sheet to find his father, purple-faced, shaking the key ring in his face.

"I don't know what your friend was doing in our hearse last night, but I have a good idea. We need to talk. Right now, I want you to get the hearse fumigated." He sneezed and dropped the keys on Frankie's head.

Emerging from the alley Frankie ran into Sal, who was off to Mott Street to shop before the festival crowds arrived.

"Hey! I was loooking for you—to say thanks, and to tell you to keep clear of my dad."

"Do you smell something funny?" asked Sal as they walked down the quiet street. "Something stinks."

"It's me. Eddie squeezed me so tight, his cologne wore off on me."

"Christ, does he take a bath in that stuff or what? You smell like a French hooker. You sure everything went well with those guys last night?"

"Yes," Frankie said, "they know something but couldn't prove it. They made me sweat a little. That's all." They stopped by a produce pushcart, where Sal placed an order for the restaurant.

"Broccoli di rabe," Sal said to the Chinese vendor.

He was met with a blank stare.

"Broccoli di rabe. I need a bushel."

Blank stare.

"Jesus, where is Santo? I need a bushel of broccoli di rabe."

The vendor picked up a handful of greens.

"That's bok choy," Sal yelled. "I don't want friggin' bok choy. I want friggin' broccoli di rabe, bitter broccoli, *bitter broccoli.*"

Thinking it would help in the translation, he said it again, more slowly, "bit-ter broc-co-li." Pronouncing it syllabically, "broc-co-li-d-rob," did not help either.

"Let's go," Frankie said. He pulled Sal by the arm.

"Jesus, can you believe this. What am I supposed to sell, sausage and bok choy?"

Frankie led Sal down the block. A crowd had gathered behind a string of police barricades.

"What now, another shooting?"

"Not that kind," Sal said. "This is great. They're filming a movie."

Francis Ford Coppola had been directing a screen adaptation of Mario Puzo's novel *The Godfather.* Among the Italian-American community, feelings about the project had been mixed; not everyone favored the spotlight. But the local leadership had begun to see the benefits, and crews suddenly appeared on location. Set decorators had swiftly transformed Mott Street into a replica of Little Italy in the 1920s. Vintage automobiles lined the street, and actors in pinstripe suits, silk ties, and fedoras rehearsed on the sidewalk before being called for a take. Cameras on booms floated high above the action, as others panned the scene from every angle on the ground.

Sal was mesmerized. "I watched them for an hour this morning.

It's about a Mafia family getting started in the twenties. They must have shot this scene a dozen times already. This guy Brando— who's supposed to be the family head—comes out of his office, buys fruit at the pushcart over there, and gets ambushed. Jesus, it looks real."

Frankie worked his way through the crowd to get a better view. He watched as Marlon Brando walked over to a street vendor and selected a few pieces of fruit. As the scene unfolded, a group of men in black fedoras moved toward him. Brando saw them, tried to get back to his car, and was gunned down in the street.

"Jeez," Frankie said, "the magic of Hollywood."

"Huh?" Sal said.

"Forget it," Frankie answered.

"Hey, there's your father."

Primo was waving furiously to get his son's attention. Only then did Frankie notice that his pager had gone off twenty minutes earlier. They made their way through the crowd.

"We got visitors," Primo informed them. "Department of Health. They're going over all our records."

A surprise inspection? On a Saturday? *They don't waste any time,* Frankie thought. Not a good sign.

"I'm not worried," Primo said. "We do everything by the book, mostly. But they can be a pain in the ass. If they want to find something, they can."

"Do you think this has anything to do with Isabella's funeral?" Sal asked.

Frankie pointed to an unmarked but unmistakable government vehicle. "There's your answer," he replied.

Roscoe Keats sent circles of smoke rings wafting out of the window of his puke-green sedan. He smiled knowingly as the car eased down the street.

"I guess there had to be some fallout," Primo said. "These guys don't like to be embarrassed. It'll blow over. The investigators asked to see the death certificate and consulate permits. It was all in order. I explained that the family changed their mind at the last minute, paid St. John's for the crypt opening and closing, all very innocent. They asked about all the hearses. I told them you did all the ordering and messed things up like you usually do."

Frankie guessed that now would not be a good time to mention his one-on-one at FBI headquarters. Instead he added, "Right. It'll blow over."

When the inspector left, Primo placed all the files back into the cabinets. He sat in his cubicle office in the basement of the funeral home and took a deep breath. It was damp. His father's portrait hung on the wall across from him. Francesco was dressed in a black tuxedo with velvet lapels, the same one he was buried in. Primo studied the ledger on his desk and ran his hand through his hair. The numbers were off, steadily declining. He looked up to his father for advice. None came. You're a big help, he thought. He closed the book.

For now, there were more pressing problems. Primo didn't think anything could have been worse than the hearse being caught in the parade. The saint's minions, as represented by the Society of San Gennaro, had already called and lodged formal complaints. But, as he himself had always believed, things could always get worse, and they usually did.

Frankie walked down the dark steps to the basement office, expecting the worst. These meetings were never good. His father did not disappoint him.

"Our hearse, have you been renting it out by the hour?"

"No, Dad, I swear." Mentioning the FBI would be a serious tactical error. He elected to endure the lecture instead.

"You gotta use your head, Strunz!" Primo reprimanded. "It's this friend of yours poisoning your mind. And don't lie to me."

"No, Dad, it's not Sal. Don't blame him."

"No, you're wrong. It *is* him, I know it. He thinks he's some kind of show-business mongrel. He's never satisfied with what he has. He's always filling your head with these crazy ideas. And now—"

"It's not Sal, Papa. It's me. I have a dream I'd like to follow. There's a voice—"

Primo put his hand up to stop Frankie from continuing. "Listen to yourself—voices, dreams. Maybe you should see a friggin' psychiatrist. They put people like you in white jackets out in Central Islip. People who have dreams are usually asleep. Wake up! This is the real world. This Sal kid, he's a bad influence. Stay away from him. He's weird, always asking morbid questions. Do I ask him how to make ravioli?"

Primo, who did not wait for an answer, was really building up a head of steam by now. "Don't you see? You're making a mockery of yourself and your profession. You're using the hearse for joyrides. That vehicle wasn't made for joy. You upset the entire feast delegation. My membership is being reviewed in the Knights of Columbus. And if the Knights kick me out, can the Sons of Italy be far behind? A life's work down the drain! The Department of Health is looking at all our records. We have funerals that look like Chinese fire drills, with hearses and limousines all over the place. You nap in the caskets, don't deny it. I see your impression in the mattress. This has to stop. You got to get more serious. It's not normal, I tell you."

And everything else we do is? Keep quiet, Frankie. "Dad, try to understand. I love you. I love what you do. But, for me, I don't know. I may not be cut out for it. Maybe it's time we did something different. We've been burying people for a hundred years."

"And we do a damn good job of it."

That's true, no one has come back. "Maybe it's time for a change."

Primo was horrified. "What are you saying? There's no future in death? Well, let me tell you, that since the day St. Joseph of Arimathea took the lifeless body of Jesus down off the cross, and prepared Him for burial in the tomb, there has been a need for our profession, and there will be a need for us until He comes back. This is our sacred duty."

Steady work, no doubt. "That's not what I'm saying, Papa. I'm just saying it may not be right for me. I'm tired of the tears, the crying that echoes through the floor under my bed every night. We go from one sadness to another. I just think there might be something more. Things are changing, Papa. Times are changing.

Maybe we should hire a Chinese funeral director."

"We are Italian, we bury *Italians!*" Primo yelled, his face flushed with anger.

"Well," Frankie said, "Maybe we'd better start changing. Look around, Dad. There are more Chinese than Italians. You've buried all the Italians. You'd better start looking for a new ethnic group."

Primo threw his hands up in the air. "What did I do to deserve this?" Then, his familiar refrain: "You will be the death of me yet. Don't you see, this is a family tradition? We have to continue, or all will be lost. Maybe we could expand, Staten Island, Brooklyn, Long Island, somewhere; but we can't close the door on three generations. We can't do that. Our people count on us. It's not what we do, it's who we are. It's who we are in here." He poked his chest as he leaned against the cabinet holding files that reached back to the nineteenth century.

Frankie sat quietly, hoping the questions would stop.

His father was still perplexed, repeating his questions in disbelief. "How could you loan the car out to that pervert? *What were you thinking?*"

"I didn't, Dad. You got to believe me. I'd—"

"Don't lie. Now he's picking up cheap hookers in our sacred vehicle. I saw him parking it last night."

Frankie knew from long experience that once his father's tirade reached a crescendo, the end was in sight. But Primo had one more card to play. He reached into his pocket, a look of disappointment on his face, and withdrew a small object. He placed the tube of lipstick on the table in front of his son. "There's what I found in the seat."

Frankie was caught. He took a deep breath. Eddie was never of fan of the approach, but Frankie decided to give it a try: the true story. "I'm sorry, Papa. It was me. I had a date with Caterina, and we went for Chinese food . . . " *Not good!* As soon as the words were out of his mouth, Frankie knew that Eddie was right: truth was not an option.

"Oh, my God!" Primo exploded again, clutching his chest. "You use our hearse to joyride with a girl, and the girl is Caterina

Ballsziti. Are you crazy? Are you friggin' nuts? He'll kill you. You got to stay clear of this guy. He's got his hands in every business in this neighborhood, and he would like to have a piece of this place, too."

Right Dad, our cash flow is tremendous. "Easy, Papa, easy. Me and JB are good friends." After I helped him ship millions to Italy, he thought of adding, but didn't.

Primo shook his head. He walked out of the office, pausing halfway up the steps. He grimaced as he pressed his hand against his chest. He took a pack of Rolaids from his pocket and downed two tablets.

He feared that Frankie was right when he talked about how the neighborhood was changing. These days in Little Italy, it was easier to get Peking duck than a meatball sandwich. The old immigrants had died off, the new immigrants were here, and he didn't recognize them. The Chinese were taking over, expanding to every available space surrounding Little Italy. Shops were changing hands, families had moved. There were fewer and fewer pushcarts on Mott Street, no more Italian fruit vendors. The Carusos, the Bacigaluppis were all gone, just memories now. Those hanging balls of provolone were giving way to dead and defeathered ducks, suspended indelicately by their bony necks.

"The death of me yet," he said aloud as he made his way slowly up the remaining stairs to the apartment above.

Frankie watched his father leave and sat trying to digest all that he had said. He agreed, theirs was a serious, serious business, yet he couldn't help thinking about a Chinese funeral director. He tore a piece of paper from the corner of the desk pad and penned, "An hour later, you want to get buried again."

Eddie sat at the Grace table, in the middle of the eggplant parmigiana assembly line. Pasquelena sliced the eggplant, Angelina dipped it in egg batter, Zizilena took the slice and dredged it in a dish of bread crumbs, and just Lena took the slice from the dish and tossed it into a frying pan, where a few seconds later

Giovanna removed the vegetables slice by fried slice and laid them in a baking pan, covering each with mozzarella and tomato sauce.

Giovanna took a moment to fix Eddie a cup of coffee. Eddie waited, polite but uncomfortable under the gaze of the Lena foursome, for Frankie to emerge from downstairs. The Lenas' noses twitched like those of Pekingese puppies as they detected an unwelcome scent overpowering the intoxicating aroma of eggplant frying in a pan—Eddie's fresh dousing of cologne.

Their eyes lit up, however, when Frankie appeared. It was like the second coming of Christ for them. They picked their heads up and wiped their hands on their aprons. "Buon giorno, Frankie. We're making your favorite dish for lunch. Che una bella faccia."

Pinch cheek, pinch cheek, pinch cheek, pinch cheek.

Eddie shook his head at the display of affection. "Frankie, sorry to take you away from your fans, but JB wants to talk with you."

Eddie got his jacket, and they walked over to the Marconi Social Club, where they were greeted by Bull and Bull. There might have been a half smile on Bull One's face acknowledging him, but Frankie was probably just imagining it. As they waited to be summoned, the bartender set two cups of espresso in front of them. *Not again,* Frankie thought.

The door opened, and a jittery if dexterous waiter from Puglia's Ristorante arrived bearing a tray with a large steel dome. The waiter rushed past them and placed the dish in front of Johnny Ballsziti, who was seated at a corner table. It was Saturday, and JB always dined on capozelle on Saturday. And he liked it hot. The waiter ceremoniously removed the dome to reveal the defeated head of a sheep, cut off at the neck. It sat steaming on the platter with its gritty teeth jutting out against a bony open jaw. Dead black eyes—the pièce de resistance, to be savored at the very end—stared out from open lids.

Ballsziti waved Eddie and Frankie to the table. "You want some?"

Frankie looked at the menacing sheep's head and noted an uncanny resemblance between JB and the unfortunate beast—the same black eyes and gritty teeth. "Naahhhh," he said, bleating sheepishly.

That earned him an elbow in the ribs from Eddie.

Eddie also refused the offer. Just as well, too. JB hated to share. He would buy you your own sheep's head, but he hated sharing. He gnawed at the cranium. Not even the smallest morsel of capozelle meat, separated expertly from the bone, escaped him. With the precision of a lion savoring its prey, he pulled hunks of meat off the skull with his teeth and devoured it. I get it, I get it, Frankie thought—a man who could eat this could eat me alive. Ballsziti picked up the skeletal shell and sucked the remaining pieces of meat from the deepest crevices. It was like lobster to him, delicate and sweet. The slurping sounds could be heard throughout the room. Frankie felt queasy.

"Maybe I should come back when you're finished eating," he suggested to JB.

"Sit."

He sat. There was much on the agenda on this day.

JB asked Eddie, "Is everything going okay on the street?" His tone was sour. JB hated controversy, especially feast-related controversy, and he tried to avoid it whenever possible. Controversy brought unwanted attention from City Hall. But it was common for problems to arise: men fighting over a few feet here or there, one stand larger than it should be, two bitter competitors located side by side. It was Eddie's job to resolve these turf battles. If a vendor didn't listen to reason, his concession might catch fire during the night, or a vandal might bust up the contents, leaving a pile of destroyed plywood and two-by-fours. Everyone knew the rules.

But today there was a problem.

"Did you or did you not destroy the goldfish stand?" JB sucked his fingers and waited for Eddie to answer. Again he asked, "Did you or did you not destroy DePaolo's goldfish stand?"

Eddie knew from the tone of the question that he had misunderstood his instructions.

"Did I *ask* you to destroy the goldfish stand?" asked JB quietly.

Eddie bowed his head in shame.

"So, you realize how perturbed I was when old lady Bella comes in here screaming. She gives me agita. She's screaming in my ear about hundreds of friggin' goldfish flounderin' in the friggin' gutter in front of the friggin' pork store, stinking to high heaven, she says. What's the matter with you? That's all I need now, is to have the Board of Health down my back."

Eddie knew he could go only so far with an explanation. "There was a problem with the pizza stand, and I only thought . . ." He didn't have a chance to finish.

"You thought," JB said. "That was your first mistake. Let me do the thinking from now on. I want you to throw some Clorox on the street. Keep the old lady quiet or she'll pray for rain. Now, do we want rain?"

Eddie shook his head no.

"Right. Now you understand. Make sure you get it cleaned up."

Eddie nodded as JB turned his attention to Frankie, who felt rather proud to be privy to the inner workings of feast control. JB patted Frankie's cheek, then pinched it. Not as gently as the Lena four. "You had a little excitement, I heard."

"Yes, sir."

"Yeah, those bastards. Are you okay, did those assholes shake you up or anything?"

"No, no, Mr. Balls...ziti. I'm fine."

"Good." He motioned to Eddie. "Two grappas. Those no-good dickheads."

Two glasses arrived. *Not this again.* Frankie picked up his and gingerly sipped along with JB.

"I'm sure they had lots of questions," Ballsziti continued. "Those government bastards always do." He coughed.

"Yes, sir, but they didn't get many answers. I didn't tell those bastards nothing."

"You told them nothing?"

"Nothing."

Now that that's been established.

"Good, that's good." JB downed the rest of his drink. "I want you should tell Eddie here if they ever visit you again." He dislocated the sheep's eyeball from its socket with a fork, placed it delicately in his mouth, and finished it off with a single audible crunch, never taking his eyes off Frankie.

Frankie felt the contents of his stomach backing up, the grappa leading the way. "Not a problem, Mr. Eyeballsziti." *Christ, what an idiot.* Sweat was pouring down his forehead.

JB leaned in. "Good, then you can go."

Frankie got up to leave.

"By the way," JB said, "nice job on Isabella. I was meaning to tell you. She looked like she was sleeping, sleeping like a friggin' angel."

Hard to sleep with such a lumpy mattress, he thought. *Keep it to yourself, moron.* "Thank you," he said.

"At first, I didn't recognize her, but then I realized I never saw the old lady with her mouth shut." JB belched sheep's breath. "Lorenzo, bring me a Fernet," he ordered, as he unbuckled his belt for relief. "One more thing I was thinking about." He paused to consume the digestive spirit. "Smell, was there any smell? I mean with the body waiting so long to be fixed up and all."

"No," Frankie explained, "the embalming took care of that and, even if there was, you could never tell once the casket was sealed in the zinc."

"Ah, the zinc, with the hermit seal."

"Right." No sense in correcting him.

"So, once something is sealed like that you can't smell nuttin' inside. Not even a dog can smell anything?"

"Nuttin'," Frankie said, to be understood.

That answer satisfied Ballsziti.

Eddie started to leave, but JB motioned for him to sit. They watched Frankie stumble his way past Bull and Bull into the daylight. Only then did JB lean over to Eddie. "I want you to tell me honest, can this kid be trusted?"

Eddie was surprised. "Oh, for sure, JB."

"Do you believe he didn't say nuttin'?"

"I believe him, JB. He's a standup kid."

JB nodded, satisfied for the moment. His mind was working overtime, wondering what kind of witness young Frankie Grace might eventually make against him. "So you vouch for him?"

"Ten hundred percent."

"Did you know," JB asked, "that he was out with my daughter last night?"

Eddie thought for a moment. "Caterina?"

"That's my only daughter," JB said.

"Right. No—no, I didn't know that."

"Were you aware he took her for a ride in a hearse? Is he a crackpot, a ghoul?"

Eddie did not answer. He had to admit it sounded odd to him as well.

"Well, I want you to make sure that don't happen no more. Understood?"

"Yes, JB." He pictured Frankie as a white pawn advancing deep into black's ranks. And it was becoming more difficult each day for that one unprotected pawn to escape notice.

Frankie put the pillow over his head. The metal bar of the foldaway bed dug into his spine. His bed was situated above the casket bier in the funeral home below. Every moan of the mourners, every agonizing cry, vibrated up through the floorboards, bringing with it his nightly ordeal. He fought it; *think happy thoughts, think happy thoughts.* He tried counting sheep, but that only made him think of JB's lunch. He even tried counting screams. He hated sleep, never knowing what the REM stage had in store for him. His dreams ranged from nightmares with blood-curdling screams and seeping bodily fluids, to fantasies with uproarious laughter and free-flowing liquor. Each night he would twist and turn until exhaustion forced his eyes shut.

As his eyes closed on this particular night, curtains opened thousands of miles from Mulberry Street. It was the "Debut at Caesar's Palace" dream. It was one of his favorites. He could live with that one, or sleep with it.

He was in Las Vegas, the main ballroom of Caesar's Palace, standing behind the curtain. He was overwhelmed by nerves, jitters, and memory loss. He remembered the Gospel According to Primo—be careful what you wish for, you may get it. As he waited to be introduced, he considered the possibility that Sal was wrong. He was the one who said Frankie had talent, could be a hit, but maybe he was mistaken. Frankie mumbled in his sleep. "Sal, get the car ready. Get the car ready!" *If I wanted my name in lights, I should have changed my name to EXIT. It would have been easier.*

"Ladies and Gentlemen, the strange comedy of Frankie Grace!"

He heard the applause, but he was paralyzed with fear, unable to walk onto the stage, tied up in the blankets, straps buckled around his arms and legs. The scene began to fade. *Please, don't send me back into the embalming pit. I can do this. I can do this.* He tossed and turned under the covers, fighting the move from Vegas to New York. The internal debate raged as he slept.

What did I get myself into? I could have been safe and secure down in the funeral home on Mulberry Street. I didn't need this stress. I should have listened to my father. I could be draining the blood out of some lifeless body, or repairing bullet holes in some mob guy's head. Hey, it's a living and the customers never complain. To think I gave it all up for show business. I wanted more; well, here it is, smartass! Now, get out there.

That's where the debut dream always ended—as he attempted to take that step from behind the curtains onto the stage. As promised in the Gospel According to Primo, all good things come to an end. He heard his father's voice page him over the Caesar's loudspeaker. *Damn, he must have overpowered the announcer.*

"Frankie!" his father shouted. "Goddammit, you're talking in your sleep again."

He woke and realized he had been dreaming. He flipped the pillow to the cool side and stared at the ceiling, remembering bits and pieces of the dream. It seemed so real . . . He dozed off again, only to be awakened by the sound of a bedpost banging on the wall.

Chapter 12

Eddie walked in and took his usual seat at the Sunday morning breakfast table as Giovanna poured the coffee. She took a better look and set a glass of Alka-Seltzer in front him as well. "This will help," she said.

Frankie joined him at the table.

"Jesus, what did they put in those drinks last night?" Eddie wondered.

"You got home late. I heard you come in," Giovanna said. "Where were you, Eddie?"

"The Peppermint Lounge, uptown. Saw the Duprees. It was all comped by *our* friend." He looked at Frankie.

Despite himself, Frankie's ears perked up. "You have a connection there?"

"You might say that. JB owns the joint."

"He does? Why didn't you tell me? I'd love to get an audition or something."

"It's a little close to home, don't you think, Frankie?" Giovanna sang.

"Yeah," Eddie agreed, "like on the same island."

"Dad will never find out."

"If your mother says okay, I'll see what I can do." He motioned for the butter and glanced at Giovanna, who gave a slight nod.

"Speaking of Dad—" Frankie was on the verge of asking where

his father was, when the phone rang.

Giovanna answered. "Who, Tony? Oh, that's terrible . . . poor Tony." Eddie and Frankie tried to make out the other part of the story. "He's right here. I'll tell him." She hung up, her face drawn in sorrow.

"Your father needs you around the corner—at Tony Branca's apartment. The police and the medical examiner are already there."

"What happened?" Frankie asked.

"They don't know yet. It might have been a robbery. Tony was found dead in the basement of the building. Someone called the police. That's where they found him, lying in a pool of blood at the bottom of the stairs. Maybe a robbery." Giovanna's hand flew to her face as she started to cry.

"A robbery? In this neighborhood?" Frankie questioned as he glanced in Eddie's direction.

Eddie only gave him a warning look.

Frankie choked on his breakfast. "Toast, the toast went down the wrong pipe."

Giovanna pounded on his back. "When are you gonna learn, you're supposed to eat it, not inhale it. You'd better go help your father."

"If you don't mind, I'll take a walk with you," Eddie said amid a flurry of eye movements and winks.

"Let's go."

They walked out the door just as the morning coffee klatch was arriving.

"Good morning, Pasquelena, Angelina, Zizilena, Lena."

"Buon giorno, Frankie."

Pinch cheek, pinch cheek, pinch cheek, pinch cheek. They didn't bother to greet Eddie, wrinkling their noses at his cologne instead.

On Mott Street, the sidewalk was cordoned off. Pedestrians who had come for the feast-day Mass and the festivities afterward gathered behind police barricades, unsure whether they'd come upon a crime scene or a film shoot. Either way, they were in the right place at the right time: they'd catch a glimpse of a dead body or a movie star.

Detectives from the Fifth Precinct were interviewing people near the scene.

"Let me guess," one of the men said to a shop owner. "You didn't hear or see anything."

Frankie saw his father in the building's hallway. Primo waved him through the barricades. "Official business," he yelled.

"I'm with them," Eddie explained.

They approached Vitagliano's Butcher Shop just as a stretcher was being carried up the stairs with the body of the unfortunate Tony Branca. The saint's blood had not boiled in time to protect him.

"We've decided to take him in for an autopsy," the medical investigator was explaining to the policeman. "Just want to make sure. Looks like an accident; might have fallen down the steps, but just to be on the safe side." He looked at Primo. "You're the undertaker? You'll have your work cut out for you. Cracked his head open pretty good."

"Jesus," Primo said, "Tony, you poor soul. I've known him for forty years, forty years."

"What was that about a rob—" Frankie began, but Eddie shot him a look that cut him off.

"Did he have any enemies that you would know of?" It was the detective.

"Enemies," Primo answered, "are you kidding? He didn't have an enemy in the world. He was a saint."

"But the medical examiner said it was an accident," Frankie interrupted.

"Maybe. The autopsy should tell us more." The detective glanced down at his notes. "Any family?"

Primo shook his head, "None that I know of. He always lived alone; never mentioned anyone, except a niece somewhere, maybe."

"Yeah," the detective said, looking at his notes. "Well, we'll see."

Frankie looked to Eddie, who was deep in thought.

The detective scribbled a few more lines as the examiner spoke to Primo. "Call the morgue tomorrow. He should be released by then. You know the routine."

Primo nodded. They all watched as the stretcher was shoved into the coroner's wagon.

"Hey, easy," Primo yelled, "there's a person in there. A good person," he added as the wagon drove off.

There were police all over the street. Eddie tapped Frankie on the shoulder. He pointed to himself, then to Frankie, then made his quacking motions with his fingers. Frankie understood; we need to talk. Even the police could decipher that one by now.

They walked toward Lucci's without saying a word.

"Hello, guys." Roscoe Keats was seated outside Café Napoli, nursing a cappuccino. He toyed with a small piece of shiny metal in his hand. "How's it going?"

"Who wants to know?" Eddie shot back.

"Gentlemen, you look like you've seen a ghost. Is everything okay?"

"Well," Frankie said, "a friend of ours just had an accident."

"Really," Keats said. "An accident, huh?"

"Yeah, that's what they think, the medical examiner, that is," Frankie replied, seeking confirmation.

"Yeah, I know. I was over there earlier, too." He took a bite of a cannoli, never taking his eyes off Frankie.

"What did you get, deported or something?" Eddie asked smugly, meaning demoted. "Since when do they call the feds in to investigate an accident?"

Keats smiled, "Yeah, we're a little slow today. But you never know what interesting things you might find. Like this morning, when the police go down to see the body, they look around the alley, and lo and behold, something shiny gets their attention."

He tossed the metal object on the table. "Do you boys know what this is?"

"I ain't no boy," Eddied retorted.

"Go ahead, pick it up. It's already been dusted for prints."

"It doesn't look familiar to me," Frankie said.

Keats picked it up. "It's a buckle for a courier's satchel. It matches one used by the United States Treasury. Ain't that interesting?"

Ah, that's where I saw it. The color drained from Frankie's face.

Eddie was looking all around. "Yeah, well this is all very interesting, but we gotta go. Let's go, Frankie. I don't want to be seen talking to this guy."

Keats continued. "Quite unusual, I'd say, to find one in an alley in this neighborhood like that."

"Right," Eddie agreed. "There's a lot of condolences like that," he said, meaning coincidences. He looked over his shoulder and began to walk away with Frankie in tow.

Keats spoke again as they were leaving. "That's how he did it, isn't it? The money came in through the cellar and out in the casket. Clever, very clever."

"He don't know what you're talkin' about." Eddie responded.

They kept on walking.

Keats called after them, getting up from the table and following in their direction. "Interesting; and now poor old Tony Branca is dead. I wonder if Tony knew something that he wasn't supposed to know."

Eddie had Frankie under the arm now.

"I wonder if anyone else knows something that they shouldn't," Keats shouted. "We're looking for that butcher fella, but it seems he took the day off."

The two came to a halt as Keats walked up behind them. The agent tried to hand Eddie one of his cards. "Why don't you take this? If you ever want to talk, or if you remember anything, you can call me."

"Shove that card up your fat ass," Eddie yelled as he pulled Frankie further up the street and into the sanctuary of Lucci's. They'd hardly had time to find a seat before Sal strode in, shouting at no one in particular.

"Christ, where the hell is this guy? What kind of businessman is he?"

"What are you talking about?" Frankie asked.

Sal picked up the phone and dialed as he explained. "Mr.

Vitagliano—he always prepares a fresh leg of veal and holds it for me on Sunday morning. I need to pick up the order for tonight's special and he ain't around."

Eddie and Frankie exchanged meaningful glances. More dots to connect. Eddie didn't want to appear nervous as Sal dialed again. Trying to be nonchalant, he asked, "Who are you calling?"

"His cousin Fretta."

Sal waited for the voice on the other end of the phone. "Hello, hello, Mr. Fretta. It's me, Sal Lucci. I'm supposed to get a leg of veal from your cousin and he ain't around." Sal waited for a response.

"When?. . . Where? . . . Why?" He listened again. "And he don't tell nobody? What kind of jamoke is he?" Sal hung up. "Can you believe this?" Angry, he sat down with a bottle of San Pellegrino and three glasses. "The guy decides to go to Italy to see his mother. Just like that, he picks up and leaves. What a clear head. Meantime, I'll be banging my meat all day."

"When?" Eddie asked.

"When, what?"

"When did he leave for Italy?"

"This morning," Sal answered. "He just took off, spur of the moment."

Eddie was doing a million mental calculations at once; Frankie could tell the effort was exhausting him. "Sperm-of-the-moment thing, huh?"

"We got trouble, don't we, Eddie?" Frankie asked.

"No, there's no trouble," said Eddie. "Trust me on this. You heard the man; the guy went on vacation; the feds just want you to believe something else. Everything is going to be okay."

Frankie filled his glass again. At that moment, there was nothing amusing to file in his comedy file cabinet and there was a good chance it would be a long while before there would be. His list of worries had just gotten longer. "I think I'll call Caterina."

Eddie's ears perked up.

"You know," Sal said, "she was a trooper, coming in here the other night and all, and letting me know you were in trouble."

"Frankie," Eddie broke in, "I don't think that's a good idea. As a matter of fact, I know it's not a good idea."

"Why?"

"Well, JB asked me to squash this thing before it goes any further. She's his only daughter, and he's very protective of her, as you might understand."

"Did he actually say that?" Sal asked.

"Well, not in so many words."

"What did he say, exactly?" Frankie asked.

"He said, 'Make sure he don't see her no more.'"

"But you don't understand, Eddie. I think I love her. She's the perfect woman. Perfect."

"Well, maybe not perfect," Sal said, as he tapped his upper lip. "I could swear—"

Frankie cut him short. "You're crazy," he said. "There's nothing there."

Eddie had never seen Frankie so unhappy. There was no smile on his face, not even so much as a wisecrack all morning. Eddie tried to console him. "It's for the best, Frankie. Don't forget, her father is from Sicily, and your father is from Naples. These mixed marriages never work anyway."

The Church of the Most Precious Blood Church on Baxter Street was the shrine church of San Gennaro, the patron saint of Naples. Gold-leaf gothic frescoes portraying fallen angels and serpent-killing saints covered the arched cathedral ceiling. Marble depictions of the crucifixion and thorn-filled crowns hung between priceless stained-glass windows featuring last suppers and shattered tombs. It was an uplifting place.

The church was manned by the Franciscan Order, its members dressed in wide-strapped brown leather sandals and full-length brown vestments with white woolen cinctures about the waist. It had been built in 1872 to deal with what the Vatican called the "Italian problem"—that was, not enough Catholic churches for the Italian immigrants to counter the growing Protestant threat.

In the darkened holy catacomb at the back of the church, long ater Mass was over and churchgoers had departed for the parade, Frankie waited, crouched behind the stone grotto where the Blessed Mother stood atop a gently flowing fountain. It was there he had asked Caterina to meet him, despite Eddie's admonition. He was uncomfortable in the tiny space, and the running water gave him the urge to pee.

He looked at the dial of his illuminated watch. He would wait forever if need be; die here if he had to, never to be found, for who would think to look for his body behind Mother Mary's holy grotto in the rear of Most Precious Blood Church? Eventually, the stench of his decomposing flesh would lead them to his lifeless corpse. And, when he was found, what would be the theory for his presence in so unlikely a place? He wondered if death in a church would entitle him to some consideration for sainthood. Nah, he reasoned, the best he could hope for would be no charge for the mass.

Each time he heard someone enter, he peeked out from behind the statue to see if it was the love of his life. Each time he was disappointed as one elderly lady after another came forth to kneel and pray before Mary. Change jingled in the collection box each time a tiny votive flame sprang to life. Once, he heard heavier footsteps make their way down the aisle. He peered out from his concealment to see Father Colapetra blow out the candles and empty the change box before more women came to add more coins, light more candles, say more prayers, and leave. Talk about cash flow, Frankie thought irreverently.

He settled back. After a few minutes, he heard a younger, softer voice in prayer. He looked around and saw her, lovely as ever, a face so angelic that it should adorn the walls.

"Caterina," he whispered from behind the grotto.

She jumped.

"Thank you for meeting me," he said. "I was afraid you wouldn't."

"What are you doing back there? Come out."

"Shush, just kneel down like you are praying. We're not supposed to be together. That's why I wanted to meet you here. Church is the last place your father would look."

"What does my father have to do with anything?"

"Don't you know? He's not too happy that we're dating." He tried to keep his voice to a whisper.

"What makes you say that?"

"Something he said," Frankie answered.

"And what was that?"

"He said he's not too happy that we're dating." *Come on, lady, you're in business school. Figure it out.*

"Well, he doesn't want me to get involved with unsavory characters," she said.

"Me, unsavory?" Considering the cast of characters at your dinner table that would be stretching things, he thought. Though what if she knew just how deeply entangled he'd suddenly become with JB's delivery network?

"Yes, Mr. Grace. He has told me about your gambling problem. I know that you owe money to a lot of shady people, and that you have other expensive habits as well."

"What habits?"

"Show business habits, and let's leave it at that," she said.

"Are you kidding?" His voice grew louder and echoed in the grotto. He whispered, "Are you kidding? I don't even smoke cigarettes, let alone gamble or do drugs."

"Well, he wouldn't just make it up."

"Do you think it's true?"

"I don't know you well enough, sir," she replied in an unmistakably coquettish tone.

"Well, it's not true. Maybe you need to talk to him. Tell him you found me to be a perfect gentleman."

"My father told me all you show business people are into things like that."

"Well, he's wrong. Please believe me."

"You tell him. He is a reasonable man." Frankie heard her giggle softly.

Beautiful, and a sense of humor, too, he thought. She was playing with him. "I'll do the jokes, if you please."

"Frankie, why don't you come out of there?"

"No, we can't be seen together for now. It's cold back here, too. You leave first, and then I'll leave." He learned that from Eddie.

"I'll go, but only after I see you. I look crazy talking to a statue."

"Believe me, that's normal in here."

"Come out," begged Caterina.

This could be her way of rebelling against her father, he supposed. "You sure you want to see a drug-addicted, gambling alcoholic?" He would hate to be used.

"Frankie," she said reproachfully. He could hear the smile in her voice.

"Okay," he relented, deciding it might not really be so bad to be used, at least not by her.

Their eyes met as he appeared from behind the grotto. In the dim light he cupped her face in his hands, tracing his fingers along her eyes and cheek. While he was at it, he ran his thumbs across her lips like a blind man reading Braille. He paid special attention to the upper one, feeling for the slightest nub or stubble, careful that his tactile investigation be seen as an act of affection. He felt nothing. Sal is crazy, he thought. If anything, it's a freckle, a beauty mark.

As the two embraced, their youthful passion sent them stumbling against a display of votive candles. Dozens of tiny flames struggled to stay alive as they rocked to and fro. In that moment, Frankie understood Adam's desire to taste the apple, the fall from grace, as he thought about consummating his love for Caterina right there before Mary's virgin eyes. Cherubs blushed and marble angels stared as silent witnesses to their reckless abandon. They could never understand, though, he thought. They were made of stone; he was not, although he could feel some part of himself start to harden. Against his wishes, he extricated himself from their embrace.

"You have to go," he said. "We can't do this here, now. I'm already on a fast track to hell. I can't do this here."

Mental note for the comedy file cabinet: a new meaning to the Immaculate Conception. He was back!

She kissed him again, drawing him close once more.

"We mustn't, not here, not now," he said. "Will you meet me again?"

"Maybe," she teased, as she turned to go. Caterina crossed herself, dropped some change into the box, and lit a candle. As she knelt to pray before leaving, he ducked behind the grotto and waited for his chance to make an exit.

Seconds later, her place on the pew was taken by another woman who must have believed that praying aloud would make it easier for the Blessed Mother to hear her plight and help her in her time of need. As far as Frankie could tell, she looked to be in her thirties, kind of dumpy, but with beautiful, plump lips. "Oh, Mother Mary," she beseeched, "help me decide; should I marry him or not? Please send me a sign."

At that very moment, Frankie's foot slipped, unplugging the motorized waterfall. The cascade stopped instantly. The woman gasped. Awestricken, she stared up at the statue of Mary. "Can you send me another sign, so I can know if that was a real sign?"

They're never satisfied, Frankie thought. Feeling godlike and beneficent, he reached behind him and plugged the cord back into the socket. The water began to flow.

"Thank you, sweet Mother," said the supplicant, her prayers answered.

✝

As Frankie was about to leave the church, he saw Father Colapetra enter the center booth of the confessional. Frankie paused momentarily and then walked in. The mesh screen opened and Frankie began, "Bless me father, for I have sinned. It has been three years since my last confession."

"Frankie, is that you?"

So much for the anonymity of the confessional. "What gave me away?"

"Three years," said the priest. "More like four, though. What brings you here?"

"Can I talk to you, in confidence?"

"That is the whole idea, Frankie."

"Right, well, here goes." Frankie spent the next few minutes explaining about the stolen money, Roscoe Keats, Eddie, Johnny Ballsziti, the buckle on the money satchel, Italy, the whole nine yards. He stopped short of mentioning his anxieties regarding Tony Branca and Mr. Vitagliano—or his fears that he might be next on the list. "And now he's telling his daughter lies about me. Why? I should have told her the truth. If she knew that her departed grandmother had wads of stolen cash stuffed up her ass—"

"Frankie!"

"Sorry, Father." He stopped long enough to consider what the curse would add to his penance. "I meant stuffed up her posterior. So, what do you think, Father?"

There was silence on the other side of the screen. "You're in deep shit," Father Colapetra finally answered.

"Do you have any suggestions?"

"Did you know there's a horse named Dead Meat running in the third at Aqueduct? You might want to put a few dollars on him to help with your legal bills."

Frustrated, Frankie protested, "Father, it was a mistake. I got some problems here. I don't know where this guy gets these ideas."

"Frankie, you've got to be careful. These guys have a way of pulling you into their web. When I was first ordained, twenty years ago, I went into Gene's Dry Cleaning and Tailor Shop to play a number. Now, understand, I'm fully vested. John Ballsziti runs in, sweating like a pig. 'They're two minutes behind me,' he announces. He slams a bunch of papers on the counter. 'Who?' Gene asks. 'Cops,' he says. 'I got all the New York and Brooklyn action here.' Gene thinks for a second, grabs the papers, and stuffs them into my capuchin. I'm shocked, but I don't think I want to refuse these two guys. 'We'll pick it up later,' says Gene. 'We know where you live.'"

"A second later the entire police department comes storming through the door. They blow past me, throw JB and Gene into a corner, and begin searching the whole place top to bottom."

"What did you do, Father?"

"I tied my vestment around by head, blessed the men in blue

for doing God's work, and hightailed it out of there. Later, they sent a kid by the rectory to pick up the sheets, and I didn't pay for dry cleaning until the day Gene died."

Jeez, Colapetra was a numbers runner for the mob! "Sounds like the hoods used your hood to make a hood out of you. This is great, father, like *Angels with Dirty Faces*, and Pat O'Brien, and Cagney. It would make some story for the *Post*."

"My larger point is that JB learned something from Gene the tailor, like how people never look for things that are right under their noses. And I learned that they will use anyone and any means to achieve their ends. Anyway, what are you going to do now? You can't go to the police. It's your word against his, and you won't even have a chance to get your word out."

"What do you suggest, Father?"

"Forget it. Go to St. Bernadette and say two Hail Marys. Trust the Lord to provide a way."

There was no response.

"Did you hear me?" asked the priest.

"Yes, yes, go to Mary and say two Bernadettes." Frankie couldn't help laughing.

"Not funny, Frankie."

There was quiet. Through the mesh, Frankie could see Colapetra thumbing through a set of football sheets.

"How are you doing, Father?"

"I'm going through a dry spell. I haven't had a winner in a week or so. I could use one, too. Hopefully today I can turn things around. The pews have to be refinished."

"Well, good luck, Father."

There was silence for a moment. Finally the priest asked, "Frankie, have you told me everything?"

"I got to go, Father."

Frankie opened the door of the confessional and realized he had been there a while. A line had formed. "Hello, Pasquelena, Angelina, Zizilena, Lena."

Pinch cheek, pinch cheek, pinch cheek, pinch cheek.

Chapter 13

In the late afternoon lull at Lucci's, Frankie and Eddie found Sal relaxing at the usual table. He was rolling olives from one side of the table to the other.

"I told you, this guy has a screw loose," Eddie said.

Frankie was inclined to agree. "Sal, what the hell are you doing?"

"Playing mini bocce. It helps pass the time. All my usual customers are out watching the parade."

"If you say so," Eddie said.

"Hey," Sal suggested, "the movie, let's go see them make that movie. I heard they're filming downtown now."

"What's wrong with you?" Eddie asked. "How can you be so stupid, so taken in by this Hollywood bullshit?"

Sal protested. "Well, excuse me! We can't all idolize real-life mobsters, like you do."

"Listen, you squirt, you want to understand real from fake? Hollywood is fake; Johnny Ballsziti and this neighborhood are real. And Johnny Ballsziti has more power than Hollywood or anywhere else."

"You are a nut job," Sal bellowed. Frankie wished he hadn't. Eddie didn't like to be called crazy. He was like a pressure cooker, always ready to blow. Frankie grabbed a bottle of Chianti and three wineglasses from behind the bar, trying to stave off a confrontation.

As Frankie poured the wine, Eddie lit into Sal. "I'm a nut job, hey? That's why before the first camera was unloaded on Mott Street, those guys had to pay twenty-five hundred to Johnny, and they had to pay it up front, in cash, and I know, because I picked up the money and delivered it. And furthermore, you starstruck sack of shit, when your hero, Mr. Marlon Brando, found out that Johnny Ballsziti was around the corner, he asked to be introduced to him. You understand? *Brando* wanted to be introduced to *JB*. I know, because I gave JB the message, and brought Brando into the café."

"Brando went to meet Ballsziti?" Sal was on the edge of his seat.

"That's right. I, 'nut job,' personally escorted Marlon Brando into the café to meet Johnny Ballsziti."

"Jesus!" Even Frankie was impressed. "What happened?"

"They played gin until four in the morning. Brando lost thirty-eight hundred. He didn't have it on him so JB said he could send it in the morning, and added two points vig. They shook hands. Next morning, I go by the set and some gofer hands me an envelope. Case closed." Eddie rose from the table, satisfied he had made his point.

An old-timer having lunch at the bar overheard the conversation. "If you're right, sonny boy, how come JB couldn't get that Chinaman out of the scene at the fruit stand? There wasn't a single Chinaman to be found anywhere on Mott Street in the twenties."

"You mean Mr. Lee?" Eddie asked. "He's with Johnny. He's a big earner, and JB protects him. He runs the biggest mah-jongg game in Chinatown. JB wouldn't make him leave, but he got him to wear a hat and turn his collar up, so you don't see he's Chinese and all." Feeling pretty good about himself, Eddie hiked up his Sansabelt pants by the waistband and adjusted his member.

The front door opened suddenly to admit Lorenzo, the bartender from the Marconi Club. He brought a message. "JB wants to see you," he said, nodding at Eddie, who immediately rose to follow him. "And your friend here, he says." Frankie broke out into a sweat as he realized who was meant.

✝

Bull and Bull nodded their heads ever so slightly when Frankie and Eddie followed Lorenzo into the café.

"I think they like me, Eddie," Frankie joked.

"Yeah, right," Eddie returned sarcastically. "Sit here for a minute."

As Eddie approached the table, JB kicked a chair out toward him. "You," he barked, "is there something you want to tell me?"

Eddie was silent.

JB's voice grew angrier. "Did the feds pick you up for questioning?"

The inquiry caught everyone by surprise; card games stopped, pool cues stilled in mid-shot.

"Pick me up? No. They stopped us on the street. I was gonna tell you, JB; it was nothing, the same old bullshit."

"And you didn't think I should know that you were stopped and questioned."

"I just thought—"

"There you go again, thinking. Don't think. There's a reason they call you Special Ed. You got nothing going on in there." He pointed to Eddie's head. JB was screaming by then and had the whole room's attention. Frankie wanted to crawl into a hole.

Lore had it that the blood of San Gennaro boils once a year, and had done so every year since his beheading in 305 A.D. In Little Italy, it was generally agreed that it was better to have Gennaro's blood boil than Johnny Ballsziti's.

"I want to know when you take a leak," JB yelled. He gave Eddie a loud slap across the face with his open palm. The impact sent Eddie careening into the bar and onto the floor, blood trickling from his lip. He lay there sprawled out and frozen in place, his back against the foot rail. The smack was meant for public consumption, a warning, to ensure order in JB's kingdom. Word of the insult would be all over Mulberry Street within ten minutes. Ballsziti wanted it that way.

As Frankie stared at JB, he saw him for what he was: the face of pure evil, a man who would rather be feared than loved.

JB wasn't finished. As he returned to his table he flung a chair in Eddie's direction. The leg cracked as it bounced off the bar. "Now get out of here," he shouted. "Get my car washed." He threw the keys at him. "Out of here, both of you."

Eddie reached for the keys and slowly dragged himself up from the floor. He left the café under the knowing stare of dozens of eyes.

Frankie did not know what he could do to help. He followed after him, but Eddie was gone, lost among the throngs of revelers in the maze of concessions. Special Ed had his own special ways of disappearing.

As was the plan, the news of the smackdown quickly spread along Mulberry Street. Johnny Ballsziti had twisted Eddie's balls. Frankie stood in the middle of the sidewalk, left to his own devices, not knowing which way to turn.

Eddie sat in the dark, past midnight, at his kitchen table. He knew the routine by now. He would have to sit and stew until some low-level messenger came to tell him that JB wanted to see him. He knew the routine because, more often than not, he was that low-level messenger, sent to summon some crew member who had found himself in disfavor. And, for all his hurt and anger, Eddie understood that not being summoned would be worse. Machiavelli might have explained the method to Ballsziti's madness, but Machiavelli was well over Eddie's head. He only understood life on the streets and what it took to survive.

At nearly one o'clock the knock on his door brought relief: it would be over, one way or another. An anonymous voice called out, "You're wanted at the café." That's all: no names, no times. Immediately was implied.

He leaned over the kitchen sink and stared into the mirror. His cheek was still red and swollen, a full handprint clearly visible. He splashed on a round of witch hazel, followed by his signature Canoe.

He crossed the room and sat lightly on the edge of the Murphy bed. He ran his hand across the sleeping form beneath the covers.

"Marie," he whispered softly, "I got to go." He kissed her cheek and patted her backside. "Marie, I'm leaving."

Groggily, she lifted her head from the pillow. "Where are you going?"

"I got to go."

"When will you be back?"

"I don't know. Best you get dressed and leave, too."

"Will you call me later?"

He couldn't answer. He didn't know the answer.

As he walked down the steps, Eddie was trembling inside. He was scared of Ballsziti and what the unpredictable gangster might have in store for him. This meeting could be the end. He thought about running the other way, but then reconsidered. What would my father want me to do? What would *he* do? Eddie decided that his father would take the heat. In fact, he had. It was the code. If there was to be honor among thieves, he would have to accept the sentence handed down. His father would have expected nothing less.

When Eddie walked into the café, the room was empty, eerie . . . no card games, no pool. JB sat alone at his table. A forlorn tune by Jimmy Roselli, JB's favorite Italian crooner, was blaring on the juke box. In a mournful, melancholy Neapolitan dialect, Roselli was crying about something or other, either his wife leaving, or his mother dying, probably both—a love song, Italian style.

Eddie stood nervously in front of the table until Johnny motioned for him to sit. The bartender brought espresso for two. "Give us a minute, Lorenzo," JB requested.

Lorenzo laid his apron across the bar, grabbed his cigarettes, and walked out the front door.

JB pushed a cup of the strong coffee toward Eddie and leaned into him. "What am I going to do with you?" he said. "You make me crazy."

"I'm sorry, JB."

"I know you are. I know you are."

Eddie recoiled as Johnny extended his hand, only to place a

gentle tap on Eddie's cheek. "You know how important it is that I know everything that's going on. You're one of my key men. How can you not tell me about something so important?" He pushed the cup closer.

"I was gonna tell you. Of course I was. It just happened. Keats just got in our faces right there on the street, asking questions. And then I was up in Harlem making that delivery you wanted me to make." Eddie was talking slowly, remembering not to say something stupid like "I thought. . ."

"So, you were going to tell me at some point?"

"Of course."

"What did they ask you?"

"It was about that same thing that they are looking for." He was proud to show JB he could answer without saying anything incriminating. "I don't know anything, that's all I said."

"Okay, because it's important that I can trust you. You are a key man to me and there are big things in the works. I need to know I can trust you."

"Of course you can. I hate those pencil-neck pricks more than anyone. My father hated them, too, but I hate them more."

"They killed him, those bastards," JB reminded him. Eddie nodded.

"Good, then," JB said. "In a few days I am planning to bring something very big back from Italy. I'm going to need your help."

"Of course, whatever you need, JB."

"Good, good," he cooed, like a benevolent grandfather. "I want you should go uptown and meet with our friends, the Chili Brothers. You know who I mean, you been there before."

Eddie nodded.

"I want you should give them a message, and more importantly, I want you to listen and tell me what they say. Remember, never say 'yes' when you can nod."

Eddie nodded, happy to be useful again.

"Do you think you can do this?"

"Yes," Eddie answered, then nodded.

JB reached over and pinched Eddie's cheek. "You make me

crazy," he said, "but you're a good kid. There are big things ahead for you. Big things."

Chapter 14

Eddie parked the Impala on 118th Street and First Avenue, in front of Patsy's Pizzeria. The east Harlem neighborhood was no longer the Italian stronghold it had once been. What the Chinese were doing to Mulberry Street, the Puerto Rican immigrants had done to the 116th Street area—slums always belonged to the newcomers. Left behind were little reminders of the old guard: a small café, a lone Italian restaurant or candy store; outposts all, under siege, but where business could still be conducted.

Eddie always combined a visit to the Harlem crew with pizza from Patsy's. He loved the way the coal-burning oven made the dough rise, and he never missed an opportunity to devour a slice. It was also a good idea not to have JB's car parked in front of an establishment that was under surveillance; the feds routinely recorded the plate numbers of vehicles whose occupants patronized many of the neighborhood businesses.

Pizza in hand, his second slice, Eddie walked from Patsy's down to 116th Street, stopping at a seemingly innocuous candy store. The metal shelves along one wall were lined with apothecary jars full of brightly colored penny candies, while the counters housed stands full of homemade lollipops and rock candy. As Eddie surveyed the impressive collection of candy bars wrapped in foil and paper, he made eye contact with the counter man who motioned him into the back room, where two other men were watching television. They were dressed in fine suits and white shirts with long collars that hid the knots of their striped silk ties. Their facial features seemed too small, obscured by the masses of skin that folded into double and triple chins overlapping lunar potholes. Diamond rings and gold-faced watches reflected the bright fluorescent lighting. The men rose long enough to greet Eddie with a firm embrace and a kiss on each cheek. One guy turned up the volume on the television, while the other motioned Eddie to sit.

"Our friend sends his warmest regards," Eddie told the men.

They smiled. "He's a wonderful man. All our respects back to him."

Eddie nodded.

"What happened to you?" the first man asked, pointing to Eddie's face.

"I took a sucker punch from some mook. He paid for it, though."

The man nodded. "We want our friend to know that we here in Harlem are very interested in his proposal. We are ready to move the . . . " They looked at each other searching for the right word.

"Produce," the one offered.

The other man approved. "Yes, produce. We can move the produce quickly and safely, and if the oranges are as good as we hear they are, the money is no problem, and the return is guaranteed."

"We understand the fruit in Afghanistan is very sweet," the first man added.

Eddie struggled not to look confused. What the fuck do I know about fruit in wherever the hell he said? They don't look like no farmers, he thought, struggling to decipher their code. Eddie knew it was important that he not mistake one word for another, so he listened carefully. "I understand," he said, although he had no idea what they were talking about, nor was it vital to his mission to know. His only job was to relay a message back to his boss. "Our friend will be happy to hear that," he offered, for lack of anything better to say.

"He is a brilliant man." They all nodded. "We just hope that he can deliver the *produce* as he has promised. We are all counting on it."

"Our friend always keeps his promises, especially when it comes to produce," Eddie assured. Again, it seemed like the right thing to say. It made them happy.

One of the men leaned in, "There is that one small problem, though."

He pointed to an article in the *New York Post* nestled alongside a picture of a gangland boss.

> In a stunning reversal of the government's case, Moe Fortissimo, reputed leader of the Fortissimo crime family, was found not guilty this morning on counts of federal tax evasion and conspiracy to distribute heroin through an international drug cartel.
>
> Fortissimo, known as Crazy Moe among his circle, flaunted his not guilty verdict, holding a block party in his Brooklyn neighborhood. Fortissimo's acquittal on these charges effectively puts an end to the federal case against him due to the risk of double jeopardy.
>
> "Mr. Fortissimo is a free man," his attorney, Roy Silverschein, stated. "The government has failed again. They cannot put Mr. Fortissimo away. The jury has seen this for what it is, a witch hunt by an overzealous prosecutor."

The man ripped the article out of the paper and handed it to Eddie, who stared at the page, pretending to read it. He didn't have to—Fortissimo's victory picture said it all.

"I will tell him about your concern," Eddie said.

He tucked the article into the pocket of his raspberry-colored shirt, and with another round of hugs and kisses, Eddie left the way he had come in. He grabbed a sucker and two jawbreakers on the way out.

The ride back down to Mulberry Street was troublesome. The FDR was jammed with traffic. Eddie turned off and went south down Second Avenue, all the while brooding over the convoluted

conversation he had just taken part in. One part of him didn't want
to know, it wasn't important. Just do what JB says: go to Harlem,
see these guys, take one message, bring another back. It wasn't
important to know more—fruit, produce, moving it safely—it was
none of his concern. And where the hell was Afghanistan? That
shouldn't be important either. But another part of him could not
help but know the truth.

He pulled the news clipping out of his pocket. He knew Moe
Fortissimo, a notorious renegade who answered to no one, not
even the feds, it would seem. Fortissimo was JB's only rival in
New York. His power and influence came from drug money. JB
had never approved of illegal drugs, but times were changing.
JB must be changing, too, Eddie thought. He knew JB had never
liked Fortissimo, with his flashy cars, gaudy jewelry, and fancy
clothes. His flamboyant lifestyle was not in keeping with JB's old-
world ways. It brought unwanted attention, and it was not good for
business to taunt the feds. They tended to take things personally.

JB was a subdued, quiet man in dirty clothes, driving an
old Impala. But smart. He'd slipped a fortune out of the country
undetected. He was all set with money and new identities in Italy,
should he ever have to lam it. But Eddie figured five million could
also buy a lot of white powder, too, turning five million into lots
more money. The calculations were beyond him. His mind was
already working overtime, debating the pros and cons. He was
going to be bringing a big payday into the country—but how? How?
It nagged at him.

JB listened intently to every word Eddie reported. He was
expressionless: no smile, no frown.

"They are concerned about one thing, though," Eddie related.
He took the article from his pocket and flattened it out on the table.
JB glanced at it, then at Bull and Bull. They walked over to the
table. He picked up the article and handed it to them with a quick
but unmistakable tug of his right earlobe. Bull and Bull crumpled
the newspaper and nodded.

"You did good," JB said. "I'm proud of you. But we have more work to do now." He leaned in toward Eddie's face. "You know, there have been some meetings, and I'm sure the books will be opening soon."

Eddie raised his eyebrows.

"You know what that means?" Ballsziti queried.

He did. It was the single driving impetus in Eddie's life, the opportunity to become a good fella, like his father. "Yes, I do," he said, then nodded.

Ballsziti leaned in closer. Eddie thought his saw JB's eyes water. "If your father was here now, he would be so proud of you, so proud." He patted Eddie's cheek. "As I am," he added. He settled back in his armchair. "Will you be ready when the time comes?"

"Yes," Eddie answered, then nodded.

"Good, but again, there is more work to do. You know Mr. Vitagliano?"

"Mr. Vitagliano? Of course, the butcher."

Johnny nodded, "The poor old guy went to Italy to visit his mother and had an accident."

Eddie only nodded, eyebrows raised.

JB nodded, too. "I'm working to have him brought home for burial. It's only right."

Again, Eddie only nodded.

"I want to talk to your friend to get help with the arrangements. Would you have him come see me when I'm ready?"

"Sure, JB."

"Good, I knew I could count on you." He pinched Eddie's cheek, "Oooooh, you make me crazy, do you know that?"

"I'm sorry, JB."

"Okay," he banged his fist on the table. "It's over then, forgotten."

Now that there was peace in the family once again, Eddie thought it would be a good time to ask a favor. "You know my friend Frankie that you want to see?"

"Yes."

"Well, he thinks he's f-f-funny, you know." Eddie was unusually nervous and noticed himself stuttering. "Yeah, he thinks he's funny and he's always trying to get a c-c-comedy job so he can make it in show business some day, you know, he thinks he funny and all . . . "

"Is there a point to be made soon?" JB asked.

Eddied nodded, "Point, oh yes, of course, a point. Well, I was thinking—" He was sorry he had chosen those words, knowing the effect they would have on JB. "I thought—"—Jesus, I said it again—"I was hoping—"—that's better, no thinking involved—"I was hoping you might be able to get him a tryout at the Peppermint Lounge, up there on 45th Street."

"I know where it is," JB said.

Eddie nodded. He nervously cracked his knuckles.

"So, the kid wants to be a comedian?"

"Yeah, he's pretty funny sometimes. It's like he hears voices telling him jokes."

"Where does he get it from? Not from his father—Jesus, I don't think I've ever seen that guy smile. A real stiff. Does his father know?"

"Well, he does, and he don't. He knows the kid did some shows here and there, but he made him promise to stop. Kind of thinks laughing is bad for business."

"And the kid will break the promise?"

There was no answer.

"I'll think about it," JB said, "but, if I do it, it's only as a favor to you. Understand—*only as a favor to you.* And only if he stays away from my daughter. In the meantime, I will be counting on your friend Frankie. We must bring Mr. Vitagliano home to rest in peace."

Chapter 15

At the back table in Lucci's, Sal brought out a pot of pasta e faggioli, a staple of his diet. "Smell those beans," he said, "fava and cannelloni, the best. Lots of restaurants only use one type of bean, but not me." He ladled generous helpings into three large soup bowls.

"Eddie, I don't like this," Frankie said. "Did he say what happened to Mr. V?"

"No, he just had an accident. Accidents do happen, you know."

Sal listened intently as he added more pasta to each bowl, allowing the excess liquid to drain back into the pot.

"Eddie," Frankie repeated, his voice lower, "I don't like this."

"Since when don't you like pasta e faggioli," Sal asked. "I can eat this stuff cold."

"Not the food, you schmuck," Frankie said, pointing to the dish.

Eddie looked around the restaurant. "You're letting your imagination run away with you."

Sal broke a half loaf of Italian bread into small pieces and put them in his dish, mixing the soggy bits with the beans and pasta. "Right, Eddie, it's his imagination. The guy ships five million out of the country under the feds' noses, and so far two of the people who knew anything have assumed room temperature, accidentally of course. You're right. It's definitely his imagination."

Eddie did not want to admit his own concerns. "Can they even do that? Bring a dead guy back from Italy?"

"Hey, they brought Lucky Luciano, and he had been deported," Frankie said.

"This ain't good," Sal mumbled with his mouth stuffed. "You don't have to be no Sherlock Holmes to figure this out. And my friend here is in the middle of it. He's in danger."

Frankie downed a glass of red wine at that assessment.

"No," Eddie said, "JB likes him. He's going to help him line up a job at the Peppermint Lounge."

Sal choked. He looked at Frankie as if he had been betrayed. "You're letting that wise guy help you? Are you nuts? You don't want no part of that guy. His kind don't do nothing for nothing. He will own you."

"Relax," Eddie said. "He's doing it as a favor to me. He don't want no piece of nothing." Knowing the ways of the streets, Eddie only half believed what he'd said. "We all got to calm down, that's what we got to do. Don't lose our heads."

"That, my friends, is my number one priority . . . literally," Frankie said.

"I got to go," Eddie said. "The old man wants me to do something. You check in with Little Anthony, tell him JB sent you."

After a round of hugs and kisses, Eddie headed out the door.

"You traitor," Sal barked at Frankie.

"What are you talking about? You're still my manager. If I get a gig at the Peppermint Lounge, that's good for both of us."

"No good can come from that guy either," he said, pointing out the door toward Eddie. "He's half a loon. Stay away from him and open your eyes. You are in danger. You know where all the bodies are buried. If anything is going to happen to you it's gonna come from the guy who just left. That's how they do it."

"Eddie?" Frankie laughed. "You must be kidding. He would never hurt me. Never. He's been protecting me since I was a kid. When I used to get beat up in school, he would save me."

"Well, that was your father's fault, and your mother's. They dressed you like a midget undertaker. What kid in sixth grade wears a herringbone overcoat, black fedora, and spectator black-

and-white shoes? I mean, come on."

Frankie had to agree. Primo had insisted he be dressed appropriately for an undertaker's son. That meant Frankie had to run home from school on more than one occasion, chased by boys with a different sense of fashion. The taunting would usually end with Eddie giving the bullies a few swift kicks in the ass. "He'd never hurt me," Frankie repeated.

"Hey, *sienta a me,* calamari brain. If you know anything, you know that this neighborhood alters your sense of reality. Around here, Capone and Ballsziti are the good guys; Eliot Ness was the bad guy. Don't assume anything. Don't assume you know anyone."

Frankie didn't want to respond. Sal was making sense and it bothered him. He tried to change the subject. "Do you know that JB told his daughter I'm some kind of degenerate? Why would he do that?"

"Simple," Sal explained, "it's the pre-whack propaganda. It happens all the time. They spread rumors about someone, so when the guy goes missing, people aren't surprised, or better still, they think the guy had it coming to him. That way no one makes a sucker's holler to the cops—they figure justice was done and it's best to mind their business."

"How do you know all this stuff?"

"Hey, I had two uncles once. They went missing in action about twelve years ago during the Carfano wars. I'm sure they're buried somewhere in the footing of the Verrazano Bridge."

"That's good to know," Frankie remarked. "The next time I drive to Staten Island, I'll pay a toll—and say a prayer."

"Ha, ha. But, you'd better listen to what I'm saying. You know I'm right. You know it, Frankie."

"I don't know it, Sal. I'm confused."

"Well, I have news that might cheer you up." He soaked up the remnants of sauce from his plate with the heel of a loaf of bread. "Try this," he said, shoving it into Frankie's open mouth.

Frankie swallowed the soggy bread, forgetting to chew.

Sal explained, "I was waiting for the right time, but I guess now is as good as any. On your last night at the San Su San, I sent a couple of talent scouts out there. You think I'm sleeping? Anyway, they're doing a movie about this Bruce guy, he was a comedian, and maybe there's a small part for you. I'm just waiting for the call."

"A movie? What the hell do I know about acting?"

"It's a comedy; you walk on a stage and tell a joke. You don't gotta be no Marlon Brando. It ain't no starring role, but it will be good exposure."

Frankie thought about it. "So what's the deal?"

"A screen test or something. You may have to go to L.A."

"L.A.?"

"Yeah, that's show business talk for Los Angeles."

"That's, like, on the other side of the country."

"I think so," Sal agreed.

Frankie headed for the Peppermint Lounge, where he introduced himself and asked to see Little Anthony. He waited in the main room while the barmaid, a petite brunette with bright green eyes and a knock-'em-dead smile, went to get him. The lounge was everything Frankie had imagined. Row upon row of cocktail tables rose theater-style from the front stage. Overhead, multicolored spotlights swung from a complicated series of tracks and booms. The whole place was awash in brass and glass.

He had goosebumps as he waited for Little Anthony. Nicknames were usually ironic, so Frankie was expecting a giant. He was wrong. He felt a tug on his pants leg and looked down. Little Anthony was a midget with pompadour hair, polished jet black. The first wave dipped over his forehead and looped back, where it met a second wave, circling up from his right ear, and a third up from his left. They all met on the crown of his head, and disappeared at the neck. *It's got to take hours to dry that,* Frankie mused.

"Hello, Mr. Little . . . Mr. Anthony. I'm Frankie Grace. I guess I'm here to audition."

Little Anthony looked up at him like Frankie had just fallen off the moon. "You're kidding me right, kid. Ha, ha, okay, I get the joke."

Frankie seemed bewildered. Little Anthony noticed the look. "Look, kid, who's kidding who? I get a message direct from Johnny Ballsziti telling me you're coming, and who you are, and what you want. What do I have to say about it? I'm only trying to run a business here. If they want to send up every half-baked amateur who thinks he can sing 'Moon River' or crack a joke, then who am I? And then they want to know why the count is off. Go figure. So you see, whatever your name is, you can suck for all I care." He looked a calendar from his pocket. "I got Bobby Rydell headlining on Saturday night. You can open up for him. Be ready to do forty-five minutes. Can you handle that?"

"Sure," Frankie said, equal parts shocked and thrilled.

"Do you do your own material at least, or am I going to hear Henny Youngman reruns?"

"My own material." *And a little Henny.*

"Good, now get out of my way. I got a barber's appointment." The little man pushed by him. "By the way," he said, "make sure you bring some people. You got any following at all?"

"Some friends," Frankie said.

"Well, bring them. I'm not running a charity. This is a business after all."

In the backyard of Lucci's Restaurant, before the dinner hour arrived, Sal was using a funnel to pour C & K wine from gallon jugs into empty one-liter Coca-Cola bottles. As he filled each one, he covered the open mouth with aluminum foil.

"What the hell are you doing?" Frankie asked.

Sal looked up. "Just giving the public what it wants. We got new people eating here, like hippies or something. They like homemade wine, so I tell them this is homemade—it looks authentic in the Coke bottles. They think I made it in the basement. They pay extra for it and get drunker drinking it. Go figure, stupid bastards."

"You know, you need serious help," Frankie said.

"This coming from a man who sleeps in a casket," Sal replied.

He placed a piece of foil over the last bottle. "Hey, while you're here, you gotta do me a favor."

"What's up?"

Sal pointed to the clotheslines that ran from building to building overhead. "It cost me a few thousand bucks to make this spot into a nice garden for outdoor dining. You know, I don't have that much sidewalk space out front like some of the other places. But, look." He pointed to the clotheslines. "See that? They belong to the merry widows. People are down here trying to friggin' eat, and these friggin' bloomers are up there waving all over the place like friggin' pirate flags. It kills the mood, not to mention the appetite."

Frankie looked up to see the brilliant blue afternoon sky sprinkled with an assortment of women's black girdles, cotton underwear, and double-D bras. "Jeez," Frankie noted, "they almost block the sun. Get a load of the size of those things. I could show home movies on them!"

"Think you can do anything about it? The old ladies, they love you. Offer to buy them a washing machine and dryer. I'll pay."

"I'll see what I can do," Frankie promised as they made their way back inside.

"Good. Now, what can I do for you?"

"I need some help. I got the gig at the Peppermint Lounge, but the guy asked me to bring some people. He wanted to know if I had any fans."

Sal stepped to the bar and filled two glasses with wine.

Frankie continued, "We got no credibility after the Rudy Vallée thing. Our friends don't trust us. Our following has stopped following."

Sal pondered the predicament as he skillfully worked a cleaver though a fresh wheel of provolone. The pungent aroma made Frankie hungry. "I thought they did big business there. Why do you have to guarantee a crowd?"

"Rydell will draw the usual wise guys. But I bet half of them don't pay, and the other half are comped."

Sal understood. "I'll give it some thought. Taste this." He handed Frankie a slice of the provolone. "Sharp, huh?" Sal sat down at last, took a deep breath, and stopped chewing on the wedge of provolone he had cut from the wheel.

"Are you okay?" Frankie asked. "You seem like you're all over the place, more hyper than usual."

"Not really. I'm a little pissed. I'm trying to compete, and it just gets harder and harder. Then there's all this trouble with the mob. If these guys got to kill somebody, why not use my restaurant? Look at this beautiful setting. It's perfect for a hit. Can't they spread the goodwill around? I could use the advertising, too, you know."

"I'll bring it up at the next meeting," Frankie joked.

Sal refilled the two wineglasses, this time from one of the recycled Coke bottles. "Try this. It's homemade, my own feet."

"How inviting."

"So," Sal asked, "are you ready for this Peppermint thing? All worries aside, it's good exposure."

"I need practice, and there isn't much time."

"Hey, there are twenty-some-odd hours in a day. Time management, that's the key."

"What do you mean?"

"Look, you can combine your nighttime comedy routine with your day job. If you play your cards right, your father will never know. You've been doing it already, but now you'll step it up a notch. Sort of, hearse and re-hearse." Sal laughed at his own line.

"It won't be easy."

"Hey, do you think you'd be the first? Think of all the famous people who have successfully led double lives. There was Jekyll by day and Hyde by night, Count Vlad by day and Count Dracula by night. You certainly have a lot in common with him: you both sleep in a coffin, and are very much involved with blood. And then there was Theresa Marufi."

"Who's she?"

"Crackerjack waitress in the daytime, dynamite Park Avenue hooker by night."

"I'm sorry I asked."

"And then, of course, there's the Wolfman, who, very much like you, comes alive at the full moon."

Frankie considered the idea. There was certainly no shortage of comedy clubs in New York City. He could easily make three or four a night. "I'm going to need some new material. The stale one-liners aren't going to fly at the Peppermint Lounge."

Sal nodded. "Listen, you can put it together. You'll find your voice. You need a hook, something that will make you stand out. That's what you need."

"*That's* a big help," Frankie said.

It could work, he thought, but the grand deception would require the appearance of absolute normalcy. That would be imperative, for Primo was a suspicious man, and Frankie walked a delicate tightrope.

Sal refilled their glasses. "So, you practice the comedy routine at night, and by day you are the mild-mannered undertaker. Your father will never be the wiser. It's simple."

Right, that's what they always say. *Look out, Clark Kent, here I come.*

"You have your yearbook from embalming school?" Sal asked.

"Embalming school?"

Yes, embalming school. You know, the place where you went for your license. Where they teach you to reconstruct people's noses and drain people's blood, embalming school."

"Yeah, I think I can find it."

"Bring it to me. I'll find you a following."

Shortly after midnight, midday for the mobsters who frequented the café on Mulberry Street, the card games were in full swing, the pool hustlers were at their prime, and liquor was flowing at a fast clip across the bar. The pay phone rang, prompting Bull to leave his post by the card table.

"Hello?" He listened but did not speak.

Café regulars knew enough not to say anything that might be overheard and later used against them in court. Phone conversations were more problematic to conduct in the usual codes or double-speak than face-to-face meetings, and the more delicate lip sync method was limited to direct conversation. It was not unusual to find men huddled in a corner moving their lips without emitting a sound. Wise guys had to be proficient in the familiar form of jargon if they had any hopes of advancement. Improvements to police electronics had made mimes of many in the mob.

Bull digested the message and hung up the phone. At the card table, JB sat contemplating his hand. He would bluff with a pair of deuces. Bull whispered the message into Ballsziti's ear.

"Our friend is on Mulberry Street, eating around the corner at Cha Cha's."

Johnny's expression never changed, except for a raised eyebrow. He had given his minions their orders when Eddie delivered the newspaper clipping from the Chili Brothers. Bull and Bull stood where they were. JB glared at them with a do-I-have-to-pull-my-ear-again look. Evidently he did, so he tugged on it again and again. They finally got it. Ballsziti always knew they weren't the brightest pair, but they served a purpose.

Bull One stepped behind the bar and slid the lower panel of a walnut storage cabinet to the left, revealing a hidden compartment. He reached in and grabbed a worn leather bag, which he brought back to the table. JB unzipped the bag and pulled out one .45 caliber pistol, then another. He checked the chamber of each before handing them to Bulls One and Two. They left without a word.

Minutes after the call, the two mob henchmen arrived at the restaurant. Bull One went in the front door of the restaurant as Bull Two entered through the back. Their target was at a corner table, two women at his side. A small cake sat in front of him, the candles just lit. The two chorus girls were singing "Happy Birth-day."

Bullets flew. Two hit the old man, one in the shoulder and another at the collarbone, as the women screamed and fell to the floor. Wounded but not down, he jumped up from the table and crashed through the front window onto the street. Bull and Bull followed, still firing. Wobbly and dazed, the victim staggered aimlessly. The force of the bullets carried his body to the middle of the street, where blood spewed from his torso and forehead. Bullets ricocheted off parked cars and unlit buildings, shattering windows in the process.

The sound of bullets and broken glass awakened the Grace family two buildings down. "Jesus Christ, not again," Primo exclaimed. The insurance company had already revoked his coverage. He would have no recourse. No one would pay to replace the busted glass. No one had paid the last three times. Primo wrote it off as a necessary business expense; gangland violence was, after all, a hazard of doing business on Mulberry Street. If he were called to handle the funeral it would help soften the blow.

Primo moved to his bedroom window on his hands and knees, motioning for Giovanna to stay put. He cursed as he saw Frankie crawl past their bedroom and into the kitchen. As Frankie peeked over the windowsill, the ambush unfolded before him as if in slow motion. Against the halo of a street lamp, he saw the silhouette of a man in the intersection of Mulberry and Hester Streets, sustained upright by a barrage of bullets. The victim fell to one knee, then struggled up again, swirling in a circle, his face upturned to the dark sky. Finally, his knees buckled and he fell straight back to the damp pavement, one leg contorted beneath his body. The firing stopped, giving the shooters a chance to appreciate the theatrics before they scattered at the sound of police sirens.

"Dad, did you see that?" Frankie whispered excitedly.

"No," Primo answered, "and neither did you. Go back to bed."

As he lay in bed, his heart still racing, Frankie thought about what he had just witnessed. Life imitated art. It was just like the scene he'd watched on Mott Street, when Brando was shot, only this time there was no one to yell, "Cut, that's a take."

Always a fan of great dying scenes in the movies, Frankie was impressed with this man's finale. He thought about Cagney, blown up on top of an oil tank in *White Heat*, or crying like a baby when he got the electric chair in *Angels with Dirty Faces*. No one was close enough to hear this man's last words, but what would they have been? In the solitude of his room, Frankie reached for his pen, and on a scrap of paper wrote: *Famous last words: Rosebud! Top of the world, Ma! Check, please!*

✝

Eddie, too, had watched the action unfold on Mulberry Street. In the darkness of his apartment, he sat by the window, overlooking the street. The only light came from the intermittent glow of his cigarette. In the morning, the world would discover the victim's identity, but Eddie did not have to wait until morning. He understood. The unspoken order had been heard and carried out. In the wee hours of the morning, his mentor, Johnny Ballsziti, had became the most powerful don in America, and the new international importer of Afghani fruit, consolidating power by way of a hostile takeover. Gray smoke from his Chesterfield floated out his window. There was a new Pope. Moe Fortissimo was dead.

Five million buys a lot of funerals, thought Eddie. He was counting the dead: Tony Branca the handyman, Mr. Vitagliano, the butcher, and this lowlife, Moe Fortissimo. And five million converted into white powder would easily be worth fifty million or more on the streets. Despite others' opinions, Eddie was good at thinking ahead, and he did not like where he imagined this game would end.

Chapter 16

As luck, or fate, would have it, it was turning out to be a banner week at the Grace Funeral Home. Six unexpected deaths, all from natural causes, was a record—not counting the grisly bonus of Moe Fortissimo. Each service had to be perfectly timed and planned around the feast activities. The bonanza made Primo rethink his earlier pessimism. Frankie had his work cut out for him.

Under his father's watchful eye, Frankie embalmed and dressed Mr. Vispucci, dead of a stroke, but he got no cooperation—from his father or the corpse. It seemed as if both were unusually inflexible, and both refused to smile. Finally, after much cutting, poking, and rearranging—coupled with one or two of his father's well-placed smacks to his head—Frankie strapped the body to a pulley, raised it off the embalming table, turned it, and lowered the deceased into the casket. He made a few final adjustments to the pillow. He folded newspaper lengthways and ran it up the pants leg, insuring that the crease fell right above the fold. Then he straightened the sleeves of the jacket and tied the tie. A little mortuary wax and cosmetics, and Mr. Vispucci looked brand new.

Before the casket could be brought upstairs, Primo had to examine the work.

"I still see a hair in his nose," he remarked. "And he still has too much of a smile."

As Frankie clipped the nose hairs, he asked his father to check the yard.

There was only one way to get the casket from the basement morgue to the parlor on the main floor. Primo opened the basement door, where a ramp in the alleyway led up to the courtyard. When all was clear, he and Frankie would have to push the casket up the ramp to ground level, then through a back door. The timing had to be perfect. Patrons of Lucci's found that dining under the stars did not come without a bizarre risk: the sight of a casket being maneuvered along the garden wall had put a damper on many an evening.

Worse yet, Annunziata Ballsziti would, on occasion, be perched outside the back door of the bakery, taking in fresh air or feeding her cat. God forbid that Annunziata should get sight of a casket. The cat would hiss and haunch its back, while Annunziata would sink her teeth deep into her palm, her hackles raised as well, as she prepared to defend against the evil omen. Her standard ritual of mal'occhian purification took the form of a Neapolitan Tourette's, complete with the repeated thrusting of two fingers, pointer and pinky, with the occasional middle finger thrown in for good measure. When she was done, she would scoop up the cat and send salt flying out the door.

"The coast is clear," Primo announced. The two quickly pushed the casket up the ramp and into the funeral home. Frankie arranged the flowers around the casket, finishing just as Mrs. Vispucci walked in. She gazed at her husband's casket.

Frankie waited for a "Well done" or "Looks like he's sleeping." Instead the widow exclaimed, "That's not his nose."

Well, it's not my *nose.* "Excuse me?" Frankie didn't know what else to say.

Mrs. Vispucci repeated, "I said, that's not his nose. My husband's nose was strong like a falcon's. That's not his nose."

"I can assure you, Mrs. Vispucci, that's the nose he came in with." *Even if from this angle it does look a bit like a two-car garage with the doors open.* "We would have no reason to replace an existing nose. It's not like we keep a supply of them on hand."

He could tell Primo didn't care for that response. His father was a bit more delicate, explaining that perhaps it was the initial shock. "You're not accustomed to seeing your husband in this position."

"Are you kidding me? This is the only position I ever saw him in—lying on the couch. The only thing missing is a *TV Guide* and a can of beer. That being said, that's *not* his nose."

The evening dragged on. After leading a prayer, saying good night to the last mourner, and assuring Mrs. Vispucci that they would find her husband's nose—even check the hospital, as she suggested—Frankie locked the door and took a deep breath, more certain than ever that there had to be a better way. He vacuumed the rugs, emptied the ashtrays, and placed the chairs back in rows. He looked at his watch. It was already nine p.m. He quickly changed into his rented tux and headed uptown, a world away.

He cruised the city on a whirlwind tour of the comedy clubs, from Stratton's on Queens Boulevard to Pips in Sheepshead Bay—anywhere in the five boroughs where he could grab a microphone. In traffic between stints, he often found himself in an encounter between the black hearse and a Yellow cab, exchanging multilingual curses and a few select hand motions he had learned from Annunziata. Frankie was not to be outdone in this vehicular jungle: a cabbie giving him the finger would get the international mal'occhio, the extended pointer and pinky. The gesture had added significance when it came from someone driving a hearse.

Next morning, he was right back in the basement. In the embalming room, he hated the quiet—so he talked out loud to keep himself company—knit one, stitch two; who's on first; I don't know; third base—anything to get his mind off the dreaded task at hand, and to keep himself awake. He tried out his act in front of his captive audience of one. At least when he rehearsed in the embalming room no one walked out on him.

The prep room, as always, was suffocating, the odors irritating. Frankie climbed out of the basement for fresh air and gravitated to the kitchen at Lucci's, where Sal handed him a wet towel and poured him a glass of red wine.

"Tough day?"

"Jesus, tough week," Frankie answered. "It's like we're having a clearance sale or something."

"That's it, that's it—that's funny. See, you can work this stuff into your routine."

Frankie shook his head in doubt.

"Why can't something be sad and funny, too?" Sal protested. "Or, can't you make something funny out of something sad? Remember when my father died? I mean, one minute he's slicing potatoes and peppers and the next minute he's face down in the casserole. It wasn't funny at the time, but looking back, you gotta laugh."

Frankie sipped the wine and pondered the question in context of his last few days. He mulled over how to work death into laughs. This week alone he'd collected enough material for three full acts.

Like helping Filomena plan her husband's funeral that morning. He had escorted her through the basement door into a display room with a small selection of caskets, each identified by its model name. He recommended the bronze.

"He was a shoemaker, not a don," she said. He thought *that* was funny. He remembered how she walked around the selection room, from one casket to another, finally stopping at the mahogany. Ah, we have the same taste, Frankie had thought as she examined the casket.

"It looks used," she said, noting a strange indentation in the mattress.

He turned the pillow. Should he explain that he had lain in it? Would she understand that the casket was more comfortable than his folding Castro Convertible with the horizontal iron bar digging into his back? The comfort angle might actually be a good selling point. Would he be able to convince the widow he'd had to try it out for quality control? *No, Frankie, let it go.*

As he recalled following her around the room, he felt it happening: the line between serious and silly was disappearing, just like Sal suggested. As he watched her make her decision, the little voice in his head was popping off jokes. He felt like the host of a morbid game show, waiting for the contestant to make the big decision. There was something funny there, he couldn't deny it.

In the bakery kitchen, where she and her mother were learning to adjust to the absence of the indispensable Isabella, Caterina Ballsziti watched the workers in chef's hats and once-white aprons skillfully knead homemade bread dough and expertly shape an array of cookies and delicate pastry shells. The ovens were working overtime to keep up with demand. Rich aromas filled the air.

She leaned against the counter, flipping through a large folder of her grandmother's recipes, as she watched her mother waddle back and forth behind the counter, serving the unending stream of customers. She kept track with her watch: each customer took a minimum of five minutes to help as they mulled over their choices between three chocolate biscotti and one éclair or two napoleons or one cannoli or possibly just the biscotti and the cannoli. She did some quick math—six to ten customers an hour, over ten to twelve hours . . . small potatoes, she concluded. They could do better.

During a brief lull she approached her mother. "Mama, when you divide the hours by the income, are we really profitable?"

Annunziata wiped her brow. "Anything you mix with water makes you money," she said. "Bread, cement, pizza . . . and pastries."

Caterina smiled as she worked her way to the back room of the bakery. Metal vats and pots were scattered everywhere. Stainless steel counters, wooden rolling pins, and overhead racks occupied much of the unused space. She peered through the cracks of a boarded-up door at the back of the storage chamber, revealing another large, empty room. She had known it was there since she was a small child, but now, as she pried loose the boards one by one, she called out, "Mama, what's in here?"

Dusty cobwebs hung from the ceiling and across the doorway. "Oh, nothing," Annunziata called back. "We never use that part of the building. Your grandmother always wanted to expand, but didn't really know how."

Caterina headed up Mulberry Street to the market. While she'd been away her childhood neighborhood had changed greatly. When she left for school, there had been only a handful of Italian restaurants, but now every storefront housed an eatery or retail shop of some kind. She paused, looking in the windows, ignoring the waiters who shamelessly hounded her to come in and eat—had they known who she was, they would not have been so pushy.

She thought Mulberry Street looked very much like Naples now, all the sidewalk dining at tables covered by Cinzano umbrellas. The area had become a hot spot and she understood the equation that made it so: the worse the publicity, the gorier the rubout, the more brazen the hit, the bigger the crowds of curious outsiders who trooped to Little Italy hoping to catch a glimpse of the mob in action. There was no such thing as bad publicity.

It was that very attention from which her mother and grandmother had sought to shield her. Her earliest memories of her father included dozens of men seated at the dining room table on Christmas Day. Each arrived with a little trinket for her—a diamond necklace, a diamond ring, a diamond bracelet—and those with less taste gave her an envelope that contained enough money for her to buy a diamond ring, a diamond necklace, or a diamond bracelet. She understood early on that her father was an important man, though she was not exactly clear as to why.

When she was old enough to start asking questions, and old enough to be the object of taunting from classmates with fewer family connections, her father agreed that it would be best for her not to be involved in his day-to-day occupational stresses. To insure that she was protected, and at the insistence of Nonna Isabella, Caterina's parents agreed to send her to school in Italy, where they had enough family to look after her needs. No matter how hard they tried to shield her from the truth, though, Caterina still read the papers that chronicled her father's life—the allegations, the arrest, the attempts at conviction. She knew.

Still, for all the changes along Mulberry Street, some things remained the same. Papalardo's Salumeria was still the place for imported dry sausage and provolone sharp enough to burn your tongue, and that was her destination.

Frankie's heart raced, his pulse quickened, and his face flushed as he saw his love enter the market. *What a lucky time to take a break,* he thought. He crept up behind her in the produce section.

"I think I love you, Caterina," he said. "And please don't tell your father."

She turned to face him, a bright smile on her face. Frankie's heart melted.

"May I hold your melons?" he brazenly asked.

"You're fresh, such a clown. My father may be right."

Frankie reached for a zucchini and feigned a smart stab at his heart.

"Aren't you ever serious?"

"Not if I can help it." He reached out to take her bags. "Will you go out with me again?"

"Yes," she said without hesitation.

He protested, "But your father is wrong. I don't know why he said those things—"

"Frankie, I said *yes.*"

It finally sank in. "Why, yes, I guess you did. Do you have time for a gelato?"

"Do you think we should be seen together on Mulberry Street?"

"You're right," he agreed. "We can go to Ferrara on Grand Street. It's not as good as your grandmother's, God rest her soul, but we can go there."

"That's fine," she said. "Then I can decide if my father has misjudged you, and check out my competition at the same time."

He set the bags down on the counter. "You are so beautiful," he said.

Then, in the deli light, he thought he saw something. He cupped her face in his hands, tracing his fingers lovingly across her eyes, his thumbs moving lightly across her lips, slowly, back and forth. *Goddamn you, Sal.*

Café Ferrara was world renowned for pastries, Perugina candies, and confectionary. Caterina wasn't kidding about checking out the competition. She approved of the white-jacketed waiters but was appalled at the prices. As they awaited their order, an espresso and a cannoli for her, a Manhattan Special soda for him, she studied the inner workings of the operation. Like an assembly line, pastries were packaged, wrapped, and tied in an orderly, efficient way. The waiter placed the coffee before her. She looked into the cup. "No foamy head," she said. "They don't pack the coffee tight enough in the filter." She tasted the cannoli. "Yesterday's," she observed. "It's not fresh." The tubular shell disappeared into her mouth as Frankie watched in amazement. He felt a stirring. She bit down on the shell. A cringe replaced the stirring.

She wiped a small trace of cream from her lips. "The shell is too thin and not long enough, and the cream does not go all the way though. They skimp." She looked at him. "Do you have any understanding of what I am saying?"

He was flushed. "Yes—good head is important, and size matters."

"Frankie Grace," she said, "you are incorrigible."

She wiped her lips and walked away. Resigned or mad, he didn't know. There was one thing he did know. As he paid the check and gazed down into the showcase of pastries, he knew he would never look at a cannoli in the same way again.

On Thursday morning both men of the Grace household left the breakfast table on separate missions. It would be a long day, and there was much work to be done.

Primo Grace remembered his words to Frankie. Sometimes people do and believe strange things. Primo had an inkling that Frankie was more involved than anyone thought with Johnny Ballsziti's daughter. The prospect of having an outlaw as an in-law was worrisome. JB would find a way to take control of his business, somehow, some way. Before he knew it, there would be a cadre of wise guys sitting backwards on folding chairs outside the parlor. That's how wise guys sat. That would be just the beginning. They would be using the chapel as an office, or a warehouse for stolen furs or televisions. It would be a perfect place for quiet craps games. Who would guess? Boxcars! Soon, he would be asked to create a double-decker casket as a way to remove an uncooperative associate. Not acceptable. He didn't mind burying mobsters—they buy big, the more the merrier—but he didn't want one as a partner. Nothing good could come from this.

It occurred to him that he had an ally who also had a vested interest in keeping the two apart—Annunziata Ballsz(ti. An undertaker in her family! Well, there was simply not enough salt in the Dead Sea to counteract that.

Primo got the chance to test his theory when Annunziata called for him. She wanted to settle Isabella's funeral bill and asked him to come see her. He was uncomfortable meeting at her apartment—he wouldn't want JB to get the wrong idea—but he dared not refuse.

Primo knocked on the door. "Annunziata, buon giorno," he called out.

Annunziata opened the door. She was in her mourning uniform: black bloomers, black stockings, a black slip and black dress. She was grief incarnate. "Come in."

He slipped on a scattering of salt granules as he walked into the kitchen.

The Ballszti apartment was atypical of the others in the building. From the hallway it looked similar, but the Ballszitis had the whole floor, combining three small apartments into a sizable penthouse. The interior looked like the showroom at Roma Furniture on Grand Street. There was no understated elegance here.

The kitchen floor was imported Italian tile, and plastic mats led from one plushly carpeted room to the other. The seating was early Gaudi and covered with plastic, from the couches to the intricately carved wooden armchairs. Ornate lamps with delicate silk shades shone from each corner. French provincial furniture flanked each wall.

Annunziata escorted Primo into the living room and motioned for him to sit. He did so, beneath a life-sized portrait of Benito Mussolini embroidered on a black velvet backing. Compressed air escaped from the sofa as he sat, sounding like flatulence. He was embarrassed until she took her own seat in her Queen Anne chair and won the whoopee cushion contest hands down.

"I have the bill here," she said. "Ten thousand, three hundred twenty dollars?"

"Yes," he said, "but that includes the airline charge, which was considerable."

She nodded. She went down the hall to the refrigerator, opened the freezer, and took out a tray of ice. She cracked the ice, revealing a package wrapped in aluminum foil. Inside the foil was a clear plastic baggie containing a stack of newly minted hundred-dollar bills—cold, hard cash. "There's ten thousand even here," Annunziata said, returning with the money and rewrapping it in the foil. "I'm sure there's a discount for cash."

Who was he to argue? As Primo marked the bill paid, he thought this might be a good time to broach the subject of Frankie and Caterina. If he was ever going to do it, he would have to speak up now.

"Annunziata, I have a small problem; or better yet, *we* have a small problem. I need your help."

Annunziata's ears perked up.

"It's my son."

She nodded. "That sonofabitch takes my daughter in that black car. Look, he's your son; you have to live with him. But he has his eye on my daughter. If I catch him, I'll kill him, never mind my husband." She was ranting by that point. "He brought her flowers from the dead. He doesn't even buy them fresh, that strunzo."

Hey, the same pet name, Primo thought.

"I tried to give him a hint, but he didn't take it."

"I think he's slow," Primo offered.

"Slow! Slow is being kind. When I think of my daughter in that car, I go crazy. *Che disgrazia. Dis strunz!* I faint right there."

"Exactamente! And that is what bringa me here," Primo said in broken English, in an unconscious bid for her sympathy. "Is there something you could do, or suggest, or I can do to—" he paused, "to put an end to this affection?"

Annunziata was intrigued at the idea. Surely there was a page in the evil-eye handbook dealing with such a request. After a moment, she sat back in her chair and placed her palms flat on the coffee table. She drew a deep breath. Her eyes rolled back into their sockets. She was in a trance, muttering and chanting incoherently. Primo felt a chill; goosebumps ran up his arm. He tried to understand the words, but the language was foreign to him. She was possessed. After a few moments, Annunziata came out of her trance.

"I've have done what I could, but you must help," she said.

"What do you want me to do?"

"Take a statue of Saint Valentine, bury him face down in the yard, cover him, then wet the ground. Do this just after midnight. While you're wetting it, say your son's name over and over."

Primo was confused. "By wet it, you mean water it? And then bury it in the yard?"

Annunziata grew impatient. "No, not wet with water, wet with *piscia,* pee. You must pee on the saint and bury him in the back yard."

Primo was stunned. "I plant tomatoes back there."

"It's the only way, the only way."

"Annunziata, I thank you for your suggestion, but I don't think I can . . . urinate on Saint Valentine."

"It's the only way," she said again.

As Eddie had instructed him, Frankie paid a call at the Marconi Café. Frankie was glad he'd avoided the lunch hour. JB called him over almost immediately. "I'm sorry you had to witness all that unpleasantness recently," he said apologetically. "That guy Eddie never learns. Do you want a drink or something?"

Frankie's knees were shaking. He nodded.

JB took that as a yes, and held up two fingers. Lorenzo brought a round of grappa in two pony glasses, accompanied by two espressos.

"I heard you want to be a comedian or something?"

"That's what I'd like to do."

"Well, that's good."

He raised his glass and tapped it against Frankie's. "Salute! Drink, drink."

JB tossed down the grappa and then chased it with the strong, steaming coffee. That must be the trick, Frankie thought. Swallow it quickly and it doesn't have time to burn your tongue. Lorenzo brought another round.

"I'm counting on you to be funny," JB continued. "I heard Little Anthony was able to fit you in for Saturday night."

"Yes, thank you very much." *How quickly you forget, moron. This guy is evil.*

"Hey, there's no thanks necessary. That's what friends do, they help each other. But, I want you should know that I'm doing this as a favor to you. I want you to understand that. I like you very much."

"You do?"

"Of course I do."

"Thank you, Mr. Balls…"—*not now, stupid*—"ziti."

"Now, I got another question for you. You know how you sent my mother-in-law, Isabella," he crossed himself, "may she rest in peace, back to Italy?"

"Yes," Frankie answered, feeling his collar tighten around his neck.

"Well, what if somebody dies in Italy, and wants to be buried back here?"

Frankie pondered the question. "Well, an American citizen would be entitled to be brought back. I guess the Italians have a similar process of permits and things like we do."

"Right, I would think so, too." JB sipped the espresso. "Probably easier, as I think about it, with all the people I know over there." He leaned in, "You know, it's Italy; you spread a few dollars around and you can buy the Vatican."

Frankie sat quietly.

"You see," JB explained, "I have a friend who died while he was on vacation. You may know him, Mr. Vitagliano."

"Oh, Mr. Vitagliano, the butcher? I'm sorry. When did it happen?" Frankie tried to keep cool. *Don't give anything away.*

JB drained his cup. "Any day now. I mean, any day now the arrangements will be made over there to bring him back here for burial. He had some family making their way to visit him. Do they use zinc like we do?"

Frankie stammered. "I . . . I think it would be a requirement for the airline."

"Right, right," JB agreed. "And that would include the hermit seal, so no smell could come out? In case he goes bad or something."

"Yes, hermetically sealed."

JB rapped his knuckles on the table, apparently satisfied with Frankie's response. "Okay, then, I will let you know what's going on. You knock 'em dead at that club, okay, kid?"

"Thank you, JB."

"Hey, you don't have to thank me; one hand washes the other and both hands wash the face." The profound statement was illustrated by an exaggerated flurry of gestures.

Frankie hated himself for being nice, but he had no choice. He got the message loud and clear—you see what happens to people who can put me away? First Tony, now Mr. Vitagliano. Who should be next to cover my tracks? You are nothing but a sheep's head to me. But you scratch my back, I scratch yours, and our hands will wash our faces, and all that good stuff. Frankie didn't know who to believe, who to trust.

He rose to leave. As the door closed behind him, JB led an enthusiastic chorus of ball scratchers.

As Primo and Frankie, reunited, walked up Mulberry Street, Frankie saw Roscoe Keats seated at Café Napoli reading the *Daily News*.

"Don't stop," Frankie said.

"Isn't that the police guy?" Primo asked.

"Yes, don't stop."

Keats saw them. "Good morning, gentlemen. Would you like

some coffee?"

"No thanks," Frankie answered, as he kept walking, holding onto his father's elbow.

"Shame about Tony," Keats said. "Him being murdered and all."

Primo stopped dead in his tracks. "Murdered?"

"Well, yes. The story is right here on page three." He pointed to the article.

"I thought he fell and hit his head."

"Well, that was the working assumption, until the autopsy. They found coal dust deep in his head wound, so we went back and discovered a shovel by the furnace. Sure enough, there was his blood on it."

"So, they think someone hit him with a shovel? What for? The guy had no money. What could they want from him?" Primo was perplexed. Frankie was not.

"Gee," Keats said, "do you think it had anything to do with the buckle we found?"

"What buckle?" Primo asked.

"Let's go, Dad."

"Yeah, you better run along. But hey, be careful. This neighborhood isn't as safe as it once was, and no one wants to be the guest of honor at the funeral luncheon."

"What the hell is he talking about?" Primo asked.

"Ignore him, Dad. Let's keep walking."

Frankie continued with his father to the medical examiner's office on First Avenue. He hated the place. The smell of the industrial-strength Clorox used to mop the floors was nauseating, especially when mixed with the odor from open chest cavities, decaying flesh, and rotting organs. *Why wouldn't anyone love this business?* he thought.

Primo had been worried that Tony would not receive a proper burial. There was no family to authorize one, so the city was about to send him to be buried in a plain pine box in the potter's field on Hart Island. That was unacceptable to Primo. "The guy deserves better," he told Frankie.

And now that the medical examiner had determined that Tony Branca had been murdered, Primo felt all the more obligated to take care of his friend. As they stood waiting at the examiner's office, he told Frankie, "He has a niece living in Pennsylvania somewhere. She kept in touch. We'll track her down." He slipped the clerk $100 to lose the paperwork for a few days.

Back at Tony's basement apartment, Frankie and Primo looked around for any sign of family. There were no photographs, no books. It was basic, almost monastic—a single bed, a lamp, a kitchen table and two chairs, and a bookcase. Primo flipped through a box on the bottom shelf of the bookcase until he came across a military folder containing a record of Tony's army discharge.

"This is good news," Primo said. "He's a veteran, saw action at Anzio. He's entitled to a grave at the national cemetery on Long Island."

Frankie was happy for his father, and for Tony. "Look," he said. He picked up a greeting card and read it aloud. "Uncle, just want to wish you a happy birthday—Love, Ann."

Primo took the card and read it for himself.

"Look for the envelope," he said. Frankie saw it on the bureau. Primo took it and read the return address. "Bingo!" he exclaimed. "We have the next of kin."

It didn't take long after that for Primo to locate Tony's niece by phone and inform her of his death. She lived in Hawley, Pennsylvania, and did not get to see her uncle very often. She was shocked at the news and too far away for Primo to console her. He explained that the city was going to bury her uncle in a pauper's grave, but he had found an army discharge and would be able to stop that, with her help.

"But Uncle Tony didn't want to be buried," she said, struggling to regain her composure. "He wanted to be cremated."

"Cremated?" Frankie knew Primo hated that word. It was the scourge of traditional funeral business.

"Yes," said Ann. "He told me that often."

"Well, okay. If you will send me a letter authorizing us to take possession of your uncle's body, we can carry out his wishes.

Afterwards, I'll have his ashes buried at the Veterans' Cemetery."

"I will," she said. "But how much is this going to cost? I have no money and was certainly not expecting this. I have three children and—"

Primo had heard it all before. He cut her short. "There is no charge. Tony was a friend."

"Thank you, Mr. Grace. I'll send the letter immediately."

Primo gave her some last-minute assurance. "As soon as we get the letter, we'll make sure Tony gets a worthy burial."

Frankie and Primo returned to Tony's apartment. Primo looked through the closet and picked out the newest of the old clothes. He told Frankie, "Clean him up nice and arrange for the cremation, and maybe we can get some prayers said. It's the right thing to do."

It had already been a long day—and there was still another evening's visitation to prepare for. As he finished parting the customer's hair, Frankie practiced his routine. He turned to look at the chapel: row upon row of empty chairs in a dimly lit room, just like the nightclubs. Life-sized capodimonte holy statues stood in every corner, in every nook, and on every shelf and table top. None of them smiled—the saints never had a smile. Must be hard to be a saint, he thought. There was no record in the Bible, Old or New Testament, of anyone having a sense of humor.

As he studied the chipped, painted faces of the Apostles, the Cosmo and Damiano Brothers, Mary, Joseph, Theresa, Ann, he wondered about the connection between comedy and tragedy, humor and mortuary art. Each was a solitary endeavor, the performer working alone, whether up on a stage or in the embalming room; working in a room with a single stiff, or full of stiffs; always hoping to hear "well done, good job, you made him smile." The line between laughing and crying was always blurry for him. As he looked around the chapel at the stone faces, he thought of another similarity: the comic, much like the undertaker, starts out with a room filled with stone faces, each daring him to make them smile.

Frankie had an irreverent idea. Why not, he thought? It was

as good a place to practice as any. With the hairbrush as his microphone, he envisioned the inanimate statues as enthusiastic patrons coming to see his act. In an Ed McMahon "Heeeeeeeere's-Johnny" kind of voice, he introduced himself to his audience. "Ladies and Saints, the Blue Room, Chapel A, at the Grace Funeral Home is proud to introduce—Frankie Grace!"

If anyone could get a laugh out of them, he could. He leapt in front of the casket, as if he had just come from backstage and worked his lines. "Hey, thanks for being here; not used to working before a live audience and in this case, I'm not. Must be a good night—you people looked stoned already." He walked around the room, acting out his gig as a nightclub performer, first to the statue of Saint Joseph. "Joey—Joey baby, great to see you. You look great! Love the whole halo thing you got going. Hey, like what's the score? Lions six, Christians nothing."

Then over to the Blessed Mother. "Hey, what a kid you got. Love that water-to-wine trick. Wish I knew how to do it. Maybe He could teach me sometime."

He stared at a picture of the Last Supper and tried to imagine what Jesus and the Apostles were discussing . . . of course, the bill, what else? "Who had the extra unleavened bread? Matthew, you had two glasses of wine. Hey, who asked for separate checks? Does anyone have change? Ask Judas. Hey, I like this resurrection idea. We can double our funeral business that way. Boy, that would sure please my father. Hey, Saint Paul, tell me, your letter to the Thessalonians, did they ever write back?"

It was all in an effort to improve his timing, deal with a heckler, improve a line. There was quiet from this saintly crowd, no laughs. He was accustomed to that, too—dying onstage; it happens.

His morbid matinee was interrupted by the ultimate heckler. "Christ, Frankie, what the hell are you doing?" Primo shouted.

Uh-oh. How long have you been there?

"Are you friggin' nuts? Have you totally lost it? Is there nothing sacred?"

A while then. Caught in the act—literally. "Sorry, Dad."

Chapter 17

For Sal Lucci, the joy had gone out of making lasagna—if not out of eating it. He was bored and he wanted more. Lucci's Restaurant had been a fixture on Mulberry Street since Sal's grandfather started it in 1920, and he had worked there until he died. His son, Sal's father, took over then, working the restaurant until he was long past retirement age. Even then, he'd stayed on as Sal's counselor and official ball-breaker. Every change, meant to keep up with the times, was met with old-world resistance. But it wasn't long before old man Lucci was content just to show up every morning, sit at a table in the back of the restaurant dining room, and peel potatoes and cut peppers. There was an endless supply; Sal made sure of that.

"It keeps him quiet," he would say.

Like a machine, day in day out, he would cut, peel, and slice. After every few potatoes, he would stop to sample the wine. In the process, Sal's father got pickled more often than not and would fall asleep right there in the chair. His eyes would close and his jaw would fall open. He was an oddity to dining tourists, some of whom even snapped his picture.

When old man Lucci died right there at the table, no one knew for three hours. The waiters and busboys hustled back and forth the whole time, thinking he had dozed off, but this time it was more permanent. By the time the truth was finally discovered, his body was cold. Sal and the wait staff huddled around him. The general consensus was that he had stopped snoring an hour or two earlier—it was important to get the time right for future betting.

Sal called his best friend, in his first year of mortuary school and, like Sal, heir to a family business. "Frankie, I think there's something wrong with my father. I think he's dead."

"What do you know? You're not a doctor."

"You don't have to be a doctor. He ain't snoring so loud, for about an hour, and he's cold and purple."

Purple, sure sign; there's a reason it's the color of mourning, Frankie thought. "I'll be right over."

Frankie walked through the crowded dining room. Sal was standing in front of his father, shielding him from the view of his patrons. Old man Lucci was stiff in the chair. "Frankie, be nonchalant. Don't draw attention," Sal said as he continued to smile and wave to customers. "Phil, a bottle of wine to table six."

Frankie felt for a pulse on his neck. Ice cold, no pulse.

"Sal, I think he's dead."

"Why do you say that?"

"He's purple."

"I put a bag of ice on his lap," Sal said. "It seemed like the right thing to do."

"Christ, I'm glad you didn't put him in the walk-in box."

"What do we do now?" Sal asked.

"We need to call the police. This is an unattended death. They have to be notified."

"Christ, I can't have the cops running around in here. The joint will empty so fast your head will spin. Frankie, you got to help me. We're having a bang-up night. If I have to empty the dining room to bring a stretcher in, it's all over. Dad wouldn't want that."

Frankie agreed. Old man Lucci was all business.

"Is he under a doctor's care?"

"Yes, Dr. Copolla."

"Okay. We'll take him out and over to the funeral home. We can say he was having chest pains and I was going to drive you to the hospital, but it was too late."

"You're a genius. How do we get him out of here without putting the kaibosh on the night?"

Frankie commandeered Phil the waiter and together they draped old man Lucci between them.

"Sing something, Phil," Frankie said.

"Like what?"

"I don't know, a Louie Prima song might work."

"I don't know any Prima—"

"Sing *anything*," Frankie said.

Impatient, Sal started to sing: "Show me the way to go home, I'm tired and I want to go to bed. I had a little drink about an hour ago, and it went right to my head." They carried the old man out of the restaurant like a drunk. It worked so well that all the customers started singing along.

"Coming through," Frankie said as he walked through the crowded dining room.

"No problem, folks, too much homemade wine," Sal called out.

Frankie marveled that even as he was carrying his dead father out the door, Sal was touting his restaurant's virtues. Sal led the way out, conducting the impromptu singalong like an orchestra leader directing a conga line.

Once outside, Sal told Frankie, "Hey, I should get a discount on pop's embalming. He's already stewed."

"*I'm* supposed to make the jokes," said Frankie, "though not while I'm carrying a corpse."

Phil, Frankie, and Sal got old man Lucci into the funeral parlor, and Sal walked back to the restaurant, thinking that his father was really better off. If he knew what the changes in the neighborhood were doing to the business, it would kill him anyway. The restaurant business was going through a metamorphosis.

These days tourists came by the busload to see the authentic neighborhood hangouts where some of the most notorious wise guys had been whacked. Mulberry Street had become a caricature of its former self, a veritable Hollywood backlot. But fame was a double-edged sword. The more people that came, the more restaurants opened. It became a struggle to compete, as the newcomers undercut the prices of the older establishments.

Sal sat at a back table musing over the restaurant's history and going over the books. As he looked at the numbers, reality set in. Business was off, except for the boost brought by the feast— and that couldn't last forever. He needed to think of something. He racked his brain until it finally hit him—Comedy Night! He would get Frankie to do a show, put a trio in the corner, and give the people some live entertainment. It couldn't miss.

As he sat contemplating his newly hatched plan, he noticed Caterina Ballsziti enter the restaurant. He was honored.

She smiled as she approached his table. "I came to thank you for helping Frankie. On more than one occasion."

"Oh, no, I should thank you. Please, have a seat. Do you want something to eat? How about some baked ziti?"

It was Sal's specialty—ziti macaroni mixed with ricotta cheese and sauce, then baked in the oven with mozzarella, and topped off with toasted bread crumbs. He grabbed a towel and moved a huge rectangular pan from to counter to the table. Steam rose as he portioned the contents into small squares with a rubber spatula.

"No, thank you," she said, "I've already had lunch."

"Oh, weak stomach? I understand. Do you mind if I eat?" He didn't wait for an answer before he started to shovel macaroni into his dish.

She stared at him, an intense, uncomfortable stare.

Seeing the look she gave him, he explained, "I can eat this stuff cold if I have to. I love it and it's good for you, too. Puts lead in your pencil." He whistled as he clenched his fist and raised his stiff forearm.

She seemed embarrassed by the gesture. In silence, she watched him add hot pepper by the tablespoon.

"You sure you don't want some?" Sal asked.

"Positive." She sat across from him, trying not to be appalled by his gluttony.

"You know your father used to eat here all the time, but then he opened up his own joint on Grand Street." He lifted his glass, recalling those bountiful checks of yesteryear.

"I've come to talk about Frankie," said Caterina.

"My favorite subject." He couldn't help staring at her as he ate. He understood what Frankie saw in her: such poise, such demeanor. She was a class act. From her head to her designer shoes, she was the total package. And her eyes, they stared right through him.

As she looked around, she commented, "The restaurant looks good. I love the flowers on the table, nice touch. How's business?"

Forkful after forkful of baked ziti found its way into Sal's mouth. He paused just long enough between bites to answer. "Not like it used to be—too many joints, too many tourists. They don't like to spend." He rubbed his fingers together. "Cheap bastards!"

She blushed.

"Sorry, sorry," he said. "How about the bakery? Does your mother find business is off a little?"

"No, actually it's quite good. My grandmother owned the building and put it and the business in my name a couple of years ago."

Smart, he thought—their estate planning took RICO into consideration.

"Well, that's good. Things are not the same here, and not owning the building and all is a problem. Those bastard landlords want to quadruple my rent. They think I'm sitting on oil or gold or something."

"Well, the bakery's numbers are on the rise."

Of course they are, genius, he wanted to say. Every wise guy from all five boroughs is required to buy every birthday cake, communion cake, confirmation cake, wedding cake, and funeral cookie from you. Even diabetic dons have a standing weekly order just to brown-nose your old man. Add the fact that your father launders another half-million or so through the books, and it's no wonder you do well.

Caterina shifted in her seat. "Do you think Frankie's serious about this comedy business?"

Sal couldn't stop staring at her.

"I mean, I don't think there is a future in it. Do you?"

"You are absolutely right," he said. "There may not be, but

what of it? It's what he loves. I think he can do it. He thinks he can do it. That counts for something. But guarantees? There are no guarantees for success." That is, unless your bakery was connected to Johnny Ballsziti.

"So, you don't think it's a phase he's going through?"

"If it's a phase, he's been going through it since first grade. He was the class clown back then, too. I remember when the teacher asked 'Who shot President Lincoln?' Frankie jumped up and said, 'I'm Italian. I'll never tell.' His mind is always three steps ahead, thinking of some funny angle to anything anyone says. He writes a million funny thoughts on any paper he can get his hands on, cocktail napkins mostly."

She nodded as she absorbed what he was saying.

Sal asked, "Have you been talking to his father? You sound like his father."

"I don't know why you would say that. It's got nothing to do with his father. It's just that I need to know if this is something he is serious about or just a childish dream, a passing fancy."

Sal put his fork down and wiped his mouth. He thought it wise to count to ten and not blow up at her.

"Childish dream?" he repeated. "Have you ever seen him on stage? He's a natural-born comedian. He can't help who he is. He has no choice in the matter. Did you ever hear him up there?"

"No. I don't think my father would approve."

"Well, then, how could you know?" Sal resumed eating, his eyes still crossed in an effort to contain his anger. He pointed to a set of pictures on the wall. They were of Frankie, taken onstage at various clubs.

"Look at him in those shots. Look at his face. Have you ever seen him so happy?"

Her eyes scanned the wall of framed photos. "So you don't think this is pie in the sky?"

The word "pie" triggered something in Sal's head. He reached into the display case and took out the ricotta cheesecake and cut a slice. "Me," he said, "I think he has a real shot. I don't know what you consider pie in the sky. I only know that he enjoys making people laugh more than anything in the whole world, and he is good at it and that's what is important. Not tradition or his father or security or . . ." Not even you, he thought, but did not say.

"Or me?"

She was smart, too. Sal said, "I didn't say that."

"You didn't have to."

"Listen, Caterina, if you care for someone you can't make conditions. You should share his dream, not stomp on it. You can't change people. If he doesn't give this a shot, he will never be happy, and anyone with him will be miserable, too. He will always question himself and wonder what might have been if he had only tried. A guy has to listen to the voice inside him, not the voices trying to drown him out."

"I guess we all have a dream."

"Of course we do. Hey, listen. Although he doesn't know it yet, I'm going to get Frankie to do a little show here in a few nights. I hope it will be good for business. Why don't you come, too, as my guest? He'll be so happy if you're here."

"Okay, Sal. I will."

"Good. Then if you will excuse me, I have to go bang my meat." He picked up the scaloppini hammer and winked.

"By the way, Sal, does Frankie gamble?"

Sal thought for a moment. "Only every time he does his act," he said.

She nodded and said good-bye, leaning in to give him a kiss on his cheek. As her face came to close to his, he spotted it. Freckle, my ass.

It was just after midnight when Primo opened his eyes. He looked at his wife, who slept soundly beside him. He slid his feet to the floor and eased himself off the bed. He found his pants and shirt in the dark and slid his slippers on. Still, she slept. It was not unusual for him to get out of bed late at night, so if she awoke, she would think nothing of it. He often had to leave in the middle of the night for an untimely death that needed tending. As he paused by the dresser, moving statues that sat atop the bureau like chess pieces, Giovanna stirred slightly. Primo found one he wanted. She turned beneath the covers as he slipped it into his pocket and tiptoed quietly from the room.

Why Saint Valentine? he thought, a saint he revered for the commemoration of the massacre and the gang war it kicked off. Couldn't it be Saint Christopher or another saint that the Pope didn't like anymore?

He walked down the steps, opening the door that led to the back. Vines clung to the fences that separated the yards. There was a small garden behind Lucci's, and lounge chairs surrounded a picnic table behind Isabella's bakery. Underwear and women's personals, hanging on clotheslines strung from the fire escapes high above, swayed in the moonlight. Nothing dries like fresh air, he thought.

In the corner, by the weeping willow, Primo fell to his knees, removing a trowel from his pocket. Slowly, silently, he chipped away at the grass and earth. Eight inches, maybe ten, maybe a few more until he was satisfied. Only then did he remove the package from his pocket. He could hardly look Saint Valentine in the face. Surely his place in hell would be reserved on this evening. He tried to remember the instructions. Put the statue upside down? No, right side up, or facing the east, or facing Chicago?

He knelt again at the miniature grave and followed the instructions, as best he could recall them. He placed the statue face down in the sandy pit and covered the hole. That was the easy part, he thought. Standing now, he looked back toward the building and up to each window. No witnesses. His head raised, his zipper lowered, he stood in wait. No results. He was accustomed to his own bathroom. His nerves had the best of him. *Concentrate,* he told himself.

Seconds seemed like minutes. Finally, the stream started, puddling louder than he had hoped, shattering the silence of the courtyard. "Frankie, Frankie, Frankie," he whispered, as instructed. It lasted longer than usual. *Jesus, what did I drink?* A small puddle flowed from the mound and made its way toward his shoe. He lifted his foot up, out of the way. His shame grew even more pronounced when he noticed a stray dog staring at him, peeing against a tree, with one leg in the air. *What have I become?* The dog did not answer, except to cock its head, confused by this strange new breed. *What have I done to Saint Valentine? I gave the patron saint of love a golden shower. I am going to hell. Furthermore, I bet this will spoil the lawn out here.* A burnt patch of grass would be eternal testimony to his pagan stupidity.

Finally finished, he returned his unholy water-maker to its rightful place with a quick bounce and shake, all the while nervous, turning, checking to see if anyone was awake. God forbid anyone should see him in the middle of this ritual—worse yet, Pasquelena, Angelina, Zizilena, or Lena. He would have to kill himself; it would be the only way.

He patted the mound with the spade, packing the damp soil tight. Finished. Success. But there was a sound, a familiar liquid sound, from beyond the fence. He was devastated at the thought that someone had seen him. He pushed himself against the fence and stretched up on his tiptoes, until his eyes were just above the top. He found himself staring directly into another set of eyes. "Mrs. Ballsziti?"

She was flushed, and she stuttered a bit. "Yes, it's me. I'm bringing out the trash."

She turned and walked back toward her building. Only then did he notice the back of her dress caught up in the band of her panties.

It had to be a joint effort after all.

Frankie quickly found himself a fixture on the circuit. Whenever his face popped in the door, the house manager would move him to the head of the waiting list—if only to get that damned hearse out of sight. He would wait with other comics for a chance to try out a new joke, work on timing, practice his delivery. "You got five minutes," the gatekeeper would say. "Make the best of it." The bartenders soon knew him and would have a fresh cognac ready by the time he reached the stage. When they called his name, he would run up to the microphone, do his shtick, grab his drink, and then high-five his way out the door.

At midnight Frankie was at the Improv, where he worked on a bit about the funeral customs of different ethnic groups. "The Italians like to pass the house before heading to the cemetery; the Puerto Ricans drive through Taco Bell. The Italians take a picture of the deceased; the Irish take a picture posing with the deceased." After a few minutes, he made his way toward the door, stopping only to toss back his after-the-show drink. Then into the hearse and uptown, to try out a bit about the first American Indian funeral on Mulberry Street, describing his father in the ceremonial headdress and a campfire in the chapel. "I had to tell my father that they were half Italian, from the Wopaho tribe."

The connection between the two sides of Frankie's life—comedy and death—grew stronger as the line between laughing and crying continued to blur. The excitement of his nightly performances sent blood pumping through his veins, until morning, when he sent blood pumping from someone else's. Hit the stage, polish his lines; hit the embalming room, polish someone's nails. Back on stage, loosen up the crowd; in the embalming room, loosen rigor mortis. It was all coming together, like Sal said it would. He was a mild-mannered mortician by day and a cut-up comic by night.

But the stress was beginning to take its toll on him. He drank more than he'd ever drunk in his young life. He was tired, running on alcoholic fumes. The clubs all began to look the same: crowded bars, smoke-filled rooms jammed with people squeezing around small, circular tables, waitresses making their way through the crowd with the agility of ballet dancers. He was never sure what crowd he was playing for—the patrons began to look like the mourners, and the mourners like the patrons. His internal clock was jet-lagged. He started to confuse his lines.

Keeping up the schedule and the appearance of normalcy was not easy. He was tired but exhilarated. He was getting home at five a.m., sleeping for a few hours, and going to work with his father. It was catching up with him fast. Still, Frankie had stayed so busy he'd almost—*almost*—put the specter of laundered cash and mob recriminations out of his mind. They had been nearly erased by dreams of the lovely Caterina.

✝

Primo was tired the next morning—he'd had a long night. He dozed off on a couch in the funeral home, leaving Annunziata's payment still wrapped in aluminum foil lying on the desk in the office.

"Jesus, Dad, where did this come from?"

Primo was startled to find Frankie standing there in the office, still rubbing the sleep from his eyes and unfolding the foil from the package. He hadn't even heard him come down the stairs. "Mrs. Ballsziti paid her bill," he answered groggily.

"Dad, you can't deposit this!" said Frankie in alarm.

"What are you talking about?" said Primo without rousing from the couch. "I'll just deposit it a little each day. I got checks to cover."

"Dad, you don't understand. *You can't deposit this.* Promise me you will not deposit this until I tell you to."

Primo rolled back over and shut his eyes again. "Whatever you say," he promised. Within seconds he was snoring again.

Frankie wrapped the money back in the aluminum foil and tucked it behind the file cabinet. He'd think of something.

✝

"How's it going?" Sal asked Frankie that afternoon, hardly looking up. He was engrossed in unwrapping a package of sliced meat, handling it as if were pure gold, stripping away one layer of wax paper after another until the prize appeared. Gently, he peeled off a slice. "Frankie, do you know what this is?" He did not wait for an answer. "Prosciutto di Parma. Do you understand? If it isn't from Parma, it isn't prosciutto di Parma, simply the finest in the world. This is flown in once a week and goes to only the finest restaurants in the city. Luckily, my cousin at JFK looks out for me."

He held a thin, delicate slice of the cured meat over his head and lowered it into his waiting mouth. "Christ, that is good." He tried to hand a slice to Frankie, who refused it.

"What's wrong? You sick or something?" He studied him more closely. "You are sick. Whatever you do, you can't get sick now!"

"I haven't been sleeping. I'm tense, jumpy."

"Well, who wouldn't be, in your situation?"

"Thanks."

It had been one sleepless night after another and days filled with worry and looking over his shoulder. He thought about Eddie, and about Sal's warning. He wondered what Eddie had done to earn his wings, or what he would do. He remembered how viciously JB had slapped Eddie, how evil Johnny Ballsziti really was.

"I have these nightmares," Frankie said. "I'm lying on the embalming table in the funeral home, and the embalmer is ready to open my carotid artery. I open my eyes to ask if he wouldn't mind using my femoral, because I'm ticklish, and the embalmer is Johnny Ballsziti, and he has an assistant. It's Eddie. Eddie is handing JB the scalpel. I wake up in a cold sweat every time."

"You know, you could put a psychiatrist's kids through college. Maybe you should stop sleeping in a casket. Maybe that has something to do with your weird nightmares." Sal lowered another slice of prosciutto into his mouth. "Jeez, do we have different dreams. My idea of a nightmare is running out of virgin olive oil. That's what wakes me up in a cold sweat: no olive oil. Have a drink."

"No, I'm not in the mood."

"Christ, there *is* something wrong with you." He wanted to help but didn't know how. "Have some more prosciutto. It's from Parma."

Frankie put his head on the table.

Sal stopped chewing. "It's going to be all right, Frankie. Things have a way of working themselves out."

"By the time I come home, my father thinks I'm just getting up and the day with him begins. This morning I told him I'd gone out to Queens for a hospital removal and had a flat tire—I even rubbed some gunk from the wheel on my shirt for effect."

"Hang in there—just one more day."

"I'm all confused. Yesterday I began a funeral with 'Ladies

and Germs' instead of 'Dearly beloved,' and this morning, before leaving for church for a Mass of the Resurrection, I told everyone, 'Hey, thanks for being here, you all look great.'"

Sal laughed as he poured two glasses of wine.

Frankie continued. "The other day, I spent an hour with a woman who was picking out her husband's casket. She broke my balls for a whole hour. My mind was all over the place. I started thinking about a new bit. Isn't that crazy, to be thinking about comedy at a time like that?"

Sal said, "Maybe not. I'm telling you to go with it. It's what you know."

Still resistant, Frankie countered, "I don't think the funeral business exactly lends itself to humor."

Sal shrugged. "You sound like your father. Maybe you're right, but maybe not. It's a jungle out there. Everybody wants to be a comic. You gotta think of something to set yourself apart. The Peppermint Lounge gig is a big deal."

"I know, I know."

"You want to be ready for that. You don't want old jokes. Go with what you know. It's new; and it's definitely different."

With his big night approaching, Frankie decided Sal was right—his humor had to come from his life experience. He began to put his thoughts on paper, starting with the widow who didn't know her husband's real name. "Bugsy," she told him. "Everybody called him Bugsy." He imagined a prayer card with the name Bugsy Marotta. Could work, could be funny. He also remembered the Jewish wife of a Catholic man who wanted a traditional church funeral. She knew nothing about the Mass and asked Frankie to pick out the hymns. He thought about the word "hymns." Why weren't they called "hers"? Was the church sexist?

He thought about the bizarre requests people have: the items they wanted to put in the casket; the things people said to survivors when they were nervous. He had had to suppress a laugh more than once. Surely there was a routine here, a treasure trove of material as he thought about it now. The incident with Mrs. DiCicci sealed the deal for him.

It had been a relatively normal funeral arrangement until the bereaved Mrs. DiCicci reached into her handbag and pulled out what appeared to be a dead rat.

"Don't forget this. My husband always wore it. He wouldn't be caught dead without it."

She pushed the brownish hairpiece toward Frankie, who squeamishly accepted it. "But . . . he's already dead."

"Everybody know's he dead. No one knows he was bald."

Placing the toupee had been an agonizing task.

"Turn it to the left," Primo suggested.

Frankie turned it.

"More," Primo said.

Frankie kept turning, first clockwise, then counterclockwise.

"Dad, maybe she gave us the wrong one."

Primo was stymied. He tried turning the hairpiece himself, and it came down over Mr. DiCicci's nose. "Go get Rocco the barber in here. He'll know how to fix it."

Frankie couldn't believe his ears. "Rocco? Are you serious? He's so afraid of the dead, he don't even like to cut *your* hair. He's a nervous wreck when you go for a trim." Rocco did find cutting the undertaker's hair difficult—with one hand on the scissors, the other on his balls.

"Get him," Primo said again. "Don't take no for an answer."

Frankie ran up Grand Street to Rocco's Barber Shop. Rocco gave him a nod as he hovered over a soaped-faced man reclined in the chair. Frankie watched as he skillfully ran a straight-edged razor along the man's throat. A few customers looked up when Frankie entered, but went back to reading their newspapers, nonchalantly attending to their balls.

I saw that, Frankie thought.

Rocco moved the razor delicately down the man's chin until Frankie approached and whispered in his ear, "Your services are needed at the funeral home. We're having a problem with Mr. DiCicci's wig."

Suddenly, a drop of blood appeared on the man's face, courtesy of Rocco's shaking hand.

"Christ!" The customer jumped out of the chair.

The sight of blood made Rocco dizzy. He was disoriented. Frankie grabbed a bottle of Bay Rum and waved it under Rocco's nose. Then he handed the bleeding customer a towel. "Put pressure on it." The blood drained from Rocco's face and the customer's neck at the same pace.

"Are you frigga' crazy?" exclaimed Rocco. "I'm no can do. Tell your father he's a crazy sonofabitch. I no can do."

"But Rocco, you took care of Mr. DiCicci's wig when he was alive."

"Ah," Rocco screamed, "that's the important word, 'alive.' I'm no touching him now."

"Rocco, I have to get this done. I've got appointments tonight. Now come with me."

He dragged Rocco from the barbershop, tunic and all, down the block and into the funeral home. Rocco would not cooperate. He fought every step forward with a step back. Once they reached the funeral home door, Primo was able to help pull him in.

"Get in here, you *gaga sotto*." Shit pants. They dragged Rocco, kicking and screaming, to the casket. He was in shock. Primo gave him a gentle slap across the cheek.

"Just fix the hair," he said. Primo slapped him again, a little harder. Then again, harder still.

"Dad, he can't help us if you knock him out."

"Rocco, just fix the friggin' hair, you *mammalucca*," Primo repeated. He shoved the reluctant barber toward the body. Sweat poured out of Rocco's every pore. His knees buckled. With his eyes closed, Rocco placed his hands on Mr. DiCicci's head and maneuvered the hairpiece until it sat perfectly upon the dead man's skull.

"That's it!" Primo yelled. "You did it."

Rocco scurried out the door. "Leave me alone! And find a new barber. You're a crazy bastard!"

"He's a little superstitious," Primo said.

"You think?" Frankie thought about it. If that wasn't funny, there was no funny.

†

Absorbed in trying out one of her grandmother's recipes, Caterina heard a sudden commotion at the entrance as her mother tried to prevent a delivery. The two men insisted that they had the right address, but Annunziata's considerable frame blocked the double doors.

"Mama, it's okay. I bought it. Let them in."

The deliverymen were relieved. They hoisted the awkward machine and maneuvered it into the shop as Caterina directed them to a spot behind the counter.

The cat hissed and ran for the kitchen as the deliverymen approached.

"Place it right here, near the register," Caterina said.

Annunziata was confused. "What is this?"

"Watch, Mama, just watch."

For twenty minutes the men assembled the contraption under Annunziata's watchful eyes.

"Now look, Mama." Caterina filled a box with pastries. She folded a sheet of the Isabella wrapping paper around the box, then placed it on the center of the new piece of equipment. Magically, automatically, string encircled the box and tied a knot.

"You see, Mama, this will save time."

"Save time for what? Where am I going?"

Good point, Caterina conceded. She gave the newly packaged pastry to the deliverymen, with her thanks.

"You'll get used to it, Mama."

"I no think so. What did this cost?"

"It's not what it cost, Mama. It's what it saves."

"A little education is a dangerous thing," Annunziata said.

"It's just the beginning, Mama."

It took hours before Annunziata was able to operate the new machine without getting her hand or fingers tied to the box. There was no shortage of profanities in the process. Progress came at a price.

✝

Frankie's first stop on Friday night was the Comedy Shop, then on to the Improv, then to Asti's; east side, west side, anywhere there was an open mic night—same lines, new audience.

"A terrible thing happened in a nursing home. The staff mixed up the Poli-Grip with the Preparation H." *Wait for it, wait!* "Now all their gums are shrinking and their rectums are stuck together." *Funny, but I should have waited longer. I stepped on it.*

Then back into the hearse to hurry across town to the next stop to try the same line again. This time, he would switch things and hold that punch line a little longer— " . . . and their gums are shrinking!" Ba-da-bump. There, that was better. It worked. Run back to the car, and over to another bar to try it again, then out the door to the next club until the last patron paid the last check after hearing the last laugh of the night. But Frankie knew that even though he was pretty good, so were the dozens of other comics, male and female, who went on stage before and after him. They all thought they were funny, too.

It was midnight when he finally made it to Dangerfield's. With the hearse double-parked on First Avenue, he elbowed his way into the popular Manhattan night spot. No sooner did the bartender see him enter than his drink was ready at the counter. The main show was over, the dining room was clearing out, and the bar was crammed with people.

"Boy, do I need this."

"Drink up," the man said.

"You think I can do a set?" Frankie asked.

"I don't think it should be a problem; Rodney gets a kick out of you."

The dining room was nearly empty except for a couple of tables. After a few minutes, the ever-jovial host gave the nod and introduced him.

"Ladies and gentlemen," Dangerfield said as he tugged at his shirt collar, "the laughing undertaker! He'll make you die laughing. Here's Frankie Grace, the kid's a real deadbeat." He looked at

Frankie. "You'd better give me a discount."

The introduction clicked with Frankie. Yes, that was it! Suddenly he felt smooth as glass, right at home, as surveyed the audience, a handful of stragglers.

"Dearly beloved," he began. It got a laugh. "Excuse me folks, I'm not used to working before a live audience."

Laugh, laugh, then some more laughs. Getting up his courage, he addressed the club's owner: "I promise you a discount, Mr. Dangerfield, but you'll never know if I honor it." People were curious. Eyes turned in his direction.

Turning again to Dangerfield, Frankie offered, "Rodney, thanks for the opportunity. Hey, you look great, nice coloring, very natural." Laughter swept across the room as Rodney's body convulsed. "Are these your die-hard fans?" Frankie asked. "They already seem pickled to me."

"Hey," a heckler yelled, "are you really an undertaker? You're not getting me. I want to be cremated."

Frankie looked straight at the man. "You can't be cremated," he shot back. "Shit don't burn."

Laughter erupted across the room. People who had been standing idly at the bar flooded into the room, filling up the seats. *Go with it,* Frankie thought. *Just talk about your day job.* He started again. "I had a rough day. I need a drink." He got one. "This woman looked at her husband in the casket and said, 'That's not his nose.' I said, 'Lady, if we could change noses, do you think I'd be wearing this one?'" The crowd roared. The audience was eating it up.

"The other day, I met with a woman to pick out a casket. Jesus, as she walked around the room, from one casket to another, I felt like the host of a weird game show—Let's Make a Wake. Okay, Mrs. F., now for that big decision. Do you want to keep the box, or do you want to go for what's behind door number three? You want to keep the box? Okay, Johnny Jacobs, open it up; let's see what she's won. It's your husband! He died hours ago in Philadelphia. We flew him back here via Eastern Airlines—Eastern, When You Need Care in the Air. While in New York, your husband will be staying at the fashionable, luxurious Y. U. Ballin Funeral Home.

Try Calling Ballin, When Someone Has Fallen. Notice the fine crushed-velvet interior on the hand-rubbed mahogany casket. His wardrobe was furnished by Botany 500—Botany, for that natural, not stiff, look—making the total value of this funeral thirty-eight hundred dollars, not including headstone or perpetual care. Thank you for helping us playyyy . . . Let's Make a Wake!"

The patrons loved it, beyond even his wildest dreams.

He was on stage a full two hours at Dangerfield's, ad libbing about nothing more than his normal day at the funeral home. He felt like he could have stayed up there forever, talking about wakes, and people, and crazy requests. He looked at his watch. *Christ, the funeral.*

"So folks, if you're ever on Mulberry Street, stop by the funeral home for a cold one. I gotta go. I have a funeral in a few hours, and I don't want to mess it up. It took me hours to get this guy's wig to stay in place, and his wife didn't know how to thank me. She wanted to pay me extra, but I said, 'Hey, what can I charge for a nail?'"

He had never heard such howling.

He rushed off the stage with a quick parting line. "Good night. God bless. I'll see you on the way out."

They laughed at that, too. He stopped by the phone and called his best friend. "Sal, you were right. I found it. I found my hook."

Chapter 18

It was nearly six in the morning when Frankie tiptoed into his room. It had been a long night with more than a few drinks.

Primo opened the door of his bedroom just as Frankie had removed his tux and changed into street clothes. "Ah, you're up early," he said to his son.

"Uh, yes," Frankie said. "I wanted to get a head start cleaning the prep room."

"Don't worry about that now. Come with me. We have time before the funeral. I want to show you something."

Frankie walked along like a zombie, accompanying his father out to the parked hearse. Frankie was grateful that Primo didn't notice the engine was warm. They rode quietly in the front seat as Primo made his way through the narrow streets toward the Brooklyn Battery Tunnel.

"Where are we going?"

"Brooklyn," Primo said. "I want to show you a surprise."

He put the radio on—string music, orchestra, Mantovani. Music to Commit Suicide By, Frankie labeled it. Still, there was something about having his father's undivided attention, on a crisp fall morning, that opened up his amiable curiosity.

"Dad, tell me about Mr. Fontana, Eddie's father."

Primo looked over at his son. "What do you want to know?"

"The story, what happened?"

"No one knows the real story, only bits and pieces and half-truths and rumors. Far as I can tell, Fontana was the wheel man, while JB went into the jewelry store. It was supposed to be empty, but it wasn't. Shots were fired and a private guard was killed. Turns out the poor guy was an off-duty police officer trying to make ends meet. JB hightailed it, leaving Fontana in the car. He was nabbed. The DA would have gone for life if he'd given up his accomplice, but he never did. So as far as the law was concerned, Fontana might as well have pulled the trigger. The rest is history. Why do you want to know?"

"Just curious," he answered. "Do you think Eddie knows the truth?"

"I can't begin to guess what Eddie knows or doesn't know, or better yet, what he understands or doesn't understand."

Frankie nodded. He settled back. "Pop, how did the ball scratching start? You see it, too. People see us and they scratch their balls."

"It's not us. It's what they think we represent."

"Huh?"

"You see, to them, you represent death. So, what's the opposite of death?"

"Life."

"Right, and where does life begin?"

"In the womb?"

"No, it begins in the balls."

"Ah," Frankie said, "life begins in the balls, not the womb." It made sense. "So keep your hand on the source of life when in the presence of death."

"Sure."

"So, it has nothing to do with a Pope who said to touch iron in the face of danger or fear and you will draw strength from it."

"What's iron got to do with balls?"

Good point, Frankie thought. "Eddie told me when faced with danger or fear or imminent harm, you should grab your testicles and you'll be protected."

"I never heard that one, and in Eddie's case I think it's just a permanent case of jock itch."

"Good . . . I don't think I would want to be caught holding my balls if I was about to be killed. It wouldn't make a good picture." Getting killed was something Frankie had found himself imagining these days a lot more than he wanted to.

Primo said, "Well, our people do a lot of crazy things, have lots of superstitions. Still, you should take what Eddie tells you with a grain of salt. He's not the best authority to interpret papal encyclicals."

Another good point, Frankie conceded.

Primo drove along the Prospect Expressway as Frankie thought about the plausibility of Primo's ball-scratching explanation. He was doing the same thing, in a way, with his comedy. When faced with death, cling to life; when faced with sadness, cling to humor. It validated his emerging comedic voice.

"What was Grandpa like?" Frankie asked.

"Ah, he was something. You know, in Italy, he was a cabinet-maker. That's how it all started. At first, when someone died, the family would call for him, and he would go to the house with the box. Later, they started asking him to put the body into the box. Before long he was cleaning, shaving, and dressing the dead, too."

"So, he was a full-service cabinetmaker," Frankie observed. "He came to America and followed his craft to its natural progression. A cabinetmaker, huh?"

"Yes, and wakes were held in the house in his day. I used to help him carry dozens of chairs up flights of steps. For every dozen I carried up, the family would return eleven. We've got folding chairs all over the neighborhood. I also helped carry the portable embalming table into the apartment. He would embalm right in the bedroom and drain the blood into wine gallons. *You* got it easy."

"Drained the blood into wine gallons? Lovely."

Frankie thought about filling Coke bottles with blood, covering them with aluminum foil, and having Sal sell it to his newfound clientele. They would probably love it. He could hear the amateur sommeliers now: what body, what color, great legs, rich, great year. If they only knew. He laughed to himself.

"Yep," Primo continued, "then I'd seal the wine bottle and put it in the bottom of the casket. The wake was held right there, in the apartment. I was just a boy then, six or seven."

Frankie felt sorry for his father. By an accident of birth, his childhood memories were of sealing blood in bottles. His own youthful memories were not much better. "Not much room in the apartments for a wake."

"Exactly. That's how the funeral home evolved. But Frankie, a funeral home is more than a room with chairs: it's the people who work there, the people who get up in the middle of the night to help someone, the people who care for other people. That's what makes a funeral home."

Frankie did not hear the last part of his father's answer. He was sound asleep. He dreamed that he and Sal were in the restaurant's wine cellar. The shelves collapsed and all the wine bottles crashed to the floor. The wine flowed toward them and they sucked it up as fast as they could. But it wasn't wine—the wine had turned to blood and started filling up the restaurant's basement and overflowing into the basement of the funeral home. They were drowning in blood. Father Colapetra appeared and fought with Frankie's grandfather, Francesco, who had jumped out of his portrait. Francesco started to mop the floor as a little boy squeezed the mop's contents back into the wine bottles. "Fifty-one," the little boy said. "A good year, great vintage."

"No," Colapetra protested, "only I can do that. Only I can turn wine to blood."

The car slowed down, and Frankie shook off the daze. The hearse entered the gates of the Greenwood Cemetery in Brooklyn. Primo turned off the radio, opened the windows, and took a deep breath. The car slowed to a crawl.

"Wake up, Frankie." Primo shook his arm.

Frankie saw trees and grass and was disoriented. "Where the hell are we?"

"Almost home," Primo answered. He took a deep breath. "Breathe," he said. "Ah, fresh air."

"Home? Have I died? This doesn't look like Mulberry Street."

A quick series of turns took them deep into the cemetery grounds. There was little pedestrian traffic on a Saturday morning. *We drove out here for a busman's holiday?* Frankie thought.

"Isn't this beautiful?" Primo asked. He drew in another long breath. "Fresh air," he said. "It's good to get out of the city once in a while."

Your ideas about spending quality time with me need work, Frankie thought.

"Take a look at these trees; they must be hundreds of years old."

"At least," said Frankie, humoring him. He stared out the window.

Primo slowed the hearse as he circled a section of the cemetery blanketed with mausoleums. "Some pretty famous people here," he said. "Anastasia, Costello."

"Lou?" Frankie asked.

"Jeez, do you know what something like that costs?" Primo asked, marveling at a granite structure that looked like a small house. It had ornate stained glass windows and intricate designs carved into the granite.

"Big money," replied Frankie. "Sleeps at least ten in there."

"Oh, at least; probably a hundred thousand," his father mused, ignoring Frankie's wisecrack. "Beautiful, just beautiful." He kept driving down the narrow, tree-lined paths. "I like this time of year. The leaves are turning. Look at those colors. And look there, see that lake? It's the biggest lake in New York City, right here in the cemetery. There are five lakes in this place. Big, huh?"

Frankie nodded. He looked over into the back of the hearse, hoping not to find fishing rods.

The journey continued. A lesser man would have been lost by now, but Primo knew each bend in the road, each intersection. He knew where he was and where he was going. They were silent for a while, just driving, taking in the sights. "Look at some of the dates on these stones," he said. "Jesus!" He read some aloud. "1812–1849; 1837–1912. Wow, that was a long life in those days." He paused by stone after stone, reading each date as if he were looking for a pattern that might offer him some insight to life, but there was none to be found. Finally, Frankie recognized the road back to the entrance gate. It was there that his father pulled over to the side of the lane. "We're here," he said and jumped out of the car. Frankie followed and stood alongside his father, who asked, "Well, what do you think?"

"About?"

Primo spread his arms wide, tracing the boundaries of a plot of land, and pointed to a twelve-foot granite stone with the name GRACE inscribed on it.

"It's ours. I bought it."

Frankie was stunned. "We could play handball on that thing."

Primo continued, "It's our burial plot, and I put your name on the deed, too. It wasn't easy, either. This section was sold out years ago. This was a resale; the family was ready to sell it back to the cemetery, but I stepped in."

"Why?" Frankie asked. "Did they decide to live?"

"Stop with the jokes, already. We can fit ten people here." Primo had become Willy Loman. "I got sixteen feet of frontage. We got plenty of room for ten here." He started walking off the perimeter. "It's the only piece of land we own outright. No mortgage, I paid them cash."

"Are you all right, Dad?" Frankie had to ask.

"Of course, never better. I just want to make things go easier for you, take care of as much as I can." He walked up to the stone. He took a can of spray cleaner and a rag from his pocket and began to polish the granite. "Barre gray, all polished. That says class, your mother likes that."

Great, give her something else to clean. She'll probably come here twice a week to mow the lawn.

Beneath the larger letters were engraved two more lines: "PRIMO born 1924–", and alongside, "GIOVANNA born 1925–".

"You only have to put the last date in. I did as much as I could for you."

Because you worried if left to me you might have an unmarked grave? "Thanks, Dad."

"This fits ten people," Primo reiterated.

Twenty if we stand them up, he thought. "Who are they?" *Please, not the Lenas too.*

Primo stopped pacing and held up his hands, counting on his fingers. "There's me, your mother, you, your wife and children. At least we'll have elbow room."

Jeez, Frankie thought. *I'm not even married, and he has my kids buried—all six of them. This is a warped idea of family planning.*

"This way we can all be together," said Primo. "Great spot, huh? Big. Look at the view."

Frankie listened. *Maybe we can put in a sausage concession,* he wanted to say. *Looks like a busy corner.*

"And we are right by the gate, so when you come in with a funeral, you can say hello. You can't miss me. You don't even have to get out of the car if it's raining!"

"Right."

"It's about planning, son. I thought about the cemetery in the Bronx, but the neighborhood has gone to the dogs. The Puerto Ricans actually picnic on the cemetery grounds. The place is full of beer cans." He walked around the plot, proud of his choice. "They wanted me to buy a plot over there." He pointed over a ridge. "But it was too close to the lake; and with your mother's rheumatism and all, I just figured this was better."

"Good thinking; can't be too careful." *Who knows how close a drugstore is up there?*

"I thought about St. John's, but too many mobsters. There are more wise guys there than in Sing Sing. Same with Calvary. I lived with those *pezzonovanti* enough." He looked around and took a deep, satisfied breath. "No, I made the right choice. I just wanted you to know—in case you worried about these things. You see, Frankie, it's all about having a life plan. Now, you should know I left all my instructions in a file, and there is a box in the basement behind the file cabinet. Don't open it until I'm dead. It's a surprise."

The surreal conversation left Frankie confused, wondering if he should be looking forward to opening that surprise soon. "Dad, are you sure you're all right? Are you feeling well?"

"Fine, I'm fine." He looked at his watch. "We'd better get back."

The ride back to Manhattan was quiet. Each man was deep in his own thoughts, each worrying about the future. Primo wondered if his son would ever settle down and take life seriously, while Frankie thought about a wife and six children—and about Tony Branca and Mr. Vitagliano and the crimes he had committed, and the crimes still to come.

As Mrs. DiCicci sobbed at the casket, Frankie prayed, ending with, "Eternal rest grant unto him, and may perpetual light shine upon him."

"His hair looks good," she remarked. "He looks handsome."

Another satisfied customer, Frankie thought.

Afterward Frankie stopped in at Lucci's for a late lunch. He handed Sal a loosely packaged assortment of leftover flowers.

Sal took the bundle, unwrapped it, and fingered through the colorful bouquet. "It's about time," he said. "Roses, tulips, daisies, gladiolas, gladiolas, and more gladiolas." He looked at Frankie. "Why do florists always use gladiolas in funeral pieces?"

"Maybe they should be called *sad*iolas. Or, to be more precise, *sadioli,*" Frankie offered.

Sal handed him a cocktail napkin and Frankie jotted down the line. "No orchids?" Sal complained. "Too bad."

Frankie only shrugged. Sal cut the stems down to fit the squat green vases. Without a word, the waiters grabbed the centerpieces and placed them on the tables.

"You don't look so hot," Sal noticed. "Hey, c'mon, tonight's the big night. You gotta be at the top of your game. How did it go last night?"

"It's hard to explain. Dangerfield introduced me as the laughing undertaker, and suddenly it hit me. A few people stopped talking and drinking and started paying attention. So, I ran with it. Two hours. I just let it all hang out. Morbid was funny, what a world!"

"I could have told you that," Sal said. "But you look like shit."

"Gee, thanks. I'm running myself ragged, drinking and laughing all night; crying, praying, and directing funerals all day. I just spent an hour trying to get this one guy's jacket on. I tell the family to bring a nice suit, and they bring the tux he wore at his wedding thirty years ago. Like, what are they thinking?"

"Hey, that could be funny, too," Sal said. "Turn it into something good. Work with it."

"You think?"

"Of course. You said you found your hook, so run with it. You could easily do ten minutes on trying to dress a guy in a suit that doesn't fit. Can't you imagine the visual?—you stumbling around stage like a stiff wearing a straitjacket?"

Frankie imitated the corpse. Sal laughed as Frankie ad-libbed. "His suit is too tight. He doesn't look comfortable. Like, I want to ask these folks, 'When was the last time he wore it? His confirmation?'"

Sal laughed. "Yeah, that's good. You want to be different than the other jamokes waiting to get on stage? I told you, go with what you know. You don't see me trying to cook Chinese food, do you? I cook what I know." He paused. "Listen, I got some good news. I met with Caterina yesterday. She is beautiful, though perhaps not perfect . . . "

"What do you mean, not perfect?"

"Never mind. She asked me if you gamble. Anyway, I invited her to your show next Monday, and she said yes."

"Gamble? My next show? What are you talking about?"

"You know, the pre-whack propaganda I warned you about."

"Thanks. And what show?"

"Next Monday night—I have a trio coming. I'm setting them up in the corner and I thought you could do an hour or so. I might even sing." He started in: *"The cement is there, for the weight, babe . . . "*

"Spare me, please."

"Listen Frankie, I got to do something to help the register once the feast is over. I got two choices. I even thought about staging a hit."

"Staging a hit?" Frankie asked.

"Yeah, yeah, it's simple. You know, I fire a few bullets through the window late at night, when people are eating. There's a mad rush for people to get out; they knock over the tables. Someone reports 'shots fired'; the cops come, question me. I don't answer, like I don't want to squeal; and it hits the papers that there was an attempt on a mobster at Lucci's, and the owner is uncooperative. The advertising would be phenomenal. I thought I could pull that off. I'd just play dumb."

You wouldn't be playing, thought Frankie. "Sal, where do you get these ideas? Are you nuts? And how can I do a show here, next door to the funeral home—next door to my father?"

"I thought about that. Your father goes to sleep early. We do the show late. Simple."

"Yes, you are."

While they discussed the details, Eddie walked through the door. Sal quickly nixed the conversation on the staged hit and made his way to the kitchen.

"That sonofabitch Keats never sleeps," Eddie said.

"You're telling me. He's everywhere I go," Frankie responded. In a strange way though, Frankie felt safe knowing that Roscoe Keats was hanging around outside the restaurant. Keats was just strolling among the booths, sampling a calzone, watching, listening, smiling every now and then at some passerby. Eddie was not as comforted.

Just then, Sal came out of the kitchen yelling in agony. His face was red and he was gasping for air.

Eddie and Frankie rushed to his side. "Sal, hey, Sal, what is it? What's wrong?"

He was clutching his throat, sticking out his tongue, pointing to it. He rushed to the sink behind the bar and stuffed ice into his mouth.

When he was able to talk, he said in a hoarse, scratchy voice, "Try those hot peppers, they're great."

The guilty dish of long fried peppers gave off an aroma that made their eyes water.

"No thanks," Eddie said, eyeing the deadly dish. "If they burn going in, they have to burn coming out."

Sal drank a bottle of water and ate a loaf of bread to cleanse his palate.

"Why do you eat those things?" Frankie wanted to know.

Sal's voice was strained. "They put lead . . . lead . . . "

"I know, I know. Lead in your pencil."

Eddie looked out the window. Keats was still there. "Let's be careful, guys. For all I know, that guy is a lip reader." He turned his back to the door and looked straight at Frankie. "Mr. Vitagliano is ready to come home. It took a while to find an Italian undertaker JB could work with, but he did. Anyway, a guy who does what you do here, but only over there, will be in touch."

"I think I understood that, but can you say it again?"

Eddie spoke more deliberately. "Our friend says you will receive a call from the guy over there, who does what you do, so you can do what you do over here, after he does what he does over there."

"I think I understand less."

Sal poured a round of cognac into Frankie's glass. It quickly disappeared. He poured another.

"The only thing is," Eddie continued, "it's like a different time over there, and they don't work all day like we do here. So, the call may come at some other time of the normal day."

"What if he speaks Italian?" Sal asked.

Frankie nodded. "That's a good question. How am I supposed to communicate?"

"Hey, I don't have all the answers," Eddie said. "Use your hands. That's how we talk."

"Eddie, is everything all right?" asked Sal.

"Sure it is." He paused. "Sure it is. Hey, see you at the show tonight. And, um . . . break a leg."

"Gee, thanks, Eddie," said Sal and Frankie in unison.

Chapter 19

With the help of Frankie's yearbook, Sal had worked the phone all week. It paid off in spades.

The traffic jam on 45th Street was legendary—complete gridlock. For Frankie's opening night at the Peppermint Lounge, his former classmates showed up from all across the five boroughs, as well as six friends from New Jersey, two from Philadelphia, and one from Maine, to see the show. And they, in turn, had called their friends.

It was Sal who had come up with the stunt. Strung along 45th, completely blocking traffic and effectively putting a stranglehold on pedestrian and vehicular traffic alike, were the conveyances he had suggested they drive—their funeral hearses. There were scores of black hearses, some gray ones, some white ones, two burgundy ones, and even a bright red number from Diaz Funeral Home in Spanish Harlem. The police were livid, ticketing every double-parked vehicle, as well as those parked on the sidewalk. Sal and Little Anthony stood out front surveying the street scene, plump cigars hanging from their lips. Little Anthony was thrilled, and Sal was practically busting his buttons, proud of his accomplishment.

It was a mortuary class reunion mixed with the usual Saturday night array of dons and their dollies, wannabes, queen bees, and could-have-beens. It was standing room only. JB sat at a back table with his longtime *coumare*, surrounded by the Bulls and their broads. Eddie sat close by with Marie.

The announcer introduced him the way Sal had suggested, "Ladies and gentlemen, a man with buried talent, the laughing undertaker—Frankie Grace!"

Tuxedoed and hyped up, Frankie bounded onto the stage. "Hey, folks, excuse me if I'm a bit nervous. I'm not used to talking to a live audience." It was a good start. His confidence growing with each laugh, he segued from one topic to another, starting slow and building the routine, brick by brick. The first brick was his family.

"My mother is a cleaning fanatic. All day long she cleans the house, mops, and vacuums. My father got her an extension cord, just to get her out of the house. Now, she's vacuuming our neighbor's house. If I want to find my mother, I just follow the cord."

The room was with him. Even the Bulls giggled.

Frankie continued, "She cleans the windows so good, we kill six pigeons a day. They fly into the window, thinking nothing is there. There's a ton of feathers on the sidewalk. We're being investigated by the Audubon Society."

He paused, just the right amount of time.

"I tell you folks, it's not easy. Ever notice Italian people have like a million statutes on the bureau? Every one of them is broken. Like, is there a statue repair place in heaven? There ought to be. And, there's a statue for every need. Lose something, pray to St. Anthony. A woman told me, if you want to sell your house, you bury a statue of St. Joseph upside down on the lawn. I asked what happens if you bury him right side up. She says, 'You'll sell your neighbor's house.'"

His timing was perfect. He waited for the laughter to just about subside before beginning again.

"And jeez, how do you get rid of roaches? Please let my mother know. You know there are all types of roaches: Italian, Jewish, Chinese. You can always tell an Italian roach. He usually hangs out on the corner—corner of the washing machine, corner of the stove, most times with a policy sheet in his hand. A Jewish roach you usually find by your underwear. You open the drawer and he says, 'I'll let you have a dozen for a steal.' There are black roaches.

You open your cabinet, you don't see nothing, but you hear a lot of tap-dancing. And then there are Polish roaches. They think they're ants."

Bull was choking with laughter. So much so, his shirt bunched up. Shameless, he stood up and began to tuck it in.

Frankie caught it.

"Hey, what the hell are you doing? The men's room is over there. Must you show everyone your shortcomings?"

He was on a roll, and Bull was his new foil. Damn the consequences, full steam ahead.

"What was that? You're supposed to throw the condom away after you use it."

"Folks," he told the crowd, "I want to introduce you to this guy. Hey, did you get here in a mafia car? You know what that is, folks? A mafia car—when you open the hood, there's another hood inside. Hey, I just figured out why the mob shoots people in seafood restaurants—the witnesses clam up. Hey fellas, it's a coat check room, not a gun check room."

The laughs overshadowed JB's more somber expression.

Undaunted, Frankie pointed to both Bulls. "You know, folks, these guys were members of the fencing team in high school. They used to sell stolen property."

The room roared with laughter. He stayed with it.

"Can you imagine trying to get these guys into a casket? I'd have to lay them sideways. I mean, it would be like closing over-packed luggage. I'd have to sit on the lid."

The visual worked.

"It's good we can laugh," Frankie said. "Life is short. Believe me, I know. Working in a funeral home all day teaches me that much. Ever notice how people attending a wake suddenly become morons who don't know how to talk? I mean, people say the stupidest things at wakes because they don't know what to say. 'Was he sick?' No, he was in great health. 'Will you be selling his car?' I mean, come on now. One time a man was standing at his mother-in-law's casket. His wife was screaming, 'That's not my mother, it doesn't look like her.' The guy tells her, 'It's her, dear, you're just not used to seeing her with her mouth closed.'"

He took a quick sip of water and continued. "Then people want to start putting things in the casket: clothes, wine, newspapers, guns, food. You have no idea. Like, where's he going, on a safari, a camping trip? Someone dies, and it's time to clean out the attic: put this in the casket, put that in the casket. I had to tell one woman that if we put anything else in your husband's casket, we'd have to take *him* out to make room. Jeez!"

Frankie moved on to his "That's not his nose" and "Let's Make a Wake" routines. His new material cracked up the whole crowd.

"I was making funeral arrangements with a woman. I asked what her husband did for a living. She said, 'He worked for the railroad.' I said, 'He did?' like I'm surprised. Not many Italians work for the railroad. She told me that every morning when he left the house he said, 'I'm going to the track today.'"

People applauded at that one. Frankie kept going. "Christ, the other day a casket was being carried up the church steps. It was so heavy, it slipped off the pallbearer's shoulders and down the church steps and rolled between the hearse and limousine. Then it kicked into second gear and somewhere along Baxter Street, it hit a hydrant, made a left onto Mulberry, and slid into the drug store. It hit the counter, the lid popped open, and the man got up and asked the druggist, 'Do you have anything to stop this coffin?'"

That line brought down the house. But he had more. "I tell you, folks, you haven't lived until you've been laid in a hearse. That's right, sex in a hearse. It's an undertaker's version of the mile-high club. Do you know how difficult it is to have sex in a hearse? The girl keeps rolling away from you. The other day, I had a funeral mass for a man who was half Jewish, half Catholic. The organist played *Oy vay Maria*. A month ago I buried a guy who died while he was having sex. He didn't know if he was coming or going."

As the jokes went on, the laughs kept coming. "Hey, do you like my tie?" Frankie pointed to it. "Last week a family came in to make funeral arrangements. They brought two ties and told me to choose one. I chose this one. Last week a wise guy told me he didn't want bugs in his casket. I told him I'd put a can of Raid in there with him."

His lines were crisp, his timing sharp. His funeral director friends were enjoying every minute of it, and Little Anthony was happy, too. The register was ringing off the wall.

He finished his stint with, "I'll see you on the way out," and, "If you're in the neighborhood, stop in for a cold one."

After two curtain calls, Frankie joined the fun at the bar. He was in his glory, getting hugged, high-fived, and slapped on the back. As he signed an autograph, someone tapped him on the shoulder. Without turning he said, "I'll get to you in a minute, champ." The unknown admirer tapped again. "Hold it chief," he said, as he scribbled his signature. Finally, he turned to see Johnny Ballsziti, who looked anything but happy.

"Hey, *capo tosta*, thickhead. What's the matter with you?"

Frankie didn't understand; he stood frozen. "You doing jokes about guys that get shot in seafood restaurants, filled with shells, hot sauce will kill you. Don't you got no respect? You make fun of the dead."

JB did not like Frankie's newfound comedic voice. He wasn't finished.

"And what is it with the condom jokes?" he said. "You're talking about condoms? I warned my daughter about you." Frankie forgot— JB was just an old-fashioned guy.

The Bull brothers escorted JB through the morbid maze of funeral wagons to where the Impala was parked on Eighth Avenue.

As they walked Ballsziti muttered, "Mafia car, mafia car. You see what I mean about this kid. He's probably gonna be strung out by the time the night is over. How can you make jokes about the dead? It's the formaldehyde, I tell you. It got to his brain."

"You want I should break his legs, boss?"

Ballsziti tossed his cigar to the sidewalk and stepped on it. He'd have to let it go for now; the time was not right. He had other plans for Frankie Grace.

✝

When JB left, Frankie returned to the bar. He leaned against the polished counter, gladly accepting his slaps on the back accompanied by "Well done" and "You're funny, man." He turned when heard giggling behind him. A group of women had gathered. They had glossy, colorful nails, professionally plucked eyebrows, and beehive hairdos layered high on their heads. This is what he wanted: the night life; the laughs; the wine, women, and song, as opposed to the crying, the widows, and the sedating organ music.

"Hello, handsome." He turned to see one of the brunettes staring at him admiringly. Her stylish hair was wound high and tightly wrapped; her long eyelashes were clumped thick with black mascara; her narrow lips were slathered with a heavy coat of candy-apple-red lipstick. "You were great up there. Can I buy you a drink?" she asked.

Frankie was on the verge of considering when he heard another voice beside him—a familiar voice, sultry and melodious. "Excuse me, but I think you've got the wrong man—he's with me." Frankie turned to see the most beautiful eyes on the planet peeking at him over dark glasses. "Don't you have grandkids to tend to at home?" their owner suggested to the intruder.

"Caterina—what are you doing here?" asked a stunned Frankie. He took in the sight of her, from the smooth shoulders revealed by her strapless black dress, to the velvet choker at her graceful neck, to her fishnet hose and knee-high boots.

She quickly pushed the glasses back up and patted a curl of her blonde wig. She raised a slender fingertip to her pink lips in a gesture Frankie found irresistible. "Shhh, my father would kill me if he knew!"

"He's gone—you're safe. But let's get outta here before Little Anthony spots me with you."

Caterina showed no hestitation at riding with him in the hearse this time. Sliding over next to him on the wide leather seat, she slipped off the wig and let her dark tresses fall around her bare shoulders. "You really were funny, Frankie," she told him.

Relieved, Frankie replied, "Thanks. I owe your father, big time."

"People have found that be a dangerous spot to be in."

Tell me about it, he thought.

She moved closer to him, whispering into his ear. "Most of all, though, I think you're a good guy, Frankie. Don't let them get to you." She leaned back to look at his profile as they passed under the street lights. "You know, I think my mother's in league with him now to break us up."

"Why is that?"

"Let's just say there's a statue of Saint Valentine that has been restored to its rightful place," she said, smiling a Mona Lisa half-smile in the darkness.

In the alley, where he was careful to park the hearse quietly, Frankie looked deep into Caterina's eyes. "May I walk you home?"

"I only live next door," Caterina said. "I've been staying at my grandmother's, though."

"Oh?"

"Would you like to come up?"

His eyes opened wide. "Your father lives in the same building."

"A floor below," she reminded him. "And he doesn't get home until early morning."

Frankie had never noticed how much noise squeaky steps made when you needed them not to. Stifling giggles, the two inched their way up to the top floor, where they had first met. Isabella's apartment was a shrine, nothing touched since her passing—no clothes discarded, no drawers emptied. Tour groups could make it a stop.

They wasted no time, kissing their way through the apartment, leaving articles of clothing in their wake.

In the bedroom, Caterina lit the votive candles on the dresser—mood lighting, sort of. The pale moonbeams filtered through the skylight and poured over her skin, confirming for Frankie that he had indeed been visited by an angel. He put his arms around her waist. The flames flickered in the little glass receptacles and their red aura mixed with the moonlight, flooding her in a spectacular hue. He looked at the bed. *I hope they turned the mattress,* he thought.

He took her in his arms and kissed her. He fumbled with her bra; the clasp wouldn't cooperate. "I guess I'm better at dressing people than undressing them," he said.

Silently, she helped him. He was momentarily worried he would not be able to perform with the audience of saintly eyes gazing, like voyeurs, from the bureau. She would think him pagan if he turned them around, but he felt inadequate in such lofty company. He was not one of them. Far from being a saint, he was sure there was a little devil in him. His likeness would never be shaped in porcelain to sit on anyone's dresser.

Then he saw her fully naked. *Eat your heart out, Saint Valentine,* he thought. There was no time to seek his blessing. In a moment they were together. On the mattress where the grandmother had so recently expired, with the tantalizing smells from Lucci's dining courtyard filling the room, the secret of life was revealed once again: sex, food, and death. *Jeez,* Frankie thought, *there was no escape.* But it did not matter. He wanted to stay wrapped in her arms forever, gazing out at the heavens beyond the glass ceiling.

Chapter 20

Primo felt a sharp pain in his chest. As he thumbed through the pages of the *Daily News* he was shocked to find, alongside Earl Wilson's column, a picture of 45th Street, taken from a rooftop, with hearses lined up as far as the eye could see. And beside the lines of type, a small snapshot of his own son.

"Aspiring comic and expiring undertaker Frankie Grace knocked 'em dead last night at the Peppermint Lounge.

In a marketing stunt that can only be described as genius, his debut was marked with a reunion of friends from funeral homes throughout the city, clogging the street and causing mayhem as a parade of morbid-mobiles parked, double-parked and triple-parked. We'll be talking about this for a long time.

The kid was not bad, great poise, and I'm sure you'll be hearing about him again. I think he has a future. I laughed out loud when he said he comes from a tough neighborhood—in a pizzeria on Mott Street, he ordered two Sicilians to go, and the cook emerged from the kitchen with two guys bound and gagged.

When he's not making people laugh, he finds

another way to put a smile on their faces. He is the
funeral director at Grace Funeral Home on Mulberry Street. As the kid says, 'If you're ever in the
neighborhood, stop in for a cold one.'"

The chest pain grew more intense. Oh, God, the family secret is
out and all over the newspapers. Shame upon the house of Grace.
He couldn't look at his father's portrait. Francesco must be turning
over in his grave. His grandson was a clown—a clown in a family
of undertakers. Somewhere, there was a defective gene. Antacids
did not help. Primo had lost the battle for his son's heart and soul.

Sal Lucci, however, couldn't have been more pleased with
himself. "Did you read that?" he asked, pointing to the article. He
had no fewer than fifty copies of the *Daily News* piled on the table.
"They called me a genius, a marketing genius. I told you I was."

Frankie only smiled, allowing him his moment.

"And there's more," Sal said. "Remember my producer friend,
Sol Weis? Well, he called. They are going to do screen tests soon,
and he definitely wants you out there."

Frankie hated to admit to himself that things were going rather
well. The Gospel According to Primo was too deeply ingrained in
him. Some of its most basic precepts: When things are going well is
when the roof falls in. If it seems too good to be true, it is. "You did
good, Sal. Real good."

"And you—I noticed you didn't stick around for the celebration?
I was starting to get worried, until you showed up today."

Frankie grinned and said nothing.

"Why do I get the feeling there's something you're not telling
me?"

By late Sunday evening the last vestiges of the Feast of San
Gennaro were being cleared from Mulberry Street. The sidewalks
were empty of every concession. The carnival trailers had closed
their huge metal doors and pulled away, taking with them all

the stuffed teddy bears that nobody won. The sidewalks had been scrubbed clean of every oil and grease stain; every leftover morsel of sausage and pepper had been swept away.

Parking again became easier. A single folding chair reserved the only parking space in front of the Marconi Social Club. Many a tourist attempted to utilize the prime spot, but when their eyes meet those of the Bull boys, they quickly decided to move on.

Sometime around four in the morning, back in his own bed, Frankie heard his father yelling in the kitchen. He woke with a start, thinking at first that he was having another of his nightmares.

"Who is this? You crackpot! You got the wrong number. Who? What, what are you talking about? Fongul you, too! And the horse you rode in on."

Frankie jumped out of bed and rushed to grab the phone. "Hello, Io sono Frankie."

The voice on the other end was jovial. "Ah, Frankie, sono. I am Fabrizio. How are you? You sound more *normale.*"

Great, he speaks broken English; I speak broken Italian. This should be interesting. "I good, but I no speak too well the Italian." *Or the English either, it would seem.*

"No problem. I speak un poco. I been to America. I have, one time, an American girlfriend. She teacha me many things, *molti cosi.* I go to Sana Frana Sisco with her. I especially like sixty-nine."

"Sixty-nine?"

"Si, si. She take me to Chinese Restaurant. It'sa beef and vegetables. *Ci sono troppo pazzo* there in Sana Frana Sisco."

Pazzo, Frankie understood. His father called him that all the time.

"In *ogni caso,* anyway, Frankie, *povero* Senore Vitagliano, *che peccato,* what a shame. He's ready to come back to you. He no look so good. We do our best, but he no looka so good."

"How did he die?"

"*Scusa?*"

"Die, die, *morte, comé,* how?"

"Ma, you never could believa. He fall fifty feet down the steps . . . two times, how you say, clumsy *bastardo,* si or no. *Che peccato!*"

There was no response.

"Hello, hello?"

"I'm here. I'm here."

"Anyway, we try putta him on a plane ina one day or two. Right now, there's big *scopero,* how you say, strike."

"When did it start?"

"Twenty minutes ago. Sometimes it lasts for a week, sometimes two hours. Anyway, we also wait for some *famiglia* who want to say good-bye. They come from Taromina. When weze ready, he come into land at Jayeffakay; I letta you know the flight number. I think zerotwofifateen. *Tutti cosi e stata pagata.* Everything been paid already. But, *di nuovo,* he no looka so good."

In a quiet corner of the café the next morning, while most of the wise guys perused the sports section, Eddie sat alone, hypnotized by the chessboard. The game helped clear his mind, and after Frankie told him about the phone call from Italy, his mind definitely needed clearing.

He studied the board before him. He was tired of the King's Indian approach. He stared at the black king, safely surrounded by his knights, two castles, and queen. Black pawns advanced ever forward, the front line shielding the realm but falling one by one. There was imminent danger that one would be lost, then his queen, leaving the king open; and there was no one he could turn to for help, not his fallen pawns and not his frozen bishops, who had long since abandoned him.

He stared hard at the possibilities before him, thinking of a way to extricate himself from this certain fate. There must be a move to be made, he thought. *Just think, Eddie, just think.* A thousand maneuvers came to mind, none good. It came down to only one option. There was but one white knight left who might be able to restore order. A risky move, but a decision had to be made. He picked up the phone and called Frankie. "Meet me at St. Pat's," he said.

✝

Frankie made his way up Mulberry to meet Eddie as instructed. St. Patrick's Old Cathedral, built in 1809, was the oldest surviving Catholic church in New York. He spotted Eddie a full city block away, the banana-yellow bowling shirt his point of reference.

Eddie peered through the rungs of the iron fence surrounding the church graveyard. A few bystanders had gathered to watch a dig in progress. The diocese's archaeological unit, generally involved with the process of beatification, was unearthing a gravesite.

"Eddie," Frankie called out.

Eddie didn't turn around.

Frankie surveyed the work being done in the graveyard. "What's going on?"

"I asked that guy wearing the dress over there," Eddie said.

"You mean the monsignor?" Frankie queried.

"I guess. He said they were looking for some guy's bones to prove he was a saint or something. They said he lived around here a hundred years ago."

"Really?" Frankie said. "Did they find him yet?"

"No, but they found three other bodies, wrapped in shower curtains doused with lye. They was buried more recent."

Only then did Eddie turn around. In the bright sunlight the red finger marks were fading but still evident on his face.

Frankie wanted to say something supportive, but he couldn't find the right words. Finally, he just asked, "Are you okay?"

Eddie paused before replying, "Oh, this?" He pointed to his face. "This ain't nothing. The old man apologized later. He didn't mean nuttin'; he just got excited. There's a lot on his plate. It's just his way, that's all. He's got a lot on his mind."

"I guess," Frankie said.

"Yeah, he apologized later, said he didn't mean it."

"Good, good, Eddie."

Eddie looked up at the church's steeple. "You know, there's a lot of history here?"

This should be interesting: Eddie's knowledge of historical facts.

"You know the Italians built this church," Eddie began.

No, the Irish did. That's why it's named St. Patrick's.

"And there was this crazy Pope named Dagger Donato who chased the Irish out of the neighborhood."

It was a bishop named Hughes who had manned the walled parapet around the church and fought the Protestants back in 1836. It was at that point that the Catholic Church began to flourish in America. It wasn't that Frankie was so smart, just that he'd read the plaque in the courtyard commemorating the event.

"You know, St. Patrick was really Italian," Eddie continued. "His name was Pasquale."

No, it was Patrick, short for Patrick.

"And he went to Ireland to chase the rats out."

They were snakes, not rats. No commemorative plaque, just catechism class.

"Then they all came here."

"The rats?" asked Frankie, incredulous.

"No, the Irish," replied Eddie, adding, "and the rats, too, I guess."

Frankie just nodded.

"Let's go for a walk," Eddie suggested. "I may have an appointment downtown."

The two strolled slowly up the block. Eddie insisted they avoid Mulberry Street, for safety reasons. He wouldn't have to tax his brain with doublespeak and hand gestures if he wasn't being watched.

"We live in a famous place, you know."

On Grand Street, Eddie stopped in front of police headquarters. "My father was booked in there. Lots of guys were sent off to college from here."

Again, Frankie just nodded. College was neighborhood code for prison, but if prison was college, then police headquarters was orientation class. *Boy, this was one well-educated neighborhood,* Frankie thought.

"Let's go this way. I feel safer." Eddie looked up to the rooftops out of habit. They walked along Grand to Greene Street, then headed south to Columbus Park.

"You know this park was named after Big Jim Colosimo, a big time gangster killed by Uale and Capone."

"Really," Frankie said. *Whatever happened to good ol' Genoa boy Christopher Columbus, duh?*

"And right here is where they found my good friend Sonny Burke slumped over the steering wheel of his car; took a bullet, right here." Eddie pointed behind his right ear. No commemorative plaque, just local history. "He wasn't a bad kid, but he was wild. His father was at college with my father."

Nice that they could dorm together, Frankie thought.

"The kid was always getting in trouble, stiffin' bookies, shys. No one would bother him because of his old man, but then he stole some money from the wrong card game, and that was it. Some of the mustache Petes had had enough. The order was given. Sonny drove a purple El Dorado in those days. Can you believe that? JB hated that car, too flashy, drew unwanted attention. Anyway, one night Sonny comes out of an after-hours joint and sees his best friend, and he asks him for a ride. Next thing you know, Sonny is dead, right on this spot. Sonny's father was JB's partner. When he graduated, he vowed to find out who had killed his son. He got whacked soon after that. I could have won a bet on that one."

"Do you think?"

"I get in trouble when I think. JB went to his funeral, too. He's very respectful that way. He goes to lots of funerals."

Frankie agreed. In fact, his father often said Johnny Ballsziti was the best thing to happen to the funeral business since the Spanish influenza. They kept going.

"Sonny wasn't a bad guy, a little wild I guess," Eddie reiterated. "Neither was Tony, I guess, or Mr. Vitagliano. But they were working guys, civilians, minded their own business. They wasn't involved with anybody; but I guess even if you're not involved, they get you involved."

Frankie was trying to follow the conversation, which itself was involved. "These guys are in their own world, Eddie. You know that. They make their own rules as they go along and convince themselves they're living up to some honored code." It was a risky suggestion.

"Well, it ain't what it used to be, that's for sure."

They found themselves on Foley Square in front of the Federal Courthouse. "You know, Frankie Uale, there was a man. He was the kind of mob guy that helped people. He was Al Capone's boss and Capone had him shot; that's how these things work, you know. They send your best friend to whack you."

Thanks for reminding me.

"That was back in the twenties, when this place was a real neighborhood, the Sixth Ward, before they put up all these friggin' courthouses. Uale had a funeral that was like nothing anyone ever saw. I think your grandfather handled it. Your father told me about it, plus I saw pictures in the café. Thousands and thousands of people came; that's the kind of guy he was. Everyone loved him. He even had a police escort."

Maybe they wanted to be sure he left the neighborhood.

Eddie continued, "When he was shot, he was wearing a belt buckle with a million dollars' worth of diamonds."

Frankie knew the story: it was diamond-studded, though hardly a million dollars' worth.

"He was a standup guy, not all good, not all bad. Most people are like that, you know, not all good or all bad. Except for these guys today; they may be a different breed, like Fortissimo and that bunch."

"They are all for themselves," Frankie agreed.

Eddie looked up toward the Brooklyn Bridge. "Capone lived around here," he said, "I think I read that someplace. There were lots of gangs then: Jews, Irish, some real tough Irish guys, too, like that Paul Kelly guy."

Right. Paul Kelly, birth name Paolo Vaccarelli. Why ruin it?

Eddie stared up the granite steps of the Federal Courthouse. "You know, the last time I saw my father, he was standing on top of those steps. I was a kid then."

"Did you get to see him afterwards?"

"No, it was hard to get up there to Sing Sing. There was a priest who brought me letters, and read them to me, and gave me messages, but that stopped. I don't know why. I guess because he was dead and all, and couldn't write no more."

They sat on a bench by the courthouse. The city's symphony of noisy traffic and cooing pigeons surrounded them. Eddie turned to face Frankie. "You know, General Patton, he was a great general, and he slapped somebody. I think it was a president."

He hadn't let it go. The smack still stung. Frankie just nodded. As for the historical inaccuracies, there were too many to correct. "I'm glad the feast is over," Frankie said, hoping to change the conversation. "I've had enough of San Gennaro."

"He was quite a guy, too," Eddie said. "You know why they made him a saint?"

Yes, but enlighten me.

"Because he refused to bow his head to some king or something, so they chopped it off. I think I read that somewhere."

Jeez, he got something right!

They sat quietly for a few minutes, until Eddie noticed the time. "Listen, thanks for taking a walk. I got to meet someone. I'll catch you later."

"Do you want me to come with you?"

"No," he said. "Got to do this myself."

Frankie said goodbye and walked north toward Mulberry Street and Little Italy. He turned to see Eddie's yellow shirt disappear into a sea of suits and attaché cases as he walked south toward the Battery. Frankie wasn't sure whether he'd just been warned—or propagandized.

Sal, the marketing genius, put the final touches on the sandwich board that would sit on the sidewalk in front of the café.

Frankie Grace, The Laughing Undertaker

You'll Die Laughing!

One Show Only, Price Fix Menu

He thought about adding "Spend a little, you cheap bastards," but decided against it. Then he worked the phones, calling anyone and everyone he knew. Eddie promised to bring some people as well. Sal reserved a special table for Caterina and then practiced singing with the Elizabeth Street Trio. The acoustics were not so good, matching his voice.

As showtime approached, Sal started getting nervous. The phone call they were waiting for had not come—Giovanna was supposed to let them know when Primo had gone to sleep. It was a full hour past his usual bedtime, but Frankie would not go onstage until he knew his father was safely tucked away.

Sal jumped when the phone finally rang. "Good, great." He hung up. "He's sleeping!" Sal yelled.

Right on cue, the waiters brought out the sidewalk sign and the trio started in on an upbeat tune. Frankie paced behind the meat-grinding machine in the corner of the kitchen. He was nervous, trying to remember his lines. The meat grinder seemed to carry an added significance tonight.

In the dining room, the crowd settled in for the show. There was no pretense of quieting the room. In the kitchen, waiters and busboys passed quickly in front of and behind Frankie as they tiptoed, raising trays of food high in the air, or ducked with trays of empty dishes, trying not to get in the way. The clatter of pots and pans from the kitchen could be heard throughout the dining area.

Sal popped his head through the kitchen door. "She's here," he reported.

Frankie looked out into the dining room and saw Caterina. The clingy blue dress she wore accentuated her every curve. God, she's gorgeous, Frankie thought. Just the sight of her made him more nervous. It had been different before, when he didn't know she was in the audience. Was his routine too raw? Could he clean it up a little? Too late now—Sal was at the microphone.

"Ladies and gentlemen, may I have your attention. What a beautiful night—the wine, the music, the food. It's great to be alive! Sorry, Primo. Anyway, it is with great pride that I introduce my friend Frankie, the undertaker. He's used to getting a cold welcome, so let's give him a warm one. Here he is—Frankie Grace!"

Frankie ran out from the kitchen through the small dining room. The place was packed. Eddie had kept his promise and brought some friends: Pete the mechanic was there—he cleaned up nice—and Pete's sister Marie, considerably overcosmetized, was all over Eddie. She didn't look half bad, but the other half made up for it. Frankie was tempted to joke about it—the rosy cheeks, bright red lips, purple eye shadow. Yuck! If he'd had his kit . . .

"The things I do for you, Frankie," Eddie heckled.

Jeez, Eddie. "Hey, if she lies down, I can fix that makeup." There, he did it, he went for the joke, damn the consequences! Eddie laughed; Marie didn't get it, which was lucky.

There were more people than Frankie could have imagined crowding the small room. "Hey, I'm not used to a live audience," he started. "It was a quiet day at the funeral parlor today. But hey, what would you expect at a funeral parlor.

"Every time we have a wake, my mother cooks for the family. They all come up to eat. What you eat depends on what casket you bought." The drummer accommodated with a rim shot.

It was an informal evening, more ad-libbed than rehearsed. Quick lines, aimed mostly at Phil the waiter, flew from the stage. "He just spent a week in the Riviera—not France, his Buick. He came from a broken home, his parents were broke. Hey, Phil, nice coloring—very natural."

The room was alive with laughter and wine was flowing; it helped. They would have laughed at anything. He hoped the ruckus wouldn't wake his father.

He talked about the last place Sal had him booked, the Polish Copa. "My first joke was about two Polish guys, and a guy in the back gets up and yells, 'Hey, I'm Polish,' so I say, 'Okay, I'll talk slower.' Anyway, people say I have a big nose—it was supposed to be a third arm. Hey, did I tell you about the undertaker's version of the mile-high club?" He joked about doing it in a hearse and how he'd considered writing a book, *Sex after Death; or, How to Get Laid in a Casket.* He looked anxiously at Caterina. Was she offended? Did she laugh?

He moved on, joke after joke, ten minutes, twenty; a heckler here or there, he put him down; thirty minutes. He was in his glory, forgetting his fears. As he said good night, the trio formed behind him and played "Every Street's a Boulevard in Old New York; I like the people you meet, on Mulberry Street."

It was Pete the Mic who noticed Frankie making his way down to the bathroom in the basement. "This is as good a time as any," he whispered in Eddie's ear.

Eddie nodded, looked around, and followed Frankie down the steps.

As Frankie washed his hands, the door behind him opened. He saw Eddie in the mirror. *Watch out when things are going well: Gospel of Primo 1:3.*

"You having a good time?" Frankie asked, trying to keep both his voice and his knees steady.

"Always, everything is great." He paused for a moment. "You okay? Your face is kinda red."

"No, no, I'm fine. I'm just a bit nervous about all that's happening."

Eddie nodded his understanding. "Frankie, I wish I wasn't the one who had to take care of this. You know how much I like you?" he said.

Frankie began to shake. He could think of nothing but Sonny and the purple El Dorado.

Eddie reached into his jacket pocket. Frankie closed his eyes and fell back into the stall. His life flashed before him. He imagined how his picture would look in tomorrow's Daily News, his head in a toilet bowl like a defeated goldfish. If he had to be killed, why couldn't it be in a barber's chair, or at a sidewalk café or, best of all, onstage? Somewhere, anywhere, that would add some punctuation to his life. Somewhere that would add a little class to his rubout, afford him a little dignity. How demeaning to be killed on a toilet seat. He imagined the clever headlines—"Comedian's Career in the Crapper." "Comic Wiped Out on Toilet Bowl." "Undertaker Gets Family Discount." Sal would be happy, though. He'd get his wish: a shot to Frankie's head could be just the shot in the arm Sal was looking for—and he wouldn't have to fake it. *The things you think of before you die,* Frankie mused.

Eddie took a step closer to him. Frankie pulled back and tucked his arms closer to his head. *Not the face; please, not the face!* He knew how long it took to repair bullet wounds using mortuary wax. Eddie's hand slid further inside his jacket. He pulled out an envelope and smacked Frankie in the head with it.

"Hey, hey, what's with you? Why are you so jumpy?"

Frankie opened his eyes and saw the envelope in front of his face.

"You never paid for the hearse repair. The Mic gave me the bill for you. I'd pay it myself but things ain't going too good this month."

Frankie took the envelope and started to laugh. "Hey, no problem. I can't thank you enough for getting that done. I'll never forget it."

Sometime later, as Caterina's head lay upon his chest, Frankie traced his fingers along her face, and while he was at it, what the hell, he moved his other hand over her hips.

"Frankie," she said, "I have to go."

He looked at the clock. It was two in the morning. "Don't you mean *I* have to go? You live here."

She looked up into his eyes. "No, I don't mean now, from here. I mean back to Italy. My father wants me to return to my studies in Bologna."

A knife into his heart could not have been as painful. He didn't believe his ears. It couldn't be. "You can't, you can't go," were the only words he could muster.

She put her head back on his chest. "I must," she said. "My father has his ways of persuading people to do his bidding. Even his family. *Especially* his family."

"But couldn't you stand up to him, tell him what you really want?"

"You're one to talk, Frankie."

She had a point. "Well, run away with me, then. We'll—"

"Shhh, we have better things to do with the rest of our time together, don't you think?"

He felt empty, hopeless, dead. *Get the floral wreath ready with the clock set to two a.m. My life is over.* Now, in a moment, from one simple sentence, he understood every heart-wrenching Neapolitan song he had ever heard, even without understanding the words. He understood the melancholy sense of loss he heard in singers' voices from the sidewalk speakers hanging outside Rossi's music store. Now, he understood the anguish of Carlo Buti, the indescribable longing of Caruso, and the tears of the clown, Pagliacci. Now, he understood heartache, love, and loss.

Chapter 21

The morning's headline could have read "Primo Is Pissed."
As he swept the sidewalk in front of the funeral home, the
entire neighborhood stopped to congratulate him on Frankie's
appearance—Primo, your son's a cut-up, but you know that; or
Primo, your son's too much. Lucci's was jumping last night; or
Primo, what a character that kid of yours is. It wasn't long before
he couldn't take any more. He propped his broom inside the gate
and marched straight into Lucci's. "Sal, was my son doing his
funny business here, under my nose?"

"Mr. Grace, I am offended by the allegation and by the alligator."

Primo looked puzzled, as well he might have.

It was about then that Sal noticed the billboard advertising
Frankie's appearance leaning against the wall. He placed his arm
around a skeptical Primo Grace and eased him out the door with
his back to the sign. "Now, Mr. Grace, I am many things, but a liar
is not one of them."

Primo went back into the funeral home, determined to find
his son. The small chapel was empty; after their record-breaking
feast week, suddenly it was famine again. He went down the stairs,
his ire growing with each step. There was a desk light on, but the
office was empty, as was the prep room. In the quiet darkness,
he heard snoring. He followed the sound into the casket selection
room, where he saw his son sleeping in the mahogany casket. *A*

million times I told him not to sleep there! At least he had taken his shoes off.

Resigned and tired, Primo sat in a chair and took a deep breath, allowing his anger and blood pressure to subside. He slouched, trying to analyze just where he'd gone wrong. Getting Frankie to follow in his footsteps had been an uphill battle from the start. Some part of him knew that, but he always held out hope.

As he stared at his son's rhythmic breathing, he recalled the time Frankie was expelled from embalming school for what the dean called deep psychological problems. He should see him now, sleeping in the mahogany casket, Primo thought. This would be his confirmation.

He remembered going to see his old friend to plead for his son's reinstatement. The dean was ready for him. He opened a closet in his office containing clay heads used in restoration class, where aspiring embalmers learned to reconstruct facial features. All of Frankie's practice heads sported a Jimmy Durante nose, Mickey Mouse ears, or Barney Google eyes.

"As you can see, he's not taking this seriously," the dean said.

Primo could only nod. Eventually he did prevail on the dean to reconsider, after explaining that his son's umbilical cord had been wrapped around his head when he was born and not enough oxygen had gotten to his brain. He promised he would personally walk his son through the program. Now he wondered if he had made the right decision.

He stared at his son in the all-too-familiar position, watching his chest rise and fall. The things we get accustomed to in this crazy business, he thought. My kid is sleeping in a casket. The predisposition must have been directly related to his birth, he decided.

Primo recalled the day his son was born. Dr. Copolla had walked into Larry's Bar and taken his usual seat. When Primo called to him from the window, he took the time to finish his beer before going up to the apartment. Upon seeing Giovanna's advanced state of labor, however, he sent Primo to get the car. What a battle had ensued when the women realized Giovanna's husband intended to take her to the hospital in a hearse! They gave in at last to the doctor's orders, but if looks could kill Primo would have been dead four times over. "It's the family car," he had protested meekly.

It was Pasquelena who had climbed out of the hearse with the infant in her hands, holding him above her head like a trophy. Primo took a deep breath. I have a son, he thought. My boy—and born in a hearse. Francesco must be smiling. Surely this was a sign from heaven, from God himself.

He thought he heard the Lord's voice on that day, like Moses did when God delivered the Ten Commandments. "Behold, I give unto you a boy, and he will be an undertaker."

Who was he to go against God's wishes? How could he have been so wrong? How could he have misinterpreted such a clear sign from heaven? How could God have been wrong?

As he gazed on his grown son now, he believed less in signs from heaven. They got things wrong sometimes. He reached for his wallet and retrieved a small newspaper article and unfolded it. It was the Earl Wilson piece about Frankie's appearance at the Peppermint Lounge. He read it over again. "The young comic shows lots of promise," it said. He folded it and tucked it back into his wallet. Hey, he figured, there are worse things than not carrying on the family business.

The phone rang, waking Frankie from his troubled sleep. He hoisted himself out of the coffin and tried to convince himself the bad parts of the previous evening hadn't really happened.

"Grace Funeral Home, Frankie speaking."

There was static on the line.

"Frankie, *tutto e pronto*. It's me, Fabrizio."

After a convoluted combination of English, Italian, and possibly two other Romance languages, Frankie got confirmation of the flight from Naples, to arrive at ten the following morning at Jayeffakay.

He hung up the phone. By now it didn't make much for him to put two and two together and come up with real trouble.

✝

At the Marconi Café, Eddie reported the conversation from Italy.

JB was most pleased. He sat quietly, nodding, thinking. He turned to Eddie and whispered, "You did good, Eddie, real good. I am proud of you. I didn't want to tell you until I was sure, and now I am sure. Now, I want you to know. I have proposed your name to the commission. The books were opened and your name was first. You've been sponsored by me."

Ah, Frankie was wrong—there *was* a book! For Eddie Fontana, it was the culmination of a life's work—recognition by his peers. Being sponsored for buttonhood by Johnny Ballsziti was equivalent to knighthood by the Queen, like being on a short list for the Nobel Prize or an Oscar. It was a promise fulfilled. Johnny Ballsziti found him worthy.

"In a few days, after we take care of some business, I'm going on a little vacation. I'm leaving you in charge—everything from Mulberry Street to the West Side. You're in charge. Do you think you're ready?

Eddie wanted to jump for joy. It's not the kind of thing you could run out into the streets and shout about, or he would have. The neighborhood would find out in due time, he was sure. There were ways of letting people know that he was a man to be respected now. "I am ready, JB. Thank you."

In front of a room of card players, pool players, television watchers, and various locals, JB kissed Eddie on both cheeks— rejection to redemption.

"Sit," JB said. "Here's what I need from you. You heard about Fortissimo?"

Eddie nodded. "He was not a good man, not a good leader—too flashy. I'm not surprised someone wanted him gone." JB winked. "You know what he was into?" He put his fingers to his lips as he asked the question.

Eddie only nodded. Finally, he got it right.

"Well," JB said. leaning in as he spoke, "I have to step in or there will be chaos, disorder. Can we have disorder?"

No, Eddie nodded.

"Here's where it gets important, Eddie. Here is where I'm going to need you, my number one man." He took a sip of espresso. "When the fruit arrives I want you to go to our place in New Jersey. Wait there."

He pointed to Bulls One and Two. "They are going to take a ride with the undertaker to accompany Mr. Vitagliano's casket from the airport. They've been with him before; he's used to them. They will make sure nottin' goes wrong and then drive out to New Jersey. I want you should empty and secure the contents of the casket."

Eddie listened, his fears confirmed.

"You understand what's at stake here?"

"I do," said Eddie, sealing the marriage.

JB looked around. "There is one more thing, Eddie." He paused. "Ooh, I can't believe this day has come. I only wish your father was here to see you get your . . ." He pointed to a button on his sweater.

Eddie nodded.

"Now, what was I saying? Oh. Oh, this undertaker kid."

"Yes."

"This kid who is doing this; he knows a lot of things. He can hurt us."

"Frank—?" As he started to say his name, he saw the whites of JB's eyes. Eddie had broken mobspeak rule 101.

JB nodded at the name. "After the coffin is emptied . . ." Eddie stared at him as JB started to raise his arm. Please no, Eddie thought. Let him scratch his nose, his forehead, please. Let him rub his neck. Let him have a speck in his eye.

But there it was, the sign, clear and unmistakable. The earlobe.

JB rose from the table, embraced Eddie, and kissed him again. He then motioned to Bull and Bull, who came over and kissed Eddie, too. It was an abbreviated welcoming ceremony due to time restraints. A more formal, invitation-only dinner would eventually be announced.

Eddie left the club, emotions whirling—elation at the promotion and dejection at the price it extracted. How could he do it? How would he do it? This was different from before. He'd been a civilian then. How would he tell Primo and Giovanna that their son had had an accident, or was missing, or—what? What would he tell them? Maybe he'd seen it wrong; maybe he misinterpreted. No, no, it was a definite tug of the earlobe, and he knew he could not refuse.

When Eddie left the café, JB turned to Bull and Bull. "When he has finished his work—" he told them. He tugged on his earlobe again. A callous was forming.

Bull and Bull looked at each other and nodded.

"Where's Frankie?" Eddie asked Sal, who was standing in the doorway of the restaurant.

"He's in a bad state," he answered. "I saw him walking toward Columbus Park. If there was a lake there, I'd be worried." Sal was determined to speak his mind. "Eddie, I think there's something wrong with Frankie. I think he's in trouble. More specifically, I think he's in real danger."

"I think you're right," Eddie said as he sat down. He rubbed his temples.

"Don't argue with me, Eddie. He's in danger, like dead, *morte*, dead danger, that kind of danger."

"I think you're right," Eddie said again. "I'm agreeing with ya."

Sal was stunned. He was hoping Eddie would disagree with his assessments as usual. Sal took a seat across from him, waiting for an explanation.

"There's not much I can say. You have a cousin at cargo, JFK?"

"Yes."

"I want you to ask him to keep his eyes open for any unusual activity, like police or plainclothes feds snooping around, staking the place out."

"Eddie, you know how these guys work. You know what happened to Tony and Mr. Vitagliano, and you know who may be next."

"Not yet, we have some time. They still need him for now."

"What do you mean 'not yet'? So, you're really agreeing with me. There's a hit on him?"

"I didn't say that."

"The hell you didn't. You know JB is already making the case that Frankie is a lowlife."

"He still serves a purpose. That's all I can say. Now, about that screen test in California?"

"Yeah?"

"Make the arrangements," he said. "Buy him a ticket for tomorrow."

Sal's face registered skepticism and worry.

Eddie reached into his pocket and took out what bills he had and counted. "Lay it out," he said. "I'm a little short this week."

That request raised Sal's eyebrows.

"And one other thing—loan me your keys," Eddie said.

"What, are you crazy? The car is brand new. I don't want you driving it."

"Give me the friggin' keys, moron. It's important."

Sal saw a sense of urgency in Eddie's eyes. He handed him the keys and got just what he feared—the GTO, clutch grinding, peeled out down Mulberry Street leaving a cloud of dust and the smell of burnt rubber.

"Hey, easy with her," Sal yelled after him. "She's my baby."

Frankie walked, without purpose, through Columbus Park, deep in the heart of Chinatown. He had gone from cloud nine to the gates of hell in the time it takes to say "I must go."

Eddie circled the park until he found Frankie—not too difficult to do, since he was the only redhead in a sea of black-haired Chinese. He gunned the pedal, popping the clutch. The car came screeching along Bayard and jumped the sidewalk, coming to an abrupt stop on the grass.

Eddie motioned Frankie into the car. "It's important," he said.

Frankie got in and they sped off, finally stopping under the Brooklyn Bridge. Frankie felt queasy as he followed Eddie's lead and stepped out of the car.

"First," Eddie asked, "what's going on with you? What are you doing down here with all these chinks?"

"It's Caterina," Frankie said. "Her father's sending her back to Italy."

Eddie processed that information to see how it played into JB's overall plan. He concluded that JB did not want his daughter in town should this plan go south; or maybe he was planning to meet up with her and start his new life; or maybe he did not want her to get involved with Frankie, knowing there was no future in that. Option three seemed most likely.

"And on top of that there's the situation with what's coming *back* from Italy."

"Frankie, there are some complications."

"No shit."

"Listen, you're gonna have to trust me on this. You're gonna have to trust me and do what I say and don't ask why."

"Why?" Frankie asked.

"I told you, you can't ask that." He looked around, up, and down. "You remember about Fortissimo?"

"Of course. It took me three hours to wax the bullet holes in his face."

"It was an open *casket*."

"Yes, what of it?"

"Don't you see? Don't you make any connection?"

Frankie was in no mood for guessing games. "I really can't keep up with all this stuff. I got my own problems."

More than you know, Eddie thought.

"Listen, Frankie. I want to tell you something, and I want you to understand what I am trying to say. I need you to focus."

Eddie just advised me to focus? Can things get worse?

Eddie felt a little safer under the bridge but still didn't want to take any chances. He spoke in a low, hushed voice. "You know how all the cabbage was sent back to Italy, you remember?"

"Are you kidding? I wake up every night remembering—"

"Enough, enough. Now, you know what line of commerce that

guy you just fixed was in?"

"Only what I read in the papers."

"Well, with him gone, you know who takes over his business?"

Frankie was about to answer but Eddie covered his mouth and said, "That same guy is now planning to fill all the fruit stands with fruit."

"You lost me there," Frankie said, confused.

Eddie tried again. "Our friend is now planning to bring baby powder into New York."

"Can you do better, Eddie?"

He gave up. "Goddammit, Frankie, JB's got a shipment of white powder heroin stuffed in that casket with the butcher from Bologna!"

Frankie suddenly felt dizzy, stunned. He fell backwards against the car, wishing he were dead. "Oh, Christ! Christ! Jesus fucking Christ!" He muttered and swore as the plan became clear. He beat his fists on the hood of the car. "Jesus Christ, Eddie. What am I going to do? This Roscoe guy is all over me already. He knows I did something. Now this. He'll be watching every move I make like a—." He pointed to his nose and flapped his arms. "I could be sent away for life. And what's worse is, my father's involved. We can *both* go to jail for life. And even if it works, JB don't like witnesses. Now I get it about Tony and Mr. V." He kicked the tire of Sal's car angrily. "Jesus Christ, Eddie, what the hell have I stepped into?"

Eddie appreciated Frankie's assessment. Smart kid, he thought. He put his arms on Frankie's shoulders and looked him straight in the eye. "Hey, dickhead, do you know I love ya? Do you know what your mother and father done for me? You know they're like my own?"

Frankie nodded.

"Then trust me, like I said. Just trust me."

"Eddie, maybe we should go to the cops—turn ourselves in, tell them what happened, how it happened. We had no choice; we can make a deal with them."

"Cops! Are you friggin' crazy? Frankie, I told you to trust me." Eddie's voice was as firm as Frankie had ever heard it.

"But Eddie, maybe they can help. They'll make a deal, put you in witness protection."

"What? And work for some farmer somewhere squeezing a cow's nipples? No, no, now don't get spooked on me. Just trust me. I can't leave this neighborhood; it's the only place I know."

"Eddie, are you sure? I mean, are you really sure? Maybe we should go talk to them."

"What are you saying? You're willing to trust Roscoe Keats and not me?"

Frankie hated when Eddie made sense. "No, I'm not saying that. I *guess* I'm not saying that. I don't know what I'm saying, or thinking."

"Listen, I know what most people think of me, maybe you, too. But on this one, trust me. Let me think for the both of us."

"What do we do now?"

"We better go see Pete the Mic." He pointed to the hood of Sal's GTO. "He's gonna have to bang those dents out."

Eddie parked the Impala a block past Patsy's on 119th Street, as usual. He stopped for a slice of pizza and then walked down to 116th. He knew his way into the back room. The two men in back of the candy store greeted him more warmly than before. There was no "Hey, congratulations! We heard you're a made man now," but there was a bigger smile, a stronger squeeze of his hand, a tighter hug, and more passionate kisses on his cheeks. They knew—word of his promotion had made it up to Harlem already.

He basked in the glory for a moment then got down to business. "The fruit is scheduled for delivery tomorrow as promised."

That was the message: simple, clear. More hugs, kisses, and pats on the back followed. Eddie felt good; he was a part of something. He belonged, even if he didn't have a decoder ring like they did. "Hey, that's a beautiful ring," he said to Chili.

Chili flicked his pinky to let the light reflect off the diamonds.

"What? This? Go see my cousin Tulio at the diamond exchange on Mott and Canal. Tell him I sent you."

As he walked back to the car, Eddie debated with himself. He was talking out loud without realizing it. If JB pulled this off—if the drugs came in okay—what would be the benefit in killing Frankie? Why not just let him go on his way? Live and let live? What harm could a pawn do, anyway? He realized what stupid questions they were, and all his wishful thinking was just that, wishful. It was all about covering tracks, he knew. And he knew there would be other tracks that needed covering as well. He paced back and forth, thinking, thinking—against JB's direct orders. He noticed strangers staring at him and realized he had been talking to himself. Not good.

He leaned against the Impala on the quiet side street until he at last came to a decision. He would have to live with it now or die with it. He looked up the street, then down. When he was satisfied no one was looking, Eddie kicked his heel into the car's right rear taillight. The red plastic shattered. He brushed the bumper clean of the telltale shards, and then got in the car and headed downtown.

Chapter 22

Early the next morning Bull and Bull, in matching leisure suits, waited in front of the café as their boss finished his breakfast. In a few minutes their ride would come down Mott Street to pick them up.

Around the corner, on Mulberry, Frankie Grace turned the key in the ignition of the hearse. Eddie looked at his watch and ran over to stop him. "Frankie, wait up."

"I got to go, Eddie. I don't want to, believe me, but I got to."

"I know, I know." Eddie looked at his watch again. "I just want you to be calm. Be calm."

"Right, that should be easy. I'm taking a hearse ride with two malcontent murderers to pick up a zillion dollars' worth of drugs in a casket coming from Italy and taking it to who knows where, and who knows if I'll ever come back."

"Hey, hey, just take it easy. That's all I can tell you. You promised to trust me." He looked at his watch again and lit a cigarette.

As they spoke, three unmarked police cars, sirens blaring, came barreling down Mott Street and pulled up in front of the café, coming to a halt directly in front of the brothers Bull. The two behemoths did not move. As Roscoe Keats and a contingent of plainclothes agents poured out of the vehicles, Bull Two dropped his pants, tucked his shirt in, then pulled them back up and buckled his belt.

"You are the epitome of grace and class," Keats commented.

"Thanks," Bull answered. He was genuinely flattered.

JB got up from his seat and went to the door to check out the commotion.

"Celestino and Philip," Keats said. "Did they call you Celeste? Gee, if I was named Celeste or Philipi, I would want to be called Bull, too."

Bulls One and Two exchanged embarrassed glances. Their secret was out—Celestino and Philip DiBullova, a.k.a. Bull and Bull.

Keats deliberately spoke loud enough for passersby to hear. "We'd like to ask you fine gentlemen, Celeste and Philipi, a few questions about Mr. Moe Fortissimo."

He was met with stony stares. "We don't have to go no place with you," said Bull One.

"That's true," Keats said. "I can stick around here with you for an hour or two and disrupt whatever business is going on—numbers, policy sheets, sports betting."

JB motioned to a low-level bookie at the bar. "Tell them to go," he said.

The guy went outside and whispered in Bull's ear.

"JB said to go," Bull told his brother.

"You see, your boss said it's okay. Now, there's an easy way to do this and a hard way."

Bull nodded to Bull. Agents opened the back door of each car. "Celeste, Philipi, after you," Keats said, extending his hand toward the cars. Bull and Bull looked at each other as each climbed into a back seat. Keats puffed on his cigar and stared at the café window. He took his time getting into the lead car, smiling as he did.

"Hit the strobes and siren," he commanded.

The driver looked at him, questioning the order.

"Just do it."

The convoy of police cars made a loud, flashy exit down Mott Street, alerting the whole neighborhood.

Eddie heard the sirens. "Wait here," he told Frankie.

"Christ, Eddie, what's going on?"

"Just sit tight."

He walked nonchalantly around the corner into the café. JB was standing by the window, reassessing his plan.

"What happened?" Eddie asked.

JB put his finger to his lips and took his seat. He pulled a chair out for Eddie. He leaned in. "A little change in plans," he said. "I want you to go to the airport with the kid. Follow the same plan. After you have the casket, take everything to where I told you to take it, take care of business, then bring the car back to our mechanic friend. He will, ah, sanitize it."

Eddie scratched his head.

"Eddie, do you understand?"

Eddie nodded. He was getting good at nodding yes instead of saying yes, probably because of his new status.

The Bull boys were escorted into separate interrogation rooms at the Fifth Precinct on Elizabeth Street. Roscoe Keats entered Bull One's room with a file large enough to choke a horse. "Quite the undistinguished career," he said. "Early education in stealing hubcaps; promoted to stealing cars; went on to study importing, with a specialty in cigarettes from South Carolina with no federal tax stamp; and finally, graduate work in union negotiations, with a minor in enforcement and intimidation. That's probably when you were noticed by the other academics and received your Ph.D., shortly after the disappearance of Carmine the Snake. No doubt you've been on a continuing education track since then."

Bull One looked up. "Fuck you," he said.

"That's it? That's all you can say? Gee, you hurt my feelings." Keats snapped the folder shut. "I'll get right to the point, Celeste. Where were you the night Moe Fortissimo was gunned down?"

"Playing cards at the Marconi Club."

Keats looked at his watch and left the office. He glanced up at the clock in the hallway as he entered the other interrogation room. "Philipi," he said, "what a sweet name." After chronicling Philip DiBullova's criminal record, which was very similar to his brother's, he asked, "Where were you the night Moe Fortissimo was shot?"

"With my brother."

Keats checked his watch. "Let them go," he said. "Save their lawyer a trip."

Bull and Bull met in the hallway; they embraced and kissed.

"Isn't that sweet," Keats said. "What a close family. Get these two candy-store gangsters out of here."

While the Bulls were being interrogated, Eddie, following JB's orders, joined Frankie in the hearse. He couldn't help but notice that Frankie didn't look so good. "You okay?"

"I thought Bull and Bull were coming with me."

"Your lucky day, plans have changed. You should be happy."

"Happy, how can I be? This is wrong. Even if we get away with it, we'll be flooding the streets with drugs. That's going to hurt people. And if I *don't* do it people will still be hurt, especially me."

"Let's go," Eddie said, "and try not to draw any attention."

Frankie looked at him like he was nuts. "You're wearing a cranberry-colored shirt, how does that not draw attention?"

Eddie looked down. "It's magenta," he said.

"Magenta?"

They approached the cargo area at the Alitalia terminal and backed the hearse into the warehouse. A few feet away, they saw the casket sitting on a skid. It was a six-sided wooden coffin with a hand-carved lid, and it was larger than Frankie had expected. Frankie wondered if the procedure in Italy had the zinc inside the casket, as opposed to the casket in zinc.

Frankie could not stop shaking. "Eddie, what if the feds are just waiting for me to take possession of the casket?"

"Don't worry about that. Sal's cousin works down here and sent us word that there hasn't been any unusual activity."

"So, we're taking the word of a guy who smuggles mozzarella?"

"And prosciutto di Parma," said Eddie. That wasn't exactly reassuring. Frankie was worried that as soon as he took custody of

the remains, police would appear from every corner. He imagined
the headline in the *Daily News*: "Undertaker Takes a Powder." He
imagined his father, dead from embarrassment, and his mother,
ironing his underwear as she warbled her musical lamentations.

Eddie tried to calm him. He held Frankie's left arm as Frankie
signed papers with his right. There was nothing unusual at the
cargo bay, and in actuality the process went more smoothly than
usual. Frankie handed a twenty to the clerk, signed his name, and
showed his funeral director's license, and in a moment a forklift
was maneuvering Mr. Vitagliano's oversized casket toward the
hearse. A bump or two later, the coffin was secured.

They left the airport, headed toward the Van Wyck Expressway.

"Frankie, don't speed; you're speeding."

Frankie looked at the dashboard. "I'm sorry, just nervous. I
want to get this over with."

"Well, don't speed, and make sure you signal when you change
lanes."

Frankie nodded.

"We don't want to get stopped for something minor."

Not when we could get stopped for something major, Frankie
thought. As he slowed down, he stole a few quick glances at Eddie,
who didn't look too good, either.

"I'm worried about my father and mother," Frankie said.

"I am, too. I asked you to trust me."

Frankie didn't respond.

"Your father is okay. He's on board. I explained some things to
him, as much as I could. He's nervous for you, but he's okay. He
understands."

"What do we do with this now?"

"I'm supposed to bring the drugs to a secret warehouse in New
Jersey after dark, then bring the hearse to the Mic; but I'm not
gonna do that just yet. For now, turn here—we need to kill some
time."

There could have been a better choice of words, as far as
Frankie was concerned.

It didn't take long for Frankie to figure out Eddie's plan. "You don't mean for me to take a casket filled with drugs to the funeral home, do you?"

Eddie did not answer.

"Eddie, you're not going to take these drugs to the funeral parlor, are you?"

"Did I say that?"

"No, you didn't say it; but you didn't not say it."

Eddie had to understand that. He was a master at double negatives. Still, there was no response.

"Eddie? . . . Eddie!"

"Frankie, I asked you to trust me."

Frankie looked forward. He had nothing more to say.

St. John's Cemetery, in Middle Village, Queens, was the last stop of choice for many mobsters, some of them before their time. Gambino, Profaci, Colombo, Genovese, Galante, Maranziti, all chose these sacred grounds, whether by coincidence or fate. Perhaps God found it easier to keep an eye on them this way, thought Frankie.

The hearse pulled in front of a private mausoleum constructed of white stone with Greek-styled columns. Marked with the name Lucania carved into the granite, it housed the remains of Lucky Luciano.

"We're in interesting company," Frankie said to Eddie. "You should feel very much at home."

Eddie pulled a laminated prayer card from his wallet. On the front was a picture of St. Aloysius holding a skull; on the back, in small print, a name and dates. "Go to section 54," Eddie said.

Frankie knew the 170-acre grounds like his own backyard. He made a series of lefts and rights and pulled along section 54.

"Wait here a minute," Eddie told him.

Eddie left the hearse and walked down between rows of modest headstones—all simple, upright gray granite. Eddie stopped at a grave, knelt down, and pulled a tin vase filled with fresh flowers from the ground. He continued walking, taking the bouquet with him. He studied each gray tablet along the way, until he found the one he was looking for, then he knelt down and placed the flowers at the base of the stone. He ran his fingers over the inscription:

FONTANA

Mario 1926–1963   Maria 1928–1947

In God's Hands

Eddie knelt with his head down then stood up, straight, erect. "I'm sorry," he said, but so only he could hear. He leaned over and kissed the granite headstone. He walked back to the hearse, leaned against the hood, and lit a cigarette. "You know, you're never really a man until you father dies," he said.

Frankie looked at him, confused. "Excuse me?"

"I mean, when you're young and growing up, and you have a father, well, you have someone to run to with your decisions. Someone to give you advice, tell you if you made the right choice. But when your father is dead, then your decisions are your own. You have to keep your own counsel; you're on your own and you live or die with your choices. That's when you really become a man."

Frankie was paying little attention. His mind was too preoccupied to consider Eddie's unique insights into family dynamics and decision making.

The ride back to Mulberry Street was quiet. Frankie thought about his future, about Caterina, her father, his father. He envisioned the headlines in the *Daily News*, the picture of him in handcuffs, the interview with Roscoe Keats, suggesting he was the head of an international drug cartel. He imagined what visiting day would be like at Sing Sing. He imagined his father furiously trying to reach through the screen to enforce his own son's death penalty. He pictured his mother weeping and worrying about his underwear. He even imagined Pasquelena, Angelina, Zizilena, and just Lena, all wondering where they went wrong.

Frankie asked, "Eddie, what are you thinking about?"

Eddie looked out the window. "Me? I'm thinking about how to keep a king out of a pawn's square, because if I don't, the pawn will be lost."

"Chess, is that all you can think about at a time like this? A board game?"

"It's not just a game," Eddie replied.

✝

Easy does it, thought Frankie, *we're almost home free now.* But at Mott Street a police barricade blocked the way. Frankie panicked. "Shit, Eddie, it's a stakeout!"

Eddie looked out the window, then up and down the street.

"Go around to Canal," Eddie said.

Frankie drove to Canal Street, then down to Mulberry. They encountered another barricade.

"Christ, what's going on?"

"Jesus," Frankie remembered, "it's the mall, the streets are closed to traffic."

"Whose friggin' bright idea was that?"

"The restaurants came up with it after the feast to encourage walk-in business—no parking, no traffic, a pedestrian mall." There were hundreds of people drinking and eating at countless tables all along the sidewalk, which had been transformed into a promenade at lunchtime. "Eddie, what are we going to do? We got trouble here."

"Quiet. Let me think. Let me think," Eddie said. Timing was critical now.

Eddie's rumination was promptly interrupted by a knock on the window. Frankie looked out to see a horse's ass as a New York City mounted policeman maneuvered his stallion alongside the hearse. From the driver's seat, he appeared to be eight feet tall. *Shit,* Frankie thought. *Why now?* He rolled down the window.

"What's up, chief?" the officer said.

Frankie was frozen with fear, his eyes fixed on the officer's black riding boot.

Eddie leaned over and spoke. "We got the funeral home down the street and have to make this delivery."

"Not this afternoon, street is closed. You'll never get through," the officer said. "Come back tomorrow."

Eddie leaned over further. "Officer, the guy will go bad by tomorrow." He held his nose.

The officer considered the possibility. He blew on his whistle and called to his counterpart on another horse. "Follow me," he said, "and go slow."

"Eddie, this is fucking crazy," Frankie said.

"Just hang tight and follow him. What choice do we have?"

The two officers on horseback directed Frankie around the barricade. Each took a position in front of the hearse and escorted it through the crowds, blowing the whistle in short bursts to clear a path. With the trappings of a state funeral, the police horses led the hearse down Mulberry Street as hordes of diners eating at sidewalk tables stared in disbelief. There was a whole lot of ball scratching going on as the hearse passed Cha Cha's, Il Cortile, Paisano's, Casa Bella, Fornaio's, Napoli, La Luna's, Paolucci's.

"Eddie, we're fucked!"

"Just calm down! If you're *nervous*, we're fucked. Just follow my lead."

In front of the funeral home, Sal was standing on the sidewalk, schmoozing with his customers. He had six tables set up in front of his small storefront and six more in front of the funeral home. He turned his attention to the street when the crowd parted, making way for the horse-led hearse to pull up.

Frankie was pale and frazzled, and Sal noticed it. Sal understood the implications of the police, the casket, and the drugs. He watched, anxious and helpless. All he could do was play along.

The policemen dismounted and helped guide the hearse into the alley. They seemed just as tall off their horses as on them. "How you guys going to get it inside? Do you have help?"

"We'll handle it from here, officer. Thank you very much," Frankie said.

"Nah, come on, let's give them a hand," the other officer said. "I work as a pallbearer a few times a week."

Find me a hole so I can crawl into it, Frankie thought.

"Hold this," one of the officers said to Sal, handing him the reins of the two brown stallions. The horses eyed Sal, stamped, and snorted.

"Hey, I don't know nothing about horses," Sal protested.

"Come on," the officer said.

Frankie opened the door and rolled the church truck toward the back of the hearse. The four slid the casket out of the hearse and onto the truck, then rolled it into the funeral home.

"Christ, this is heavy," one of the officers commented.

"This is something I've never seen before," the other officer said as he ran his fingers along the casket's hand-carved wood top. "Different shape, too."

Frankie was starting to stammer. "It's Italian . . . a coffin from Italy . . . Italian . . . from Italy."

"Guys, thanks a million," Eddie broke in. "We want to buy you dinner." He reached into his pocket then looked at his companion. "Frankie, you got fifty dollars?"

Frankie took out some bills and began counting. Eddie grabbed the money and handed it over to the police officers. "Guys, you want a drink or something before you leave?"

"Why not?" They took off their helmets and sat.

Eddie was not interpreting Frankie's frantic eye-movement codes. *That's not fair. I always play when you want.*

Instead Eddie asked, "Frankie, doesn't your father keep that bottle in his desk?"

Frankie hurried down the stairs and came up with a bottle of anisette and several Dixie cups. Eddie took the cups, placed them on the casket lid, opened the bottle, and poured. The officers took the drink.

"Here's to Mayor Lindsay," Eddie toasted.

"He's a prick," one officer said.

"Well, fuck him then," Eddie answered.

They all laughed, except Frankie.

"What's with you, kid?"

"I'm not political," he said, hoping that would account for his reluctance to toast.

"Well, we'll drink to this guy," the one officer said, indicating the casket. "What's his name?"

Frankie was beginning to shake. The name might ring a bell. They might want to see more, make him open it. "Uh, this is Mr.

Fullanarco," he finally said. "From Italy."

He was saved by the sound of loud swearing from out on the sidewalk. The two police officers finished their drinks, grabbed their helmets, and ran out into the alley. Sal was yelling at one of the horses, which had just left a considerable calling card in front of the restaurant. The tables emptied quickly.

"Phil, Phil, get hot water, hot water."

He lifted his arm back, ready to give the horse a right hook.

"Hey," the officer yelled. "Hit that horse, you're a dead man." He grabbed the reins.

"The horse just shit all over the sidewalk. My afternoon is ruined."

"It's a horse, asshole. Sometimes they shit."

Sal turned to see the other officer writing a summons. "What the fuck . . . ?"

"Sorry, sir, you don't have the proper permit to have tables on the sidewalk."

✝

Inside the funeral home, Frankie poured himself another drink, and then another. His hands were shaking, his knees too. The lights were off except for a single candelabra in the corner, and the fully drawn drapes threw the parlor into an eerie gloom. Frankie was spooked, more so than ever. Saintly shadows seemed to be closing in on him from every corner of the chapel.

"I can't take this," he said.

"It's over now." Eddie peeked up the alley. "They're leaving. If that moron friend of yours stops arguing, that is."

"I want to die. I just want to die," Frankie said. "What's with the drink? Why not offer them a toot? While you're at it, why not just open this up and hand them a few packages and say, 'Thanks for the help, guys. Have a ball. It's on us!'?"

"They would have taken it, too."

"I wish I was dead."

"You can't die yet."

"Did you say 'yet'?"

"Yes, because we got to open it," he said to Frankie.

"Right here? Are you nuts? Why?"

"Frankie, we got to open it. And I told you not to ask that question. What do we need?"

Frankie looked in a closet and grabbed a Phillips head screwdriver, a chisel, and shears.

"You got any of those plastic gloves?'" asked Eddie. "We'll need those too. Put 'em on."

Frankie grimaced, wondering what gruesome contents Eddie expected to encounter. He placed the tools on top of the casket and started unscrewing the top. Forty screws held the lid in place, so it took some time. Frankie was sweating, and not just from the intense labor. Finally, both men lifted the casket top off, exposing the zinc liner. Eddie punched a hole into the corner of the zinc with a chisel, enough to get the tip of the shears in to begin cutting.

Cutting through the zinc was a slow, tedious task, like opening an enormous can of plum tomatoes. Frankie took the shears and helped until his wrists were tired, then Eddie took over again. Back and forth they cut, until finally the zinc top was free. They paused, not wanting to see, or smell, what lay beneath. Together they lifted the zinc top off, revealing pouch after pouch of white powder.

Frankie dug deeper, gingerly thrusting his hand into the coffin, expecting at any moment to encounter Mr. Vitagliano's cold body. "Christ, Eddie, where is he?"

"Don't you see? Looks like he took up too much space. It wasn't cost-effective. It was either him or another couple hundred pounds of this." He picked up a pouch.

"But where is the body, then?"

"We'll probably never know. They used him as a way to get permission to get this casket into the country. At some point, I guess they took him out and got rid of him."

"So, I was supposed to bury a casket with no body in it."

"No, at this point you weren't even supposed to know."

Frankie fell back into a chair, digesting that last comment. "What do you mean, I wasn't supposed to know?" There was noise from the hallway. "Eddie, someone is coming. We were followed, we're f—"

Eddie put his hand over Frankie's mouth. "Shush." The footsteps got closer and closer. Eddie turned off the light, leaving them in total darkness.

"Frankie? Eddie?" a familiar voice called.

"Dad, don't—wait a minute, I can explain—"

Primo switched on a lamp and walked over next to the casket. Frankie's mind was racing for a way to account for the unsealed coffin and its incriminating contents.

"It's alright, Frankie. Eddie told me. We've got work to do."

Relieved but still puzzled, Frankie watched his father make the sign of the cross. "No need for that, Dad."

"What do you mean?"

"I mean, he's not in there."

Primo looked in and moved the pouches around. "Then where—"

"Probably off the coast of Syracuse by now," said Eddie. "Looks like he gave up his seat on the plane." He picked up a packet of powder as though he were weighing it in his hand.

"Have you done what I asked?" Eddie questioned.

"Yes, he's over there." Primo asked.

Frankie looked puzzled.

Primo walked to another corner of the funeral home, where a large oak casket stood on another church truck. "I got the extra size, like you wanted," he said. He rolled it alongside the other and opened the top. Inside, dressed and cleaned, his head wound closed, was the lifeless body of Tony Branca, the handyman.

"Let's go," Eddie ordered. He started loading the pouches of heroin into Tony's casket, filling every nook and cranny. Frankie got the idea and began to help. Primo joined in.

"But Eddie, how are we going to get away with this? JB is going to know. How are we—"

"Shush," he said, "I asked you—"

"I know, I know, to trust you."

It took fifteen minutes for every pouch to be transferred from Vitagliano's casket into Tony Branca's. The Italian coffin was empty now. Primo shone a lamp's light into the casket to be sure.

Only a single shoe remained. "This must have been Mr. V's," said Primo. "May he rest in peace at sea."

At that they were all quiet until, led by Primo, they each made the sign of the cross. They cleared the tools and closed Mr. V's coffin. They put the shoe into Tony Branca's casket. Just before it was closed, Eddie reached a gloved hand in and removed four of the pouches, which he dropped into a small grocery bag. Frankie looked at him skeptically.

"Don't ask," Eddie said. They closed the casket and sat. "Now, this is important," Eddie said to Primo. "What time is the ceremony?"

"Scheduled for four," he answered. "You and Eddie get this loaded. I'm going to call Father right now."

Primo left, and it was Frankie's turn again to be puzzled.

"Frankie, there's one more thing," Eddie said in an unfamiliarly determined voice. "I need you to be gone for a few days. I need you to be dead for a while."

It was becoming clearer. "Christ, Eddie, you're supposed to kill me. Christ, Eddie. How could you?"

"I didn't," Eddie noted, correctly.

Frankie's eyes began to water. "Eddie, you are supposed to kill me, *me*. That's what you meant when you said I wasn't supposed to know the casket didn't have Mr. V in it. Where were you supposed to do it? New Jersey? How were you going to do it, a gun, or were you going to strangle me and leave me in the Meadowlands? Was that supposed to be me in that casket over there? How could you?"

"Hey, mook. *I didn't do it.*"

Frankie backed off. "Just how am I supposed to disappear?"

"Sal has a screen test arranged for you in California—he's got your plane ticket and everything. My friend, Mr. Ho, runs a car service in Chinatown. He's a good guy. I trust him. He will be waiting in front of Lucci's in one hour to take you to JFK," Eddie said. "Just lay low out in L.A. for a few days until I think it's safe for you."

"A few days? How many?"

"I don't know; how many are in a year?"

"A year!"

"Calm down. I didn't *say* a year. I said I don't know yet. I got to let this thing play out or we're both gonna never be found."

"I can't stay away that long. I can't." And Caterina—how would he live without her? How would he know how to find her? He didn't dare call her, not now.

"Again, mook, I'm gonna tell you. Three days or thirty-three hundred; I don't know yet. When it's safe I'll know, then you'll know. Now get outta here and go pack."

He kissed Frankie, picked up the bag, and left.

Johnny Ballsziti waited at the bakery for word from Eddie or the Bull brothers, whichever arrived first. Confident of his plan, he sipped espresso and ate anisette cookies. The cat was smiling, and so was Annunziata.

Eddie looked up Mulberry Street, then down, then up to the rooftops, before taking a seat across the café table from Johnny.

"The fruit is on the fruit stand," was all he said about the day's doings. "My friend is away on vacation," was all he said about Frankie. That was not such a lie.

Satisfied, JB nodded. "I will meet you later at the café, and we will celebrate with a drink," he said.

Caterina emerged from the back of the bakery and took a seat at the bistro table next to her father. She was dressed in workman's overalls and her hair was pinned up under a baseball cap. It was time to make her intentions known. "Papa," she said, "I would like to talk to you about Frankie. I don't know who told you he's a gambler or any of those other things, but I don't think it's true. I would like to see more of him. And I don't want to return to Italy."

"Why are you dressed like that? What is that on your face? Paint?"

"I'm doing some work in the back. Sprucing things up."

He looked at his wife, who just shrugged.

Caterina continued, "I'm serious about Frankie. I'm not a little girl who needs protection."

Ballsziti sat still. This is what he feared. This is why he got the big bucks, for thinking ahead. "Caterina, I am so sorry I have to be the one to tell you this. Frankie is missing. I just got word. This is what I was afraid of. It seems he owed the wrong people money, big debts, and somebody decided to make an example out of him."

Tears began to flow from her eyes before he even finished.

"I want you to know," he said, "I am going to turn over every stone to find out who did this to this kid. I will not rest until justice is done."

As Caterina ran from the bakery, Ballsziti looked at his wife again. This time he saw daggers in her eyes. "She's young," he said to her. "She'll get over it."

Caterina ran straight to Lucci's restaurant, pulling the ball cap down to hide her red eyes. "Sal, where is Frankie? Where is he?"

Sal, uncharacteristically silent, was sitting at his usual table. He hated to see her hurt—but if he gave away Frankie's whereabouts, both of them stood to be hurt far worse.

"There's something wrong, isn't there? You're not eating or drinking. Sal, what's wrong? Where's Frankie?" Then, afraid of the answer, "No, don't tell me, don't tell me."

"He's . . . taking a trip, Caterina. It'll be alright."

She looked up at him from under the brim of the cap. "You think I don't know what that means?"

"It's not—" Sal had no chance to finish, as she turned and ran out, down the sidewalk, and up the five flights of stairs to Isabella's old apartment.

Within the hour she was packed, dressed in black pantsuit and dark glasses, and on her way to JFK for the next flight to Rome.

The driver from Ho and Ho Car Service pulled up in front of the restaurant at three forty-five. Frankie, in black suit and dark glasses, was a reluctant passenger. He had his marching instructions from Sal: under no condition was he to phone home;

three successive beeps on the pager would be the signal for him to check in with Sal. His life—and the lives of those he loved—depending on his being dead.

Frankie got into the Lincoln and it pulled away, passing the bakery as it left Mulberry Street. *I never said good-bye to Caterina,* he thought. *Or my parents.* Ahead, he saw the Empire State Building. The sight would have to last him for a while.

Mr. Ho was accommodating. "Mr. Eddie say take good care of you, Mr. Frankie. You very special, very special. I do, I do. I got nephew like you. He do same work with dead people. He crazy too. I put radio on for you, Mr. Frankie."

He did, just in time to hear Tony Bennett finish singing. *"But when Joanna Left me, May became December."*

Events were happening too fast. Frankie couldn't think straight. A few blocks away, he yelled, "Stop the car, Mr. Ho," he said. "Stop the car!" Ho pulled over, leaving the engine running.

California was too far away at a time like this, Frankie realized. It was on the other side of his world. Hollywood would have to wait. "Change in plans," he said to Mr. Ho. "Take me to the Port Authority Bus Terminal."

Ho was adamant. "I no can do. Get in trouble, big trouble. Mr. Eddie, he not right up here sometimes." He tapped his temple. "He kwazy."

"Don't worry, Ho. It will be fine. I'll never tell."

Ho looked into the rearview mirror and muttered in his native tongue. Frankie had no trouble understanding the Cantonese. Ranting is ranting in any language. "You get me in big friggin' trouble if you tell Eddie Fontana."

The Lincoln made a U-turn on Delancey Street and headed toward the West Side Highway. Frankie ripped the airline ticket in half.

✝

At Lucci's, promptly at four o'clock, Eddie pulled a chair up to the restaurant window, lit a cigarette, and stared out onto the street.

He watched as Johnny Ballsziti walked out of the bakery and climbed into the waiting Impala for the long ride around the corner, with Bull Two at the wheel. Bull One, back at his duty station, closed the door to the back seat and took his place in the front of the car.

As the car pulled away from the curb, Bull noticed a police car behind them, strobe lights flashing. He stopped dead in the middle of the street.

"What the hell does he want? I didn't do nothing."

JB did not respond at first. "Just take whatever ticket they want to give you and let's move," he finally said.

Roscoe Keats climbed out of the police car and stood a few feet behind the uniformed officer who approached Bull One's window.

"What's the fuckin' issue?" Bull asked.

"Is this your car, sir?"

"No," JB offered from the back seat, "it's my car."

"License and registration, please," the officer requested.

"What is this bullshit? Just write the ticket, if that's what you need to do," JB yelled from the back.

"Whose car is this again?"

"Mine, mine. I told you this is my car," he screamed. "What, are you dense? Now, what's the problem? What did he do?"

"Well, it seems you have a broken taillight."

"Taillight? Is that a federal crime now? Big deal, I'll have it fixed." JB was getting impatient.

"License and registration," the officer said again.

Bull Two opened the glove compartment and handed over the documentation.

"So, you are Mr. John Ballsziti?"

"What, are you stupid?" JB asked. "I told you this is my car. That would make me John Ballsziti."

"Would you mind stepping out of the car," the officer told Bull. "And keep your hands where I can see them."

More police cars gathered in the intersection. Passersby on the sidewalk stopped to see what was going on. Clerks and shopkeepers peered out of doorways. Women paused from taking in their laundry and leaned out of upper-story windows to get a better look.

Bull One got out of the car.

"Would you mind opening the trunk?"

"Hey, what is this about? It's just a broken taillight. What do you need to look in the trunk for?" JB complained.

"Looks like the wiring might be damaged too."

Keats chewed on a cigar as he observed the developing scene.

"Just do what he says," JB ordered, "and let's get out of here." He turned and recognized Roscoe Keats. "Hey, they got you writing traffic violations now?" he laughed.

Bull opened the trunk and the police officer looked inside.

What's this?" the officer asked. He picked up a pouch tucked behind the wheel well and held it up for Keats's inspection. "Looks like heroin to me," he said. "And there's more: one, two, three . . . "

JB, reaching the end of his patience, jumped out of the car. "Hey, what is this?"

Keats was only too happy to answer. "It looks like conspiracy to distribute illegal drugs."

"What are you talking about? That ain't mine. How did they get there? These ain't mine."

"Keep looking," Keats commanded.

The officer took out his flashlight to continue the search of the trunk and drew out a brown paper bag. He opened it and handed it to Keats, who reached for his pen and used it to maneuver a handgun from the bag.

"Gee," he said, holding the gun by the barrel, "looks like a .45 caliber—two of them, as a matter of fact. Does anyone remember what was used on Moe Fortissimo?" He answered his own question. "I think the shooters used .45s."

Bull One moved closer to Bull Two. "You were supposed to put them back," he whispered.

"I did. I did put them back."

"Gentlemen, gentlemen, let's not quibble," Keats said.

One of the agents turned JB against the car and started to put the handcuffs on his wrists. Then he stopped and turned to Keats. "I think you should have the honor," he said.

Keats dropped his cigar to the sidewalk and ground it out. He took the cuffs and snapped them tight around Ballsziti's wrists. "You have the right to remain silent," Keats began. At that moment his life was complete.

A local crime reporter, working on an anonymous tip, found himself in the right place at the right time. The lucky journalist snapped the picture that would grace the front page of the *Daily News* and every other major newspaper across the country the next morning: Roscoe Keats cuffing mafia lord Johnny Ballsziti, and in the background, the don's wife standing in the bakery window, flipping the bird. Whether Annunziata's gesture was directed at Keats or at her husband, only she knew for sure.

Primo drove with Father Colapetra to Woodlawn Cemetery in the Bronx, where the cremation would take place. He thought a prayer was in order and convinced Colapetra, against his better judgment, to offer it. "It goes against all we believe," Colapetra explained. "Resurrection of the body—what's to resurrect if we have no body, just ash?"

"Father, don't you think God, with all His power, can reconstruct us? From dust we came—remember when He said that?"

Colapetra finally relented when Primo said that Tony deserved a prayer after all he'd gone through. The ride to the Bronx was quiet. Primo was nervous and did not feel like having the usual "What's new, Father?" conversation. Just as well. Father Colapetra was not his usual gregarious self either. He opened his Bible, revealing the daily race form. At the cemetery, Primo helped the crematory attendant roll Tony Branca's casket from the hearse onto a lift. Father Colapetra watched as they slid the casket into the brick-lined retort chamber.

"Jesus," the man said, "what the hell do you have in there?"

"Sadly, a victim of greed. A terrible sin, don't you think, Father?"

The attendant reached to press the ignition button.

"Please," Primo asked, "may I do that?"

"Sure, go ahead." The attendant wiped the sweat from his forehead.

As Primo pressed the button, the burners ignited and Father Colapetra prayed. "Eternal rest grant unto Antonio Branca, O Lord. May perpetual light shine upon him. May he be lifted high in Your presence. May he rest in peace."

The flames grew brighter and brighter until the retort was completely ablaze. The casket, its occupant, and its ill-gotten contents were instantly engulfed in flames burning at two thousand degrees Fahrenheit, generating an exhilarating air quality over the Woodlawn section of the Bronx as the cremation was carried out. The vapors put the usually morose funerary gathering into a New York state of mind.

"May his soul, and all the souls of the faithfully departed, rest in peace." Father Colapetra finished with a sign of the cross. As they left the crematory, the good Father started to giggle, as did Primo. Neither knew why.

The ride home was filled with lively conversation. "How's Frankie?"

"Don't ask."

"What's wrong?" Father asked. "Is it about the stolen money Ballsziti sent to Italy in his mother-in-law's casket? Frankie confided in me a little."

"What stolen money?"

"You didn't know?"

"Not about the money, but it makes sense now. They paid me in new bills, wrapped in aluminum foil. When I showed Frankie, he hit the roof. It makes sense now." Primo, in an uncharacteristically chatty mood, opened up about all he knew—about Vitagliano and Branca, about the drugs they'd just incinerated. "I didn't know everything until you told me your end," he explained. "But now I can put two and two together. I don't know how we ever got involved with this Ballsziti guy."

"They have their way," Colapetra observed.

"It is touch and go for now, Father, touch and go. Before long Eddie's plan should become clear."

Colapetra looked at him quizzically. "Eddie Fontana? This was all Eddie's plan?"

"Yes."

They both giggled—Eddie's plan, that was funny.

Colapetra went back to reading his Bible, the part about the loaves and the fishes. "I'm hungry," he said.

"Me too," Primo answered.

They giggled again, all the way back to the motherland.

Within the hour, news crews set up shop outside the bakery on Mulberry Street. Sal carried a tray of veal cutlet sandwiches out to the reporters. "Thought you guys might be hungry," he said.

"Hey, thanks. If I can do something for you, just say the word."

"Well, now that you mention it, don't you think you'd get a better camera shot from this angle?" He motioned to his storefront.

The reporter got the message. "Hey, guys, let's set up over there."

The news crew moved their cameras, and the evening's broadcasts prominently featured the neon sign that read "Lucci's Restaurant," along with a placard advertising the nightly special: The Cod Father—flounder oreganato served with arborio rice and a side of cooked goose.

Reporters from every station in New York City tried to interview reluctant passersby, but they got nowhere. "Johnny who?" was the standard response. Not a single shop owner or neighborhood resident had anything to add.

Chapter 23

The neighborhood, the day after Johnny Ballsziti's arrest, was adrift like a rudderless ship. The Marconi Social Club did not open for business as usual. JB's crew waited, leaderless and confused, and like nervous Apostles who went into hiding after Christ was crucified, all thought it best to stay home until the situation made itself clear.

No one knew what else the feds had in store—what other subpoenas were waiting to be served or what other arrests would be made. If JB offered anything it was stability, and without him there was uncertainty. But his faithful believed he would find a way to extricate himself from his present dilemma or make his wishes known, and they bided their time while awaiting the word.

Eddie, venturing over to Lucci's at dinnertime, found Sal sitting motionless with the phone in his hand, a worried look on his brow. "What's with you?" he asked.

"I got a call from Sol Weis. Frankie hasn't showed up for the screen test. I called the hotel where they had him booked. He never checked in. He was supposed to be there last night, and he should have been at the studio hours ago."

Eddie sat down. "Could be a million things. Don't have to be what you think it is. Could be a million things."

"Name one," Sal shot back.

Eddie considered the possibility that JB had had a backup plan to deal with Frankie all along. But that would mean other possibilities as well. It was too much for his brain cells to deal with right now. "He's gonna call. I'm sure of it. Don't say nothin' when he does. Be careful of the phones, but find a way to keep him under wraps until I say it's clear."

"You're assuming he will call. He should have been there by now, and he isn't."

Sal was making sense, but Eddie refused to admit he might have miscalculated.

"Maybe we should check with Caterina, see if she knows anything."

"Are you dense or somethin'? We don't know where she stands in all this. Blood is thicker than water. If this chick gets to see her father, he could find out that Frankie is still alive, and his wheels will start turning and like that Hansel and Gretel story, the whole thing will come tumbling down."

"Don't you mean Humpty Dumpty?"

"Them too."

In Atlantic City, New Jersey, the 500 Club was the legendary hot spot that had helped launch the careers of comedians like Dean Martin and Jerry Lewis. Frankie asked for some details from the hotel concierge, then reached for his wallet and took out the business card from the Peppermint Lounge. Little Anthony had said it would open doors for him, and that was just what he needed it to do now. Living on the lam, without the largesse of Sol Weis's expense account, would require quick cash.

It was nearly dark before Frankie ventured out on the unfamiliar streets, still wearing his dark glasses. By now, West Coast time, he should've been standing in front of the cameras, a ball of nerves. Instead, here he was in Jersey, a ball of nerves, and wishing he could call home. Still, he was sure he'd made the right choice. He felt better, somehow, being a little closer to home.

At the club Frankie asked for the manager. He held out his hand to introduce himself. "Mr. D'Amico, I'm—" he began, catching himself just in time. "I'm Sal Lucci from Miami. Just flew in from a stint in the Big Apple."

Skinny D'Amico read Little Anthony's card and gave Frankie the once-over. He studied the back of the card where Little Anthony had written "Friend." D'Amico knew the Peppermint Lounge implied a connection to Johnny Ballsziti, who had a silent interest in a dozen clubs on the strip in Atlantic City. To check Frankie's bona fides, D'Amico asked him a series of questions. He flicked his thumb on the edge of the card as he talked. "Little Anthony's a piece of work, ain't he?"

"An original copy," Frankie answered.

"Do you think he wears a piece?" He pointed to his hair.

"A weave, my guess is a weave."

Skinny nodded. "How's the weather in New York?" he asked Frankie. He wasn't referring to the temperature.

"Hot, very hot right now."

"I heard," he said. "Quite a storm last night."

Frankie kept to the climatic metaphor. "Temporary heat wave. It will blow over."

The man nodded, never taking his eyes off Frankie. "So, they think it will cool down?"

Jesus, how far can this go? Frankie thought. "Once the barometric pressure drops, the humidity will probably dissipate and cooler winds will come out of the east, moving the high pressure out to the ocean."

"Huh?" Skinny looked confused. He tried another course. "Word is his house is full of rats."

"The whole city's full of rats. His house has fewer than most."

"Well, that's good. He always had good exterminators."

"You know it. They work on weekends, too."

"Still, it's not like it used to be."

"Nothing is."

Skinny nodded. "Temporary, that's what you hear?"

"He's got too much up here," Frankie said, tapping his head.

"One of the smartest," Skinny agreed. "So, New York's not worried? You see the papers this morning?"

He hadn't—but he played along. "Clear and sunny in a few days." *I hope this conversation ends soon,* he thought. *I feel like a friggin' weatherman.*

Skinny handed the card back to Frankie. He reached out his hand and pulled Frankie in closer to kiss his cheek. *What? Just like that?—a kiss, but no dinner? No flowers?* Frankie understood the complicated relationship that made kissing acceptable between strangers, between men no less. I know somebody, a friend, who has a friend, who knows somebody, another friend, that you know, which allows us to kiss. Eddie had taught him that.

"We got a singer in the lounge, every night," Skinny said. "Name's Vinnie something or other, a wise guy's son, from down your way. If you ask me, he sucks; but hey, the kid's father knows your rabbi, and you know the rest. I think the kid's a fugazy, too." He let his wrist go limp. "But hey, live and let live. Go see him. Tell him I said to work you in."

For forty minutes that night, Sal Lucci of Miami had the audience in the palm of his hand. It was textbook comedy, a comic's dream. Frankie was in the zone as never before. He tweaked his routine, using a different neighborhood, family, friends, leaving out all references to his lately developed funeral hook. The audience laughed until they cried. Frankie's world centered around two opposite emotions, joy and sadness. Laughing turns to crying—just like Primo always said.

The five-piece band started on cue. The house swelled with applause, and the patrons were on their feet, calling for him to take a curtain call. Acceptance—the most gratifying experience in his new world. What a rush! Frankie jaunted back from behind the curtains, bowing and throwing kisses to the audience.

What D'Amico had said about the news nagged him, though. What was going on back in New York? He had to risk a call. He found a telephone booth in the hotel lobby and dialed.

"Where the hell are you?" said Sal. "It's after midnight. We're sick to death here worrying about you. I haven't even eaten dinner."

"No dinner? Sal, you must really be worried! But I couldn't be so far away with all that's going on."

"Where are you?"

He hesitated. "Atlantic City."

"Atlantic City!" Sal yelled. "You're supposed to be dead, so you go underground in Atlantic City? That's Ballszitiville. Why don't you just go hide out in the Marconi Social Club? Or better yet, put a target on your back."

"I'm using an alias," Frankie said. "I got a gig but I'm not telling funeral jokes. I'm being careful. Why are you getting so excited?"

"Are you kidding? I told you, I'm sick to death about you. I get a call from my people, who say you didn't show up for the shoot and I figure that's because maybe you've been shot. I didn't know what to think."

"Your people?"

"Show business talk. Get with it. Weis is pissed. You know, he's a bigwig with the Philip Morris Agency. He's got connections up the wazoo. He told me that if all had gone well with the screen test you could have broken out. The guy knows Carson, damn it! Do you understand? You blew it, and I'll be making meatballs for the rest of my life. And here you are standing on some Jersey stage putting out a sign saying 'Come get me!'"

"I'm sorry, Sal, but you know me better than that. I should be up there, and I can't be. I had to stay close. I had to."

There was silence. Frankie took that to mean Sal understood. "What's going on up there?" he asked. "What do you know?"

"JB's in jail. Keats picked him up right after you left. Seems somebody got careless and left some fruit rotting in the trunk of his car. The neighborhood is buttoned up tight. Smart money has him out in a few days. Papers are talking about a snitch in the family."

"Wow," said Frankie. "I wonder . . . "

"I gotta tell our friend I heard from you. He's walking around with his thumb up his ass. He sits at the chess board hour after hour. Thinks his friend had a backup plan in case his original plan didn't work. And if that was the case, he would have a plan to deal with all parties involved, if you know what I mean."

Amazingly, Frankie did.

"The old man must be thinking overtime now," Sal said. "If he even suspects you're alive, he's got to figure you're a guest of the feds."

"Careful," Frankie said.

"Right, sorry."

"How's my mother, my father?"

"Your mom's fine. Your father don't look so good. Your mother and all the Lenas know you're gone and he can't tell them where you are. Those broads are ready to take their black wardrobes out of cold storage already. This whole thing's pretty stressful. Did I tell you, I'm not eating like I usually do?"

"I'm coming back."

"No, not yet, no way. Ed—*our friend* will let me know when it's right."

"What's he waiting for?"

"He doesn't know if his friends will be back from college for spring break."

"How is Caterina? Have you seen her?"

"I'm sure she's fine," Sal lied. If Frankie had an inkling of the truth, Sal was sure wild horses wouldn't keep him from returning to New York on the next bus.

One of the roving reporters appeared in the doorway, and Sal quickly changed gears. "Okay then, Mr. Baciagulope, add another case of Chianti to that order and have it delivered."

"What are you talking about?" asked Frankie.

"Right, Mr. Baciagulope, that's fine. Your check will be here. 'Bye. And don't forget to bring back some taffy." He slammed the receiver down.

✝

Eddie waited in the entryway of a building that was deserted at midday. He looked at this watch to verify the time and checked the street signs to make sure he was in the right place. One o'clock Thursday afternoon, corner of Elizabeth and Houston—that's what he was told. He took a deep breath. He was in the right place; it was the right time.

He lit a cigarette after fidgeting with the pack. A few minutes after one, a black Cadillac limousine with dark-tinted windows slowed to a stop on Houston Street. The door opened. Eddie looked up and down, east and west. When he was satisfied that no one was watching, he extinguished his cigarette and ducked into the back seat of the car. Roy Silverschein extended one hand in greeting and placed the other around Eddie's neck in an awkward show of affection. The hand lingered on his neck just a moment then fell off, sliding gently down Eddie's back.

"Hello, Mr. Silverschein," Eddie said uncomfortably.

"Call me Roy."

"Hello, Mr. Roy Silverschein," he said, pronouncing each syllable, clear and loud.

Eddie sank into the soft leather alongside Silverschein. A glass window separated the two of them from the driver. Silverschein poured a Scotch for Eddie and another for himself. They raised their glasses.

"Salute!" Silverschein offered.

"Lock'hymen!" Eddie answered.

Silverschein was dressed like a movie star. His tie screamed money; his shirt was white on white, and his elegant suit had Brioni written all over it. He looked and smelled like he had just left a barber's chair—Pinaud aftershave, Clubman talc, and not a hair out of place. As often as Eddie had seen him on television, he felt like he was in the presence of a celebrity.

"Our friend sends you his best regards," Silverschein said. "He told me you got heart." He placed his perfectly manicured hand on Eddie's chest and patted it. "Heart," he reiterated, reluctantly pulling away. "He told me you're his number one man."

Eddie blushed. "You're keeping up with things, I assume?"

Eddie nodded. The car moved down the Bowery.

"Not good," Silverschein said.

He took out two cigars and offered one to Eddie. "Cuban," Silverschein explained. Eddie refused. Silverschein bit the tip of his cigar and spit it out, lighting the other end. He took a few deep drags. "I got to tell you, JB is worried. I've represented him for twenty years, and a hundred guys like him, but this is different. I'm not used to seeing him sweat these things. In fact, I'm not accustomed to seeing him so sloppy. He's always so cool under pressure because he has alibis up the gazoo. You know what I mean?"

Eddie nodded and sipped at his drink.

Silverschein leaned in. "He's confused. Johnny's trying to figure out what went wrong. He thinks one of the Bulls went bad on him. Do you think it's possible?"

Eddie nodded and drained his glass. Silverschein poured another round.

"How can a man smart enough to send millions in stolen currency out of the country and bring a shitload of heroin back in— in a casket, no less—misjudge his own people? He must be slipping up here," he said with a tap to his forehead. He puffed on his cigar. "The Johnny Ballsziti I knew was always four times removed from suspicion."

Eddie sighed in agreement, and scratched his head.

"Anyway, he wanted to know if the goods are safe?"

Eddie nodded.

"Good, good," Silverschein said. "He'll be happy to hear that."

Eddie finished his second drink. Silverschein fixed him a third.

"Listen," Silverschein said. "He wants you to start moving it. He wants some cash on hand. When I get him out on bail, he has an exit strategy."

Eddie nodded affirmative.

"It's not good right now," Silverschein said again. "JB's in solitary with nothing but time to think and think. The Bulls, everything points to the Bulls. He wants them gone. He told me to tell you to go to the Chili Brothers. They have connections inside the walls. They can make it look like a fight in the jailyard, or however they want to handle it—a murder-suicide would be perfect. They'll know what's best. Do you understand?"

Eddie took a swig of his drink and nodded.

"Good, good," said Silverschein. "I told him, with them gone I'll have a better chance of confusing a judge, and I can at least get bail. I can lay it all at their feet." He conjectured out loud, dramatizing for effect. "Your Honor, the DiBullova Brothers were working independently, got caught, blamed each other. They fought; one killed the other. The surviving sibling was consumed with grief, realizing he had killed his own brother, and decided to take his own life. It's the stuff Greek tragedies are made of. I'll have the judge eating out of my hand. The fact that the judge recently spent two weeks' vacation in a villa in Taromina won't hurt either. It was all comped. JB is always thinking ahead. Anyway, is it fair to say you will take care of his request?"

Eddied tossed back the last of his drink and gave a thumbs up.

"Good, my man, he knew he could count on you. The car will take you back."

The limousine came to a stop in front of the Federal Courthouse in Foley Square. Silverschein exited amid a contingent of media, while Eddie hung back in the shadows. The reporters and photographers were falling over themselves, shouting questions, aiming mics, knowing Silverschein was always good for a sound bite. Silverschein answered question after question in his glib, nonchalant style.

One reporter shouted, "Is your client guilty, Mr. Silverschein?"

Silverschein stopped and turned toward the gaggle of reporters. "Yes," he said, "he is guilty . . . of having a vowel at the end of his name—no more, no less." Those were the last words Eddie heard as the limo's window closed and the car pulled away from the impromptu press conference. A block later, Eddie knocked on the glass. "This is far enough, chief," he said.

The driver pulled over to the side, and Eddie got out on Worth Street. He could still see the host of reporters following Silverschein up the courthouse steps. The man relishes the spotlight, Eddie thought.

As he walked back to Mulberry Street, Eddie remembered the last time he was downtown. He thought about JB, Frankie, Giovanna and Primo. He stopped at a hot dog stand. "One with everything," he ordered. "Extra relish." The vendor proceeded to put a frankfurter in a bun with mustard, sauerkraut, chili, onions, and extra relish. "Orange soda, too."

Frankie's one-night gig at the 500 Club was extended for a week. Except for his feeling of impending doom, it was the experience of a lifetime. His nights were filled with laughs and music, a full 180-degree difference from his life at the Grace Funeral Home on Mulberry Street. But every morning he woke with the same worried feeling in his gut. The newspapers suggested that Ballsziti was going to walk any day. There was conjecture that a gang war would ensue as he cleaned house. There go the windows, he thought.

He walked aimlessly on the boardwalk, recalling the time he was parked off the Brooklyn Belt Parkway with Caterina, and worring about his mother and father and Eddie and Sal. Maybe the coast was clear enough . . . he stopped at a phone both and dialed the bakery. He needed to talk to her. He *had* to talk to her.

"Pronto." It was Annunziata.

Frankie disguised his voice. "May I speak to Caterina?"

"No, she's no here," she said suspiciously. "Who's this?"

"Oh, just an old friend from school."

"Well, she'sa not here. Who's you name?"

He started to sweat. "Baciagulope, tell her Mr. Baciagulope called."

"Mr. Baciagulope," she repeated. "I give her a message." Click.

He wondered if he'd made a grave mistake. If he had, it was too late to undo it now.

The following night, after the midnight set, Frankie was approached by a gentleman who handed him a business card.

"Hey Lucci, Lucci," the man called. Frankie didn't respond at first, forgetting his alias. "You don't know me," the man said. "I'm K. Broder. Call me K. I'm Jerry Vale's agent. I think you would be a good fit for Jerry. He's looking for an opening act. Can we talk?"

Frankie's mouth dropped open.

"I actually brought Jerry here last night to catch your act," the man said.

"That was him?" Frankie said. "I kinda wondered. Wow, if an angel had hair, it would look like his. But I already have a manager."

"Good," the man said. "but you still need an agent. I took the liberty of booking you this weekend." He scribbled some information on a piece of paper. "It's not far, South Philly. A place called the Black Banana. You got Friday night. I'll pick you up."

At One Federal Plaza on Friday morning, a recalcitrant Philip DiBullova, nattily dressed in orange, sat at a table quietly conferring with his attorney. His beard was thick; he hadn't shaved in days. The whispering stopped when Roscoe Keats entered the room.

"My client has nothing to say," the young attorney stated matter-of-factly. "We will be making a motion for bail. Mr. DiBullova maintains his innocence and asserts he was just a passenger in the car."

"Save it," Keats responded. "I don't even want to know what excuse he has for his fingerprints on the weapon that killed Moe Fortissimo."

"We will answer that in the appropriate venue."

"Don't tell me," Keats said, "JB handed you a brown bag, so you reached in and instead of zeppoles there were guns."

The attorney rose from his seat. "We do not have to subject ourselves—"

"Save it," Keats said again. He sat quietly for a moment. Timing was everything. "You know what? Go for bail. The government will even recommend it."

Bull looked at his lawyer, confused.

Keats pulled a tape recorder from his pocket. He set it on the table, turned up the volume, and pressed the play button.

A familiar voice on the tape revealed Ballsziti's plan for the Bulls to an unidentified listener. "JB's in solitary with nothing but time to think and think. The Bulls, everything points to the Bulls. He wants them gone. He told me to tell you to go to the Chili Brothers. They have connections inside the walls. They can make it look like a fight in the jailyard, or however they want to handle it—a murder-suicide would be perfect. They'll know what's best. Do you understand?"

"That fuck!" Bull shouted. The tape continued to play.

"I told him, with them gone I'll have a better chance of confusing a judge, and I can at least get bail. I can lay it all at their feet."

Bull whispered in his attorney's ear.

"My client is open to a deal. What are you offering?"

Keats smiled, put the recorder in his pocket, and walked out. "I'll think about it," he said.

With K behind the wheel, they drove to Philadelphia. Frankie was quiet and just stared out the window.

"You know, Sal," K said, "for a comic, you look pretty gloomy."

"I'm sorry," Frankie said. "I'm not a good driving companion. There's a lot going on in my head. Some problems with my family up north, my girl, my best friend, a long story. And I was supposed to be in California this week. I was going to take a screen test for a movie role. It could have been a big break, but I blew it. I came here instead. "

K nodded. "North? I thought you said you came from Miami."

"Yes, north Miami." He was nothing if not quick.

"Well," he said, "show business is a funny thing. One door closes, one door opens."

Frankie nodded and kept quiet. K continued, "You know, Jerry has just signed with Caesar's. He'll be doing six weeks there then going on tour. Things may work out for you yet."

Frankie slept the rest of the way into Philly. K knew the city well and gave Frankie a tour, ending up in the small Italian section of the city. Frankie stopped into a salumeria, deliciously familiar with its aromas of provolone and dry sausage. The smells reminded him of Mulberry Street. He surveyed the Italian delicacies—

packages of Stella D'Oro cookies and Perugina candies.

Among the varied pastas and sauces with fancy labels he spied an appealing package of cannoli shells. He did a double-take at the label. "Isabella's Home Cooking." He read more: "Made from a family recipe. Manufactured in New York City."

"You can buy their cannoli filling, too," the clerk said. "It's in the refrigerator."

Caterina, he thought, one smart cookie and beautiful too; and he had let her get away.

He excused himself to find the men's room—and a pay phone.

"Pronto." It was Annunziata again.

"Is Caterina there?"

"Who's this?"

"Mr. Baciagulope."

"Mr. Baciagulope my ass. My daughter don't know any Baci-agulope. Stop calling her or I breaka your legs by myself."

"Could you give her a message, then?"

"She'sa not here, she'sa back in school. In Italy."

He clicked off the receiver and stood silently in the phone booth. *Italy.* He felt a grief as raw and fresh as if she'd died. Would he ever see her again? He was swearing off moo goo and thai foo forever. Not to mention bufala mozzarella.

In the strangely quiet enclave of Mulberry Street, Eddie wandered the streets, at times talking to himself. The neighborhood was different, something was missing. He stopped at Lucci's, where Sal was sitting at his table. There was no food in front of him, no wine, no delicacies. There was no big hello, nothing. There was something missing for Sal, too. With the slightest acknowledgment, Eddie slid into the seat across from Sal. There was nothing to say.

Finally Sal broke the silence. "Frankie called me again last night, Eddie. He's getting restless. And he's asking questions about Caterina. I don't know how much longer I can convince him to lay low."

"Just tell him it ain't right yet. If he doesn't want to get us killed he'd better just stay put. JB may beat this thing and he's gonna have a lot of questions and I ain't good at giving answers."

The door to the restaurant swung open. It was one of the reporters from the *Daily News* Sal had been courting who brought the news—literally.

"Listen, Sal, buddy, you've been great about all the free meals and stuff. Thought you'd appreciate this, hot off the presses."

Eddie looked over his shoulder at the afternoon front page. The lineup of photos was unmistakable: there was the face of Johnny Ballsziti alongside mug shots of the Bull Brothers, and one of Roy Silverschein as well.

Sal read aloud. "In what federal officials call a deathblow to organized crime in America, Mr. Johnny Ballsziti was indicted this morning on counts of conspiracy to distribute narcotics and conspiracy to commit murder. Testimony from two key figures in Ballsziti's organization, Philip and Celestino DiBullova, sealed the grand jury's decision. Pending trial, Mr. Ballsziti has been remanded to the custody of a maximum security facility."

Eddie and Sal exchanged looks as Sal ushered the journalist out, with his thanks and a meatball sandwich wrapped to go. Eddie attempted to read the rest of the story.

"C'mere, Sal, help me out here. I left my glasses at home."

"Well, it goes on to say that 'In an unprecedented move, attorney Roy Silverschein has surrendered to federal authorities, who have accused him of conspiring with the Ballsziti crime family. Prosecutors asserted that Mr. Silverschein was the target of a criminal investigation, and wiretaps from his office and chauffeured limousine have convinced a judge to remove him from the Ballsziti case. Silverschein will be defending himself against charges of criminal solicitation and conspiracy. He will also address charges by the New York State Bar Association, which has started disbarment proceedings."

"Sal, I'll have some wine," Eddie said, almost cheerfully.

Sal brought a bottle of Montepulciano to the table and poured two glasses. He sensed a cloud was lifting. He waited and watched as Eddie sipped. He took a swig, too.

"Are we toasting anything?"

"Maybe," Eddie answered.

Frankie's act that night turned out to be perfect for Vale's audience. Except for the fact that they talked funny, Frankie found the inhabitants of Philadelphia's Little Italy similar to those of New York's. He even picked out the usual café types in the audience. His jabs worked on them just like in New York, and they got the inside jokes, too. He left the stage to great applause.

In the dressing room K had just brought in a congratulatory bottle of Dewars when there was a knock on the door. Frankie was caught completely by surprise when Bobby Rydell walked in and clapped him on the back.

"Frankie, Frankie Grace, you son of a bitch, how are you? I came to see Vale, and Christ, was I shocked when I saw you. I'm still telling the story of the night you opened for me at the Peppermint." He looked over at K. "A thousand hearses!" he exclaimed. "A thousand hearses all over the street. This kid's a New York original."

K shot a look at Frankie.

"It's a long story," Frankie said. "I can explain."

K nodded. "Well, whatever your name is, Sal or Frankie, from New York or north Miami, I have some good news for you."

In the closet-sized dressing room, Frankie had just kicked back with a scotch on the rocks to bask in his success. Vegas. The Strip. Names he had only seen on TV. The big time. If he couldn't have Caterina, he could at least have Caesar's. And he could afford to drown her memory in Dewar's every night.

He heard the pager go off—once, twice, three times—the signal from Sal. He practically leapt out of his chair for joy. Was the coast clear for him to return home? He dashed out to the pay phone in the lobby and dialed Sal's number.

"Hey, Sal, chef! I saw the news about JB. And I've just been pegged—"

"*Compare,* I have to tell you something."

Frankie caught the serious note in Sal's voice. "What, what?"

"Your father's in the hospital. Might be his heart. Your mother called Eddie, and they left just now with him in the ambulance. For a while it looked like your dad wasn't going to let them take him."

Frankie recognized his father in that statement. "I'm coming back," Frankie said.

"I know. You do what you gotta do. But you still have to be careful. We'll watch out. So you're good to go; I mean come. I mean you're good to go . . . shit, just come home, *amico mio.*"

K got Frankie on the last flight out that night. Frankie stared out the window as the big DC-8 brought him back to his world, by way of LaGuardia. He was hypnotized by the humming of the engines. His eyes were fixed on every movement of the giant mechanical wing. The grinding motor coincided with the flaps on the silver arms as they rose to slow the aircraft. He felt suspended in air as the plane slowly banked left, then right. He could make out the Fifty-ninth Street Bridge and, moments later, the Empire State Building and, lower on the horizon, the amazing outlines of the World Trade Towers. The plane was flying low now, suspended just above the rooftops. The panoramic view of the earth below condensed through the small window as the plane descended.

He strained to locate Mulberry Street—he zeroed in on the Manhattan Bridge, followed Canal Street, and, for a moment, was sure he saw it. Some part of his mind heard the pilot's admonition as they began their final descent, and he knew he had complied; his seat belt was fastened. But another part of his mind was on a stage in front of an audience. He was working the crowd, making them laugh. It was clear, real, except that it wasn't. The drummer's ba-da-bump rim shot after his final one-liner was actually the landing gear locking into place. When he heard the applause, he was sure he hadn't imagined it—and then he realized it had come from the other passengers when the plane was safely on the ground.

He was home.

Frankie hurried up the corridor, his few clothes and belongings in a carry-on bag slung over his arm. Though Sal was waiting for him at the gate, it took a moment for the two longtime friends to locate each other.

"Frankie, over here!" he heard Sal call out at last. The two embraced. Sal had started to grow a goatee, and a diamond stud glistened in one pierced ear.

"I go away for a few days and you become a freak?"

"I missed you, too," Sal said. "And what's with the crew cut?"

"Disguise. Best I could do, since I can't change this nose."

"Come on, hurry," Sal urged, trying to change the subject. "This friggin' airport crossing guard thinks he's a federal agent. I gave him twenty bucks to look the other way so I could park at the curb."

Sal floored the GTO. In the car, they were quiet at first. Finally, Frankie said, "You know, for years I would to go to sleep every night thinking about death, thinking about someone I love dying. It's the worst part of the funeral business. Sooner or later, you have to bury everyone you love. I've always dreaded the day I had to face it."

"Hey, you gotta keep your hopes up." Sal gave Frankie the full report on his father, on the toll the past week had taken on him. "He kept his word not to let on about you. That hasn't been easy, what with everybody in the neighborhood asking after your stint at my place. He'd just shrug and say it looked like you'd gone off to follow your dream. And your mother, she's just about ground the floor to sawdust, between pacing it and cleaning it."

"And Eddie?"

"He told me to give you a message, but it was so convoluted, I didn't understand a friggin' word," Sal said.

"Give me the gist of it."

"He said, 'Tell Frankie not to look for me. The leak hasn't been found, and there may still be plumbers working on it. The crabs are gone.' He said his balls don't itch right now, and he don't think the itch will come back. Jeez, who's he been banging? And he said when the sauce is ready, he'll call, and you will eat together."

Frankie smiled. Classic Eddie—mixed metaphor, double negatives, and all.

"I'm not as good at this stuff as you, but basically, he wanted you keep laying low until more time passes," Sal said. "He don't want nobody to put two and two together. The old man still has some friends on the street. You should have seen that morning when they all got pinched. Johhny Balls looked like a bumbling fool when that guy cuffed him. Like, 'How the fuck did this happen?' I mean, the feds pull out a load of drugs from the trunk and two guns used in a murder; how stupid is this guy? And these criminals call themselves organized. Ha! Anyway, he's in lockdown, no bail. We can call him Johnny Balls now; it's safe. Balls, Balls, Johnny Balls, Giovanni Cogliones, Giovanni Culones! Hey, that's got a nice ring to it. Anyway, they got him dead to rights, excuse the expression. He won't see daylight again. Bull and Bull are making deals—must be the prison food got them to talk. They got a pass on the Fortissimo hit by pointing to JB. They may wind up in witness protection. It shouldn't be too hard to hide those giant miscreants somewhere in Iowa, selling Avon, right? Anyway, like I said, the feds got JB dead to rights now. And Eddie is the last guy standing. Go figure. And there might not be no San Gennaro festival next year. There's a new sheriff in town, claiming the whole thing is a front for the mafia. What nerve! And there's this Guiliani guy; he's with the feds—supposed to be some mad-dog prosecutor. An Italian going after his own, go figure! And, of course, now the friggin' mayor thinks he can run the festival better. Hey, for all their faults, the boys ran a hell of a festival."

Sal was rambling on like he hadn't seen Frankie in years. "Sal, Sal, slow down, take it easy. How are you doing, Sal?"

"Eh, *porca miseria*. I didn't want to tell you. I'm losing the restaurant. These prick landlords don't want to listen to reason. I can't make the nut anymore."

"Jeez, Sal, I'm sorry."

"Don't be. I got a job lined up with a talent agency as a publicity agent. That Weis guy helped. Go figure."

Frankie yawned, exhausted despite himself.

"Catch some winks," Sal told him. He turned off the radio. "We'll be home in no time, safe in the motherland."

"No, I'll be fine. And we should go straight to Beekman."

"You got it."

"And Caterina? Do you hear anything from her?"

Sal was silent as he passed the turn for Mulberry and continued on to the hospital.

"It's okay, Sal. I know. I already know."

The usually antiseptic lobby of Beekman Downtown Hospital had been transformed into an all-you-can-eat buffet. In a belief that treating the staff well insured they would treat the patient well, half a dozen of Little Italy's dining establishments had sent food to the emergency room, along with a coffee urn, plates, and utensils, the minute they'd seen the ambulance leave with Primo Grace.

Frankie embraced his mother and bent to kiss her. She looked much older to him, and there was no song in her voice despite her pleasure at seeing him. In act five of her opera, the hero was in mortal danger. On the waiting room couch beside her sat Pasquelena, Angelina, and Lena. Zizilena took turns keeping Sternos lit under the trays of manicotti and eggplant parmigiana.

Annunziata had just arrived with a box of pastries. "Frankie," she asked him, "did you eat anything, are you hungry?" She pushed a piece of fruitcake in his direction, but he ignored her.

He walked through the swinging doors into the emergency room, toward the curtained area the nurse had indicated.

Rocco the barber met him on the way out, red-eyed. "I shave you papa," he told Frankie. "No charge." He walked by with his head down.

Frankie was afraid to pull the curtain back. At his father's bedside, the hum of a window fan broke the ghostly stillness, and the bright overhead fluorescent lights only emphasized the pallor of Primo's face. God, how many times had Frankie seen that look? He was struck by the effort it took Primo to turn his head.

"Papa." He reached for his father's hand and squeezed it gently. Primo did not squeeze back. His hand was cold, wet. Frankie knew.

Primo cleared his throat with difficulty. "Frankie?" He spoke with measured breaths. "What are you doing here? You're supposed to be in—"

"Quiet, shush! I leave you alone and look what you go and do to yourself."

"I don't know, I don't remember." His voice was weak.

"Hush, save your energy. You'll be fine. I'm here. I'll be here."

Primo spoke again. "How did you do with the movie test?"

Frankie was stunned at Primo's condition. Each word took effort. Frankie used a moist towel near the bed to pat his father's brow and lips. "The screen test? I did fine, Dad, just fine."

"You know where the deed is, in the file downstairs. I showed you the plot and there's a box—"

"Shhh! We're not going to need the cemetery deed. You're going to be fine."

Frankie heard the nurses discussing tests with the doctor, who appeared at the bedside. His face was grim, conveying all Frankie needed to know. And he was Chinese.

"Where's Dr. Copolla?"

"Retired. I took over his practice."

"What about his son? Wasn't he studying to be a doctor?"

"Oh, he changed his mind. He decided to study film at NYU instead."

The doctor reached out his hand to Frankie. "I'm Dr. Wong Wing. I've been treating your father."

Primo reached out and pulled Frankie close enough to whisper in his ear. "We wanted to call him, but were afraid to wing the wong number."

It took a moment to settle in. Then Frankie lost it. The silliness of the joke and its unlikely source were just too much to bear. Frankie started laughing uncontrollably.

Wong was clearly perplexed. Every time Frankie looked at him, he'd bust out laughing. Frankie laughed so hard there were tears in his eyes. He placed a kiss on his father's forehead and whispered in his ear, "I'll do the jokes, you just get better."

Primo smiled and closed his eyes.

Sometime during the dark hours, and as prophesied by the Gospel According to Primo, the laughing turned to crying as Primo Grace passed away peacefully in his sleep. The smile never left his face.

Chapter 24

Frankie walked up Mulberry Street. He stopped by Rossi's Music Store. There was something different: there was no music blaring from the sidewalk speakers. He looked down the street and saw Italian and American flags flying at half-staff, from Grotta Azura on Broom Street to Cha Cha's off Canal. Shop owners stood speechless in front of their establishments—no scratching—as Frankie walked past them. Primo Grace was dead. How could it be? It was the end of an era.

Clara Pella moved her sidewalk table away from the funeral home and hung a sign in its place: "No Rice Balls. Death in Family. Will reopen Tuesday."

Frankie walked back to the funeral home and sat in the office. He found his father's file, written in his own hand, with the specific instructions for his burial. Three pages' worth, including the suit he wanted to wear, the cufflinks, the prayer cards. He was directing his funeral from beyond. Frankie laughed, seeing that his father chose the mahogany casket. *That's one way to stop me from sleeping in it, Dad.* There was one more thing in Primo's file: a newspaper clipping—the review from the Peppermint Lounge, three copies.

Frankie sat and cried. He did not notice Eddie standing at the doorway, but the smell of Canoe could only mean one thing.

"I'm sorry, kid. I really am. I'm sorry about this whole thing."

Frankie looked up, tears running down his face. "Do you think it was my fault? Do you think all this stress . . ."

"Hey, don't think like that. You should know better than most: when it's your time, it's your time. You know when you're born, your name is in a book on two different pages. You can't change it."

"There you go with those books again."

Eddie sat down across from Frankie. "What's that you're reading?"

"My father's instructions, right down to the letter."

Eddie looked at the papers. "Don't look like he forgot nothin'."

Frankie flipped through the pages. "Too bad the feast is over with."

"Why?"

"He wanted the San Gennaro Street Band to follow him to church."

Frankie put the papers down. "I'm sorry, Eddie. I never thanked you for getting me out of the heat."

"Well, I couldn't let him hurt my family."

"You took a big chance, Eddie. How do things look now?"

Eddie shook his head. "I'm callously opt . . . opto . . . opto . . . I feel pretty good so far. I know JB will never see daylight no more; but now there's a vacuum at the top, and I'm just waiting to see what kind of strength he has from inside. Something like this makes everyone run for cover. Still, there's always a chance someone will put things together and try to earn his stripes by taking care of me."

Frankie nodded.

"Your father was a big help," Eddie continued. "He was a standup guy. You know, he took a huge risk taking all the heroin up to the crematory. Jesus, I swear his eyes were glassy for two days when he came back. He and Father Colapetra were laughing like school kids. I don't think I'd ever seen him laugh before—both of them—it was a sight."

"You got my father and Colapetra high?" Frankie laughed.

"Christ, with all that stuff going up in smoke, the whole Bronx must have been high."

"Jeez, I wish I could've seen that." Frankie looked at his watch. "I have work to do."

"You're not gonna embalm your father?"

"God, no . . . I called his friend, the dean of my school. He's in there now."

Frankie rose from his seat; Eddie followed. As Frankie turned, he saw a box from the corner of his eye. "Wait," he said. "That's the box my father told me about. He said he had a surprise for me, a gift."

He moved the file cabinet and pulled out a large package. Eddie took a knife from his back pocket and helped him cut the edge open. Frankie pulled out a framed likeness of his father. Primo had commissioned a portrait in the same tuxedoed pose as his grandfather.

"It's a self-portrait," Frankie said.

"Jesus, it looks like your father," Eddie said.

"Yeah, that's the idea, Eddie."

"Where you gonna put it?"

"I'm gonna hang it here, next to my grandfather's."

"Come on, I'll help you."

"I'll get a nail," Frankie said.

"No need," Eddie said as he looked at the space alongside Francesco's portrait. "There's already a picture hanger in the wall. Your father thought of everything." Together they hung the portrait on the wall. It was a wonderful likeness. Frankie found it strangely comforting to know his father was where he belonged.

Eddie put his arm around Frankie. "When's the Mass?"

"Thursday. I think Thursday."

"Will your friend be able to do the Mass?"

"Father Colapetra? Sure, why not?"

"Oh, you haven't heard. Word is, he's about to be arrested."

"Arrested! For what?"

"It seems he has a little problem. He took a beating on football last week—a big hit. He lost on the Saints, go figure. Seems the church account is short about nine large. Can you imagine? A gambling priest. You know, those weren't hymn numbers he put up in the church? They were the over, under for Sunday's games. Anyway, word is the accountants from uptown are going over the books all week, and now they've called in the D.A. It's larceny, you know. Father may be serving his next Mass in prison."

Frankie looked at his father's portrait and remembered another tenet of the Gospel According to Primo: when you think things can't get worse, they do.

Frankie thought the last night of the wake would never end. No one wanted to leave the small chapel in the Grace Fun. Home— leaving would mean it was over, it was final, and that was hard for any of them to accept. They lingered long past closing hours. Throughout the evening, Frankie could hear Filomena muttering to anyone who would listen, "You see, for their own they don't lose noses."

Hundreds came to pay their last respects, and every face at the wake brought back memories for Frankie. It was like turning the pages of a photo album. Only one memory was missing for him, the one face that could have made a difference: Caterina's. But he could manage only one heartache at a time.

When Frankie climbed into bed, he was too exhausted to sleep. There was no more bedpost banging against the wall. Instead, he heard his mother's muted crying. The painted mural of the Bay of Naples, barely visible by the dim rays of a streetlight, had faded, and the lines were blurred where the sea met the shore. He felt closed in. He had outgrown this room.

He didn't remember closing his eyes or exactly when he began to dream. He felt guilty, but had no control over the dreams, as if even they were not supposed to let him escape reality. In this dream, he was back at the 500 Club. It was all so clear, so real, and so close. He watched himself take center stage. He saw the lights and heard the crowd. He heard his voice, his routine. He heard the laughs. It was so real. But the calls from the announcer prodding him to take a curtain call faded into his mother's voice.

"Frankie? You've got to put the 'No Parking' cones in the

street." He knew she was right and he knew he wasn't in Atlantic City. There were no scantily dressed waitresses, only his mother shrouded in black; no crowd, just the Lena four; and no laughs, only the loud, rumbling sounds from Zizilena's stomach. He was burying his father today, and the parking spaces needed to be reserved early, a task usually handled by Primo.

As the pallbearers carried Primo Grace out of the funeral home, solemn music filtered through the neighborhood. The sound came closer and closer, until at last the San Gennaro Street Band turned the corner onto Mulberry, playing a dirge. Frankie looked across the street at Eddie, who acknowledged the deed with a wink. He was dressed in a shiny gray sharkskin suit with a black bowling shirt. His hair was neat and combed, his nails were polished, and a diamond ring on his pinky reflected the sun.

Frankie and Giovanna walked down Hester Street behind the casket. The band followed, and the shopkeepers and neighbors fell in behind. It would be the last of the old-world funerals, all according to Primo's instructions.

In front of the church, the hearse stopped in the middle of the street as the pallbearers marched, like a military unit, to the back door. Frankie led them up the steps. He helped his mother down the aisle to the front of the crowded church. There, in each of the pews, were parts of Frankie's recent past—Pete the mechanic, Tony Romo, Little Anthony, Annunziata Ballsziti.

The assembled mourners waited in the church. They waited and waited. Word had spread through the neighborhood about Colapetra's woes. Who would say the Mass?

They had their answer as the organist segued from the Ave Maria into the call to the gate. Father Colapetra emerged from the sacristy, fully vested. He walked past Primo's casket and stood face to face with Frankie. From his vestment pocket he pulled out a ball of aluminum foil and put it into Frankie's hand.

"Thank you," Colapetra said. "You saved me from certain religious convictions."

"I'll do the jokes, Father."

A few minutes later, the chimes sounded. "Dearly beloved," Father Colapetra began. Eddie sat in a back pew. There were a few men around him who Frankie did not recognize. They looked uncomfortable and always lagged behind during parts of the Mass where people stand or kneel or sit.

Suddenly a series of sharp explosions from the street startled everyone inside the church. Thinking it was yet another mob hit, mourners quickly ducked under the pews. They were all equally embarrassed when they realized it was only the Chinese celebrants outside causing the noise. The dragon was awake, breaking out of its confines below Canal Street, parading boldly into new territory. The Chinese were beginning their Mid-Autumn Festival, complete with a parade and firecrackers.

Eddie left his pew, upset that the unanticipated revelry was interrupting the solemn ceremony. From atop the church steps, he tried to wave off the heathen invaders. "Hey, there's a friggin' Mass goin' on!"

But they did not know him, and did not know enough to obey. The dragon gyrated its way down the street, with the Chinese musicians in tow. This was their turf now. This was their feast, this dragon their San Gennaro, these moon cakes their zeppoles. It was a changing of the guard. He walked back to his pew, shrugged his shoulders, and shook his head.

Colapetra was at his oratorical best, almost like he believed what he was saying. "What happens to a community when the caregiver is gone? When the man we called at three and four in the morning when we didn't know where to turn, or who to turn to, is gone? When the man who made it possible for us to see our loved ones one more time, just one more time so we could say good-bye, is gone? Who will we turn to now to help us say good-bye? How can we go on?"

Colepetra looked straight at Frankie, but Frankie looked away. *Not me, he thought. Don't look at me. You can't mean me.*

The funeral procession, led by three flower cars, crept down Mulberry Street and paused in front of the funeral home. Frankie opened the back door, a custom meant either to let the spirit out of the car or let the spirit in—he was never sure which. Mrs. Marotta leaned out the window, waved, and blew a kiss. She did the same thing for every funeral.

The cortege proceeded down Mulberry, where the tourists focused their Kodaks and home movie cameras at the passing funeral. They would return home, back to Italy or France or California, and play the reels and show the pictures and tell their friends of the funeral they'd seen on the New York City's Lower East Side. They would wonder and speculate aloud about who had died—a politician, an actor, or better yet, a mobster. No one would guess that it was just a man, a family man who gave his all for the community he loved. Frankie stared out the window of the limo. It came to him that through the snapshots and films, Primo, in death, would travel farther than he ever had in life.

In Greenwood Cemetery, Primo was laid to rest. "Not too close to the lake," Frankie explained to his mother, "because of your rheumatism."

The pallbearers carried the casket from the hearse and placed it over the open ground. The gravediggers at the cemetery were more solemn than usual. Normally dressed in sagging tank tops and dirty dungarees, they typically hid behind nearby trees during the interment, smoking cigarettes like a band of thieves and waiting until the priest had finished before returning to their work. But today, they wore button-down shirts and joined in the prayers.

The flower cars were emptied, the floral tributes placed all around the casket. The easels of the large standing sprays were pressed into the ground, serving as a fragrant altar in front of which Colapetra stood and offered a final blessing. Frankie had heard these words so many times, but this time he listened more intently: "In my Father's house there are many dwelling places."

In my Father's house. Frankie felt the words were speaking to him directly, while at the same time feeling as far away from God as he had ever felt. He watched as the priest sprinkled holy water on the casket at the final blessing. Giovanna knew what to do; it was time. She approached the casket and placed a single long-stemmed red rose upon it. The rest of the mourners followed her lead.

When they returned to the limo, Giovanna directed the driver to take her and her companions to stop at various graves so Pasquelena, Angelina, Zizilena, and Lena might visit their respective husbands.

Frankie remained at his father's grave, with Sal and at his side and Eddie nearby. There was a driver standing by the Impala waiting for Eddie—finally he had an inheritance.

The casket had been placed on canvas straps that were secured around the steel frame of a lowering device at the open ground. When all had left the gravesite, the foreman released a small lever, and the casket descended. Frankie watched as the casket was lowered into a concrete encasement. When he was in charge, Primo had never left the grave until the vault was closed and sealed. He was from the old school; he made sure things were done right. Frankie stayed and watched and made sure.

Two men stood above the grave and held onto thick ropes that were secured to the vault lid. On cue they lowered the huge concrete slab. Its weight strained their arms and shoulders. A loud thump echoed as the cement door landed, sending a puff of loose earth up from the hole. The door was closed, secured. The process of separating Frankie's past from his present was complete.

Frankie sat in the front row of the chapel alone, unmoving, until darkness fell. He stared at the empty casket bier, hidden in shadows in the silent room. Suddenly he heard the voice of an angel saying to him, "I thought you were dead, Frankie Grace."

He bowed his head to hide his tears.

The voice came closer, until the angel was standing over him. "I thought you were dead."

He looked up and saw her: a vision—Our Lady of Fatima, Lourdes, Medujoria, all in one, there before him. His Caterina was there, cradling his head in her arms. He looked up to see her face, radiant in the darkness. It was really her. "I thought you were dead, I thought you were dead."

She was crying, but among the fear and sadness were tears of joy. She brushed her hand over his cropped hair. "Why didn't you call me? Why didn't you let me know you were alive?"

"I tried, I tried. Mr. Baciagulope."

She laughed, "Mr. Baciagulope, *you're* Mr. Baciagulope. My mother told me there had been calls . . . she thought you were a pervert."

"Right."

She sat down next to him and explained. "The morning my father told me you were missing, it felt like a part of me died. I know what 'missing' means in my father's world. I ran to Sal, to Eddie, but I learned nothing. Now I know it was for your safety."

"I'm sorry about what happened to your father," Frankie said, thinking he should.

"No, don't say that. I'm sorry about *your* father. And I am the one who must be sorry for what mine got you involved in. Can you ever forgive me? It was his way, but his ways were never mine. I'm so sorry he put you through this."

"Your mother must be pissed at me. Your father won't be coming home for a long time."

"She's the one who called me in Bologna to tell me your father had died. I couldn't get a flight back until today." She sighed wistfully. "My father was hardly home anyway . . . they had a fight a while ago, and it was never the same after that."

"When did they fight?"

"The night they were married."

Frankie laughed. "I'm sorry, I didn't mean to laugh."

"No, I want to hear you laugh. I missed hearing you laugh."

"I wondered if I would—laugh again, that is."

"I understand that, and I understand so much more," said Caterina. "When I thought you were dead, I had so many regrets. I tried to bargain with God, telling Him that if he gave me another chance, I would do things differently. I prayed that if He brought you back from the dead, I would make sure you had no regrets, ever again. And He did bring you back from the dead."

"But then He took my dad," said Frankie. "It's like, that's it. I bury him and boom, the neighborhood is back in business. It's like nothing happened, like he never lived. Like I want to shout, 'Hey, Stop! My father's dead!' But the world doesn't stop, and for as much of a difference as he made in people's lives, he will never be remembered."

"That's what death does," she said. "It is the ultimate paradox, it changes everything and it changes nothing. The rhythm of life begins to fill in the empty spaces left by death."

"It's so hard to believe I won't find him sitting behind the desk. He won't be here to break my balls every day. I never thought I'd say it, but I'm going to miss that."

She nodded. "I can do that for you," she said, smiling.

"Would you?" he said, suddenly serious.

"Till death do us part," said Caterina. "I solemnly promise."

The two of them burst out laughing. "You're too much," Frankie said. "And I'm so proud of you. Even when I was in Jersey and Philadelphia, I felt I was close to you. I gained four pounds eating Isabella Breakfast Treats, nicely packaged, with lots of shelf space. I felt close to you with every bite. I would smell them, hoping to get just a whiff of you. I swear I did. I smelled you in the pignolis, tasted you in the tri-colored cookies, loved you in the cannoli shells."

"I think I get it," she said. "You need not go further." She smiled. "We all have dreams," she said. "Mine was to apply my business education to my grandmother's business. I've been working on it for a long time. I'm onto something. We're already deep into production, and I was able to contact some family friends in trucking for distribution. Dad was good for something, after all. I'm even getting offers from big companies who want to swallow me up—when I was in Italy I met with executives of Bindi. We will have no financial worries, no matter what course you choose."

"I'm jealous. I'd like to swallow you up, too."

✝

Over the next few days, in the solitude of the funeral home, Frankie relived every routine, every punch line, remembering the laughs, or sometimes the lack of them. Each day, at noon, he would hear tapping on the steam pipes. His mother was telling him lunch was ready. In the midst of confusion and tumult, there was still routine and organization: like the chimes of the Church of the Most Precious Blood, always there to bring him back from whatever faraway world his mind had traveled to.

Messages were piling up from K, and a few from Sol Weis. A fruit basket came from Jerry Vale and a condolence card from Bobby Rydell. Frankie smiled at Father Colapetra's note that a horse named Primo had won the eighth race at Belmont on the third day after his father's burial, although he, personally, had not bet the race. Colapetra seemed both proud and regretful about this.

One afternoon, while Frankie was brooding downstairs, his father's portrait suddenly fell from the wall. Frankie jumped, as if he'd seen a ghost. The framed portrait landed at his feet. He picked it up and stared into his father's eyes. His father had found a way to get into his face once again. *I get it, Dad,* Frankie thought.

That's the sign. I'm needed here. I get it. He secured the portrait back to the wall and stepped back. It hung crooked on the nail. He balanced it left, too much. He balanced it right, too much. Back and forth, left, right, left; the frame was not cooperating. *Okay already, I get it. I get it. I'll stay, I'm not leaving.* Finally, the portrait hung balanced on the wall.

A few hours later, as he locked the doors of the funeral home, a middle-aged woman he did not know approached him on the sidewalk. She had a look of shock on her face. "Excuse me," she said. "Is Mr. Grace here?"

He had to think for a moment. For him, Mr. Grace always meant his father, and now it didn't. "No," he said to the woman. "My dad has died."

"Oh, I am so sorry."

She had a man's suit draped over her arm. "I'm Elizabeth St. John. Your father buried my father, a week ago. Now," she said shakily, "it's my husband. It happened this morning and . . ." She could not finish the sentence at first. When she had recovered herself somewhat, she resumed. "Your father took care of everything when my father died. Now, I don't know what to do next. What do we do? This was so unexpected, so sudden."

Her eyes were red and puffy, like his own. Frankie recognized the look of eyes when they had no more tears to shed. "How did he die?"

"A freak accident. A policeman's funeral procession. I just got word."

"Was your husband a policeman?"

"No, he was just going to work. He got caught up in the funeral procession and was run over by the motorcade. The driver said he just lost control."

Jeez, killed by a funeral procession. What I wouldn't have done with that a few weeks ago. But he couldn't think of a single funny line now. He looked at Elizabeth St. John and thought, All right, I can do this. He reached for the clothing.

"His underwear is in there, too," she said. "They're cleaned and pressed."

Of course, Frankie thought.

✝

The following night, Frankie stood at Mrs. St. John's side as she cried at her husband's casket. She was easy to deal with: no complaints about a missing nose, no complicated instructions on what to leave in the casket and what to take out. Her husband's suit fit him nicely. She was easy.

He helped her to a seat and sat alongside her. He listened as she talked about her husband—when they met, where they married, his work, his hobbies. He had been an accountant, but his true love was music. He was a lead guitarist in a band. He loved music, and his group played every weekend. Nothing made him happier. Unfortunately, he couldn't pursue his dream. Life got in the way.

And now death got in the way, Frankie thought.

"Wait a minute," she said, "I thought you were in show business, too."

"Excuse me?"

"It's funny," she explained. "When my father died, I sat here with your father, and we talked, like we're talking now. We talked about everything: life, family. I told him my husband was traveling back from Florida, where his band had been playing. And he told me he had a son who was in show business, too—a comedian, yes, a comedian. That's you, right?"

Frankie nodded.

"He told me he didn't want to make you nervous, so he would sneak out to the San something or other to see you perform. He made sure you never knew he was there. He said you were pretty funny, and he was so impressed with your ability to get up in front of all those people and put yourself out there. And he told me you were in California, trying out for a movie. He even showed me an article from the newspaper. It had your name and picture. He was so proud. I didn't know you were in the funeral business. He didn't make it sound that way."

A rush of tears flooded Frankie's eyes. His father's death meant he was truly a man now and had to make his own decisions, just as Eddie had said.

Was Elizabeth the sign, Dad? Was that my release? Your picture fell; you scared the crap out of me. But you weren't trying to tell me I was needed here, or that I had to stay, were you? I misinterpreted it, didn't I? But did you have to have her husband killed to clarify the message? Couldn't you just have told me? A note maybe?

Epilogue

Standing on the sidewalk in front of the funeral home, Frankie attempted to embrace Caterina. His arms were not long enough to reach all the way around her growing belly. She placed his hand on her stomach. "Did you feel that? He kicked."

"He?" Frankie asked.

"I think so. My mother says I'm carrying high, so it's a boy."

He placed both hands on her stomach. "You seem to be carrying high and low and sideways."

"Will you be using *this* in your Vegas act?"

"Do I have a choice?"

"Is this what I have to look forward to? Are audiences going to know every time I pass gas?"

"Maybe not *every* time."

"Oooh," she said as she held her stomach. "The kicking never stops."

"Maybe I should stay."

"Who are you kidding? Go, I'll be fine. I have built-in, round-the-clock nursing care." She pointed to the building where the Lena four were perched at respective windows. "And besides, the crews aren't finished on the restaurant renovations. I've got rent to pay, you know. And the feast is less than a month away."

"Trattoria Isabella. Cannelloni to cannoli. I like the sound of it. But can your salami sandwich ever measure up to Sal's?"

She laughed. "Will you be okay?"

"I'm nervous, a little nervous, but I'll be fine. Sal is there laying the groundwork already. He says it's really something, to see my name right there on the bill with Vale's."

Mr. Ho pulled up to the curb in the Lincoln. A slender young Chinese man stepped out of the passenger side. He was dressed in black suit, white tie, and striped shirt, and he carried himself with an air of dignity and warmth.

Frankie shook his hand. "Hi, Ho," he said. "Good to see you again."

"Hello, Mr. Grace," replied Ho. "I can't thank you enough for this opportunity."

Frankie handed him the keys to the funeral home and the hearse. "This is your neighborhood now," he said. "Good luck— knock 'em dead."

Frankie looked up to the building, waving to his mother at her window on the first floor, then to Pasquelena in 2-B, Angelina in 3-B, Zizilena in 3-C, and just Lena in 4-B. There was no representation from the fifth floor.

"Mother sends her best wishes," said Caterina, handing him a bakery box neatly tied with string. "She wouldn't let her son-in-law go off to Sin City without her special recipe to make sure he'd come back."

He gave Caterina another kiss. There was too much of her to hug. He put his suitcase in the trunk and kissed her passionately again before getting into the car.

In the rearview mirror, he caught a glimpse of his future. As Caterina stood on the sidewalk, waving good-bye, he realized just how much she now resembled her mother, rotund, with a *beauty mark* on her lip. His own mother had warned him, by way of an ominous aria, hadn't she? He recalled her voice: "If you want to know what your wife will look like, just look at her mother." But he had no regrets. None.

✝

Later that day an unmarked police car cruised down Mott

Street and parked in front of the Marconi Social Club. Roscoe Keats stepped out. He was dressed in khakis, a flowered Hawaiian shirt, and sandals. He wore sunglasses and a straw Panama hat. He looked up and down the street, extinguished his cigar on the sidewalk, and walked in.

At a back table sat Eddie Fontana, attired in a custom-tailored blue sport jacket over a darker blue knit shirt. He was staring at a chess board. He looked up, only slightly acknowledging Keats's presence at the edge of the table.

"Hello, Mr. Fontana." Keats studied the chess board. Recognizing Eddie's defense, he said, "Interesting. The Sicilian Gambit. You play it well."

"Nice shirt," Eddie said. He looked back at the chess board. "What do you want?"

Keats sat down.

"Don't make yourself comfortable," Eddie said.

"I won't," Keats answered. "I just came by to congratulate you. You heard Johnny's getting life, no parole? He'll be incommunicado for the rest of his life, stuck in a two-by-four cell, and only allowed to walk around the prison yard for an hour a day until he dies. But I heard you got a promotion. Your picture is on our chart now, right up on top. A flattering snapshot, I must say."

"I don't know what you're talking about," Eddie said and looked down to the chess board.

"Right," Keats said. "It's the Peter Principle."

"I don't know any Peter." Eddie moved his knight. "So, what, are you going to start busting my balls now?"

Keats smiled. "Me?" he said. "No, not me. I'm retired, off to Boca. You're someone else's problem now."

"Well, enjoy yourself. Stay out of the sun. They say it's not healthy, especially you being Irish and all."

"Yeah, you be careful, too. Try to stay out of trouble, especially you being Italian and all." Keats rose and started to walk away.

"Keats," Eddie called to him. "This is yours." He slipped Roscoe's business card from under the chessboard and handed it back to him.

"Why don't you keep it, Eddie? The number still works."

"I don't think so," he said. "That was a one-time thing. I kept my word, you kept yours. Let's say there were exterminating circumstances."

Keats took the card, tipped his hat, and left.

"Lorenzo," Eddie called, "Where's Communicado? Is that someplace in Italy?"

Acknowledgments

I would be remiss if I did not take this opportunity to thank everyone who helped me complete *Die Laughing,* and there were many. It was my first attempt at a novel and I enlisted an army of amateur editors, from my friend Jim Leonard, to my brother Joe. I would like to express my sincere gratitude all those who helped me, especially Catherine Hiller, Barbara Brannon and her editorial team, the talented Curtis Fennell—and the photographer who airbrushed my photo! I thank my daughter Jennifer for her vision and insights.

I am embarrassed to reveal just how long it took me to write this book. My wife Ann Marie and my children Jennifer and Vincent will be happy to tell you. To them, I offer it as a lesson in perseverance. —VINCENT GRAZIANO

This book was set in the Century Schoolbook and Bernhard MT Condensed faces in Adobe InDesign CS4 for the Macintosh computer, and digitally printed.

LaVergne, TN USA
24 September 2009
158971LV00002B/1/P